Snow in the River

By Carol Ryrie Brink

Buffalo Coat*
Harps in the Wind
Stopover
The Headland
Strangers in the Forest*
The Twin Cities
Château Saint Barnabé
The Bellini Look
Four Girls on a Homestead**
A Chain of Hands*

*Published by and available from the Washington State University Press.

**Published by and available from the Latah County Historical Society, Moscow, Idaho.

Snow in the River

Carol Ryrie Brink

With a Foreword by Mary E. Reed

Washington State University Press
Pullman, Washington

Published in collaboration with the
Latah County Historical Society
Moscow, Idaho

Washington State University Press, Pullman, Washington 99164-5910

Copyright © by Carol Brink, 1964

This edition is reprinted by arrangement with Macmillan Publishing Company, a division of Macmillan, Inc.

Foreword and cover copyright © by the Board of Regents of Washington State University

Cover illustration from a photo by Robert Hubner

Library of Congress Cataloging-in-Publication Data
Brink, Carol Ryrie, 1895-
     Snow in the river / Carol Ryrie Brink ; with a foreword by Mary
E. Reed.
        p.   cm.
    ISBN 0-87422-097-1 (pbk.)
     1. Scottish Americans—Northwest, Pacific—History—Fiction.
I. Title.
PS3503.R5614S65   1993
813'.52—dc20
                                        92-46243
                                            CIP

Author's Biography

CAROL RYRIE BRINK was born in Moscow, Idaho, in 1895 and spent most of her life there until her junior year in college. Her youthful years spanned the settlement period of rustic one-story, wood-frame buildings lining Main Street to an era of paved roads and automobiles. At a young age her father died of consumption; a crazed gunman murdered her grandfather, one of the town's builders; and her mother committed suicide after an unfortunate second marriage. Carol's maternal grandmother and aunt raised her in their Moscow home.

Brink wrote more than thirty books for both adults and children. Her most acclaimed work, *Caddie Woodlawn*, won the Newbery Medal as the outstanding contribution to children's literature in 1936. It details and synthesizes in fictionalized form the stories her grandmother told her about growing up in Wisconsin. In addition to the Newbery Medal, Brink was honored with the Friends of American Writers Award in 1955, the 1966 National League of American Pen Women's award for fiction, and an honorary degree of Doctor of Letters from the University of Idaho in 1965.

Brink wrote three stories for children based upon her experiences growing up in Moscow. She also wrote an adult series of novels about her family in and around Moscow: *Buffalo Coat* (1944); *Strangers in the Forest* (1959); and *Snow in the River* (1964). In 1993 the Washington State University Press, in collaboration with the Latah County Historical Society in Moscow, Idaho, reprinted the latter three novels, along with Brink's previously unpublished reminiscences about characters she knew in Moscow, *A Chain of Hands*.

Carol Ryrie Brink died in 1981 in San Diego. Her home town recognized her posthumously with the naming of a building on the University of Idaho campus in her honor and with the naming of the children's wing of the Moscow-Latah County Public Library after her.

Among Brink's contributions to Western American literature are her works about her native state of Idaho. In view of the relatively few Idaho writers of this period, that is of interest in itself. But there are more important considerations for recognizing Brink, especially her portrayal of a West between two eras.

Although many writers concentrate on a colorful pioneer period and the heroic feats of those who plowed virgin ground, opened the first mines, and platted towns, the chronicle of those who followed is certainly equally or more important. These were the people who established the libraries, invested their lives and fortunes in the new communities, and generally created civic life as we recognize it today. Brink's portrayal of the lives and experiences of men and women in an Idaho town during this crucial period of growth and maturing serve as an antidote to numerous works about the wild American frontier. In her three Idaho novels and *A Chain of Hands* she shows us a small town whose citizens had to weigh justice with empathy, who had to learn that the resources of the West were not entirely at their personal disposal, and who discovered that the promise of these new lands was at times ephemeral.

Acknowledgments

In 1987 the Washington State University Press and the Latah County Historical Society collaborated in the publication of two books, Richard Waldbauer's *Grubstaking the Palouse* and Keith Petersen's *Company Town*. The recognition those two works received, including awards from the American Association for State and Local History, the Idaho Library Association, and the Council for the Advancement of Secondary Education, greatly pleased both institutions and led the two to seek ways in which to collaborate again. This reprint of *Snow in the River* represents another such venture.

Carol Ryrie Brink wrote more than thirty books for children and adults. Idahoans frequently point out that Ezra Pound was born in the state, although he left as an infant, and that Ernest Hemingway lived here for a while. Both writers were obviously accomplished, but neither wrote about Idaho. In seeking true regional writers—writers who knew the state and wrote about it—Idahoans have virtually ignored Brink.

In the late 1970s and early 1980s the Latah County Historical Society undertook several projects, including giving presentations about Brink throughout the state, with the goal of bringing recognition to this talented writer. Those efforts have largely been rewarded with renewed recognition for Brink in regional anthologies, with the recent publication of a biography of the author in Boise State University's Western Writers Series, and with the posthumous naming of two significant buildings in Moscow in Brink's honor.

In 1992 the Historical Society and WSU Press agreed to collaborate on a major publication venture that would bring back into print Brink's three adult novels about Idaho, *Buffalo Coat* (originally published in 1944), *Strangers in the Forest* (1959), and *Snow in the River* (1964). In addition, the two collaborated in the publication of Brink's previously unpublished reminiscences about characters she knew growing up in Moscow, *A Chain of Hands*.

This publication venture would not have been possible without the kind assistance of the Brink family, and we are indebted to Carol's son David and daughter Nora Brink Hunter for their encouragement and help.

The Latah County Historical Society has gained a national reputation for its publications program. Special thanks are due to its publications committee and board of trustees for their foresight in recognizing the importance of regional publishing in general and Carol Brink's work specifically. I would especially like to thank our two longtime friends, Carolyn Gravelle and Kathleen Probasco, who maintained unswerving faith in this publication venture for almost a decade. I have greatly profited from their encouragement and affection for our native author. I also wish to thank Bert Cross, who supported this project when others became discouraged.

At the WSU Press, I would like to thank my colleagues and friends director Thomas Sanders; assistant director, Mary Read; editors Keith Petersen, Jean Taylor, Glen Lindeman, and John Sutherland; designer Dave Hoyt; and promotions coordinator Vida Hatley. All of them proved not only receptive but also enthusiastic when approached about a possible Brink publication project. We at the Historical Society want them to know how much we have appreciated their support and collaboration over the years.

Mary E. Reed
Latah County Historical Society
Moscow, Idaho

Foreword

TWENTY YEARS AFTER writing the first book in her Idaho trilogy, Carol Ryrie Brink began the third. The first novel, *Buffalo Coat*, published in 1944, explored her grandparents' lives and a raw western town in the quiet process of becoming civilized. The second book, *Strangers in the Forest*, published in 1959, examined the western landscape of timber speculators, homesteaders, lumberjacks, and forest rangers through the experiences of her aunt, who took up a claim in the isolated mountains of North Idaho. Then, six years later, Brink completed *Snow in the River*. While the other two novels had also focused on her family history, only in the third novel did Brink give herself a role and a voice by writing in the first person. In 1981 she admitted that this was the closest she would ever come to an autobiography, and, indeed, the fictional events fit fairly closely with the real historical and personal ones.[1]

The title is taken from a poem by the Scottish poet, Robert Burns. Snow in the river, like the petals of a poppy, is an ephemeral pleasure; the bloom is shed as soon as the flower is grasped, and snowfall in the river is only white for a moment before melting forever. Brink knew well the meaning of the poem, for her early memories were of sudden tragic disruptions of a tranquil childhood. The choice of a Scotsman was fitting, too, because among the pleasures and wonder of her childhood were the three brothers who came from this island to the small Western town in northern Idaho.

The maternal side of Brink's family dominated her childhood. After her father's death in 1900 and her mother's suicide in 1904, Brink lived with her grandmother and unmarried aunt until her senior year in college. Her mother's unhappy life and untimely death haunted her; not until *Snow in the River* did Brink feel she could come to terms with this tragedy. The experience of finally being able to write her mother's story and the effect it had on the shy and introspective child proved to be a therapeutic experience.[2]

Snow in the River reveals the unpleasant truth that Henrietta Ryrie was neither a caring nor a nurturing mother. She remarried only a couple of years after the death of her upright and civic-minded husband,

Alexander, this time to Nat Brown, a man-about-town who, with his wife, enjoyed Moscow, Idaho's (Opportunity) gayer social life, and in an age when temperance dominated, even drank. Brink alludes to the emotional abuse of her stepfather and her mother's weakness, but in the novel as in her oral history interview, she is restrained in describing this traumatic period in her life.

In her last work, *A Chain of Hands*, Brink goes farther in describing her mother's lack of affection for her "homely child who did not occupy the center of her heart." In fact her mother was so distant that Brink had few memories of her.[3]

Consistent with her personality and her own life, Brink does not make the fictional Henrietta Ryrie the central theme of this work. In the novel, after the mother's funeral the child Kit remains silent while others try to comfort her. "It was only in this way that I was able to pull what shreds of resolution I had left about my naked wretchedness."[4] The statement reveals Brink's resolve to get on with her life, refusing to let the past dominate her. Nonetheless, she was in her sixties before she could put these painful circumstances on paper. And even then, the spur seemed to have originated as much from her curiosity about the other side of her family, the Scottish Ryries, as from the need to write about her mother.

Brink had always been interested in her father's side of the family. Alexander and three brothers, Donald, Henry, and a third who soon returned to the old country, left the impoverished Scottish croft in the 1880s for the American West. Donald Ryrie became a central figure in her Moscow years. He was the father she had lost, and he reciprocated her love by lavishing affection and presents on her. Although she thought the story of the brothers had a romantic appeal, she found it difficult "to get at," and worried that "there were people still living that I thought might be hurt or involved and I put it off for a long, long time."[5]

As a young married woman with an infant son, she finally visited Scotland and met her father's family. Growing up in Moscow, she had suffered many unfavorable comparisons with her dark-eyed, musically talented, and beautiful mother. In Scotland she found the intimate link with her past. She had always thought the name "Ryrie" strange and unusual. But in Glasgow a large sign advertising "Ryrie Wines and Spirits" impressed her with the fact that she shared a common surname with other Scots. A photograph taken at the Ryrie home with her among all the uncles, aunts, and cousins revealed to her the undisputable truth that she was indeed one of the "solid Scots."[6]

After she resolved to write the book, Brink struggled with the beginning chapter. She originally began the story with the Ryrie brothers in Scotland. Then one time as she was shuffling cards the image came to her mind of "myself as a little girl coming down the dark stairs and climbing in bed with my uncle." Her uncle, who was playing solitaire, showed her how to shuffle cards. After writing a new first chapter, Brink read it to her writers' group, who severely criticized it for various reasons. Later she felt vindicated when her Macmillan editor told her that it was "the best first chapter of any book he had ever had on his desk."[7]

The image of the little girl in a white nightgown, afraid of the dark and finding refuge with her uncle in a setting of "light and warmth and friendliness" is an inspired beginning for a story that intertwines their lives. The first chapter takes the mature Kit back to Scotland to the farm where her grandfather—as had happened with Brink's own pilgrimage—still lived with an unmarried daughter. Sleeping in the front parlor, Kit is struck by the photographs of her ancestors, especially of the young Uncle Douglas, and his picture twists her heart with love as she reflects on what had befallen the young, hopeful faces in the picture frames.[8]

The trip to Scotland deepened Brink's resolve to write about the Scottish brothers, and indeed, the story of the three McBain men is the driving force of the novel. Through the stories of these three young immigrants, Brink expands the last part of her trilogy both historically and geographically. In *Buffalo Coat* she had wondered at the circumstances that brought people—namely the French and English doctors—from different parts of Europe to Moscow. In *Snow in the River* she uses the lives of the two Scottish brothers to explore how the West, with its seemingly boundless opportunities, could affect men of different personalities and ambitions.

Her relationship with the Ryrie brothers gave Brink a rare insight into the various mechanisms by which immigrants became integrated into new towns of the American West. Donald Ryrie epitomized the familiar Western entrepreneur who speculated in land, married attractive but self-centered women, schemed to make a fortune, but finally succumbed to scandal and failure.

Uncle Henry shared the more common fate of the newcomer who didn't quite make it. He worked for a time in the harness shop of Gottfried Weber in Moscow and later moved to a dryland farm in central Washington. Brink remembered a visit to this farm near Wenatchee where they enjoyed eating watermelons, a crop her uncle couldn't sell because of the high shipping costs.[9]

In the novel Brink adds many details of how her good-hearted uncle was unable to adapt to new opportunities. Henry's fictional counterpart also begins his new life in Moscow as a harness maker who continues his trade, unable and unwilling to adjust to the new machine age of bicycles and automobiles.

In developing the character of the third brother, Brink brings to life the solid citizens of the West who are highlighted in pioneer biographies. Alexander Ryrie, her father, like the fictional Angus McBain, is a mayor of the small town, surveys its streets, teaches Sunday school, and works for a Scottish Life Insurance Company. He is a leading citizen of the town, and his death is a great civic and personal loss.

But it is the fictional Donald Ryrie who becomes the pivotal character in the novel. Brink knew him much better than her own father or her Uncle Henry. Soon after her mother's suicide in 1904, Donald invited Brink, her grandmother, Caroline Woodhouse Watkins, Brink's Aunt Elsie Watkins, and a widow who had been living with the Watkins family to move to Spokane (Manitou City) and keep house for him. Donald enjoyed buying expensive clothes for his little niece, taking her with him to the horse races, and showing her off to his friends. When Donald remarried, Brink, her grandmother, and aunt moved back to Moscow to resume their peaceful, somewhat reclusive lives.[10]

During her relationship with Donald Ryrie, Brink matured from the orphaned child to a girl more aware of the outside world. After his second marriage Donald Ryrie lived "very highly." He and his wife had a cottage on Coeur d'Alene Lake in north Idaho and owned the fastest boat on the lake. Brink remembered staying at the cottage for a week with strangers while her uncle left to return to his business in Spokane. Until then she had been his favorite; but after suffering from shyness and embarrassment with people whose lives were very different from hers, she painfully realized that she was no longer a part of his life.[11] The novel expands this experience with the girl making the decision that her life belongs with that of her prudent grandmother and not with the faintly decadent uncle and his friends.

This theme of personal choice appears in the other two Idaho novels. In *Buffalo Coat*, the heroine who represents Brink's grandmother decides against a relationship with the French doctor. In *Strangers in the Forest*, Brink's fictional Aunt Elsie must overcome her frivolity and learn to be resourceful. The processes of maturing and self-knowledge are more complete and compelling in *Snow in the River*. While the bereaved child Kit learns how to survive and indeed overcome her own misfortunes, her uncle learns humility.

xii

If *Snow in the River* departs from the other two Idaho novels by presenting an intimate portrayal of the author, it also takes on a larger geographical scope. Although its location is the same small town (Moscow, Idaho) that appears in the other two novels, the story encompasses much more territory. Moscow was relatively isolated, but an electric railroad firmly connected it with the regional trading center of Spokane. The influence of that city on a rural town was both economic and cultural. Brink shows this in *Snow in the River* by contrasting the boredom of her fictional Opportunity with the high-society life of Spokane and Lake Coeur d'Alene. Differences between small-town society with its small businessmen, and the big business and grand parties of the Spokane scene, are made more poignant through the character's longing to escape, and finally, through Kit's recognition of her uncle's failings.

In many ways, *Snow in the River* is the culmination of Brink's adult fiction. It is arguably her best adult work and an excellent example of regional literature. The West she portrays is distinct and richly detailed. The intertwining of opportunities, speculation, and personal greed and failure is superbly drawn. But within the skillful dissection of a historical place and time Brink is able to make us feel very deeply about the characters who are part of her own life. The ability to look backward without rancor but with a sense of what has been gained and what has been lost insures the lasting appeal of this novel. In many ways *Snow in the River* is a statement of a woman who has reached the end of a life filled with much pain and joy, at peace with herself.

The first chapter ends with one of Brink's most moving passages. Through the reminiscence of a visit to her Scottish ancestors she skillfully connects her contemporary life with the past lives of those who have shaped and molded her existence. The passage is an epitaph for the Scottish Ryries from a gifted novelist who was intimately linked to them by blood, history, and remembrance:

> All of the faces in the old photographs looked hopefully alert and eager, but I knew that the eyes of most of them were closed in death. Better than any other living person, perhaps, I knew how they had been gay and happy or cheated and sad, thwarted or successful, good or mistaken, and what strange and interesting things had befallen all of them. If I could tell it, as it really was! But I can only make a fiction of it, and write down how it seemed to me that it must have been. So any tale is a shadow of real life, and what we write an echo of a sound made far away.

MARY E. REED
Latah County Historical Society, Moscow, Idaho
April, 1993

Notes

1. Interview with Carol Brink by Mary E. Reed, July 1981, San Diego, California, transcript of tape 4, p. 10. The tapes and transcripts of a series of interviews with Brink in July 1981 are in the collection of the Latah County Historical Society library, Moscow, Idaho. Macmillan published the three Idaho novels: *Buffalo Coat* in 1944; *Strangers in the Forest* in 1959; and *Snow in the River* in 1964. The Latah County Historical Society republished *Buffalo Coat* in 1980. Brink completed the manuscript of *A Chain of Hands* in the 1970s, but Macmillan decided against publishing it. After her death, her daughter Nora Hunter donated it to the Latah County Historical Society. In 1977 the Historical Society published *Four Girls on a Homestead*. This was a reminiscence Brink wrote for the Society of a summer she and three high school friends had spent on her Aunt Elsie's homestead. For a short biography of Carol Brink and a discussion of her writings see Mary E. Reed, *Carol Ryrie Brink*, Western Writers Series (Boise, Id.: Boise State University, 1991).
2. Brink oral history transcript of tape 4, p. 11.
3. *A Chain of Hands*, p. 23.
4. *Snow in the River*, p. 190.
5. Brink oral history transcript of tape 4, p. 10.
6. Brink oral history transcript of tape 1, p. 8.
7. Brink oral history transcript of tape 4, p. 10.
8. *Snow in the River*, p. 3.
9. Brink oral history transcript of tape 8, p. 3.
10. Brink oral history transcript of tape 2, p. 6.
11. Brink oral history transcript of tape 8, p. 3.

Caithness

1

I NEVER SHUFFLE a deck of cards but I remember my uncle Douglas and how he taught me to handle cards. I see myself in a long, white outing-flannel nightgown coming down the dark stairway from my room above to the lighted bedroom on the first floor where my Uncle Doug was sitting up in bed playing solitaire. We were alone in the house in Manitou City because my aunt and grandmother had gone out and left me in Uncle Doug's care. This was unusual, for he was the goer; they were the stay-at-homes. Perhaps that is one reason why I remember it so clearly.

Uncle Doug was my father's brother; Aunt Connie and my grandmother were my mother's people. There was no blood relationship except as I formed the link. But, when we three females had been overtaken by disaster, Uncle Doug had brought us to live with him and keep his house; for at that period he was between wives, and he did not like bachelor rooms. I am sure that there was great kindness of heart in the arrangement, though he put it on a rational basis and gave us to understand that we were doing him a favor by looking after him.

I was perhaps ten years old at the time, and this small irrelevant scene is a brightly lighted vignette among many scenes of memory in which my uncle plays a major part. The great thing that plagued me in my childhood was loneliness, and the silent house must have seemed lonely to me that night. I remember

1

the dark, narrow stairs to the upper rooms in various ways: how I came reluctantly down them on days when I was unhappy with school; how I used to dislike being sent on errands up them after dark; how, after I had been taken to the stock company production of *Trilby*, Svengali's hideous face used to float bodiless in the darkness of the stairs to leer at me as I went by.

But on this night all was light and pleasantness in the bedroom below. Uncle Douglas sat enthroned in his bed in the manner of a monarch at a levee. Like myself he wore a large, white outing-flannel nightgown which he had asked my aunt to make for him because he disliked the skimpy, store-bought nightshirts of the era before pajamas. He had begun at that time to put on a little weight from indulgence in the good things of life. Although he had not entirely lost the slight Scottish burr in his speech, he had already lost the leanness of poverty into which he had been born. But the added weight became him, and he was an exceedingly handsome man. He had a firm-lipped, humorous mouth, a finely shaped nose of the kind we used to call Roman, clear blue eyes under a broad brow, and thick brown hair. He had a good Scotch chin with a cleft in the middle of it. When he smiled at me my heart turned over, for he was the nearest thing to a father that I had known since I was five.

That night I climbed into bed beside Uncle Doug and he put the cards in my hands and worked with me patiently until I had learned to make them slip together with smooth precision.

I have called the scene irrelevant because my uncle was not a card player. He gambled in larger things, in horses and property and women's hearts. Cards were only a pastime when he was obliged to spend an evening at home. I am sure that he was scornful of these bits of colored pasteboard. Cards have meant only stopgap entertainment to me too, so it is odd that this little colored picture remains so bright and returns to me so persistently among my many other memories.

Whether I went to sleep there and was carried up to my own bed later, or whether of my own accord I climbed, drowsy but unafraid, up the dark stairs, I no longer remember. It is only the light and warmth and friendliness that come back to me when I mix a deck of cards.

I have thought about my uncle very often, because much that

2

he did was ill-timed and unfortunate, scandalous if not actually bad, and yet I loved him inordinately, and all of my memories of him are sound and good.

When I was grown I went back to Scotland and spent a week on the meager farm where my grandfather McBain still lived with his unmarried daughter and the one lame son who had remained at home to run the croft. I saw the bleak, treeless country near John O'Groat's whence my own father and Uncle Douglas and Uncle Willie had emigrated to the United States in the late nineteenth century. I smelled the peat fires and felt the fresh, chill wind that blew from the direction of the Orkneys across the Pentland Firth to Thurso and Wick. I saw the strange night sun above the turnip and oat fields, and the cold blue shadows that lay beside the stone slab fences.

I slept on an oat-husk mattress in the parlor of the thatched cottage. This was a room where only relatives from America slept between other ceremonial occasions such as funerals and weddings. It was a room of mementos too, and on the mantelpiece were the pictures of those sons who had gone away, and beside them the wives and children who had not been born in Scotland. My father was there, a thin and serious young man with hair so blond as to seem almost white and eyes of so light a color that the pupils pricked out black by contrast in the quiet face. Beside him were my mother, with her great dark eyes of tragedy, and I, a little white-haired child looking more Scottish than American.

Then there was Willie, smiling and carefree, with a stray lock of wild light hair falling across his forehead, and beside him Alma, a sour, prim wife and four gangling boys.

But the picture that twisted my heart with love was that of the young Douglas, darker than the other two, more eager and demanding, more handsome, more intent on wringing something difficult from the future. Beside him was his first wife, Mamie, and even in the inexpert photography of the 1890's, she sparkled with a bright vitality. It would be difficult to find two handsomer young people in any of the old albums, on any cottage mantelshelf.

All of the faces in the old photographs looked hopefully alert and eager, but I knew that the eyes of most of them were closed in death. Better than any other living person, perhaps, I knew

3

how they had been gay and happy or cheated and sad, thwarted or successful, good or mistaken, and what strange and interesting things had befallen all of them. If I could tell it, as it really was! But I can only make a fiction of it, and write down how it seemed to me that it must have been. So any tale is a shadow of real life, and what we write an echo of a sound made far away.

2

Caithness County lies north of the Highlands in Scotland. It is a flat, treeless country that is rarely visited by tourists. Old tales relate that the county was once covered with a dense forest, but, because wild beasts preyed so fiercely on the few inhabitants, the whole forest was burned away in order to destroy the beasts. Ancient logs and stumps found in the peat bogs seem to verify this theory, but I know of no written records of such a time. During the great days of the Viking ships, the marauding Norsemen used this part of Scotland as a base for raids on the richer lands of the south, and fought each other for power or spoils among the islands that are seen offshore.

Names like Swanson or Anderson are still common in the County, and most of the people are as blond and silent as the Swedes. They are a different race from the dark, volatile Gaelic people of the Scottish Highlands, with their clans and their tartans. I think that each man in Caithness is alone in himself, no matter what his love of family or mankind in general may be. The loneliness of the land and of the ever-present sea surrounds each man and sets him beyond the claims of clan or kin.

So little changes year by year in Caithness, that I feel sure I saw it as my father and uncles must have seen it thirty years before.

In summer the midnight glow bathes the little scattered houses in a strange golden light. Set in their fields of oats, these houses are built of the gray stone of the region and are thatched with rushes. Peat smoke rises thinly from their chimneys in the clear air. Orange lichens spread themselves in delicate webs over the gray surface of the slate, and in midsummer tiny elf-faced pansies spring up in the shelter of the stone fences.

4

Daisies and other minute, jewel-like flowers lend an air of tenderness to the closer view which is absent from the wide, bleak stretches of the larger landscape.

When the herring come around the north of Scotland, the two largest towns, Wick and to some extent Thurso, wake into frenzied life. The harbors are full of fishermen; boats come and go; men on shore are busy building packing crates, and the fish-wives who follow the herring gossip as they clean and pack the fish. Then the tinklers in their jingling carts, with dogs and children running beside, jog down the rural roads and spread their wares to tempt the fishwives. There is an air of carnival in the staid gray towns. After the herring have passed on south, quiet descends again, and remains unbroken through the long dark winter.

Grandfather McBain worked a small farm about halfway between Wick and Thurso. From his doorstep he could look far away to the sea where the light from Dunnet Head flashed; and, farther still, in the blue of the sea, he could see the Orkney Islands floating like purple clouds on the horizon. He never owned the land but he lived most of his life on it, serving it faithfully until he died, and the lame son continued on it for years after him.

Grandfather McBain was a quiet, bearded man who read his Bible and the daily papers, knew what went on in a wide world he had not seen, and respected a learning to which he laid no claim. He and my grandmother had six sons and two daughters. A seventh son, the eldest, had died in infancy. This made my father the eldest living son, my Uncle Douglas the next.

The small bleak farm could not support so many people for long. Yet sons were a form of wealth, if their careers were managed adroitly. As the lads reached an age to be economically useful, my grandfather apprenticed them out in the town of Thurso. In 1885 young Scotsmen were emigrating to Australia, New Zealand, Canada, and the United States. So many had gone that opportunities were opening up at home, and my grandfather hoped to keep his sons in Scotland by apprenticing them in various essential trades.

Angus, my father, was learning surveying and mensuration in the county surveyor's office, and on his own initiative he was studying at night for the ministry. He was deeply religious and

5

wanted to become a missionary and go to spread the Word in Darkest Africa. When I was told, as a child, that he had had this plan, I used to think very gravely of what might have happened if he had carried out his intention. "What would have become of *me*," I used to think, "if he had gone to Africa instead of Idaho? Would he have married an African, and would I have been half black? Or would that half-black child not have been me at all? And would I—*I*—not have existed?" I never shared these thoughts with anyone, but they were very real to me and they were my first intimation of the terrible chances of existence or nonexistence. They made my life precious to me. That I might not have existed was a thought more frightening to me than the other awful realization that stars were other worlds and that earth hung in a space to which we could assign no limits.

My uncle Douglas, then about eighteen and a well-grown lad with a strong body and a ruddy, handsome face, was apprenticed to the gardener of Thurso Castle. My uncle Willie was apprenticed to a saddlemaker, and Geordie was promised to a watch and clockmaker. He and the two younger lads, who were destined to be farmers, were still at school and at home. The older boys lived during the week where they were apprenticed, but returned to the farm for Saturday night and the Sabbath day.

Douglas had been the hardest one to settle into an apprenticeship. Nothing that was offered really pleased him, and he was not pleased now. To be a gardener was too near to being a farmer in his opinion, and he had already had his fill of turnips and oats and the spreading of cow dung on reluctant fields. He wanted something better from his life, and he did not have Angus' belief in eternity to give him patience.

Douglas was more like the mother's people than he was like the McBains, and the other members of the family recognized without envy that he was the mother's favorite. She shielded his whims as best she could from the necessary logic of a hard existence. But, when he finally agreed to become apprentice to the gardener, they were all relieved and thankful that Douglas was at last settled into a life's work.

The castle stood up bare and ugly on a rocky promontory at one end of Thurso's crescent beach. The Sinclairs who owned it spent much of their time in Edinburgh or London, and they had done very little to change the medieval appearance of the place. Still, it had its lawns and ivies, its rockeries, its gooseberry and currant bushes and its rows of kale on the windswept cliffs.

The gardener was a dour old man who would sooner have been alone, but the work was too heavy without some strong lads to put his plans into execution. His knuckles had grown crooked and his back bent in the service of the castle. The long, wet winters, with the darkness falling at four of the afternoon and not dispersing before ten of the next morning, played hob with a man's bones. If the consumption did not take them, the Caithness men generally lived a long time, but their joints grew thick and their backs twisted.

Whatever might be said of the castle garden, in midsummer it had the most superb view one could wish, with the white crescent beach and the little cramped gray slate and granite town at its back, and before it a wealth of turbulent blue sea and islands the color of ripe grapes thick with bloom. Whenever a fishing sloop or a larger steamer, staining the sky with her black smoke, put around the promontory, Douglas leaned on his spade and watched her go. He hated digging in heavy ground, and he knew that there must be easier and pleasanter ways for a lad to make his living if he used his brain instead of his back muscles. The ships on the horizon symbolized freedom for him. They were going somewhere while he stayed behind. He watched them with discontent and longing, and gradually with an emerging purpose which crystallized on the day the gardener sent him to Wick. He was to take the two-wheeled pony cart and go to the larger town to fetch a consignment of hawthorn bushes which the laird had shipped up from Edinburgh as a windbreak for the last terrace.

Douglas cared not a farthing for the laird's hawthorns, knowing that they had a slim chance of survival in the wild air from the sea, but he was delighted to be going into Wick in the herring season.

It was a bright crisp Friday morning in June, and the gulls wheeled, screaming and crying, in the blue air. The Caithness wind, not gentle even in midsummer, seemed today to swoop and sail and cry with the gulls. Douglas sat at ease in the high cart, slapping the reins over the pony's back. His cap was pulled down sturdily against the wind but at a carefree angle, his lips

7

had a twist of good humor at the corners, and his eyes a gleam of anticipation. He kept the startled pony at a trot, and took pleasure in passing slower and more cautious vehicles. Children and dogs poured out of a tinkler's shambling encampment with a chorus of shouts and barks as he went smartly by. This little demonstration gave him a sense of power and well-being out of all proportion to his status as gardener's apprentice.

When he came into the town, he let the pony take its own gait over the resounding cobbles, and he looked about him with alert eyes. Wick was the largest town he had known. Its herring-season crowds, its smell of new wooden boxes and salt fish, of peat smoke and roasting coffee, of stale groceries and grog shops and the damp sanctity of Protestant chapels, excited him unreasonably. Thurso had no such fine harbor and only the smallest fishing boats did business there. Among his various yearnings, Douglas felt the lust for cities stirring in his blood. What was just out of reach seemed more desirable than what lay near at hand. So Wick was more desirable to him than Thurso, and the dirty little steamers that came from Leith or Thameside were more desirable still.

Looking down the street that led to the harbor, he saw now that one of these was berthed among the fishing craft. Although she was powered by steam, she carried sailing masts for running with the wind. Her masts looked beautiful against the sky. He drove down to the port and gazed at her. Her name was *Lacy McDonald*. Men were loading her with boxes of salt herring. A man in a greasy apron that had once been white leaned on the rail smoking a pipe.

"When does she sail?" Douglas called up to him.

"Midday, Sabbath, when the tide turns," answered the man at the rail.

"Are ye shorthanded?"

"Aye, I doot. We're a'ways that."

"Whereaboots can I find the captain?"

"Captain, is it?" grunted the man. "Captain's up yonder at the *Twa Corbies* taking his morn's encouragement. Have ye ever shipped before, lad?"

"There's a first time for everything, meester," Douglas said. "I'm strong an' able."

8

"I see that. But will ye puke in the galley the first time a wave hits broadside?"

"Not I," said Douglas stoutly.

"You're a bit cheeky for a cabin boy an' cook's helper, but that's soon taken out o' ye. Yon's the mate, overlookin' the stevies. Go ask him, if ye'd like to sign on."

It was true that the *Lacy McDonald* needed a cabin boy and cook's helper.

"Be here before the tide turns Sabbath, if ye want the berth," the mate said. The pay was little; the risk and the break with home were very large. Yet Douglas saw the *Lacy McDonald* as the key to the vast unknown world for which he longed.

He drove back to Thurso in a ferment of excitement and indecision. All the next day, planting the hawthorns in a struggling row along the wind-swept terrace, he wrestled with his future. He was strongly swayed by hatred of the monotonous labor of setting uniform roots in straight rows in unfriendly soil. If he had had a more congenial task that Saturday, his decision might have been different.

One thing he knew well, his father would disapprove of his going to sea. He was apprenticed to the gardener for a year. His word had been given, and a Scotsman's word was supposed to be sacred. Moreover, the McBains had always been landsmen. They looked upon the fishermen as people of a lower order, and upon a sailor's life as too unstable and uncertain to be carried with dignity. The wishes of a Victorian father were not lightly put aside.

It was eight o'clock on the Saturday eve before Douglas was free to fare homeward. If he hurried he knew that he would catch up with Angus and Willie somewhere in the town or just beyond, and that they would walk on to the farm together as they did each Saturday night. He counted on speaking to Angus privately and asking him to intercede with the father.

At that season it was still as broad daylight at eight of the evening as any man needed for reading fine print, and Angus was reading as he walked homeward from the surveyor's office. Douglas saw the elder brother ahead of him, walking slowly, his shoulders a little bent, his light-blue eyes deep in the small book, and his mind many miles away. Yet Douglas knew that "A", as they called him, would put the book in his pocket and give him his attention when they were together. There was such grave steadfastness in A that one was never in doubt about where he stood, and his word carried great weight with the father.

Both Douglas and Willie brought their troubles to Angus, and did not suspect, for his extreme quietness, that he had troubles of his own. Angus' troubles were all of the mind and spirit. He had already gone a long way intellectually beyond the usual cotter's son; but he took no pride in this, for it had only given him a vaster appetite and a sense that he would never be appeased. He had reached a first peak from which he looked abroad and saw such beauty and strangeness of knowledge and experience as he could never hope to compass in a little span of life. The brevity of life struck him so strongly that he reached out for a heaven which might give him the eternity that seemed too short. The family had been only mildly Calvinistic, as Presbyterian as a good Scotch family can be and still live comfortably and get the crops in on a Sabbath when the need be. But Angus had taken Christ into his heart with a kind of mystic detachment that was not unusual among serious young Scotsmen of his day.

Yet he had begun to realize that to become a minister required money and leisure which he did not have. He had begun to think that a man might have as great an influence for good in the business world, working among his fellow men, as in the ministry. Certainly, the more he saw of business, the more Angus felt that it wanted the spirit of Christ in it. For weeks he had been in this quandary. When he could lose himself in a book, he was content. But, when he was in the field surveying, half of his mind was free to wrestle with the problem of his future. At such times he asked himself if it was only the prompting of the world that made him waver in his vocation for the ministry? Was it fear of the long struggle? Was it a temptation of the devil?

He went over the problem carefully, methodically, scanning all of the movements of his mind, lest he should find some evil. If he were base at heart, he wished to face it honestly and try to set himself right. There was little in Caithness scenery to distract the mind from its own preoccupations. In the clear, keen air that smelled of the sea, a thoughtful and lonely man could pursue an inner conflict peacefully.

The three brothers were within five years of an age, and they were so similar in build, clean-cut features and general family resemblance, that the differences in their characters stood out the more boldly.

If Willie had a soul, it had never given him a moment's anxiety; so long as he could eat and sleep and laugh at another chiel's crack, he was delighted with the world. He was almost as blond as Angus, but his face was ruddier, his eye a deeper blue. His mouth turned up at the corners with mirth or down at the corners with drollery the whole day, and he was not troubled with any ambition. Everything pleased Willie. His oatcake and haggis pleased him, and his mattress of husks in the little loft under the thatch. He was pleased with his work as a saddle-maker and was apt at working up the leather into thistles and roses or finishing it off with a nice glaze. He thought the saddle-maker to whom he was apprenticed a royal good fellow, and never minded that his breath was sour or that he was exacting with his apprentices.

A dozen Thurso lassies pleased Willie equally well, and this liberality of numbers had preserved his sanguine innocence. For Willie had never liked one lassie enough better than the rest to go too far with her. So the girls ran out as he went by, with havers an' clavers and tag ends of gossip; and sometimes the mothers and grandmothers ran out too to offer him a hot scone or a fresh-turned pancake. He was the jolly lad they would all have liked for a son.

Yet often, while the young girls chattered with Willie, their eyes wandered beyond him for a glimpse of Douglas. Douglas was hard to please, and young girls dream of pleasing the difficult one. His scorn and detachment were provocative. The lassies could have let these perversities pass in a plain lad, but to see them in a handsome one wrung their hearts.

Douglas had no great opinion of the Thurso women. With their plaid shawls over their heads, he thought them a dowdy lot, and, although he had not seen any others, he was sure that the ladies of Edinburgh and even of Glasgow would be more to his liking.

Falling in step beside Angus on the Saturday night in June,

11

Douglas slowed his pace to fit his brother's. Angus put his book in his pocket and looked around with a slow smile.

"Aye, Doug?" he said. "You've had a good week?"

"The same," said Doug laconically, "digging, planting, pulling weeds. I'm not fit for it, A."

"Why not then?" Angus asked. "I thought you were pleased to be a gardener, Doug. You'd find it less to your liking to sit hunched over a desk in a counting house, would ye no?"

"Aye," said Douglas, "but you know yourself, A, there's more opportunity to be found out yonder than in Thurso, or even Wick, poor towns both of them. We're wasting our time here, A."

"No, no," said Angus. "A man need never waste his time, wherever he is, and we've no money to take us far off. 'Twill have to come slow for us, Doug, but we'll watch for our opportunities here. They willna be long on the way."

"That's what I'm saying, Angus. Mine's come now. I'm sorry it's come before yours, for I ken ye want to be away from here as much as I do. But likely you wouldna take this way out. I will, that's all."

"What do ye mean by that?"

"I can sign on with a Glasgow steamer that's in Wick harbor. She sails the morn, and it's a fair way of getting out into the world at no expense to the family or myself."

"But you're bound for a year, lad! You canna go back on your word. I think to go myself when my work's done at the surveyor's office. Bide a little. Save your wee bit and learn your trade, and in a few months we'll go together."

"I canna wait, Angus," Douglas said. "Be a good brother to me. Speak a fair word to Father. He'll listen to you and weigh your opinion. I've no heart to tell him myself."

"Are you telling him, or asking his permission? I think he'll no give the permission to you, lad."

"You must try it for me, A. I'd rather have his permission than to go without it. But I'll go in any case. It's myself I'm thinkin' on."

"Yourself, aye," said Angus gravely, "but there are other people in the world beside yourself, man. You must also think of them."

They heard Willie whistling and running along the cobbles after them. A couple of friendly dogs cavorted beside him.

"Hey, Doug, I've a message for ye from Annie Swanson."

12

"What like?" asked Douglas carelessly.

"That she's a new bonnet for kirk and you're to give her your opinion on it, because you've the keenest eye for style of any lad in Thurso. What do you think of that, eh?"

"The lassie's daft," said Douglas calmly. "Besides, it's like I won't be here when the church bells ring again."

"What?" cried Willie, his mouth falling open in astonishment.

"Doug thinks to leave us," Angus said mildly.

"Whereaboots to?" asked Willie. "Can I go along?"

"No, but I'll send for ye, when I've set mysel' up in a good establishment across the water."

"Across which water? Is it Canada you're away to? Or Australia? Where?"

"I've no idea yet mysel', so dinna press me," Douglas said.

"Father will be sore fashed."

"A is going to speak to him for me."

"And the mother," Angus said quietly. "How is she to take it? Have you thought of that?"

"I canna stop to think," Douglas said. "We'll all go soon. You know that. There's no life for so many of us here. You'll stop a bit, and maybe you'll do better than me. But now I must go without too much thinking on it."

"They'll all be fair upset," said Willie. "Mither an' Jeanie will be the worst."

"Dinna tell a body at home until A has spoken to Father," Douglas said. "You *will* speak, will ye no, A?"

"I'll do what I can," Angus said gravely.

3

During the midsummer days turnips, oats, and kale grew with the eagerness of things held long in darkness. The day was no longer measured in hours, but only by the span of the sun. The men came in for dinner at noon, and in the afternoon the women took tea and oatcakes to them in the fields. At six they all trooped in again for tea with eggs or herring or a bowl of crowdie, and then they went again to the fields for the long golden light before the sun was set. About eleven o'clock the sun dipped below the horizon, leaving the world blue and chill with an unchanging twilight, and only then they dragged their weary bodies in for a supper of cold scones and tea, and bed.

The three boys who were apprenticed in Thurso were usually at home for the six o'clock tea on a Saturday night, and then Willie and Douglas turned to and lent a hand in the fields or helped with the chores about the byre and sty.

The father always sat awhile after tea to read his newspaper in the evening light. He was a sturdy man, not so tall as his three eldest sons, but broad of shoulder and deep of chest. Although his own part in the world was a humble one, he never let the world go swiftly by him without knowing something of it.

Angus sat with him on the wide slate doorstep underneath the thatch. No one resented the fact that Angus should continue to read his book and sit beside the father while the other boys were employed physically about the farm. With the same devotion that an Irish Catholic family would dedicate a son to the priesthood, the Protestant Scottish family liked to dedicate a son to intellectual pursuits. They liked him to be a minister, but that was not essential. He might be a schoolmaster or a scientist or an engineer so long as he had learning; for they respected books, and although most of the family had no skill in them, they honored the son who had.

Tonight Angus and the father sat together silently, each deep in his own thoughts, but, although they were habitually silent, something warm and sympathetic flowed between them. An old shepherd dog lay at their feet, his nose laid sideways on his outstretched paws, and behind them in the kitchen the mother and Jeanie washed the cups and plates. Lottie, the eldest daughter, had been married in the autumn, and had gone to Glasgow where her husband was a worker in a cotton-thread mill. Now there were only the mother and twelve-year-old Jean to do for all these growing men. When the cups and plates were washed, they would go out to help with the milking, for, like cooking and childbearing, that was a part of women's work.

When the father and son had been silent for some time, Angus put down his book and said in his gentle voice: "Father, I'm thinking that Douglas is no so very well pleased wi' his apprenticeship at the castle."

14

"No?" said his father. He lowered his paper slowly, and his eyes met Angus' eyes in a questioning look.

"No," said Angus. There was another silence. They both knew how difficult it had been to get Douglas established, and it was useless to put it into words. The father knew, too, that Angus would not have raised the question now if it had not been urgent.

"He's unco' hard to please," he said presently. "What is it now?"

"There's a boat put in at Wick harbor and the skipper is short-handed. He's offered Douglas a berth on her."

"The lad'll no be thinkin' of signin' up for a sailor?" cried the old man sharply. "I've promised him for a year to the castle gardener."

"He's fair set to go," said Angus. "He bade me tell you."

"Aye, an' what good will it do to tell me?"

"He wants your consent to go, Father."

"Nae, he winna have that."

"I told him myself ye'd never consider it," said Angus quietly.

"Then ye may tell him so again frae me. Tell him to put these notions out o' his head and buckle to like an honest fellow. I've fashed mysel' sufficiently wi' his whimsies."

Angus went into the kale patch and told Douglas what his father had said. Douglas went on weeding to the end of the row, then he straightened his back and flung the weeds from him with an angry gesture. A deeper red had risen under his wind and sunburned skin, and his clenched hands were white along the knuckles.

"I've my own life to live," he said fiercely.

"Bide a little," begged Angus. "Save your shillings, lad. Another six months an' we might take ship to the States together."

Douglas looked at him, bright-eyed and angry still. "I've no stomach for biding," he said, but he bent to his row again and made short work of the weeds in it.

When twilight fell at last and all of the workers had come straggling in, the mother heaped more peat on the fire and filled their cups again with tea. They were all tired and stained with the yellow earth that nourished them so frugally, and they sat stolidly and ate.

The three younger boys gulped their food and yawned. Geordie was a sharp-eyed boy, darker than the rest and clever with his

15

head and hands, Charley had a round head and red cheeks and a slow-moving mind, and Davie was a pale lad with a lame foot and a quiet smile. Before they went to bed the father asked an evening blessing.

"Lord keep us safe th' nicht, and make us sensible of a' our blessings. Let us not stray like foolish sheep, but do Thy will. Amen."

As they went up he put his hand on Douglas' shoulder. "Be steadfast, lad," he said, "be steadfast."

The mother watched them with bright, anxious eyes. She needed none to tell her that Douglas was astray again.

Douglas made no reply to his father, but his heart beat heavily, and he lay long awake in the loft where the boys slept. Their measured breathing rose all about him. The smell of oat husks and peat smoke mingled together in the heavy air, and through the little dormer window he saw a pale white moon hanging mysteriously in the midnight dusk.

" 'Tis my own life," he repeated to himself doggedly, "and myself the only one to live it."

4

When he came down from the loft, Douglas had his few important belongings tied together in a sack. The little house was full of the deep twilight between midnight and dawn, and he trod carefully, for it was also full of the soft sound of sleepers. But when he reached the foot of the stairs, something stirred in the kitchen, and he knew that it was his mother.

"Och, Douglas!" she whispered. "Can ye no bide wi' us?"

"No," he said. "I canna stick it any longer." He wanted to tell her that he would be rich some day and that he would send her money and a fine dress, and that all of them would be proud of him; but such things are hard to say at any time, and now his tongue was tied.

"Och! Och!" said his mother softly to herself. But she went to the cupboard and made up a hasty packet of oatcake and cheese to put in his pocket. Her competent hands trembled and fumbled

16

at the task. He saw her anxiety with pity, but he would not allow it to soften his resolution.

"Och, Douglas, if I never see ye again, my lad!"

"Dinna take on, Mother. 'Twill not be long until I'm home again." Hastily he bent and kissed her.

She stood in the cottage door with a plaid over her head, and watched him go away. He was straight and tall with a long, purposeful stride, and, after he had said goodbye, he never once looked back. She could see him for a long way, the only figure moving in the flat landscape, the only stir in the uncertain light of the small hours. Sometimes she wiped her cheeks with the back of her hand, but she made no sound of crying, for she wanted her grief to herself. Why must the one she loved best be the one to love home least? She stood in the open door asking herself this question over and over, until she began to shiver and knew she must get to bed, for this would be another day in the fields.

By the time the sun was up again Douglas had reached Wick and gone down to the harbor. But it was still too early to present himself to the skipper of the herring boat. He sat on the cliffs beside the harbor and drew in long breaths of the keen air. He felt like a caged thrush which has been set at liberty, and as if, at last, great things were going to happen to him. He spread the oatcake and cheese which his mother had given him on the rocks beside him and made his breakfast.

The sun sparkled and bobbed from wave to wave, and already behind him sounded the clang of hammers in the box and barrel factory on the wharf, and the clatter of wooden-soled shoes on the cobbles. Life began to stir on the boats, and the smell of herring, mingled with the salt of the sea, was in the air.

Opposite him in a half cave in the cliffs, he saw two fish girls making their morning toilet. God knew where they had spent the night, but now one sat at the other's feet, her full skirts spread about her, while the other combed and recombed the first girl's long black hair. Farther on, in a pool below the town, three small boys had flung aside their clothes and plunged naked into the cold northern water. Douglas watched them dive and bob for shore, and his own flesh tingled as if he had made the icy plunge himself. The sun on the sea, the forest of masts, the long black

17

hair of the fish girl, the vicarious prickling of the salty water, all etched themselves on his mind in a lasting impression that would be with him all his life.

5

A small smoky lamp swung to and fro in the cabin. Douglas' eyes followed it. Beyond it a jacket on a peg swung to and fro also, and the ship creaked with an almost human sound of lamentation. The air in the cabin was cold, but heavy with the smell of coal oil, damp woolen, and stale humanity. In the bunk below him a man was snoring, and across the way the occupants of the other bunks were exchanging lewd reminiscences. Douglas only half listened.

In the first days of the voyage such talk had excited him and he had given it the avid ear of inexperienced youth. In Caithness they knew the facts of life, but there was none of this obscene embroidering of them. So long as the novelty lasted Douglas was amused, but with too much repetition lewdness can become as dull as a chapel sermon. He had begun by envying the men their erotic experiences, but already his interest was fading to disgust.

The only thing he still envied the sailor who was speaking was the full-rigged ship tattooed upon his arm. Douglas leaned out of his bunk and looked at it, every mast and spar pricked out correctly in purple ink on the hairy forearm, and he was determined to have one like it if he could afford it.

Tomorrow they were to put in at Leith to unload the herring which they had been collecting in the little ports of northern Scotland, and there they would take on goods for the Canary Islands. In Spain, the cook told him, they would ship a cargo of oranges. Oranges, Spain, the Canary Islands! To a Caithness lad oranges were almost as strange as mountains and trees. An orange was a coveted thing, small and hard and round, the color of the night sun as it dropped through mist toward the horizon on Midsummer's Eve. It symbolized the strangeness and brightness of the world toward which the steamer lurched and wallowed.

The crowded cabin, the hard work and heavy odors, the vast

18

rolling greenness of the sea, and that uneasy misery of a landsman's stomach in a ship's galley were all worse than the clean-swept freshness of the garden at Thurso castle. Yet they were leading to something that Douglas wanted, and so they were more endurable than the castle garden had been. Just exactly what it was that he wanted, he did not know, except that it had to do with cities and a full life. Lying in his bunk he tried to imagine cities and what part he would have in them, but he had a poor imagination and no experience on which to found it.

When they reached Leith and finished their unloading, most of the ship's men went to taverns or brothels or to poor relations on dark side streets. A few walked into Edinburgh, but they were used to mountains and the glitter of cities. They walked unseeing because they did not care. But it is not strange that a Caithness lad, who had never seen anything but long flat stretches unfolding interminably without a tree over marsh and peat bog to the sea, should stop to gaze in wonder at his first uneven ground.

Coming upon Edinburgh from Leith Walk, Douglas loitered to stare in silence upon its seven hills. Later he climbed to the top of Castle Rock and leaned with his elbows on the parapet to look and look. The castle itself interested him little, except as a part of the general glitter of an ancient city. But he was fascinated by the rolling swell of town and circling hills. Even on a summer's day the many chimney pots of Auld Reekie sent up a thin blue smoke that lay like mist across the miles of gray stone streets. Beyond, more sharp in the cold light of distance, jutted the great hump of Arthur's Seat like a lion couchant, and to the south the Braid Hills rolled, and farther still, fold upon fold, melting into the distance, were the Pentlands.

Below him on the other side of Castle Rock, Douglas looked down on the gardens and shops of Prince's Street, and the national monuments where eminent men sat in timeless marble with the smiles of past achievement frozen on their faces.

It was almost dusk when Douglas came down from Castle Rock. Summer dark came earlier here than in Caithness. There was a warm golden flush in the sky, and every little tree and hill stood separated from the one behind it by a touch of mist, slipping from purple to indigo and far away to the most tender, heavenly blue. From away towards Heriot's Hospital came the

19

sound of bagpipes and the rolling of a drum. It seemed to pierce him like a cold, swift steel and brought the sudden tears to his eyes.

"I'm here! I'm alive! I'm livin' my own life!" he said to himself. He no longer said it with rebellion as he had said it in Caithness, but only with wonder and a startled satisfaction.

The gas lamps were being lighted along Prince's Street as he went down, and carriages were moving smartly to and fro. He was very hungry, and the lighted windows of a pastry shop took his eye.

He was gazing at the bright array of shortbread and plum cake and raisin scones, and wondering if he dared go in with his old homespun jacket smelling of herring and tar, when a young lady came out of the pastry shop, stepping daintily to the curb where her carriage stood. Her silks rustled with a little hushing murmur, and there was an odor like fresh-pulled violets about her. Her hair fell in a long cascade of ringlets under her tiny hat where, poised as if for flight, there was a hummingbird. She was his first fine lady, and coming thus after his first mountains, she seemed the greater miracle.

Douglas pulled off his cap and opened her carriage door for her, and in return she flashed him a dazzling smile, without making the mistake of tossing him a penny. For, in spite of his homespun jacket, Douglas had the eye, the nose, the turn of chin that made most women look at him a second time.

He walked on in a daze; his hunger did not trouble him for several streets and then only as something vague and secondary. But at last he found a small tavern on a dark side street that looked as if it matched his pocketbook, and he sat down to a greasy muttonchop with scones and tea.

A thin girl with untidy hair and a pair of sailor's boots on her feet sat in a corner opposite, and looked at him with calculating eyes. He avoided her gaze, and, when she followed him into the street, he had no patience with her. He shook her plucking fingers off his sleeve.

"Nay, lass, ye're too easy," he said. "I like to pick my own."

20

6

My uncle Douglas never had much to say to any of us about his nine months at sea. It is to be supposed that he liked the life of a cabin boy on a tramp steamer as little as he liked the life of a gardener's assistant. The only permanent mark of the sea that he carried with him through life was a small green anchor tattooed on his left forearm. It was probably small because at the time he could not afford a large one, but it became him well, as everything did. Being a tasteful tattoo, not a garish one, it later affected the women who knew him with tenderness, just as his slight limp did, and the romantic scars on his temple and the backs of his hands. Whatever misfortunes befell him seemed to add to his charm, and the tattoo, although more of an indiscretion than a misfortune, was of the same nature.

I imagine him in a small hot room beyond the swinging bead portiere of a wharfside dive, sitting opposite an old man in a skullcap and thick spectacles. Douglas' bared arm is stretched under the lamplight among the bottles of colored ink, and he has just reluctantly abandoned the idea of the full-rigged sailing vessel in favor of the small anchor. He is saving every shilling he can toward a passage to the United States. He has seen Spain now and the Canary Islands, and many other places. He has had his fill of swabbing decks, and peeling potatoes and emptying slops into heaving green water. His ideas are crystallized and his imagination developed to such an extent that he sees what he wants to do. The anchor now is only a romantic souvenir, a youthful extravagance to recall to him the hard way of his deliverance.

In the stormy dark as the steamer plowed through the black mountains of water and the foam-flecked wind roared by, he must sometimes have thought of his mother and the little sister Jeanie whom he loved. He must have remembered the warm hearth of the cottage and smelled the peat smoke and the oatcakes baking. He must have thought of his father, too, possibly with guilt and with somewhat less tenderness than he lavished on the mother, for his father represented restraint, and he had always been impatient of restraint. He remembered Willie's

21

laughing face and Angus' grave one, and he heard Angus' quiet voice saying, "Bide a little. Save your wee bit and learn your trade and in a few months we'll go together."

He did not write home at all. If he could have expected letters in return, he might have written, for he must often have been homesick enough even to relish a scolding or any sort of advice or reproof. But he was on a tramp vessel without a fixed course, and to get word to Caithness and back would take a long time.

That his mother would worry he knew, but he thought less of that than of his own plight, and he never got around to borrowing pen and paper from the mate until the end of his service was in sight and the vessel headed for Glasgow. Then, after he had counted his savings and looked into the possibilities of his future, he posted a brief line by the fast mail packet to his sister Lottie in Glasgow. He said he was well and hoped she was the same, and that he expected to see her in about a fortnight when his boat came in. There seemed no reason to say more.

7

When he was finally paid off and went walking up the wharf with his bag of belongings slung over his shoulder, Douglas felt a little strange and unsteady on his land legs.

There was a smoky March sunset beyond the sheds and warehouses and crowded masts of Glasgow harbor. Douglas took a deep breath. He was glad to be free again, and he told himself that he was a man of experience now who had seen the world. Yet in his breast a very young heart was beating quickly with the expectation of seeing his sister, and he was beginning to calculate the cost of a train fare to Caithness and how much of a hole it would make in his savings for America.

Glasgow could outdo London in the matter of belching chimney stacks, clatter of shipbuilding and factory-shadowed streets, but the plaid shawls over the women's heads and the broad familiar burr of the men's speech told Douglas that he was in Scotland, and he was glad. He had never known before how much he loved Scotland until his heart warmed to these sour-smelling streets.

Lottie lived up two flights of bare stone stairs in lodgings. The wooden-soled shoes of children continually clattered up and down the stairs in the echoing hallway. Douglas ran up the stairs lightly and quickly now and pulled the bell. His heart was in his mouth lest Lottie should be out or moved away or he have mistaken the number. But the door flew open almost at once and there was Lottie herself, laughing and crying, and trying to kiss him all at the same time.

She pulled him into the first of the two small rooms which comprised her home. This was a combination of living room, kitchen and company bedroom. It was unlighted now except for a warm glow from the open grate of the cooking stove which was set into the wall like a fireplace. The room was spotlessly clean and there was in it a savory smell of mutton collops. Copper pans on the wall caught the light, and the turkey-red tester on the wall bed caught it also. The warm light fell on the white cloth of the spread table, and surprisingly it fell too on the beaming face of a young man who sat in the only armchair. The young man was smiling very broadly and looked ready to leap up as soon as the intended surprise had taken effect.

"Willie!" cried Douglas, throwing down his bag and leaping forward. Willie came out of his chair with a bound, and they caught each other about the shoulders, laughing and tussling like a couple of young animals in a very small den.

"Look to my table, lads," cried Lottie. "You'll upset it sure!"

"Well, Doug," cried Willie. "I wondered how long ye'd be gawpin' around before ye set eyes on me!"

"Willie! Willie!" cried Douglas. "How come you in Glasgow, lad?"

"You'd no be interested," said Willie, "and yourself so secretive we ne'er heard a word from you this nine months past. Shall we tell him at all, Lottie?"

"Not yet," said Lottie, laughing, "give him his supper first."

"I've no appetite until I know."

"Too bad," said Lottie, lifting the cover of the pot and letting a warm aroma of collops permeate the atmosphere. She was a sturdy, pleasant-faced young person, too much like her handsome brothers to be a beautiful woman.

At this point Tom, her husband, came in and there were more greetings all around. Tom was an honest Caithness lad, wide between the blue eyes, generous hearted and laughing, and bound to be a thread-mill worker and live in two rooms all his life.

"Come to table, all of you," cried Lottie. "What a family I've got this night! Ye're fair bonnie, you three lads, if I do say so myself!"

"And are you away to the States, Douglas?" asked Tom, when the blessing was out of the way and their forks were busy with the stew. Douglas looked up in surprise.

"That's my plan," said Douglas, "but I thought first to go north to see Mother an' speak with Angus before I left."

Willie and Lottie burst into peals of laughter.

"Tom, he knows nothing," said Lottie. "We've not yet told him."

"If you've something to tell," said Douglas irritably, "for God's sake, out with it, and have done laughing."

"Och, Doug, it's your own fault for not writing," said Willie. "We knew not where to send you word, but Angus has been away to the States this six months. All settled he is, in the far West, and he's sent back money to help you and me along to join him."

"And I was swabbing decks an' emptying slops into the sea the while," said Douglas darkly. The others continued to laugh, and presently he had to join them. "And you, Willie? You're on your way?"

"Aye," said Willie proudly. "I'm on my way to America. That's why I'm here, lad, that's why I'm here!"

"Then I'll no waste time by going back to Caithness," Douglas said. "I'll return one day when I can make a brave show, but now I'll go with you. What does Angus say?"

"Here's his letter," cried Lottie, running to the sideboard to fetch a much-thumbed letter with a strange stamp. Douglas took it slowly and looked at the beautiful, small handwriting which was almost like seeing A's face.

"I am located in Opportunity, a promising new settlement in the Idaho Territory. . . . Saddlemakers are in great demand and Willie will find work to do. . . . If Douglas is not fixed on the sea, he can find all manner of openings here, for young men are needed in every line. I stay at a boardinghouse kept by a fine, godly Scotswoman, so I do not want for oatcakes and porridge, nor lack my countrymen for company. . . . The Presbyterian kirk is shepherded by an excellent minister, whose dedication makes

24

up for any deficiency in theology. . . . Near the kirk lives the doctor, whose wife, a kindly soul, has already befriended me, as have his two daughters. The eldest, a dark-haired girl with a great musical talent is just at home from boarding school. . . . I hope this finds all well at home, as it leaves me. . . ."

Douglas skimmed over the letter, his eyes bright with interest. "If Douglas is not fixed on the sea . . . young men are needed in every line."

"So Angus is already gone!" he said, still marveling.

"Aye, and the Young Men's Christian Society of Thurso gave him a testimonial dinner an' presented him with a Bible before he left," said Tom proudly, glad to shine in the reflection of his brother-in-law's glory.

Willie drew his mouth down at the corners in one of his droll smiles.

"I didna notice that anyone thought of presentin' me with a Bible when *I* left," he said, "no, nor you neither, Douglas. No Bibles for either of us!"

"Yet I dare say the two of you had the most need of them," said Lottie dryly.

"But what is Angus working at?" asked Douglas.

"He's gone out for the North Scottish Life Insurance Company," said Tom. "They've a great business in the States, I'm told."

"Aye," said Willie, "the Americans have been so busy chasin' gold an' buffalo an' shootin' each other right and left, they havena had time to insure their own lives, it seems like."

"Send a few Scotsmen out there, an' 'twill put some law an' order into 'em," said Tom. "I've almost a mind to go myself."

"Oh, no, Tom!" cried Lottie. "Never think of it! Thousands of miles over sea an' land to a wild, strange country full of savages! An' mother and father half the world away in Caithness. We're far enough in Glasgow!"

"Aye, lass, we're well enough here," said Tom, pressing her hand. He had no real stomach for far and savage places, either, and it was a comfort to have a sensible wife to hold him back. Let the McBain boys go trailing off to the other end of the world if they wished, but they were not already married and securely tied to a job in the mill as he was.

Later that evening Douglas wrote a letter to his mother. He was not a very good letter writer. He had neither Angus' beau-

25

tiful penmanship nor his ease of expression. But he told her that he was going to America with Willie to join Angus. He mentioned the state of weather then existing in Glasgow and informed her that Lottie and Tom as well as Willie and himself were enjoying good health and that he hoped that all of the family in Caithness were enjoying the same. Yet the mother in Caithness must have read, between the lines, the unexpressed love and uncertainty, the regret at parting and the ambition for the future that fluttered behind Douglas' pen as he wrote. She folded the letter away among the treasures in her parlor, and she was satisfied. Nothing could ever be so hard again as had been the parting on the morning when he ran away to sea.

8

The day that they sailed for the States was heavy with cold, white mist. The buildings along the wharves were festooned with it, and the masts pricked through it like the spokes of a cobweb. At the last moment Willie lost heart and flung himself weeping into Lottie's arms, but Douglas shook him impatiently and led him up the gangplank.

"Och, Willie! Ye're no longer a bairn."

Lottie had seen Angus go, his pale face grave and calm in the moment of departure; and now, through a mist of tears, she saw the next two take their leave. Angus was nearest to her in years, and dearest, too, she thought, and yet she had not wept at his departure. One did not weep for Angus, for there was something quiet and planned about Angus that seemed to make him safe. Whether it was the Lord's doing or his own, she did not know, but he could walk through the valley of the shadow and fear no evil. One need not shed tears for a man like that, even if one remembered how cold he used to get digging the peat in the spring, or how he hated the lack of water in the summer when the rain-water barrels ran low, or how he used to save a bit of porridge from his bowl to feed the old dog who had lost his teeth.

But it was different with Willie and Douglas—Willie blubbering like a lassie betrayed at thoughts of leaving home, and Douglas with his proud head held erect defying a world he meant to conquer. Lottie did not analyze it to herself, and yet she knew beyond telling that Angus had gone armed and girded to a far land, and that Willie and Douglas were open to all the slings and arrows that the world could throw.

She pressed her handkerchief against her quivering chin and tried to smile at them as they stood beside the rail of the vessel. Willie had already grown cheerful again at something Doug had said, and Douglas' eyes were bright with the glitter of anticipation.

They waved their caps at her as the vessel moved slowly away from the dock, and Lottie waved her handkerchief and called goodbye. The foghorn was sounding now with mournful regularity, and the waters were foaming about the ship's stern. Lottie stood in the cold fog that was beginning to pelt her with tiny stinging drops until the vessel was lost to view down the misty intricacies of the Clyde.

"The new world," she said to herself softly. "Opportunity—western territories—" No, she didn't want Tom to go, and yet she was a McBain, and in spite of herself she heard the allure in the words.

Second class on a small Scottish steamship in 1888 was far from luxurious, but Willie and Douglas were content. All of their experience had been of the most primitive kind. Willie found friends on every hand, and was soon bouncing babies and fetching shawls for old ladies and listening to the heart's secrets of unhappy young girls with plain faces. He had not been away from shore an hour before he discovered that there was nothing to weep at in departure, for life went on wherever he was and seemed as full of interest as it always had been.

Douglas stood often beside the rail watching the waves spin by. The sea was no novelty to him now, but its ceaseless movement stimulated the flow of his thoughts. He was glad to be a passenger and see other poor devils swabbing the decks and balancing trays in the dining saloon. He felt that he had made his first step upward, and he had a long climb to the place he wished to occupy. In the midst of his satisfaction, however, there was a sharp core of anxiety. He knew himself untried, and, much as he desired it, he could not see the face of his success with any clarity nor put into concrete terms the manner of its achievement.

27

But Caithness had given her lads one priceless gift. It was a Scotch gift, wrought from poverty and deprivation. Having nothing to look back upon but frugality and a treeless place of hard-won crops, the Caithness men saw even the meanest land they came upon in the new world as a betterment. Poverty had shoved them out of their native land and they had inherited the rest of the world. No beginning was too humble for them, and they saw no limit to the heights they might scale. By giving her lads none of the opulence of other lands, Caithness, in very niggardliness, had dealt them their greatest good fortune.

Opportunity

1

IT HAS NEVER quite lived up to its provocative name, yet I myself have seen it grow from a small town to a reasonably successful larger one. I remember the unpaved streets of my childhood, dusty in summer, frozen into ruts in the winter, and such a welter of mud in the spring that we used to do our romantic strolling on the railroad tracks. The trains were few, and the tracks led into buttercup and pussy-willow country impossible to penetrate by road.

In town the high board sidewalks bridged the rolling hills. I remember that hornets sometimes built nests under these narrow planks and flew up to sting unwary children who were on their way to school. Everywhere in summer there was a smell of blooming clover.

When the McBain boys came to Opportunity, it was even more primitive than I can remember. Then I was not even a thought for the future. Yet my fate had so far been decided that I was destined to be born in Idaho instead of Africa.

The streets of Opportunity are well-paved now, and automobiles go up and down. There is even a small airport; and, farther and farther out into the hills, the people are building ranch-type houses with picture windows. Yet I think that the sunset light on the blue mountains which encircle the town is the same. The wheat fields that roll and billow like the sea are still tawny gold in the harvest season. The pines and fir trees are still glossy green beneath the heavy snows of winter. These things do not change.

It was late spring when Douglas and Willie reached Opportunity, but it had been raining heavily, and the air had a sharp tang of high places. The sea voyage had been long, as had the journey by slow train across the continent of North America. Had it not been for Angus awaiting them in that incredibly far place, Douglas and Willie might have stopped off in any one of half a dozen towns along the route.

Manitou City in the Territory of Washington was the last stop before Opportunity. There had been no other way to come at their destination than by going farther west and then swinging eastward again. After a long wait on a chilly platform, with the whistle of wind in telegraph wires in their ears, the two young men climbed into the branch train for Opportunity. The engine ran smoothly at first, and then, for three hours, it chuffed and labored through mounting uplands, lifting them the last two thousand feet into higher country.

"Old A went far enough," said Willie with a yawn.

"Aye," said Douglas, "Darkest Africa could not have been farther. But it's bonnie all the same."

Everything was green and yellow in the clear light under a gray sky full of heavy, moving clouds, and far away the hills were deep blue.

"Aye," Willie said, "it's bonnie."

At the end of the line they saw a small wooden station with a swinging sign that proclaimed the name of the town. A man was backing a dray and cursing the horses for their clumsy floundering in the mud. In the door of the station stood the agent with a green eyeshade and a pencil behind his ear, and the ticking of telegraph instruments behind him. A hack, pulled by a couple of steaming, plunging horses drew in beside the platform, and then they saw Angus, with hands outstretched, running to meet them.

Angus had grown a little sandy red mustache, and somehow he looked less grave and more warmly alive than he had looked in Scotland.

They wrung each other's hands for a long time, laughing and clapping each other on the back, before Angus remembered to gather their luggage together and board the station hack.

"But where's the town, A?" asked Douglas, rubbing the steam off the hack window to look about him. Yearning for cities, he had passed through many of them, and come so far for this. There was disappointment in his voice.

Angus laughed. "Och, man, they plan things large out here. The town's a half a mile away. They've left room to grow."

2

Mrs. McAllister's boardinghouse was a square frame building with windows that rattled in the wind and drafty floors, but it was as good as the West afforded in those days and the company it sheltered was young and hopeful. A kind of devil-may-care gaiety and hope was the keynote of the West at that time. Only the young and hardy came out so far, and each man knew that he was on the upgrade. That some of them were doomed to disappointment had not yet been discovered. The days of the Gold Rush might be over, but every hearty young feeder about the checkered cloth of a western boardinghouse was still a potential president of a corporation, a lumber king, or baron in real estate.

Mrs. McAllister was not the least hopeful of the lot, although her husband had died three years before, leaving her without enough money to get back to Scotland. But she was a robust woman who believed in the West; and, having no sons of her own, she had a motherly feeling for all other women's sons. She was putting by a little money for her old age, and gathering about her at the same time a group of homeless young men who warmed the cockles of her heart.

She timed her Sabbath meals to fit the hours of worship in the Presbyterian kirk, and she saw that her lads attended, although some of them would have liked to leave kirk behind them when they left Scotland. She had made a good Presbyterian out of more than one New England lad whose excuse for not going to church was the lack of a Congregational meetinghouse; but whether this was due entirely to Mrs. McAllister or partly to the doctor's daughters and the other pretty girls who decorated the

31

Presbyterian choir and attended the young people's meetings, only the Lord and His angels could tell. Certainly the Reverend Mr. Horner had not had a great deal to do with the matter.

Mrs. McAllister attended to her young men's gaiety as well as to their piety, and her New Year's Eve watch parties and Halloween routs were major social events in Opportunity. The crowdie and oatcakes at Mrs. McAllister's were as good as any you could find in Scotland; but she still had some trouble with her haggis and black puddings, for the butcher could not seem to get them right in spite of all her telling.

Largely because of the personality of Mrs. McAllister, whose exterior at first glance was as forbidding as a Caithness moor, the nondescript character of this raw western town had taken on a definitely Scottish slant. Literature for Opportunity consisted of the Bible, Bobbie Burns, and Sir Walter Scott, and the Presbyterian assembly room had worsted the saloons as a convivial gathering place for the young.

Mrs. McAllister was at the door to welcome the newcomers when the hack drew up. There was a sea of mud between the hack wheels and the board sidewalk, but the McBain boys leaped it lightly. There was a green picket gate between high wooden gateposts, and another short stretch of plank sidewalk, a small gingerbread porch with a blooming lilac bush on either side. Mrs. McAllister was in the doorway. She was tall and flat in a gray calico dress, and her faded blond hair blew a little untidily above uncompromising gray eyes. She had a square chin with a cleft in the middle, and a light down on her upper lip like an adolescent boy.

"Good day to ye, my lads," she said, holding out a firm hand. "Don't tell me now. This'll be Douglas, and this, Willie. Am I right, Angus?"

"You're right, Mrs. McAllister," said Angus. His face was glowing with pride and family affection.

"Och, 'tis a breath of wind over the heather to look at ye!" said Mrs. McAllister. "Come in now an' get yourselves washed for supper."

A large kerosene lamp with a tin shade was suspended over the table by a brass chain and a hook in the ceiling. It threw a warm glow over the red-and-white checkered tablecloth and a

32

circle of shadow in the center where the vinegar cruet stood. Mrs. McAllister sat at the end of the table and served the repast from large steaming tureens, which the little Swedish hired girl replenished as the young gentlemen's appetites warranted, for there was nothing stingy about the McAllister table. The young gentlemen paid a fair price for it and they were not stinted.

There were a dozen young fellows ranged around the table, busily plying knives and forks. Not one of the lot had seen the weightier side of thirty. They were full of friendly jokes and friendlier advice in regard to the future of Douglas and Willie.

"You'll have the pick of the town as far as business is concerned," said a small red-cheeked fellow with black hair, "but the choice of young ladies is strictly limited since your brother Angus has taken to calling at the doctor's house."

"There's still the doctor's younger girl," said another, "but I'll admit all the beauty's on the other side." A slow flush went up Angus' transparent cheek, and Mrs. McAllister said briskly:

"We'll have no talk of young ladies now, and they not here to defend themselves. It isna their fault if there are not enough of them to go around amongst the lot of you."

"There's a place in the cobbler's shop where you can set up your saddlemaking until you've got established, Willie," said one.

"He'll do better in that empty shed next to the furniture store," said another.

"Och! that's where they put the corpses while the furniture fellow is making the coffins!"

"Well, nobody dies in Opportunity. Willie might be well started on his way to fame and fortune and a shop of his own before they'd have to turn him out for a corpse."

"And what are you going to do, Douglas?"

"I'm goin' to get rich," said Douglas with a grin. They burst into roars of laughter.

"So are all of us. But we usually start out with a business."

"I've not found mine yet," said Douglas, "but I'm a promisin' young man. Has anybody got a job to offer?"

"Aye, I've got one," said the small dark fellow with the red cheeks who sat across the table stowing away the food. "My business is expandin'. I've got more than I can handle alone. I'm lookin' for a smart young Scotsman to go partners on it."

33

"Is yon the mon who makes the coffins?" asked Willie.

"No, but he's the lad who puts folks in 'em," shouted somebody, and they were all laughing again.

"What kind of business would that be?" asked Douglas.

"It's the mortgage business, and no joking matter neither, if a man wants to get rich," said the little fellow.

"I didna think they needed mortgages out here in a new country where there's so much land."

"That's just where they do need 'em," said the mortgage man, waving his fork. "How are they going to buy new land without a mortgage company to lend them the money for it? 'Tis a great business, and a man's got a good chance to pick up a bonnie bit o' land for himself here an' there as he goes along."

"What's your name?" asked Douglas. "I've met so many of you the night, I've fair forgot."

"Johnny Buxton," said the small dark fellow with a flourish of his fork, "an' I'm a Glasgow man myself."

"You can all bid for Douglas later if you like," said Angus, "but just now he's coming in with me until he gets his bearings."

"You couldn't have a better tree to anchor to in a storm than Angus here," said a tall fellow at the end of the table.

"But don't forget Buxton," said the Glasgow man with a cheek full of bread and meat, "when you want to make some money."

"Go on with you," said the tall lad. "Angus is making as much money as Buxton or anyone else."

"He's making more," laughed someone else, "because all the widows and orphans trust him."

"But he lays it all out on books and the kirk, so he'll never be rich."

Angus smiled his quiet smile. Their raillery had not touched him at all, except for the mention of the doctor's daughter. Now he took up his own defense mildly but with his customary thoroughness.

"Riches are more than money to me," he said. "We got little education in Caithness except what we gave ourselves, and if I can buy books to keep on educating myself, I'm rich enough."

"Are *you* a bookish fellow, too?" asked Buxton, looking at Douglas with his small twinkling black eyes. Douglas flushed a little and laughed.

"No," he said, "I'm more a doer than a reader, it looks like."

34

The three McBain boys were to share a large room on the upper floor. Mrs. McAllister had put three plain cots into it and there was a woodbox and a small wood stove, a high pine dresser with a mirror which was somewhat the worse for damp, a washstand with a large pink and white crockery pitcher and bowl, and a white linen splasher embroidered with red storks standing one-legged among water lilies. Angus had furnished his own study table and student lamp, and he had made his own bookshelves. Bookshelves of the practical kind were not available in the Opportunity Furniture Store, which sold whatnots and little hanging shelves of bamboo for the ladies. The men of Opportunity rarely demanded bookshelves for themselves, and the furniture dealer had never thought to stock them.

Angus had built a large bookcase and most of it stood empty, but it had been laid out like the town, with room for growth. Beside his Bible was a row of religious commentaries and inspirational works; but on another shelf were collections of poems by Burns and Browning; Scott's *Border Ballads, Lady of the Lake* and *Marmion*; a life of Gladstone, a history of Caithness, a life of Robert Bruce; Gibbon's *Rise and Fall of the Roman Empire*; and Carlyle's *Sartor Resartus*. There were novels by Scott and Dickens, George Eliot and Robert Louis Stevenson.

Whenever Angus came into the room his eyes strayed to his books. They gave him a sense of warmth and anchorage, and at the same time a sense of voyaging and adventure. He had always been a nighthawk, and he often sat now until past midnight lost in his reading, arising in the morning at Mrs. McAllister's gong to sell life insurance and appraise land or survey town property. His only hesitation in sending for his brothers had been caused by a momentary reluctance to part with his cherished privacy. But he had waived that as of less importance than having his brothers with him, and seeing them launched on careers of their own.

They seemed to fill the room to overflowing on this first night, with their boots under the beds, their caps and bags flung every which way. Yet Angus was content to have them there.

Before they undressed for the night Angus opened the window and for a moment the three stood looking out over the fences and muddy streets and jumbled tin roofs of Opportunity. The clouds had dissolved and the moon spread a luminous haze over everything. There was a softness in the air that they had not felt in the afternoon.

The sound of a piano passionately played came from a house farther up the street.

"Listen!" said Angus. "It's Dr. Hedrick's daughter playing." They paused and listened. "It's one of the Hungarian rhapsodies," said Angus again quietly. "She loves that wild music."

"Is that the lass they twitted you about?" asked Douglas curiously.

"Aye," Angus said. "Her name is Abigail."

Angus sat on after the other two had gone to bed, reading his pocket Testament and sometimes making marginal notes in a minute, clear hand that matched the fine print on the page. Finally he drew a sheet of paper toward him and in his same small, unhurried hand began to write lines that fell into certain lengths and grouped themselves into a pattern. Perhaps it was the haunting echo of the rhapsody that made his thoughts fall into poetry instead of prose.

3

Willie was easily established in the shed next to the furniture store with a couple of hides and some saddle trees to begin on. He had to learn a bit about putting together a western saddle; but there was no competition for miles around and plenty of men were anxious to get their saddles and harness locally without having to order them sent from the coast. Willie was a skilled workman and a prince of good fellows. It didn't take the town loafers long to discover that it was as amusing to listen to Willie's funny stories in his broad Scotch brogue as it was to watch his clever fingers sewing or fitting wet leather, or stamping and tooling it with monograms and roses. There was always somebody perched on an empty crate from the back of the furniture shop watching Willie work, and often there were a half-dozen young blades shouting and laughing and spitting at the stove. The corpses wouldn't have known the place.

Douglas went in with Angus in his small office between the butcher shop and the bank. Angus had a plain table and a couple of chairs, a large wall calendar, a clock, a wood stove and a spittoon (for his clients, not himself) in a tiny, boxlike room with a door and window opening on the street. In the window, which caught the sunshine, he had a Christmas cactus given him by Mrs. McAllister, which he took great pains to cover from the cold on winter nights. He was the first insurance man in town and he was doing a good business. He did a little business in real estate, too, when opportunity offered; and people were beginning to ask him to invest money for them, for they sensed that he was honest and yet had a canny faculty for getting them more interest than the bank would pay.

He went over the little business step by step with Douglas, and Douglas made himself valuable almost at once. Douglas had been forced into gardening and had escaped by way of seafaring; but no one before had ever set him to a column of figures nor got him tangled in percentages and assets and liabilities. He was like a duck finding his first pond.

The first afternoon they went around to the livery stable and took out a couple of horses. Douglas knew the feel of a heavy farm horse between his knees, and he had even ridden the shaggy "shelties" that the tinklers brought to Caithness in the spring; but this was his first western cayuse. He liked the spring of him and the wild roll of his eye. Douglas held a firm rein and sat easily, as if he had always ridden spirited horses, and his blood ran warm and swiftly through his body.

They were going out to look at some farm machinery on which a homesteader wanted to borrow money.

"What do you ken about farm machinery, A?" laughed Douglas.

"I'm learning," said Angus quietly, but with a twinkle in his eye.

"But that's what Johnny Buxton's in—the moneylending business, isn't it?"

"Aye, the same," said Angus, "but I'd rather you got started with me, Doug. Buxton's a good lad, but he's all for making money at anybody's expense but his own. There's two sides to every question, it looks to me, and if a moneylender does not take the human side into consideration as well as the cold cash, he's like to be nothing better than a Shylock."

They spent an overly long time talking with the homesteader, Douglas thought, and before they left they knew his history from

37

the cradle to the grave. Angus asked few questions; but the man seemed eager to tell them everything, and A stood quietly listening long after Douglas' patience was exhausted. In the end Angus promised the man his money.

The roads were deeply rutted and heavy with mud. The horses' legs and the men's trousers were well spattered before they reached town. The air was sharp and clear and every pine and evergreen upon the hills had its own identity; it was not a forest bound together by hazy atmosphere, but a collection of trees each clearly delineated in the fresh-washed air. Great gray and white clouds scudded in a brilliantly blue sky, and shadows of clouds passed like moods across the rolling landscape. Scarcely a house was to be seen, but not, as in Caithness, for want of fertility or promise. And everywhere ran water, gushing from springs, trickling beside the road, winding in loops of blue through lush green fields.

"It's all new," said Angus, drawing in a deep breath and sweeping his arm in a half-circle toward the hills.

"Aye, all new," repeated Douglas.

Something that he could not express moved him almost to the point of tears. All of this beauty and promise belonged to him and to the young men who had come to take it. He had left behind him the old, old country that could no longer give its sons the riches of life. He had come to the right place.

"They say it's the best farm land in the West, too," said Angus. "Look at that mud. It's not a bonnie sight, but it can't be better for growing wheat."

"I believe that," said Douglas gravely.

When they rode into Opportunity sunset had turned the restless clouds into a dramatic turbulence of glorious color. The muddy horses walked slowly now, side by side down the street. They passed the church and the doctor's house on the way to the livery stable. As they went by, the door of the doctor's house flew open and a young girl ran out with a hastily caught shawl flung over her shoulders.

"Oh, Mr. McBain!"

"Yes, Miss Hedrick!"

Angus drew his horse in beside the hitching post and mounting block and lifted his hat. Douglas drew rein also, noting with a little amusement A's heightened color. The calm and gentle gravity of Angus' face never betrayed him, but the shifting of color under his transparent skin did.

"I just happened to see you riding by, Mr. McBain—"

"I'm glad you did," said Angus. "I want to present my brother to you, Miss Hedrick. He's come, you see—it's Douglas."

"I'm pleased to meet you, Mr. McBain," said the girl, giving Douglas a flash of her great dark eyes. Then she laughed. "I'm afraid I knew they had come, because Connie happened to be looking out of the window yesterday when the hack went by."

Douglas had time to look at her because, after her first glance, her eyes were all for Angus. She was not exactly pretty, for she had irregular features and a large mouth; but one never thought of anything but her eyes which were of a most extraordinary size and velvety dark. They seemed almost too big for the delicate, triangular face, the slight frame and slender hands and feet. She wore her hair in a dark, curly mop of bangs on her forehead, and in loose curls which were drawn away from her ears and hung almost to her shoulders behind.

"Mother wanted me to ask you—that's why I ran out—if you would bring your brothers to dinner with us on Sunday after church. Father would be very pleased to make their acquaintance. It's such a long way to have come from Scotland!"

"We'll be happy to come, Miss Hedrick, and thank your mother most kindly for us, if you please," said Angus. He still held his horse to the curb, his hat in his hand, his eyes fixed on Miss Hedrick's face, and she looking at him as if she had never seen his like in the world before. Douglas' horse tossed its head and moved its feet impatiently, and Douglas himself couldn't help clearing his throat and coughing.

"Oh, I'm so glad!" said Miss Hedrick. "I mean, Mother will be so pleased. I'll see you after church on Sunday then, Mr. McBain." She gave Douglas a fleeting smile. "I'm proud to have met you, Mr. McBain."

There was a little flurry of full skirts and slender ankles, and the doctor's daughter disappeared into the house.

"So that's the one who plays the wild music," said Douglas, for want of anything more to the point to say. If this had been Willie instead of Angus, he could have thought of plenty to say, but one kept a respectful distance with Angus.

"Aye, that's the one," said Angus.

39

They rode in silence as far as the livery stable. The horses were steaming in the chilly yard. There was a sound of stomping and munching inside the stable, and a startled horse tossed up its head and rolled the white of an eye at them over its stall boards. Douglas liked the smell of fresh hay and horses and manure and mud that rose in the sharp air. There was a smell of kerosene, too, and the yellow glow of a swinging lantern in a man's hand.

"Well, she's fair bonnie, A," said Douglas.

"So I think myself," said Angus mildly, "and she's a very fine Christian character, too, Douglas."

"Indeed?" said Douglas. He had seen the great eyes, but the Christian character had not been so apparent to him.

Their legs were stiff from the long, chill ride, and they swung out smartly on the walk to Mrs. McAllister's. Douglas felt very hungry and for almost the first time in his life quite contented with his lot.

4

Whether or not John Knox would have approved of the particular brand of Presbyterianism which flourished in Opportunity one can only surmise. But certainly it afforded a much gayer atmosphere than that which prevailed in the chilly stone kirks of the old country. The Opportunity church was a small frame building with a bit of a steeple that suggested the country school-house more than the mansion of God, and it was already outgrown and full to bursting with enthusiastic young members. There was never any difficulty in getting pious young men to stoke the big sheet-iron stove with chunks of wood on a Sabbath morning or to perform a bit of voluntary janitor service on a prayer-meeting night. As for the young ladies, such as there were in Opportunity, they were always on hand to sing in the choir and dust the pews and arrange the flowers or paint violets and lilies on satin book markers for the pulpit Bible. For, purely aside from doctrine or theology, the Reverend Mr. Horner's church served an important function as social clearinghouse and matrimonial agency; and perhaps it came nearer to achieving the true Christian ideal of the Good Life than many churches do.

40

Certainly godliness was more attractive here than Douglas had ever found it before. Angus presented his two brothers to everyone within reach before and after service. There was a great deal of warm hand shaking and clapping on the back, and half a dozen invitations to dinner. But Abigail Hedrick stood by, her great eyes watchful and darkly triumphant, and presently she said:

"Mother and Connie are waiting for us. Shall we go now?"

Mrs. Hedrick was a quiet woman, sturdily built, with keen hazel eyes which made quick and accurate appraisals. She was not what one would expect of the mother of Abigail, but Douglas instantly liked her. She was a New England woman, but there was something about her so like the solid, enduring strength of the Scotch women he had known that she seemed familiar. Half behind her, and obviously just emerging from the shy and awkward age, stood the other daughter, Constance. She was a square, well-built girl with gray eyes and a straight, square-cut bang of ash-blond hair on her forehead. She was not pretty, but she was of an age which was in flux and offered possibilities rather than finished effects.

Douglas found himself walking beside Connie as they left the church. Mrs. Hedrick and Willie went ahead, "to dish up," Mrs. Hedrick said; and Abigail and Angus walked slowly as if it were June and they strolling in the midst of warmth and roses. Abigail wore a long dark-blue cloak faced with scarlet and held her hands primly in a little muff. She did not quite come to Angus' shoulder, and he bent his head to her as they walked.

"Well, how do you like us?" asked the younger sister. "Opportunity, I mean," she added with a little giggle.

"Och! fine now!" said Douglas. "Ye've the most elegant mud I've seen the like of, the world around."

She burst into delighted laughter.

"Wait until you see the dust, though, in July or August. You'll be here then, won't you? You *are* going to stay, aren't you?"

"Aye, I'll be here," said Douglas. "You never thought the town would let me get away so soon, did ye?"

"No," she said, "I guess that's all the town's been waiting for, Mr. McBain. Now that you're here, it can go right ahead. Maybe you'll even dry up the mud for us, and blow away the dust."

41

"I'll bring my mind to bear on it, if you like," said Douglas pleasantly.

"Do you like fried chicken?" she asked. "Because that's what we're going to have for dinner. And tapioca pudding with custard sauce for dessert. Abbie *would* have that, because she thinks your brother likes it. Right now, whatever your brother likes, Abbie likes, too, but don't dare tell him I said so."

"I'll guard my tongue," said Douglas.

"I'll bet you've never eaten fried chicken before, Mr. McBain. Your brother never had."

"Nay," said Douglas. "We put our fowls in the stewpot in Caithness. But tell me now, have ye never eaten haggis?"

"It sounds like something awfully unpleasant."

"Only moderately so," said Douglas, "but after dinner I'll be wiser than you are, for I'll ken both haggis and fried chicken, and you'll ken only fried chicken."

"Now, I don't think you're a bit nice, Mr. McBain."

"I never set up to be, did I?"

"No, you didn't—but there's something about you all the same."

"What-like?" he asked, his eyes twinkling.

"Well, you're not so polite and well-mannered as your brothers, but I expect some of those crazy girls of Opportunity will like you better for your bad manners and your good looks."

"But not a sensible girl like yourself, Miss Constance?"

"Don't be silly," she said. "You're just trying to tease me."

Dr. Hedrick was walking up and down the narrow front porch of his house.

"How's this?" he said. "People have been coming by from church for fifteen minutes by the watch. When am I to have my dinner?"

"Hold your horses, Doctor," said Mrs. Hedrick good-naturedly. "You won't go to church, but someone has to uphold the honor of the family, and you'll just have to be patient about your dinner."

Douglas saw at once where Abigail got her eyes. The doctor was a great dark man with blazing black eyes of unusual size, and a pair of black muttonchop whiskers which accentuated the ferocious aspect of his face. But his ferocity was easily appeased and he was soon shaking hands and playing the host with the greatest charm and amiability.

42

Mrs. Hedrick and the girls disappeared in the direction of the dining room and kitchen, and soon a meal, the like of which he had never dreamed of in frugal Scotland, was steaming on the table. A little hired girl helped with the serving of it, and sat down to eat with them when everyone else was taken care of.

Douglas had never been a guest in so fine a house. It was thrown together flimsily with wood and shingles instead of the sturdy stone and slate of Scotland, and, like all of the houses of Opportunity, it had the temporary appearance of a place which expects soon to be supplanted by something finer; at the same time it had a careless atmosphere of luxury and well-being, such as he had never seen in the cottages to which he was accustomed.

Willie was openmouthed in his admiration of the lace curtains and Brussels carpets, the silver coffeepot and the mahogany piano; but Douglas would rather have bitten his tongue off than to have betrayed by so much as the flicker of an eyelash that he was impressed.

It was a jolly meal, for the Hedricks were easy people with whom to feel at home. The two girls were anxious hostesses and watched their guests' plates.

"Mother, Mr. McBain will have another leg of chicken, and, Father, do pass the other Mr. McBain the hot biscuits."

"Now, which McBain is to have chicken and which biscuits, or had we better pass both to all three?" asked the doctor jovially.

"Ye'll have to put labels on us, Dr. Hedrick," said Willie. "Mr. McBain number one, Mr. McBain number two, and Mr. McBain number three, and then all ye'll have to do is call numbers."

"The formality of you young folks makes me laugh," said Mrs. Hedrick. "When I was a girl we all called each other by our first names. There was none of this dillydallying about 'Miss' and 'Mister.' I never protested before, but now that we have three McBains to 'mister,' it does seem very unnecessary."

"Let's try it," said Angus. "Do you know my given name, Miss Hedrick?"

"Angus," said Abigail, flushing, "but you weren't fair—you called me Miss Hedrick. Maybe you don't know mine."

"Abigail," said Angus, ticking the syllables delicately off his tongue like something he relished.

"And now may I call them Douglas and Willie, Mother?" cried

43

Connie, the round eyes under the straight bang full of excitement.

"If *they* don't object, I don't," said the doctor's wife calmly.

"I've been dying to do it all along," said Connie. "Is Willie short for William? and does anybody mind if I say Doug instead of Douglas?"

After dinner they went to the parlor and the doctor offered them all cigars. Douglas took one to prove that he was a man of the world, and smoked it through like a soldier; but the three McBains never acquired the American taste for tobacco.

With a little coaxing Abbie went to the piano and began to play. Music was another experience almost as new to Douglas as the cigar, and somewhat more pleasant. He had never enjoyed hymns, but sometimes the bagpipes stirred him strangely, and now he found that Abigail Hedrick's playing did the same thing. Perhaps it was because she did not play sentimental things, as most lassies did, but wild, strange pieces that danced and spoke of war and pain and human delight. It was not often that Douglas was taken out of himself and set afloat on the larger world, but something untamed in Abbie's music could do that to him.

5

Douglas threw himself into business as he had never set himself to anything in his life before. He knew that he had been considered the wastrel of the family, and, now that he had found something that he liked to do and in which there seemed to be a future, he meant to show his good intentions. He began to study, too, for the first time. In the school at home he had done well without the bother of applying himself, and he had never cared, as Angus did, to explore the world through the eyes and minds of other men. But now he purchased some elementary textbooks in mathematics and English grammar. He did not wish to talk like a Scotsman any longer than he could help, and he wanted to be the master of those rows and columns of figures which symbolized the power and the privilege of the world.

Angus made a place for him at the other end of the study table, and now there were two of them who often sat until midnight. Willie tried sitting up to study, too, but neither mathematics nor the Bible interested him greatly, and he already knew the harness and saddle business from A to Z. His feet began to swell and his shoes to hurt him, sitting so long with them stretched toward the stove. First he would pull off one shoe and then the other, and then the warm glow of the lamp would begin to make his eyelids itch; and presently he would toss his English grammar to the ceiling with a loud yawn and a laugh. Sometimes he took one of Dickens' novels to bed with him, but in any case he was soon asleep with one hand tucked under his cheek and the other arm flung out over the bed clothes in complete relaxation.

Spring hurried in with a rush of wind and sunshine here in the West. Buttercups, yellow bells, lambstongue, and dandelions flowed in a green and yellow carpet under the dark pines. The misty purples of Scottish heather-clad hills and islands, the somber colors of an older land that has grown tired of striving were not present here. Here everything was yellow and green and the very petals of the wild flowers shone as if burnished by the ecstasy of being new. The sky was brilliantly blue, and definitely shaped clouds moved across it in a windy procession.

Douglas began to take over the country rides of inspection while Angus kept the office open for town business. Sometimes he met and rode along some distance with Johnny Buxton when their roads led the same way. Johnny sat awkwardly on a horse and never got the easy feel of it between his Glasgow legs; but he was good company and full of bits of worldly wisdom which Douglas filed away for future reference. One might live and work with Angus for years and not acquire a tenth of the worldly wisdom that Johnny could toss off in a single hour's ride.

Sometimes Douglas met Doc Hedrick, too, driving down the mountain from a homesteader's cabin or an outlying farm.

"Well, I got a bouncing boy that time, Douglas. They named him after me, too! Randolph Hedrick Jones!"

"Och, Doctor, that's fame for you!"

"Well, I'd rather they'd pay my bill," said Doc with a laugh, and slapping the reins over the horse's back, he jogged along.

In May a company of Indians wandered into town and set up camp on the hilltop near the Presbyterian church. They were the greatest curiosity to Douglas and Willie. Willie, whose money was coming in pretty freely now, bought beaded moccasins to send to Jeanie and Lottie in Scotland. The Indians had spotted cayuses for sale also, and Douglas was sorely tempted to stretch his money to buy one. But Johnny Buxton had told him about a bit of land he could get cheap if he would keep up the payments on it, and he finally gave up the idea of the cayuse. Regretfully he saw the Swede butcher buy the horse he had picked out, a smart little animal with an arched neck and one white eye. But Douglas' business instincts were already sound. Three days later the Indians packed up in the night and went on their way, and all of the horses which they had sold to townspeople mysteriously disappeared with them.

Douglas and Willie took turns walking home with Connie Hedrick after prayer meeting on Thursday nights. She was a rather amusing little rattlebrain with a continual flow of thoughtless chatter. And there was old A always squiring sister Abigail. When one of them was walking home with Connie and teasing her the other usually took Viola Martin, the postmaster's daughter, or Mary Gallup, the liveryman's girl; and there were several other nice young ladies with seemly giggles and neat wrists and ankles who might be had for the asking if some of the other young men from Mrs. McAllister's did not get there first.

In June the young ladies' society of the church sent out invitations to a box supper, the proceeds to be used for buying a large map of the Holy Land for the Sunday school.

"Here's where we shake up all the usual combinations!" said Johnny Buxton hopefully. "I'm no' a great hand wi' the lassies, and I always find mysel' stuck with a sour-lookin' auld maid like Sophia Wintergarten. But I can bid as high as anither man when it comes to buyin' a basket."

"How do ye ken but the auld maids will trim up their baskets as bonnie as the handsome lassies does?" asked Willie.

"Happen I'll have better fortune by relyin' upon my pocketbook than upon my face," said Johnny.

"What color is Abigail's box to be, Angus? Because we all want to bid on it," said someone.

"She's not told me," said Angus, "but 'twill be the bonniest one."

The Thursday night before the social, which was to be on a Saturday, Connie took Douglas' arm.

"Walk home with me after prayer meeting," she said, "and I'll tell you a secret."

"A secret? I thought you never kept a thing like that at all."

"Well, I don't keep them very long. But will you?"

"Bold as brass, aren't you?" Douglas laughed. "Aye, I'll walk you home."

"Oh, I'm not really bold," Connie said, "only I do have to look out for myself. And no one else will do it for me."

It was not far to walk from the church to the Hedrick's after prayer meeting, and Connie came right to the point.

"Douglas, I'm having fried chicken in my box," she said.

"What! no haggis?"

"No, I couldn't find one in town, and anyway you said yourself they're horrid things. I know you like fried chicken better. And there'll be a cake, too. A cake I made myself."

"Come now, are ye trying to drive me off?"

"Now, don't be tiresome. I can make an awfully good cake, much better than Abbie makes. I'm quite domestic, even Papa says so, and he doesn't often praise me. He thinks Abbie is the cleverest one, and I expect she is—"

"Well, tell me, then," interrupted Douglas, "what's the color of this famous box of yours?"

"The idea," cried Connie outraged. "Do you suppose I'd tell you? Why, no one is supposed to tell the color of her box!"

"You said you were going to tell me a secret," teased Douglas. "You've tricked me into walking home with you under false pretenses."

"Well, ask me some colors, and I'll tell you if you guess wrong," said Connie.

So by a process of elimination Douglas arrived at the conclusion that Connie's box was to be black, and, as there was only one black tissue paper-covered box in the midst of quantities of pink and blue and lavender and green ones, he got it at an exceedingly low price. The most beautiful box of all was a pink one covered with pink tissue paper roses. Johnny Buxton finally got it for $3.75, and, upon opening it, found that he had drawn Sophia Wintergarten as usual. Abigail and Angus had been strictly honest. The minister bought her box and Angus, hoping desperately that he had the right one, had bought Mary Gallup's and was obliged to eat the contents in Mary's company.

47

"I think it was real smart of me to think of black," said Connie. "Abbie said: 'What a horrid-looking box, Connie. No one will buy it.' But I knew that, if I worked it right, the person I wanted to have it would be able to get it cheap."

"Connie, did it ever occur to you that you talk too much?" asked Douglas.

"No! Do you think so?" asked Connie, her round eyes suddenly stricken. "But then you bought my box."

"Aye," said Douglas. "But let me give you a wee bit of fatherly advice. Your fried chicken's fine and even your cake is the best I've eaten, but you're too free with your tongue. If you really want to get a man, you've got to learn to dissemble."

"But you're very horrid," said Connie hotly. "I'm not trying to get a man, and I don't know anything about dissembling."

"Well, learn, lassie, learn!" said Douglas. "You'll find it will come useful."

Connie looked at him seriously, the anger dying out of her amiable round face.

"Well, I'll try," she said. "I know I talk too much but I can't help it. It's just the way I am. It sets poor Papa crazy. When we were little he always used to take Abbie with him in the buggy when he had a long country drive, and finally one day he let me go. I was terribly pleased and I never realized I was talking all the way. There was such a lot to see and talk about and I really wanted to please him. But when we got back, he said to Mama, right in front of me: 'Don't ever urge me to take this child again, Susan. She talked my head off. These country drives between patients are the only things that rest me. But Connie drives me crazy.'" She laughed. "I can't help it," she said.

"You should learn," said Douglas seriously.

"I'll try," she said again, a trifle mournfully. "But I get tired of having people always after me. 'Connie, do this, Connie, do that.' I want to be ladylike, I really do, but I never seem to know where to catch hold."

Douglas looked at her and laughed. "You're a good-tempered wee thing," he said.

Just then Willie and Viola came along with Viola's basket, and they were caught up in the general gaiety of a picnic spread among the pews.

48

6

That summer Willie got himself a gun and two yellow and white hound dogs with flapping ears. Mrs. McAllister let the dogs sleep in her woodshed and fed them with scraps from her table, and the other boys declared jealously that she wouldn't have done it for anybody else but Willie. All of the McBain boys were happy in the new world, but Willie was the happiest of the three. He had a talent for happiness. It was something positive with him, and not simply the absence of unhappiness.

He whistled and sang at his saddlemaking and argued or joshed with the idle fellows who loafed in his shop. The two dogs stretched their bellies in the sun at his front door and thumped their tails on the ground at the approach of customers. After working hours, which depended on the number of orders Willie happened to have on hand and which were in no wise rigid, Willie took up his gun, whistled to the dogs, and they started off for the woods and fields. Prairie chickens, quail, and rabbits were abundant, and no one in Opportunity had as yet thought of such a refinement as game laws.

Mrs. McAllister cooked his game for him, not because she liked to bother with it, but because he brightened up the kitchen when he came into it and put her in a good frame of mind. And then she made considerable profit off Willie, too, for he was forever taking dinner out with this one or that one, not always in the best of society to be sure, but always enjoying himself. He even had dinner with the Catholic priest one night, which in Mrs. Mc-Allister's opinion was carrying democracy a little too far.

"But he's a braw, bonnie man," said Willie in answer to her protests, "and I'm verra sorry for him livin' all alone in that wee hoose with no women to look after him and devil a bit of a con-gregation except a few Dagos who are workin' on the railroad. He's as full o' droll stories as an egg o' meat an' the poor chiel's got nobody but a Presbyterian to listen to them!"

As with all kind and happy people, Willie was beset by men with axes to grind and women who needed love and young girls who were plain and wanted sympathy. He was too modest him-

49

self to tell them to be about their business. He listened to them all and thought with a very merry heart that there was certainly a lot of sadness in the world.

"You'll get hooked by one of those mealy-mouthed lassies one of these days," said Douglas impatiently. "I've got no sympathy with people like that who don't know how to help themselves."

"Och! I'm no better than they are," said Willie. "A mon canna refuse to listen, if it gives the poor souls any pleasure."

7

Toward the end of August, when Opportunity baked and crackled under a bright western sun, the young people of the church prevailed upon Mrs. McAllister to chaperone a two week's camping party in the mountains.

The boys rode out the day before and set up tents and cut balsam boughs for beds. The young ladies came the next day on a hay wagon, in calico dresses and sunbonnets or straw hats with ribbons, their belongings tied up in bundles in the hay beside them.

The young ladies' tents were on one side of the mountain stream and the young gentlemen's on the other, with a plank and some slippery stepping-stones between; but they all dined together on plank tables near the campfire on the young ladies' side. Someone had been thoughtful enough to arrange the camping dates for the period of the waxing and full of the moon. Perhaps it was Mrs. McAllister herself, for she was a sensible woman in an age of affectation, and she thought that young people deserved as much romance and pleasure as they could get in a world which all too soon turned sour.

She was a strict chaperone, but at the same time she knew her young people and she had an eye to particular cases. It was Mrs. McAllister who insisted that Angus and Abigail should get the milk every day from the farmer farther up the mountain, and who saw that they got away for lonely moonlight strolls sometimes. She thought that they had gone on quite long enough in the state they were in, and that it was time something definite came of it.

50

On the day before camp broke up, Abbie and Angus announced their engagement. It was quite all right to announce it, Abbie said, blushing happily, because her father and mother had already given their consent, even if Angus hadn't spoken to them. As a matter of fact nobody was surprised, unless it was Angus, who was still filled with wonder that Abbie would have him. He always did things slowly, with a good deal of thought and prayer, and, when he had chosen his course, he was sure. That he could have had Abbie three months ago did not occur to him, and, if it had, he would have waited anyway to be absolutely certain of himself.

They were so happy in their decision that the whole camp caught the infection, and on the last night the moonlit woods were full of sentimental strollers.

"Just think," said Connie dolefully, "I'm losing my only sister. If you think that's nice, you may just think again. I'm simply brokenhearted."

"Well, if it comes to that, I'm losing a brother, too," said Douglas.

He and Connie sat on top of a rock at the edge of the pines, looking out over a misty gulf of moonlit valley. Far off a few winking lights came and went in Opportunity. He did not quite know why he and Connie were here alone, but he felt uncomfortably that she must have arranged it and that undoubtedly he was expected to do something about it.

"That's not at all the same thing," said Connie. "You've still got Willie and ever so many brothers and sisters in Scotland."

"You're a very nice lassie, aren't you?" he said, lazily, leaning back on his elbow and watching her earnest round face with amusement. "Nothing but a child, really. It's a fair shame for me to be robbin' the cradle by takin' you out all alone in the moonlight."

"Oh, I'm entirely grown up!" cried Connie eagerly. "I can't help it if Mother makes me wear these childish bangs. I understand all about love and marriage and every sort of grown-up thing. But it's just that I hate to see my dearest sister rushing into matrimony and all these things and leaving me behind to be an old maid."

"Old maid!" scoffed Douglas. "You'll never be an old maid, Connie."

51

"I'm not very pretty," said Connie, looking at him out of the corner of her eye.

"No, you're not," said Douglas, "but you've a long enough tongue to talk a man into anything."

"Oh, you *are* mean!" cried Connie. "I've been trying, really I have." Suddenly he saw that there were glistening streaks running down her cheeks in the moonlight. All in a moment he was sorry and ashamed of himself.

"Och, Connie!" he said, sitting up and leaning close to her. "I was only teasin' you. Can ye no take a joke, honey? Here's my handkerchief. Now dry your eyes, like, and look at me."

"I know I'm not pretty like Abbie," she said, wiping her eyes with his handkerchief. "Everybody tells me I talk too much, and I'm always hearing myself called the plain one. It's no joke at all. Not a bit of a joke to me."

"Let me look at you," said Douglas turning up her round chin so that her face was close to his. "You're fair beautiful to anyone who's fond of you, Connie."

"Does that mean you, Douglas?" she said in a very little voice.

"Everybody's fond of you, sweetheart," he said. "As fond as this." He put an awkward kiss on Connie's upturned lips. They both sat quiet for a moment, close together, without speaking. It was a first kiss for both of them, and neither knew just how it had come about. Suddenly Connie leaned forward and kissed him back with a warm, moist mouth. Then she sprang up.

"I'm going back to camp now," she said in a shaky voice, "so—so nothing will spoil it." She scrambled off the rock and ran away through the woods as fast as she could go.

Douglas sat awhile and thought, and, for all the sweetness of the night and Connie's lips, he was not very comfortable. A kiss was almost the same as a proposal, and he was certainly not ready to jump off the small end of the plank into matrimony. Especially with an easy little thing like Connie.

Everybody was up early the next morning, and there was a great bustle and stir of breaking camp. The tents were down and folded by ten o'clock, when the hay wagons arrived to take the campers home. The wagons were so loaded that some of the boys had to take turns walking.

"I'm saving a place for you, Douglas," called Connie from the second wagon, but Douglas did not seem to hear. He was talking

52

to Viola Martin, who sat in the first wagon, and, when it started to roll, he continued to walk along beside it.

"Is this seat reserved?" asked Willie, jumping into the second wagon and sinking down on the hay beside Connie.

"It's reserved for you, I guess," said Connie ruefully. She was trying hard to learn to dissemble. Dissembling did not come easily to her, because her mind and her tongue hung on the same thread and every breeze set them in motion.

Later, when Douglas looked back, Willie was doing imitations of his hound dogs for her, and the whole second wagon was convulsed with laughter. The next time, when he looked back, Connie was teaching Willie how to make a cat's cradle out of string. Everything seemed to be all right, and probably the least said, the soonest mended, Douglas thought.

8

Abigail and Angus were married in September. They planned a ten o'clock wedding at the doctor's house in order to catch the noon train for Manitou City, where they were to spend their honeymoon. Angus was up late the night before, packing his bags and putting his books in a box to be ready for moving to the new house. The next morning he overslept, and might have missed the wedding altogether if Douglas and Willie had not routed him out.

At five minutes to ten the Reverend Mr. Horner arrived and everyone was there but the McBain boys. Dr. Hedrick was walking up and down the porch at the back of the house wringing his hands.

"By gad!" he said, "if he deserts her at the altar now, I'll break him into a thousand pieces! I'll—"

"Be still, Father," said Abigail. "You don't know Angus at all. He wouldn't desert anyone—not anyone. He doesn't go rushing into things the way you do, but he'll be here."

A few moments later Angus arrived, a little red in the face from hurrying, but otherwise perfectly calm and collected.

Abigail didn't wear a veil, but she had a becoming white mull dress, shirred in softly at the waist and with cascades of lace

53

about the neck and sleeves. The curly brown hair was drawn back into a loose knot at the nape of her neck and a white rose was thrust into it behind her ear. She had a bouquet of late white roses which had been culled from several gardens.

Angus looked at her and smiled. He hated being the center of a ceremony of any sort. It was almost as bad as the time they had given him the testimonial dinner in Thurso and presented him with the Bible before he left for the States. In spite of the embarrassment, he had been proud then as he was proud now. But today he felt more than pride, for he loved Abbie dearly and he thought that he had never seen a woman look more beautiful. And she loved him enough to give up being Abbie Hedrick and to become Abbie McBain!

Douglas and Connie stood up with them, and Dr. Hedrick, looking even more fierce and determined than usual, gave the bride away.

Most of the young people who had known them were there, and as it was the first wedding in the group, there was a good deal of feeling about it one way and another. Some of them were sad and some jovial, but it was a genuinely important occasion. Afterwards there was a wedding breakfast, with chicken pie and homemade ice cream and bride's cake, spread in the dining room, and the wedding presents were on display in the best bedroom. There was a cuckoo clock, and there were vinegar cruets, hand-painted spoon holders, antimacassars and celery jars, fruit knives and hand-illuminated texts in rustic frames. In the center of all was an enormous silverplated tankard which swung in an ornate frame and had two silver goblets as big as the communion cups at church sitting on small connecting disks in front. This was the most impressive thing the doctor had been able to find in Opportunity to give his little daughter upon the occasion of her marriage. On each of the goblets he had caused to be engraved, "From Papa to Abbie."

In the midst of the festivities Abbie was whisked away and helped to change into a brown serge suit trimmed with black braid and a little brown hat with a feather. The doctor's horse was ready, harnessed to the carriage in the barn, and Doug brought it around to the side door as quietly as he could. Angus and Abbie and Connie slipped out, and were on their way to the station before anyone missed them. They had just time to make

54

the train, and it seemed only a moment until the bride and groom had gone, leaving Douglas and Connie alone on the station platform. They had that empty and embarrassed feeling which comes when a day has reached its climax at too early an hour, and one wonders how the rest of it is to be endured until it is time to go to bed.

Connie wiped her eyes and tried to smile.

"Well, that's my first wedding," she said. "I wonder how soon I'll go to another?"

"They'll be coming thick and fast now, I dare say," said Douglas, laughing a little awkwardly, "but the next one won't be mine —I'm sure of that."

"Nor mine either," said Connie. Suddenly she blushed and there was an uncomfortable moment when they both thought of a kiss in the moonlight on a mountain. Then Douglas squared his shoulders.

"Well, yon horse will be weary of standing," he said. "I'll take you home and then I must be away to the office. I'm head of the firm while Angus is gone."

"So you are!" said Connie. "Don't you feel important?"

"Sure," said Doug easily. "Do ye not feel it, too? You're a *sister* of the firm now, you know. That makes you and me brother and sister, does it not, Connie?" He looked at her a little doubtfully, wondering how she would take it.

"That's right," said Connie loyally. "I always wanted a brother, and now I've got three."

Perhaps her color was a little brighter and her head a little higher on the drive home, but he could see that what he had said had really made no difference to her. He went on telling her how he meant to get on in business and be rich before he thought of settling down; how he might even be a bachelor in order to get where he wanted in this world; how a man must make sacrifices to achieve success. Connie agreed to everything he said. For the moment she was a patient listener.

9

When Angus and Abigail returned from their wedding trip, they moved into one of two small new houses which had just been built at the edge of town. Each house was painted bright pink and had a large square window in the parlor surrounded by semicircular bits of colored glass, so that the general effect of the window was round. The porches and eaves were trimmed with a great deal of jigsaw ornament in the best "Lady's Book" tradition. The two houses were in one large yard with a pink picket fence surrounding the whole, and red brick walks leading from separate gates to the two front doors.

The other house stood empty for a short while, and Abigail used to tell Douglas and Willie that there was still time for one or the other of them to find a nice girl and settle down in it. But they laughed and told her that she needn't think she must be a matchmaker just because she'd got the best man in town.

"Doug's going to be a bachelor," said Willie, "and as for mysel', the lassies are all so bonnie that I canna make up my mind."

The question of the house was soon settled for them, for a young man with a wife came out from the East to help edit *The Opportunity Knocker*, and his wife found the twin pink house as much to her liking as anything in town. Its stained glass and scrollwork partially satisfied the homesick longings of a bride who had "known better things" in the East, and who found Opportunity heartbreakingly crude and raw. Even the name of the paper on which her husband was to work filled her with dismay. To have to write home that Charles was engaged upon a paper called *The Opportunity Knocker*, instead of the *Weekly Gazette* or *The Morning Star*!

Abigail threw herself with delight into the mysteries of housekeeping. If Angus' meals were not equal to those he had had at Mrs. McAllister's, they were salted with merriment and sweetened with love, and merriment and love were much more important to him than food. But, in spite of her enthusiasm for the domestic arts, there were days when Abbie let the dishes stand in the sink and the dust pile up while she played the piano. Connie was not musical, and the doctor had had Abbie's piano moved from his house to the pink cottage while Abbie was on her honeymoon. Most young ladies let their music go when they were confronted with the serious duties of life. Music was one of the embellishments of an attractive young female; when it had served its purpose by helping her to ensnare a young man, it was thought very proper to let it slip away, together with her ringlets and her slender waist.

But Angus liked to have Abbie keep up her playing, and, whether he had wanted her to or not, Abbie could not have helped herself. She floated in music as a swimmer floats in the sea or a bird in the high blue reaches of the air. It bore her up and filled her with a kind of ecstasy that even marriage had not given her.

Sometimes she played in concerts at the church or in musical afternoons for the Ladies' Aid. She was always asked because people recognized her as the best musician in Opportunity, except perhaps for old Professor Baumgartner who lived over the Bon Ton Dry Goods Store and gave lessons to the young. And yet when she played, the ladies were often uneasy, and somehow glad when she had finished and another performer came up to render "The Maiden's Prayer" or "The March of the Brownies." Only Professor Baumgartner listened to her with the same ecstasy which she felt herself. His eyes closed, his hands clasped across his stomach, he looked like an old man asleep; but in reality he was living more intensely than he lived at any other moment in his daily round.

"*Wunderschön! Wunderschön!*" he murmured to himself, and afterward he would go up and discuss with her minute points of tone and technique which she did not always understand, for she had only had as much instruction as they could give her in boarding school, and the rest she had done herself. But she always listened very carefully, for this was her language, and she took his suggestions and put them into practice.

"But you have feeling," he said, "which will destroy you. Discipline it, Mrs. McBain, discipline it."

Abbie laughed at him after he had gone away. "Discipline?" she thought. "I've never had anything but that with Papa and Mama and all the churchgoing I've had to do, and Angus so quiet and steady." When she thought of Angus, her eyes grew tender and she laughed again very softly. He certainly wasn't the dashing kind of fellow she had told the girls at school she meant to marry—someone with sparkle and verve who could be cruel and proud. How silly schoolgirls were anyway! They knew nothing at all about a woman's heart.

Angus settled down to work now very seriously. He was making good money, but, now that he had a wife, he was even more cautious with it than he had been before. He was sure of his investments before he risked anything, and whatever he could spare he put into life insurance. This made Abbie feel very dismal.

"But Papa doesn't bother with life insurance, Angus," she said, her eyes full of tears, "and he's much older than you. It isn't nice of you to make me think about death at all. I couldn't bear to go on without you. I should probably kill myself if you died first, and it would be so much more fun to spend the money on pretty clothes now to fascinate you with while you're alive."

"You're fascinating enough to me in that blue calico, Abbie. I've the bonniest and cleverest wife in town, and I mean she shall be provided for if anything happens to me." His steady blue eyes were level and serious. There was nothing Abbie could do about it but turn her wedding suit and look to her butcher's bills, and be happy.

It was a gay winter for the young people. Mrs. McAllister had started it off with her annual Halloween party, at which each young lady had to go down the cellar stairs backward gazing into a hand mirror and carrying a candle. Strange as it may seem the face she saw in her mirror was always one of Mrs. McAllister's young men. The kale stalks had been left standing in the back garden, so that the young folks might pull them to find whether their wives or husbands would be straight or crooked, tall or short. Everyone bobbed for apples and came up wet and spluttering and completely devoid of the dignity and good breeding which were supposed to characterize the social gatherings of the time.

There were piles of oatcakes and scones and pancakes, as good as you could find in Scotland, and, as a concession to America, there was cider to drink. After they had eaten, they all sat about in chairs and upon the floor while Angus read "Tam O'Shanter" aloud with a running accompaniment on the piano by Abigail.

After the party Douglas took Connie home; but he was rather

sorry that Mrs. McAllister had asked him to do it because Connie jumped so rapidly to conclusions. He did not want the kind of girl who was always tied about his neck with a red woolen string, and because one McBain had married a Hedrick was no reason another should.

Connie was very sedate and walked with little mincing steps on the far edge of the sidewalk, her little muff held up beside her nose. She was growing somewhat taller and rounding out like a real young lady. At her father's gate she held out her hand.

"So nice of you to see me home, Douglas," she said in a very ladylike voice.

"The pleasure is all mine, Connie," said Douglas in the same vein. He held her hand just a tiny bit longer than he needed to do because it was soft and warm and rather small. She hesitated as if she wanted to say something else, and then she tossed good manners overboard.

"Douglas," she said with a rush of enthusiasm, "the girls are planning to give you fellows a return party. We're going to send out invitations and I oughtn't to tell, but all the girls will want you and I thought I'd see if I could get you first."

Douglas drew a long breath and put his hands on the gateposts out of danger.

"When will it be, Connie? I'm out of town a good bit now."

"Two weeks from tonight," said Connie eagerly. "That's the second Saturday in November. You won't be out of town then, will you?"

"I'm afraid I will," said Douglas. "I've to look over some farm land near Wapago. I told the man the second week in November, and the end of the week is the only time I can spare for long trips."

Connie gazed at him with that stricken look which always made him want to shake her. Why couldn't she keep her feelings out of her face? He didn't like girls to make an embarrassment of their feelings.

"Ask Willie," he said. "He'd love to go."

In the course of the week the mail for Mrs. McAllister's was full of little scented billets doux. Douglas had one from Viola Martin which he politely declined.

"What ails ye, man?" asked Willie, "gangin' off to Wapago in the middle of November?"

59

"Business," said Douglas shortly.

Willie was elated over an invitation from Connie. He went around to all of the dry-goods stores and made a collection of boxes that would fit one inside another from a large-sized hatbox on down. The next day Connie received a large package through the mail. She opened one empty box after another until she came to the smallest box of all. When she opened this one, she found a slip of paper upon which Willie had written with flourishes, "Barkus is willin'."

10

After supper one evening that winter Mrs. McAllister called Douglas back into the dining room as the others were going upstairs.

"I've a wee bit savings here, lad, that I wish you'd invest for me," she said. She took two hundred dollars in small bills out of her worn old purse.

"You want *me* to do it, Mrs. McAllister?" asked Douglas.

"Aye, you, Douglas," she said, a little note of excitement in her steady voice. "Angus is too cautious and Johnny Buxton is too wild. You're the one who's going to make the money." He accepted her money and went upstairs, his mind already busy with plans. That lot out on south Main—somebody was going to want that badly in a year or two. He'd had his eye on it ever since he came to town, and he was sure a couple of hundred would buy it now.

He felt unreasonably pleased by Mrs. McAllister's confidence in him. She was not a woman to indulge in visions or flattering remarks. If Mrs. McAllister thought that he was going to make money, he felt a greater confidence in his own instincts which had told him the same thing.

In three months' time he had sold the lot for five hundred dollars. He came in all smiles and counted out the five hundred dollars into Mrs. McAllister's hand.

"Och! but ye've taken nothing for yourself, lad!" said Mrs. McAllister, when she had gotten over the first glow of her pleasure.

60

"Eh, now, my dear," said Douglas. "What would I take? You've been a mother to me."

"No, but I won't have that, Douglas. It's a business proposition for us both, and I want to see *you* get on as well as myself. You must take your fair percentage, and then I'll give you back the first two hundred and let you invest it again."

It was a small amount, but business, and life, are made up of small amounts which produce a cumulative effect. It was Mrs. McAllister's confidence more than anything else that marked this as the beginning of Douglas' financial career.

11

"Have ye never thought seriously of marriage, lad?" asked Willie. He was lying on his back on the bed with one leg crossed over the other knee and a worn carpet slipper dangling from the tip of his toes. His eyes were dreamy and remote, and he had been humming snatches of "Annie Laurie" under his breath:

> " 'Her throat is like the swan
> Um-te-tum-tum
> And her face it is the fairest
> That e'er the sun shone on.
> Tee-dum-dum.' "

"No," said Douglas, looking up from a paper full of figures which he was doing very neatly in red and black ink. "If I stopped to think seriously about it, I should say it was an institution for softies and men who'd made their mark in the world and could afford it. Have you got a new girl?"

"Och, no," said Willie, dreamily balancing the slipper, "only I see old Angus so happy, like, an' spring come greenin' up with a' the birds. Weel, even the Bible says 'tis nae sae gude for man to live alone. And there's Connie an' Mary Gallup an' half a dozen lassies would make clever wives. I'll find mysel' proposin' one of these days before I've fair made up my mind."

Douglas snorted, and went back to his figures. In the past few months he considered that he had become a calloused man of affairs, and Willie appeared to him as still the softest adolescent.

"I'm makin' a gude livelihood," pursued Willie contentedly. "I needna be ashamed to ask a lass to share it."

There was another pause, and then Willie said, "About Connie now. I think she likes you best, Doug. I know you dinna wish to get involved in matrimony now, lad. But happen Connie was to wait for ye?"

"If you're asking my permission to court Constance Hedrick, you go right ahead," Douglas said. "She's a pleasant wee lass, and I'd be greatly pleased to have her for a sister-in-law."

"Weel, Doug," Willie said, "it's nothing serious at all. Happen nothing will come of it. Happen she wouldn't have me if I asked her. It's just that spring's a bonnie time for a wedding, and, weel, 'Barkus is willin'.' "

Douglas got up, took a book from the shelves, and thrust it into Willie's hands.

"There. Read yourself to sleep, my boy. You'll be better in the morning."

Willie was better in the morning. He continued to play the field, and all the lassies loved him like a brother.

In the first sweet days of June, Willie took the train over to Wapago to see the livery man there about a large saddle and harness order which was pending. Willie might have made the liveryman come to him, but he liked to be obliging to everybody and the thought of a holiday from the shop appealed to him. He put on his best clothes with his hat on one side of his head, and committed his hound dogs to the tender mercies of Mrs. McAllister, for there was no train back until the next day, and he would have to spend the night in the Wapago Commercial Hotel.

He was gone for three days. Mrs. McAllister was in anguish about him, and Angus and Douglas were on the point of taking the train to Wapago to hunt for him. When Willie reappeared in Opportunity, he looked none the worse for wear except that his smile was a little sheepish and his hat a little straighter on his head.

"I was delayed by business," said Willie heartily to all inquiries. "I got a verra considerable order from the Wapago livery stable. 'Twas worth waitin' over for."

62

"There's something else, Douglas," said Mrs. McAllister. "The lad's been up to something. You'd better get him to tell you."

Douglas was of a like opinion, but at the same time he respected Willie's privacy. Tolerance of other people's affairs was one of the McBain boys' virtues. However, in this case, Willie needed a confidant. After dinner he said:

"Let's go walkin', Douglas."

They swung off toward Angus' house, but they didn't go in. There was a light in the kitchen, and through the window they could see Angus' head in silhouette, and then Abbie's going by. Abbie was setting her bread for tomorrow and Angus was reading aloud to her.

They pushed on into open country. There was a vast field of starlight overhead, and a fresh smell of clover and dewy earth in the air.

"Look, Doug," said Willie in an anxious voice. "I've fair got myself promised. I thought 'twas only right to tell ye."

"Promised?" said Doug. "Engaged to be married?" A little stab went through him. "To Connie?"

"Na," said Willie slowly, "that's the worst of it, she's no one you know, an' I doot ye will not approve of her."

Douglas could not be sure whether it was relief or chagrin which he felt most strongly. But he kept his voice casual.

"Well, you're in love with her I hope?"

"Oh, aye, I'm in love with her all right, I guess," said Willie, "but over an' above that I was fair swept off my feet with pity for the poor lass."

"Pity!" said Douglas. "You'd never marry a girl for pity, would you, Willie?"

"Weel, someone's got to help her out," said Willie in a hoarse voice. "She's in the family way, and going to kill herself unless I marry her."

Douglas stopped short. He was hot with anger and disgust.

"And are you the father of the bairn, Willie?"

"Och, no!" said Willie in astonishment. "What put that into your head, lad? I only kissed her once when she fair dared me to, and then she out with the whole tale an' wept on my shoulder, like, an' declared to God she was aboot to kill herself. What was a mon to do?"

63

"Where's the man who got her into trouble?" asked Douglas hotly. "Has she got no father to see justice done?"

"Na, she's alone there, that's the worst, and the mon's run off with all her savings. He took her by force, she says, an' not of her own free will."

"But, *God!* Why should *you* have to clean up after him, Willie?"

They had forgotten to walk, and stood facing each other in the road, their faces pale and drawn in the starlight.

"You dinna understand, Doug. She's a bonnie, gude girl. I was fair drawn to her, and you canna let a lass destroy herself."

"How long have you known her?"

"Three days," said Willie unhappily. "She's a chambermaid in the hotel at Wapago. Her name's Alma."

"*Alma!* Alma what?"

"Weel, it's Shorkey or Sharkey, I'm no sae sure which," said Willie dismally.

"I'll go over to see her tomorrow," said Douglas hotly. "I'll get you off if it's the last thing I do."

"You'll do nothing of the kind," said Willie. "I've give the lass my promise. I mean to keep my word. I've told you a' this, because you're my brother, not because I wanted you to mix yoursel' up in it."

"But you can't do this, Willie. You'll ruin your life."

"I'm no afraid of that," said Willie, "and after all 'tis my own life to live, as you're so fond of sayin' yourself."

"At least we must talk it over with Angus," said Douglas heavily. The whole thing seemed very sordid and distasteful to him.

"*You* tell him," said Willie. "A's so good, he'll no understand the kind of mess this poor girl is in."

But Angus understood. He sat at his desk, tilted back with his coat thrown open and his thumbs caught in the armholes of his vest. His lean, pale face did not change at all when Douglas told him, and his mild blue eyes continued to look thoughtfully into Douglas' troubled ones. Douglas was still red-hot with anger and disgust as he had been all night. To think of Willie taking up with a servant girl and sacrificing himself for the honor which she had been so careless of herself! It made him hot all over.

Angus straightened himself in his chair and brought the tips of

64

his fingers together like a tent which he tilted slowly backward and forward.

"Willie's a good boy," he said. "He does not have the best of judgment, maybe, but his heart is right. I'm sorry about this, though, for Abbie and I had hoped he'd make a match with Connie someday. But man proposes and God disposes."

"You mean, Willie proposes and you and I sit here like nincompoops and do nothing," cried Douglas angrily.

"No, lad," said Angus quietly, "I didn't say that we should do nothing. I think it would be a very good thing if you went over to see her. But cool off first, man, cool off."

"How much money do you think it will take to buy her off?"

"I'd take a little money with me," said Angus, "and if she's easy bought off, then Willie is well rid of her. But don't insult her, lad, just look her over. You're a clever judge of character when it comes to lending money, see if you're as clever in gauging a lassie's good intentions. If Willie marries her, you're like to have her in the family for a good many years, and there's no use starting off on the wrong foot."

12

Douglas took the train to Wapago in calmer spirits. If A was willing to accept this monstrous proposition of Willie's there was nothing for him to do but accept it, too. But he certainly meant to see what kind of girl she was and do his best to buy her off. He and Angus had scraped together a small sum for this purpose, but it was agreed that he was not to mention it, if the girl seemed well-intentioned and devoted to Willie. In this respect he thought that Angus was too mild, but Angus' mildness was harder to overcome than all the noisy blustering of a more quick-tempered man, and Angus was determined that they should do nothing to shame or compromise Willie in the eyes of the girl he had asked to marry him.

Douglas felt vigorous and self-confident. The world was full of fools, but thank God he was not one of them, Douglas thought to himself as the train swayed and rattled along the rough roadbed. Beyond the window sped a country of raw dusty roads and carelessly slashed forests, of cabins in clearings and farmhouses in wheat fields from which the stumps had not yet been cleared. Everywhere there was a blaze of sunshine and yellow weeds and wild flowers, but the mountain air saved it from sultriness.

Douglas forgot to think of Willie and his problem. This country always gripped him with a feeling of power and excitement. Here was so much promise, so much lay open for the taking. It would not long be rough and wild. There would be more settlers, better railroads, and money would flow here, rushing and leaping like the mountain streams.

Wapago lay higher than Opportunity and was an older settlement, as places went in the Territory. Men came into it from the lumber and mining districts as well as from the homesteading country, and it had never had a Mrs. McAllister to impose her cheerful Scotch Victorianism on its society.

Douglas walked up from the station and left his bag at the hotel. This was a gaunt frame building with a narrow porch across the front, a hitching rack on the street, and plenty of spittoons in the lobby to accommodate commercial travelers.

Beside the desk he met Johnny Buxton who had been gone from Mrs. McAllister's a week on one of his land-inspecting tours.

"What brings you up here, Doug?" asked Johnny, slapping him heartily on the back.

"Business," said Douglas shortly, thinking that he would rather meet the devil than anyone from the boardinghouse while he was on this fool's errand for Willie.

"Well, you'll be free the night, won't you?" asked Johnny. "They're having a dance in the Odd Fellows' Hall, they tell me. With no train out until tomorrow, we're in luck. I'll meet you here in the office after supper, and let's go. Do no harm to see a sample of the Wapago lassies, eh? What say?"

"All right," said Douglas, "if I get through my business in time. What are you up to now?"

"I've a twenty-mile ride to make before the dance the night. I must be off now, but it's lucky I saw you, man."

Douglas saw Johnny onto a lumbering mare with heavy feet and shaggy fetlocks, and he drew a long breath as Johnny's departing back diminished along the road. Now for it!

Alma was a thin little girl with a small head set on a long neck, and sly, narrow eyes. Douglas did not like her, but he knew that

66

he was prejudiced, and, remembering A, he tried to see her good points. She had light hair and high cheekbones with a good fresh color on them. Her hands were large and roughly chapped from working in cold water on back stairs. She had small, round breasts, set high, and a long slim waist. He thought that she was a calculating girl rather than a passionate one.

Her mouth was a little sulky when she looked at him. She knew as well as he did why he had come, and she preferred to do her business with Willie.

"Your brother promised me," she said almost at once. "I guess a promise holds good anywhere, don't it?"

"Yes, but you've not known each other long," said Douglas with as much patience as he could muster. "You both might want to change your minds."

"Does *he* want to change *his*?" she asked fiercely.

"I don't know about that. He didn't know that I was coming up to see you. I took it upon myself."

"Snooper, eh?" she said, curling her lip. "Well, take a good look at me. I ain't much to see, but your brother seemed to like it. I'll say your brother's a right friendly young man, which is more than I'd say of you at a first look."

"I came to get acquainted with you, lass," Douglas said with hard-held patience. "You're not making it very easy."

"Well, nothing's been easy for *me*. Why should I make things easier for other folks?"

Douglas resisted a strong impulse to take her by her thin shoulders and shake her.

"I'm sorry things have not been easy for you," he said, "but that's no reason you should refuse to hold a civil conversation with a body."

"I've had to fight for what I've got, an' don't tell me you ain't here to make me fight again. You've come to make me give him up, but a promise is a promise, I tell you!"

"I wouldn't ask you to give him up for nothing," said Douglas. He felt convinced now that she was the kind of girl to whom an offer of money would be a business proposition, not an insult.

"Well?" she said.

"Look! What you need is money, not a husband."

"Is that so?"

"I think it is."

67

"Well, I ain't the kind of girl you think I am, mister. You can't buy me off, if that's what you came to do."

"I didn't come to buy you off, but if you'd take a gift—"

"It's no use for you to talk at all. I'm in love with Willie!" She said it defiantly, sure that he would not believe her; but he had a strange, uneasy feeling that perhaps she spoke the truth.

He continued to argue and persuade for ten or fifteen minutes, standing outside the back door of the hotel, beside a bed of straggly sweet williams in a litter of empty crates and rubbish cans. Then the voice of the proprietress, bawling down the back stairs for Alma, brought the interview to a close. Douglas was conscious that he had not come off well. He went up on the hill behind the hotel where there was a pleasant pine grove, and he lay down in the pine needles and pulled his hat over his eyes. He disliked Alma acutely and he was impatient with Willie. How could you save a fool from his fate? If it didn't catch up with him now, it would later. "I should have made some effort to get him and Connie together," he thought. "Only a little push would have done it. And now he's got mixed up in this!" He realized vaguely that he was a coward where Connie was concerned. He didn't want her, but he didn't quite want anyone else to have her.

The pine trees whispered and sighed in the breeze, and over and above the fresh scent of the crushed needles was a smell of dog's fennel and clover. He took his hat from his eyes and lay, looking up into the vast empty sky. Two little clouds were slowly dissolving and melting away into the blue June nothingness.

Suddenly he felt lonely. Lives touch here and there, he thought, but each one is shut up in a shell of aloneness that no other can quite break down. It was a novel thought to him. He lay still, playing with it awhile: No one can ever know what I think now, how I feel. When I am dead it will be gone. No one will ever have shared it. Douglas McBain—what is he? Other people ken his face better than I do, but he is all alone inside. No one but myself kens myself, an' how far does that go? He felt unreasonably sad and adrift. He rolled over on his stomach and rested his face on his arms. Presently he was asleep.

When he woke up, the shade of the pine tree had drifted away and the late afternoon sun was hot on his left side. He turned over again, feeling stiff and dull and conscious that he had failed in something which he had meant to accomplish. He was hungry, but the sun told him that supper at the hotel would not be ready for another half-hour. He sat up and stretched, feeling his mind as empty as his stomach. He thought of Caithness, and that they would all be working in the fields in the pale golden light of the midnight sun tonight. He had thought very little about the Caithness folk of late, but his trip from Opportunity with no business in hand, except this unfortunate mess of Willie's, seemed to have set his mind adrift from the usual channels. He wondered what his mother would think of Alma. She had been pleased, they said, with the pictures and the accounts of Abigail. But they would not understand a girl like Alma at all.

He rose, dusting the broken pine needles from his clothing, and went down to wash up for supper.

Alma was waiting on table. Her cheeks were quite red and her eyes looked as if she might have been crying. She tossed her head and made as if she did not see him, but he got a much better piece of pork than the drummer who sat next to him, and a bigger piece of pie. He felt that she was making an indirect effort to propitiate him.

After supper he made a pretext to return to the dining room to see her.

"Will you come out and talk with me after you've finished up here?" he asked.

"I'm sorry," she said with lifted eyebrows and a crook in her little finger, "but I don't never make appointments with young gentlemen after hours. I've got my reputation to look out for."

She was putting on propriety for the effect it would have on him, and Douglas couldn't resist a parting thrust.

"Well, your virtue's perfectly safe with me, lass, but if your reputation's not already spoiled, I'll see you before train time in the morning."

He stalked out of the dining room with murder in his heart and thunder on his brow, and there was Johnny Buxton searching the office for him.

"Come away, lad," he cried slapping Douglas on the back. "The fiddle's tuning in the Odd Fellows' Hall. We'll be just in time for the dance."

69

13

Douglas and Johnny stood near the door at the end of the long, roughly boarded hall. Loops of faded bunting and yellowed evergreen from some previous occasion hid the rafters, and below these uninspiring decorations surged a crowd of eager dancers. There were men in rough boots and jackets from the lumber camps and the mines, and there were storekeepers and traveling men in checkered suits and cravats. The women were fewer in number and very much in demand. It seemed to Douglas that they had bolder eyes than the Opportunity girls, and they wore whatever they had, from lavender shot silk to brown calico, without much regard to fashion or propriety.

He watched Johnny tap the shoulder of a stocky fellow with a two-day beard and whirl away with his partner, a heavy-set girl in a bustle and black bangs. Apparently one did not stand on ceremony in Wapago, but he was in no hurry to join the perspiring throng. He knew how to dance after a fashion, but he had done very little of it and it did not particularly interest him.

"Aren't you dancing, handsome?" a girl said to him over her partner's shoulder as she whirled by. Douglas only smiled at her and thought to himself that they didn't interest him if they came too cheap.

At the other end of the room on a raised platform a piano and violin ground out a popular waltz. *Rum*-tum-tum! *Rum*-tum-tum! A small cool breeze came in the open windows and stirred the fetid air about the dancers. Douglas played with the idea of going to the hotel to bed or out on the hill where he had spent the afternoon. His feeling of solitariness in the world came back to him. What was he doing here among these strangers? He shrugged his shoulders and made his way through the crowd of onlookers to the door. There was a wide landing here and then a rough stairway leading down to the open air.

At the head of the stairs he stopped, for a girl in a yellow dress was running up them. With her two hands she held the yellow skirt in front of her to keep from tripping, and it billowed behind her as she ran. She looked up at him as she came, and her eyes were wide and strange, dancing with little lights. They were gray

70

eyes and the dark lashes about them gave them a wild, starry look.

"Dance with me," she said in a low, urgent voice. "Dance with me."

Behind her with his foot on the lowest step, he saw a grim-looking man purposefully beginning to mount.

As she reached the top of the stairs Douglas slipped his arm about her and they began to waltz. With a hard elbow he forced a way for them through the surprised loiterers at the door, and they continued to waltz onto the dance floor and around among the whirling dancers.

She moved very lightly and gracefully, but her breath came quickly and he could feel the rapid rise and fall of her breast as they danced. A little vein on the side of her neck beat the staccato tempo of her pulse.

They did not speak at all as they danced, but once she looked full in his face and flashed him a dazzling smile. There was a look about her like sunshine after rain, something washed clear and with a sparkle on every point. She had strong white teeth between red lips and warmly colored cheeks with dimples in them, but that did not in any adequate way describe her. It was only the sparkle that he saw and remembered. Her hair was brushed softly back from her forehead, but there was an artful curl on either temple.

The piano and violin were still playing the same tune they had been playing when Douglas had made up his mind to go back to the hotel to bed. He realized this with wonder, for it seemed as if a long time had elapsed since then.

Looking over her head, as they circled nearer the door, he saw the man who had followed her up the stairs. He was a tall, well-set-up man, dressed in the city clothes that traveling men normally wore. His eyes followed them angrily as they danced.

The girl saw him, too, and she tightened her fingers on Douglas' arm and looked up into his face.

"Don't let him take me," she said. "Look what he did to my arm. Look!" She raised her right arm for his inspection, and Douglas could see the red imprint of heavy fingers on the white flesh.

"What's your name?" he asked.

"Mamie."

71

"Mamie what?"

"Mamie Stephens—but Mamie's enough. What's yours?"

"Douglas McBain."

"Thank you, Douglas," she said. Her head drooped softly to one side; she lowered her eyes; a little half-smile sparkled about her lips. They continued to dance.

When the dance ended two or three young fellows made a sliding rush across the floor toward Mamie.

"Mamie, give us a dance! Let me have the next now. I was here first."

Mamie's hand continued to lie along Douglas' arm. She smiled at them all.

"Now, boys, no crowding," she said. "Let's proceed in an orderly manner."

One of the young men held up his hands like begging paws and began to bark.

"Down, Rover, down!" said Mamie, shaking a finger at him. "Mr. McBain, do you have my dance card handy?"

Douglas took an envelope out of his pocket and quickly numbered the back of it. He wrote "Miss Stephens' card" at the top and initialed "McB." on every other number. Mamie looked over his arm as he wrote and nodded her approval.

"Now, Harry," she said, "you may have the next one after this, and Clem, the fourth, and you, Rover, the sixth if you will sit up and beg ever so politely and promise not to bite. Yes, Mr. Tucker, the eighth, if you like—"

In a moment the back of the envelope was scrawled with initials.

"Ain't you saving none for Buck?" asked the young man addressed as Harry.

"Buck?" asked Mamie, her brow contracting into a puzzled frown. "Buck who? Oh—you mean Buck Clayborne? Why should I save one for *him*?" She said the last a little loudly and defiantly, Doug thought, perhaps for the effect the words should have on someone. He raised his eyes and saw the man of the stairs coming toward them through the crowd. People drew aside to let him pass through.

He was as tall as Douglas and a little heavier. He was perhaps ten years older, and his face was dark and strongly marked by

72

his emotions. He kept his voice steady now, but there were anger and possessive passion in his eyes and around his mouth.

"Mamie," he said, "the next dance is mine."

"You flatter yourself, Mr. Clayborne," said Mamie lightly. "You're just a little late, I think. Look over my card, if you like." She handed him the envelope.

He read it slowly and intently, then he tore it across and flung it on the floor.

"You came here with me," he said. "The next dance is mine."

"I beg pardon," said Douglas, "but Miss Stephens is here with me tonight. I'll ask ye to return her card and let her make her own engagements."

"Here with *you?* And who in hell are you? No one *I* ever saw before."

"Well," said Douglas dryly, "I don't inhabit the regions you mention, Mr. Clayborne; maybe that's why you're not familiar with my face."

Mamie looked from one to the other with sparkling eyes. Color lay warm and high on her cheeks, and her lips were parted over her white teeth. A little circle of spectators had begun to draw around them, and Douglas saw Johnny Buxton's gaping mouth and round eyes staring in astonishment.

"Fresh, are you?" said Clayborne angrily. "That don't go with me, fellow. Come on, Mamie."

The music had started again, a lively polka that dissolved and re-formed the dancers into new combinations. Douglas caught Mamie about the waist and began to dance. He heard her laughing and felt her hair against his cheek. But they had not freed themselves of the loitering crowd before Buck Clayborne laid violent hands on them.

He caught Douglas' shoulder with his left hand while his right fist shot out and grazed Douglas' cheek. Douglas whirled about, pushing Mamie aside, and struck back, quick and hard. The dancers scattered about them, and for a few moments, like performers in an opera, they fought to music. Then the music stopped with a discordant squawk. People began pushing and striving to see. To a western crowd there was nothing more entertaining than a dance-hall fight.

Buck Clayborne was the heavier of the two men but Douglas

73

was the tougher and more agile. They were pretty well matched and they might have gone on for a long time, striking and swaying, landing blow after blow. But the town marshal pushed his way through the yelling spectators and several of the young fellows laid hold of them and pulled them apart. They stood back, panting and angry, looking at one another with hot eyes.

"What's the trouble here, Mamie?" asked the marshal.

"They're fighting over which one brought me to the dance," said Mamie.

"Well, you ought to be able to settle that as well as anybody. Which one did?"

Mamie laid her hand on Douglas' arm.

"Mr. McBain did," she said. "Please see Mr. Clayborne out so he won't make any more trouble, Marshal." She gave the marshal one of her flashing smiles.

Douglas wiped the blood from a scratch on the side of his face. The music had begun again. They found themselves dancing.

Sometimes he stood by the wall and watched her dancing with another man—how the full yellow skirt floated out from the shapely waist, how the body swayed and the white neck curved to the dark hair. And when she whirled about so that she saw him watching her, she flashed him one of her sun-after-rain smiles.

Then he had her in his arms again and they were moving in rhythm. It was a kind of dream, unrelated to any former existence. It was compounded of bad music and intolerable heat, and the dim light of kerosene lamps swaying under faded bunting and withered evergreen, and a girl in a yellow dress warm on his arm, her body moving with his, sometimes her breath and sometimes her dark hair soft against his cheek.

The evening lasted forever. It was gone in a minute.

They were walking along a dark road by a river. There were millions of stars overhead, and pine trees black against the starlight. The river made a rushing sound, like the sound the wind makes past a man's ears when he is falling through space.

They had been laughing all the way from the dance hall in town at nothing in particular. But now Mamie grew quiet.

"Ugh! the river!" she said. "I hate the sound of it. I wouldn't live near it if I could get away. I like gay things, don't you, Douglas?"

74

"Aye," he said, knowing for the first time that it was gaiety and sparkle that he had always wanted; not the solid Scottish virtues, but something that danced and glittered.

She was silent again for a long time. "I guess I didn't treat Buck very well tonight, but I wanted to get even. He had it coming."

"What's Buck to you, Mamie?" Douglas asked in a low voice. "I've a right to know that, I think, after the set-to we had tonight."

She laughed again, a little tinkle of lightheartedness.

"Why, nothing—nothing at all!"

He was relieved to hear that. He didn't question her any further. His fingers trembled on her arm.

"Because you're *my* girl now," he said.

"You've a funny way of rolling the 'r' in 'gir-r-r-l, haven't you?"

"Would you rather I said lassie?"

"Oh, no! That's funnier still."

They had come to a gate in a picket fence. Behind it in the starlight he could see the dark bulk of a house and barn and the graceful shadows of trees. She went inside the gate and, shutting it between them, stood with her face turned up to his, laughing. He tried to pull the gate open, but one of the pickets came loose in his hands.

"Be careful," she warned. "Everything's falling to pieces here—everything but me."

"Let me come in a moment."

"No, you've seen enough of me tonight. Go along now."

"I'll see you in the morning then."

"Well—maybe."

"Remember, you're mine now—for always."

"That's what they all say," she mocked.

"This one's different."

"I wonder?"

"Mamie! It's true," he said hoarsely.

But she had run up the path and disappeared around the dark house. He still seemed to hear her laughter in the rushing of the river. Slowly he returned to town, and all the way he saw her face in the twinkling of the stars overhead.

75

14

When he first awoke in the morning he could not overcome the feeling that he had dreamed the events of the past evening. He dressed and went down to the dining room for breakfast.

Another girl had taken Alma's place in the dining room. But news travels fast in a small town. The new girl looked at him curiously. She knew that he was the brother of Alma's intended and that he and Buck Clayborne had fought over Mamie Stephens at the Odd Fellows' Hall the night before.

By the time Douglas had finished a cup of coffee and a plate of ham and eggs, the feeling of dream left him and he began to experience an acute desire to see Mamie again. She was real now, so real that he would have rushed off at once to see her, had he not realized that one did not call on young ladies before nine o'clock of the morning.

He returned to his room and shaved himself with unusual care, doing what he could to minimize the ugly scratch and bruise on his cheek, which proved beyond anything that the events of the evening had been real. He packed his bag, and brushed his hair until it shone, and still it was too early to go calling upon a young lady. But his train left before noon, and, decorous or not, he had to have all the time with her that he could manage.

Leaving his bag in the hotel office, he swung out along the quiet Sabbath street. Sunshine came golden through the trees to pattern the plank walks and the dusty patches of sorrel and dog's fennel. He had followed Mamie blindly through the starlight the night before, and now by daylight he was uncertain of the way.

At first he took a wrong turning and missed the bridge across the river. Then he wasted five or ten minutes wandering up and down before he found the crossing, and he was beginning to sweat with impatience and exasperation before he felt certain of his way. The sound of the river excited him and made him happy. He threw a chip into it as he walked and saw how it was carried away to some unknown destination. Under bridges, over stones, how strongly and sweetly the water flowed! He wanted to run, but he held himself down to a steady stride.

There was a bend in the river and trees, before he came to

Mamie's house, so that he could not gloat over it in advance. Cowbells tinkled from the pastures on his left, and above the din of the river came the sound of church bells ringing back in Wapago. It seemed to him that the air was full of bells. Even the meadowlarks thrust insistent, bell-like flutings into the ringing air. He felt as if he were swimming in sound and in long waves of yellow sunshine that washed him in recurring swells toward the house by the river.

When he came around the bend, he saw that Mamie was standing by the gate in the same yellow dress she had worn the night before, and with her was Buck Clayborne.

Douglas went steadily forward until he was quite close. They did not hear him coming, with the noise of the river and the bells in their ears. Buck was holding her wrist as a man holds something he owns and has almost ceased to value. He was speaking to her earnestly, roughly, and Mamie was looking up at him with an expression of terrible humility upon her face. There was no sparkle in her eyes or around her mouth, only submission.

As if someone had dealt him a sudden blow to the pit of the stomach, Douglas felt physically sick. But it was too late now to go back, for Mamie saw him and called out to him.

"I see ye're busy, Miss Stephens," he said stiffly. "I'll not bother you long."

A slow tide of color went up her cheeks and she pulled her wrist free. "Come in, won't you?" she said.

Buck looked at them with a kind of detached amusement. His anger of the previous night seemed to have cooled.

"Mr. Clayborne just stopped by to say goodbye. He's taking the noon train east," she said. "Come in, now. I want you two to be friends." She had begun to smile and sparkle again.

For a moment Douglas could not speak. Then he said stiffly: "I'm taking the noon train west, Miss Stephens. It's hardly worth your while to urge us to be friendly, like."

An awkward silence descended on them. The church bells had ceased to ring and the river had passed momentarily out of their conscious hearing. Douglas looked at her steadily with his level blue eyes. Then he said:

"I'll be bidding you goodbye now, Miss Stephens."

"Douglas!" she called. "Stop a minute." She flung herself through the gate calling, but he had already turned around and was going back to Wapago. Buck Clayborne looked at her, and laughed.

Just before Douglas reached town the second bells for church began to ring. They filled the air about him with intolerable sound. He got his key at the hotel desk and went back to shut himself into the untidy bedroom until train time.

He did not make any attempt to see Alma before he left. Willie's affairs had dwindled into insignificance beside his own.

15

Johnny Buxton came swaying down the aisle of the train for Opportunity and clapped Douglas on the back.

"Well, you were the life of the party last night, my lad," he remarked, making himself easy in the seat beside Douglas, "and a mighty success wi' Buck Clayborne's girl, too."

Douglas shrugged his shoulders and continued to look out of the window at a blur of flying trees and stones and yellow wild flowers.

"There's mony a young fellow would like to be in your shoes," continued Johnny. "She's the bonniest they've to offer in Wapago, aye, or Opportunity either for that matter. Poor lass! I'm a bit sorry for her mysel', however."

Douglas looked around at him but said nothing.

"Her father was killed, like, in a train wreck about six years ago. He was the brakeman, I'm told, and it's them always gets it first when there's a smashup. Her mither's married again to the most inebrious mon in the Territory, an' they've got them a bairn for every year they've been hitched. Mamie's a proud girl, an' they tell me she's fair vexed with the life she's got to lead amongst them. She'd be married an' gone ere now, I dare say, but they tell me Buck's got a wife an' family in the East. Whether the lassie knows that or not I couldna say, but she's that proud, she'd no let on if she knew."

Johnny took a quill toothpick out of his pocket and thoughtfully picked his teeth. Douglas looked out of the window again in silence. He felt shaken, as if he had been through a long illness. All he could see, as he gazed at the slipping landscape, was

78

the possessive hand on Mamie's wrist and the look of abasement on her face.

"You'll have had a wee bit too much gaiety last night, Doug," said Johnny. "You're no very lively company the day."

"I've nothing to say at all. Is it small talk you wish me to invent for you, John?"

"Na," said Johnny. "But I'll shove along down the line a bit now. Yon drummer will have some new tales, I dare say."

The week in Opportunity began as usual. Douglas made a perfunctory report on Alma to Angus. His anger and resentment against Willie's girl had cooled. He did not care a tinker's damn whom Willie married. Every man had his own problems.

"You thought she was all right, Doug?" asked Willie anxiously. He had spent an uneasy weekend, knowing that, when Douglas took French leave of Mrs. McAllister's for a few days, he had undoubtedly gone to Wapago to meddle in his brother's affairs.

"Aye, she'll pass on a dark night, if you've no lantern," said Douglas carelessly.

Willie was overjoyed. He felt as if Alma had been handed a bouquet of long-stemmed American Beauty roses. His own courage needed considerable bolstering, for he was not madly enough in love to be immune to family opinion. Even the faintest praise from Douglas, who was noted in the family for not sharing Willie's optimistic turn of mind, could raise Willie's spirits to the skies.

"She'd a neat little figure, didn't you think?" asked Willie, "and a very clever turn of mind?"

"Aye, clever all right," said Douglas. "You'd best not leave your wages in your trouser pockets when you go to bed wi' her. They'll be gone in the morn."

Willie laughed uproariously, and slapped his thigh. The hound dogs capered and barked about him.

"Aye, she's quite a lass!" cried Willie joyously.

But, as the week progressed, Douglas grew more and more restless. The fever mounted higher and higher. He could not sit still but tramped the streets by day and the fields by night.

Angus watched him with quiet, surprised eyes, saying nothing. Johnny Buxton had brought home some cock-and-bull story about Douglas stealing another man's girl at a party and fighting for her in front of everybody; but Johnny was always full of scan-

79

dalous tales. Still, Angus wondered. He thought, too late, that he should have attended to all of the family business in Wapago, and left his brother in Opportunity. The lassies of Wapago must be mighty bonnie. And then he smiled to himself a little as he thought of Abigail. The lads had a right to their own love affairs, and, although he did not see life with Willie's rosy glasses, he had confidence in the goodness of human nature and the power of right to triumph.

During the early part of the week Douglas wrestled with the thought of Buck Clayborne. He wondered over and over again with passionate uncertainty just what Buck was to Mamie. He hated him so violently that it was like a physical pain. He even thought of killing him, sometimes with a gun, but more often with his bare hands. He felt Buck's flesh under his fists as he had felt it at the dance. If they had only let him finish the fight! He was quicker and harder than Buck; he might have killed him then.

But by Thursday Buck had begun to fade into unimportance. Mamie's face, lovely and artless, floated before his eyes wherever he looked. He saw it sparkle and flash with the little dancing lights in the gray eyes and the dimples about the mouth. He felt the quick come and go of breath in her breast, and saw the tiny vein that beat so wildly in her throat. The dandelions along the roadside were the color of her dress. When a meadowlark sang, it stabbed him with the sweetness of that Sunday morning before he had seen her with Buck, when he had thought that he was going to her alone.

Finally he knew that Buck did not matter to him at all; that it was only Mamie who mattered and that he would have to make her love him, because he could not live without her.

It was late on Saturday when he reached this decision. The daily train for Wapago had gone. He went to the livery station and hired a horse. All night long he rode the rough lumber road to Wapago, with the stars overhead and the smell of pine slashings and clover and wild roses fresh in his nostrils. He felt very quiet and at peace, happy for the first time since the early church bells had stoped ringing in Wapago last Sunday morning.

80

16

Douglas breakfasted and shaved himself at the Commercial Hotel, and had his horse stabled and fed. Alma was on duty to shove him his ham and eggs. She looked at him curiously and her shrewd eyes told her that he was no longer in the least concerned with her. This made her a little angry, for, although she disliked him very much, yet she wanted him to notice her.

It's that Stephens girl, she thought, slamming down a thick cup of coffee and flourishing a napkin. She ain't no better than I am, for all her mincy airs, but the men are all locoed on her. He was fightin' Buck Clayborne for her the last time he was here. Well, I hope he gets her. Maybe he'll leave *me* alone then. She flounced her skirts and crooked her little finger.

He let the church bells ring before he started for the Stephens place. He had never really looked at the place by daylight before. It wanted paint and was exceedingly dilapidated. Chickens scratched about neglected bits of farm machinery. Two very small children sat on the doorstep spooning dirt into a can. They looked at Douglas solemnly as he approached and one called, "*Ma.*" The smallest one upset his spoonful of dirt on his ragged shirt and stuck his fingers in his mouth.

A woman came to the door, hastily tying a clean apron over a greasy front. She did not look like an old woman but she had seen hard use. When she smiled there was a faint flicker of Mamie's sparkle.

"You're one of Mamie's beaux, I expect," she said. "Set down on the porch and I'll call her."

He sat down in a paintless rocker with his hat on his knees.

"Oh, Lord!" he thought, "this is where she lives, in this awful ignominy! How soon can I take her out of it?"

She came to the door, and the strange eyes with the dancing lights were wide with something that was almost anger.

"Douglas!" she said. "Why didn't you let me know? I'd have met you somewhere."

He sprang up and took her hands.

"It's best here," he said awkwardly. "I had to see you an' this is your home."

81

"It's where I stay," she said, dropping her eyes.

He continued to hold her hands and his eyes went hungrily over her. The curling dark hair was blown loose about her cheeks, and one sleeve of her dark calico dress was split from elbow to shoulder, displaying the white, round flesh of her arm.

"You'll not be here long," he said. "I've other plans for you."

The gray eyes lifted again, mocking and laughing.

"You're a funny fellow, aren't you?"

"Smile like that, an' I'll put on bells an' a false nose."

"You don't need them."

They laughed, their eyes clinging together in understanding.

"Will your young man stay to dinner, Mamie?" asked her mother from the doorway.

"He'd rather go back to the hotel, Mama."

"No, I would not," said Douglas. "I'll be very pleased to stay, thank you, Mrs.—."

"Johnson," she supplied. "Well, we're pleased to have you, but it'll be potluck."

"I'll take my chances."

"And live to regret it," said Mamie. "You might have taken me to the hotel!"

"We'll do that later," said Douglas. "We've a long life of dinners ahead of us."

It was not a successful meal, either gastronomically or socially. The stewed chicken was tough and the dumplings were soggy and underdone. Only the boiled potatoes were plentiful. The vegetable was a bitter compound of turnip tops and dandelion greens and there was no dessert.

Four little children and a baby in a high chair sat about the table in various stages of untidiness, and at the end of the table sat a red-haired man in his undershirt who was, even this early in the day, somewhat the worse for liquor.

"Maw, you give one drumstick to the man and the other to Pa. Where do I come in?" demanded the five-year-old boy in a querulous tone.

"Well, Tom, I give you part of the thigh. It's the same meat."

"But I want a bone to suck."

"Here, let the lad have the drumstick," said Douglas.

Mamie laid a swift, restraining hand upon his plate.

"*No,*" she said fiercely, "no, you don't."

"Well, sir," said Mr. Johnson in a loud, unsteady voice, "have you heard about the new post office they going to put up here?"

"No, I've not," said Douglas. "We're building a new one in Opportunity also."

"So you come from Opportunity, do you?" asked Mr. Johnson. "Dullest town in the West, Opp'tunity. Not a saloon or a dance hall to compare what we got here. Bunch of Pres'terians over there. Lord! are they holy!"

Mamie hastily passed her stepfather the bread, but he waved it away.

"When I want a piece of bread, I'll ask for it," he said. "You seen our Odd Fellows' Hall, mister?"

"Yes, I've seen the Odd Fellows' Hall," Douglas said, "it's where I met Miss Mamie."

"She meets a lot of fellows," Mr. Johnson said. "Maybe some day she'll marry one. Seems it's about time."

"Bubber," Mrs. Johnson said, "leave Mamie alone now."

Mamie began to speak quickly and brightly. "Did you see the Dixie Belle Opera that came around last spring, Mr. McBain? They put on *Pinafore* and *Chimes of Normandy*. It's almost as good as being in San Francisco when things like that come around, don't you think?"

She was trying hard, and Douglas answered her. Together they kept the conversation on impersonal ground, but Douglas felt disgusted with himself for not taking her to the hotel. He had had some idea of wanting to know her family, but he saw now that they were better not inspected too closely. He had wanted to please her, and he realized that she was suffering much more acutely than he was. Alone and in a better dress, she might be anybody, he thought. She had the beauty and the grace of a fine lady. She had the rudiments of tact and of social consciousness, and she was, like himself, a person who might go a long way up from a low beginning. Her surroundings had shocked him for a moment, but now they only made her gallantry appear the more desirable. Suffering for her embarrassment, he knew now how much he loved her.

When the meal was over, Mrs. Johnson said:

"Put on your yellow dress, Mamie, and take your young man walking. I'll manage with the dishes."

They made their way through the untidy barnyard to a path

83

that led up through woods to a pine-clad bluff overlooking the river.

"This is my path," said Mamie.

"Do you like the woods?" he asked. He wanted to tell her about Caithness and how he had never seen woods or mountains until he was a grown man.

"No," she said, "but I've got to get away somewhere. It's either go to town or up here. You've seen them now, there's no use pretending with you. I didn't invite you, you know. I never ask my fellows out here by daylight, and they don't get farther than the gate at night."

"All except Buck?"

"Buck only comes through town once in a while. He doesn't really matter."

"Is that the truth?"

"Do you think I'd lie to you?"

"I think you might."

She flung herself down under a pine tree and spread her yellow dress around her. She leaned back, resting on her hands, her face tilted up to him, her throat full and white. A smile rippled across her face like a breeze across water on a shining day.

"You think I'm very bad," she said. "I don't know why you come here then, because I'm sure you're very good."

"I think you're an angel," he said in a choked voice. "There's no man good enough for you."

"Lots of them think they are," she said pertly. She was laughing at him now.

"Are you never serious, Mamie?"

"Sometimes."

"When?"

"When you don't expect it."

"Be serious now. I'll not expect it."

"I don't dare. Life's much better when you keep laughing. It can't catch up with you then and punch you in the nose."

He sat beside her, breaking pine needles and little sticks between his fingers. The scent of pine was strong and hot above them; and the sound of the river made a background to their light talk, as the undercurrent of the horns and bass viols flows forever behind the chatter of flutes and violins in a symphony.

84

"Tell me about yourself now," said Mamie. "I don't know you at all. You've seen the worst of me. Now it's your turn to tell me the worst about yourself. That's only fair, isn't it?"

It was easy to tell her about himself. He had never cared to put himself into words before her invitation; but now the words flowed easily. There was a quiet look of listening in her face. Sometimes she asked a question, and sometimes she looked into the sky at the drifting clouds as if she heard only the river and the summer birds, but he had never had a better audience. He made the midnight sun shine for her over the oat fields of Caithness, and the wind blow through the gardens of Thurso Castle. She saw his father sitting beneath the thatch and his mother bending over the open fire. She felt the swaying of a ship tossed on a dark night sea.

They lay on their stomachs now, with their chins in their hands, looking out toward the river with eyes that saw only the pictures Douglas' words evoked. He paused and loosened his sleeve to let her see the anchor on his arm.

She put out her hand and touched his flesh. Her finger traced the anchor delicately.

"How wonderful! I never knew a sailor."

He closed his free hand over hers, holding her fingers against his arm.

"I'm not a sailor anymore; I'm a businessman. I'm going to go up in the world, Mamie. I'm going to be rich."

She let her hand lie in his, but she turned on her back and flung the other arm up over her head.

"Rich?" she said. There was a note of excitement in her voice. Douglas heard it, and he pushed this slight advantage.

"Yes, rich," he said. "I'll need someone to help me spend it some of these days."

"How do you know?"

"How does any man know he's going to succeed? A voice inside tells him."

She laughed and sat up.

"Let me have my hand now. I've got to fix my hair. Look! it's getting late."

"I'll let you have your hand when you've kissed me."

"You don't want much!"

85

He held her close a moment, his arms trembling with the wonder and excitement of it, but her lips were laughing and they only brushed his cheek as she pulled away.

"Have supper with me at the hotel!"

"Maybe I will."

The air was all golden with descending sun as they went down the path through the trees.

"It's serious with me, Mamie," he said.

"You mean about supper at the hotel?" They ran the last way down the path, and brought up, breathless and laughing, by the pigpen and the untidy barnyard.

A child was crying in the house and there was a clatter of falling pans in the kitchen. One of Mr. Johnson's legs hung over the side of a weather-beaten hammock on the front porch. The rest of him was in eclipse. Mamie ran in hastily for a hat and met Douglas at the gate. Her eyes were shining, and she laid her hand along his arm as she had done on the night of the dance.

The green gold of the sky was caught in the bright path of the river. Robins gave their troubled prayer for rain and a varied thrush sent up a clear, wild fluting. All of the shadows about the trees were deeply green like things seen under water. The moon was a small curved thread of silver in the vast, green sky and the first star was a point of white. Douglas, who had talked all afternoon, was silent now, but Mamie chattered as she walked, a flow of gay inconsequence.

Men lifted their heads from their plates as the couple came into the hotel dining room. Mamie's face was the kind that would always lift men's eyes from meat and drink. It touched another of the primal hungers in them.

All through supper Mamie was a beautiful, fine lady—a gay, fine lady, such a one as should be seen dining luxuriously in a hotel. It might have been a hotel in New York instead of the Wapago Commercial. In either case Mamie would have graced it and been at home. All the awkwardness of the noon meal had fallen away from her. She was not so much Mamie Stephens as what Mamie Stephens fancied herself to be. Therein lay much of her charm, for she was like water under changing skies.

They walked back slowly in the starlight, and subtly Mamie's mood changed. She began to talk about her father and her childhood in halting, broken sentences that betrayed her emotion.

86

"I had plenty of pretty dresses then—and spending money—and good things to eat. He was crazy about me. He used to call me his dancing doll. And now it's like you see it at home. Oh, God! sometimes I wish I'd been in the wreck, too, and died when he did."

Douglas put his arms about her.

"*No*, Mamie, no!" he whispered.

He drew her down beside him on the riverbank and for a long time they sat still, her head lying against his shoulder. When he finally spoke, his voice was strange with emotion.

"How soon can you marry me, Mamie?"

She lifted her head and drew back from him, as if this were a new idea which frightened her.

"I'm not sure yet that I love you, Doug."

"You will, Mamie," he said. "I've love enough for two until you do."

She sat away from him in silence for a few moments, letting him play with her hand, her face turned away from his eager eyes.

"I can't marry," she said at last in a hard little voice. "I can't marry and be like Mama is. I've seen enough of that to last me a lifetime. Babies and diapers and no clothes and not enough food and God knows what else that's beastly. If ever I do marry, I've got to be sure it'll be different."

"It will be different, Mamie. I swear it will," said Douglas earnestly.

"How can I know?"

"You must trust me, I suppose."

"I want to be gay, Douglas! I want to be alive, and laugh and dance, and wear pretty clothes. I've got to know before I jump in blindfolded."

"I've two thousand dollars in the bank," Douglas said, "and I'm making good money all the time. I want to be gay myself. I'm willing to work for it, but I'll not be satisfied with half a loaf. I'm offering you the best I've got."

She sat silent a long time, her head bent forward on her graceful neck. Her hand strayed idly among the white clover blossoms that made little luminous globes in the darkness of the grass.

"What's troubling you?" he asked gently. He leaned close to her, so that he seemed to enfold her, although he was not touching her at all. He could smell the personal fragrance of her hair over and above the scent of crushed clover.

Suddenly, as if she had come to some decision in which he had had little part, she turned and put her arms about his neck. A long kiss trembled between them. The sound of the river seemed to rise up and set them adrift, as a strong tide lifts vessels and sweeps them out to sea.

17

It was not a long courtship. By the end of July both Douglas and Willie were married.

Willie took Alma to live in a little three-room house just off Main Street behind the harness shop. It was a bare, forbidding place and, under Alma's hands, it never achieved any further graciousness, but she kept it scrupulously clean, and got her meals on the table on time. It was late for a garden, but around the front door Willie set out a few tomato plants which flourished and bore fruit. Plants responded to Willie as animals and lonely people did.

Douglas and Mamie were married in the hotel at Wapago with only her mother and the proprietress of the hotel as witnesses. Douglas' heart misgave him at not having asked Angus and Abbie and Willie to be present; but now his main consideration in life was Mamie, and he had laid his plans carefully for her.

After the wedding they took the train to Manitou City. Her mother had managed a decent gray going-away dress for her and a little gray hat with artificial cherries and red ribbons on it. In a worn traveling satchel, which had belonged to her father, was the yellow dress, freshly done up, and some lace-trimmed nightgowns and underwear.

The next day in Manitou City they went out to the shops which seemed very wonderful to them after the limitations of Wapago and Opportunity. Laughing and leaning against each other or secretly touching hands beneath a counter, they looked at fashion plates and materials and consulted a dressmaker. In a week Mamie had a trousseau that would make Opportunity sit up and take notice. And it had been a wonderful week, eating in hotels, riding on trolley cars, going to see a stock company play *East Lynne*, lying in the park under the horse chestnut trees with newspapers under their new clothes and a bag of opera creams and caramels between them. There had been the fittings and tryings-on, with Mamie looking lovelier in each thing she tried; and there had been the nights in each other's arms, with the faint clatter of a distant trolley, and the street light making a high pattern of windy leaves upon the wall. There was no world but this, and they were the first man and woman to inhabit it.

Mrs. McAllister took Mamie and Douglas in when they returned to Opportunity. She was in a constant state of bereavement this year, for since Angus' marriage, she had lost a number of her young men in the same way, and most of the rest of them were courting. Mrs. McAllister sometimes wished that she could regulate her lads' love affairs as she regulated their food and drink and their religious habits. She thought that she could do better for them in most cases than they did for themselves. She had approved of Abigail for Angus, but she had had her heart set on Connie for Douglas and Mary Gallup for Willie, not to mention several other matches which, to the detriment of all involved, she felt, had not come off. Men were like cats, she thought, leaving good cream on the doorstep to prowl in the woods and bring home something wild.

She dismissed Alma with a shrug and a regretful shake of the head. Good, honest Willie with his heart of gold deserved better than that. But it was not so easy to make up her mind about Mamie. Mamie was undeniably beautiful and good-tempered and generous. What more could a man expect? And perhaps it was only a kind of jealousy because she was losing her favorite lad that made Mrs. McAllister distrust her.

Certainly the boardinghouse table was livelier for Mamie's presence at it. The boys took to shaving and changing their collars before they came down to dinner; and there was no reaching and bawling for dishes, as there sometimes was when they were alone. The conversation was much spritelier and there was more laughter. Each fellow brought out his best story and polished it off for Mamie, and if she didn't have a better one to cap it, she sparkled at him and he felt repaid.

Yet in spite of this increase in jollity there was less peace at the boardinghouse than there had been before. Mrs. McAllister

89

felt that a handsome young bride would be better off with a house of her own and some honest work to do than idle in a house full of impressionable young men.

But it took her some time to bring herself to say this to Douglas. It was early in September and she was still thinking how she might put the matter to Douglas, when he stopped one morning after breakfast to speak to her. Mamie often had her breakfast in bed and only appeared at lunchtime, and now Douglas and Mrs. McAllister were alone in the dining room.

"I just wished to tell you, Mrs. McAllister," Douglas said, "that we'll be leaving you in a few days now."

"So, Douglas?"

"Yes. The little house next to Angus' is for rent, and Mamie and I are going to housekeeping."

"Good!" she said heartily. "I think you'll both like that better, lad. What happened to the young couple from the East?"

"They couldn't stick it here, it seems. So 'twas our good luck. Abbie can help Mamie in so many ways."

"Yes, that's right. It's always hard for a bride getting started."

"You don't think it will be too hard on Mamie, do you, Mrs. McAllister?"

"No. She's a woman like the rest of us."

Douglas smiled. Mamie like Mrs. McAllister? But he loved Mrs. McAllister, too, only in a very different way. He wanted to tell her now how he meant Mamie's life to be better than most women's, gay and utterly carefree; but Mrs. McAllister went on speaking.

"You mustn't spoil her, Douglas. A woman's like a horse, you can ruin her by giving her too much rein."

"No danger of that," he laughed. "How often do ye recommend beating her?"

"Not more than twice a year," she said, smiling her dour Scotch smile. He caught her by the shoulders and kissed her lightly on both cheeks.

"You're a good lass," he said, "and as Scotch as a dish of porridge." They were both laughing as he went out, and Mrs. McAllister couldn't remember for the life of her what she had intended ordering for dinner.

18

Abbie did everything she could to be nice to Alma, and she fell in love with Mamie at first sight.

"She's so beautiful, Angus—so dashing! And she wears her lovely clothes so well. It's no wonder Doug fell in love with her. I'm glad you didn't see her before you saw me."

Angus smiled his quiet smile. He was not very clever at rising to bait, but sometimes his honesty turned the compliment just as neatly.

"She's an elegant lassie, but more Doug's style than mine. Seeing her first wouldn't have changed my life a jot, Abbie."

Perhaps this honest sentiment of Angus' was the final brick that cemented Abigail's firm and enduring friendship for Mamie. They took each other to heart almost from the moment they saw one another.

Abbie had almost as much fun helping to furnish the second pink cottage as Mamie and Douglas did. She was called in for advice on nearly every point, and she and Mamie took delight in making the dry-goods store clerks turn out their shelves for them when they were choosing drapery material; or in having every picture in the lumber room of the furniture store brought out for their inspection before they finally selected one. If the clerk was a man, Mamie enjoyed giving him a provocative glance and watching his ears turn red. She and Abbie would laugh all the way home at his confusion.

Sometimes Connie went with them and was gay, too, but more often she stayed at home. She had been begging her father all fall to let her take up nursing, but Dr. Hedrick would not hear of such a thing.

"A daughter of mine doing all the dirty things a nurse has to do? Well, I guess not! Lifting naked men around in bed and wiping up after them. Is that a lady's job? By God, no! I've got money enough to keep my daughters ladies, thank the Lord!"

But Connie seemed perversely determined upon some kind of career, and, since no other presented itself, she suddenly took up the violin. Beginners on the violin are notoriously incompatible with their families, and this was doubly so in Connie's case. The musical talent, which had fallen so lavishly to Abigail, had skipped poor Connie entirely. She might have taken up china painting or gilding rolling pins, but she had no talent there either and she wanted to distinguish herself at something.

Dr. Hedrick had a particularly nervous and easily offended ear. If Connie's incessant chatter annoyed him, her fumbling efforts to find the right note on the violin infuriated him.

"Abbie was a nice quiet girl," he said. "She used to do the right thing at the right time. But I can't read my newspaper in peace in the evening without some damned racket that Connie makes."

"Now, Doctor," Mrs. Hedrick said, "you have to be patient with her. No two people are alike in this world. You and Constance just set each other's teeth on edge. Remember she's your daughter."

"I never have a chance to forget it," the doctor said.

Connie learned to do her practicing while her father was away from home, and this usually kept her in on the afternoons when Abigail and Mamie went shopping.

"I wish Connie would get married," Abigail said to Angus. "Ned Taylor asked her last summer, and father was furious with her for turning him down; and Johnny Buxton would ask her, I'm sure, if she would only look at him."

Angus shook his head and said nothing. He was reading one of his books, and Abbie was not even sure that he had heard what she said. That was one annoying thing about Angus. If he had his nose in a book, you could talk and talk to him, and you never even knew whether he was listening to you or not. But this time he must have heard after all, for he closed the book, with his finger between the pages to keep the place, and said in his quiet voice: "I'm sorry Doctor won't let her take up nursing. Connie would make a good nurse."

"Oh, Angus! how can you? That's an awful business for a woman. Being a doctor, Papa should know better than anyone. Why, nobody goes into nursing who can do anything else."

"But that shouldn't be so," Angus said. "With so much pain in the world, a woman should be proud to help allay it. A woman like Florence Nightingale—."

"But, Angus, Connie's no Florence Nightingale."

"I think sometimes that Connie would do better if all of us expected more of her," Angus said. "She wants to feel important, and none of us has ever tried to help her in that way."

92

"I love her," Abbie said, "but she's such a chatterbox, and there's nothing she can really do. This violin now—she simply murders it. It's terrible to listen to her."

But Angus had opened the book again and was reading.

Abbie was fascinated by the amount of money Douglas was spending on the furnishings for the pink cottage. There had not been so many wedding presents to start with as Angus and Abbie had had, although, of course, wedding presents were sometimes more of a problem than a help, thought Abbie. But Douglas was determined that everything should be right. Abigail had a set of Haviland china with a design of poppies and wheat on it, and Douglas bought Mamie a similar set with a delicate design of lavender sweet peas. He had good taste, and he also had a Scotchman's instinct for getting the best value for his money, but without the traditional reluctance of the Scotchman to part with it.

"Just look what Douglas is spending, Angus!" said Abigail, "and I don't think he's making as much money as you are. Their carpets are ever so much nicer than ours and their furniture much prettier, and look at her clothes."

"He's taken all of his savings out of the bank, Abbie, and he's spending everything he makes. We're putting something by."

"I don't care. I like to enjoy life. When we are dead, what good will our savings do us?"

Angus took both of her hands. "We'll get there, Abbie," he said. He kissed her and coaxed her into a good humor again.

Douglas laid out his money on the new house with pride. He saw the pink cottage as a temporary dwelling on the way to something better, but, although it was not an end in itself, he wanted it to be as perfect as they knew how to make it. He remembered the little Caithness parlor that was used only for company and state occasions, and he was determined that his parlor should be enjoyed. He remembered the open hearth where his mother had stooped to cook the oatcakes, and he purchased a fine black range with shining nickel trim and a tank for heating water.

Water! It had been so scarce in Caithness that every drop had counted in the summertime. But here water ran in prodigal rivulets down the mountains; it pounded and churned in the big storage standpipe on one of the town hills; and Douglas made sure that it ran both hot and cold into the white enameled bathtub with the claw feet and into the hand basin beneath the plate-glass mirror. Free-flowing water on his skin was a luxury that never failed to elate him.

In Caithness they had not even had a proper outhouse, but only a corner of the stable partitioned off from the animals. Here the device that flushed away everything at the pull of a chain seemed to him symbolic of the new life he meant to live.

To Mamie the house was a wonder, too, and, while she was helping to bring it to completion, her interest and enthusiasm were engaged. She had come a long way from the untidy farm in Wapago, as Douglas had come a long way from the bleak croft in Caithness. Each had a material past which needed to be obliterated in a material way.

But at that point their experiences parted company. For, more and more as he grew older, Douglas thought back to the warm family unity of the McBains, and how they had worked together and appreciated each other and thought high thoughts, despite a lack of plumbing. In his plans for the future there were sons and daughters, well bathed and tastefully dressed and thoroughly educated. There would be no apprenticeships to gardeners and saddlemakers for *his* boys. They would be doctors or lawyers or statesmen, Douglas thought.

But Mamie had no happy family memories to project into her future. What she wanted was a good time with no strings tied to it. As yet she could not bear the thought of bringing children into the world. Douglas loved her and respected her wishes. To himself he thought tenderly that she would change as time went on. A time would come when they would live in a finer house and have children and be respected members of the best society. They had surely not come so far, so fast, for nothing.

19

One evening after an early supper Willie called his two hound dogs and went up to Dr. Hedrick's. The leaves were blowing in the wind, and he whistled to himself as he went along. He whistled as he worked in the shop and he whistled as he walked.

Had he not stretched his mouth so much with laughing and smiling, it might have had a perpetual pucker. Yet tonight the sound of his piping dissolved in the wind and seemed to lack its usual authoritative good cheer.

The two dogs trotted along behind him with their ears flopping and their tails wagging.

When he reached the doctor's house, Willie went around to the side door, where through the lighted window, he could see Connie helping the little Swedish girl to do up the dishes. He gave a bobolink whistle outside the window, and saw Connie's head jerk up and her face turn listening toward the darkening pane. He whistled again and she came out.

"Willie!" she cried. "Who dug you up?"

"I scratched my own way out, lass."

"How's Alma? We never seem to see her—nor you either, Willie. Why don't you bring her up to see us?" She reached her hands out to the dogs and they began to fawn upon her.

"Why, Alma's fine, but she's a real homebody. I canna get her across the doorsill. It's yourself must come down, Connie."

"Well, Papa will be delighted to see you, Willie. Come in now."

"No, listen, Connie, it's no the doctor I've come to see. It's you, Connie. I just thought—"

"Go on, Willie. It's something I can do for you, isn't it?"

"It is that," said Willie eagerly. His face looked troubled as well as eager, and he was having a hard time saying what he wished to say.

"I'll do anything I can," said Connie.

"Look! You've always liked my dogs, haven't you, Connie? You're the only one they'll go to as easy as they'll go to me."

"I know," said Connie. "Dogs always like me. I guess it's because I'm as brainless as they are."

"Never run yourself down, lass," Willie said. "You've a good heart, and that goes a long way in this world."

Connie was touched. Tears were never far from the surface with her, and a kind word from anyone was likely to spill them. But, if she talked fast enough, she could choke them down.

"Oh, dogs!" she said. "We had a dog named Mac once, black with curly hair. I don't know what kind he was, but Papa took time and taught him all kinds of tricks. Only then the crazy dog

95

would come into the parlor whenever we had company and sit up and beg and roll over and bark his head off for attention. Poor Papa couldn't get a word in for Mac's showing off. Papa gave him away, then, and I was the only one who cried for him."

"Connie," Willie said, "would your papa let you have a dog now—two dogs, say?"

"I don't know," said Connie. "Why?"

Willie hesitated. Then it came out with a rush. "I've got to give my dogs away, Connie. Alma's dead set against them. They frighten the poor lassie, and I've got to rid myself of them somehow. I thought if they could go to a friend—"

"Why, yes," said Connie. "Yes, I'll keep them for you, Willie. I'm sure that I can fix it up with Papa. And you can still come and get them when you want to hunt."

"You will?" cried Willie in happy relief. "You're a grand girl, Connie! You're sure the doctor won't mind?"

"That's all right. I'll keep them out of Papa's way. It's parlor competition that he doesn't like. Can they sleep in the wood-shed?"

"Sure. They've been on the cold ground since Alma and me were wed. But now the winter's comin' on, and my heart fails me to know they're cold at night. The woodshed will be a palace to them."

It never took much to make Willie happy, and now his spirits soared like birds in spring.

Willie and Connie took the two dogs to the woodshed where they found an old packing case, and Connie brought gunnysacks from the cellarway and made a bed. The dogs jumped in and out of it, wagging their tails, whining and turning around.

"That's it, lads," said Willie gaily. " 'Tis your new home, and ye've a kindhearted mistress to keep ye in good cheer."

"What the devil is going on here?" thundered Dr. Hedrick, standing large in the woodshed door, his black eyes blazing.

"Papa!" cried Connie, "you're not to say a word now, do you hear?" She could be brave when someone else's interests were at stake. "Willie is giving us his dogs, and they're wonderful hunters. When you want to go shooting you'll find how useful they can be. They'll never come into the parlor, I'll see to that."

"I'll pay for their food, Doctor," put in Willie.

"No such thing, Willie," said Doctor. "I'm not so poor I can't support a couple of good hunters. But why are you getting rid of them?"

"Weel, Doctor," Willie said, "the truth is my wife doesna like dogs."

"So who's the master in your house, eh, Willie?" thundered the doctor.

"Och!" said Willie, laughing good-naturedly, "there's no one master, I hope. The thing is to get along as fair and sweet as possible."

"Connie!" ordered Dr. Hedrick, "go get the dogs something to eat. They won't know they belong here till they've taken food. Aren't there some supper scraps?"

"Yes, Papa!" cried Connie, hurrying away.

"Now, Willie," Dr. Hedrick said, "we'll be good to your dogs. But, a word to the wise now: Don't let your wife run over you. Keep women in boots and bonnets, man, but never let them get the upper hand."

"Why, sir," said Willie, "no one's got the upper hand. I like to please my lass, that's all."

Connie came, bringing a plate of scraps. In the night she woke and thought probably the scraps had not been enough for them, so she got out of bed and warmed some milk over a chafing dish and took it out to them. She had something to "do for" now.

Willie did not whistle as he walked home. Perhaps it was the windy night with its feeling of autumn sadness that kept his lips from their familiar pucker. But he missed the dogs, too. It troubled him more than he cared to admit to have to give them up. On a night like this, when they walked together, he had only to put down a hand to feel the friendly thrust of a cold nose or a warm tongue on his palm. Their galloping and wagging somehow expressed the galloping and wagging feelings which he had always enjoyed in himself.

He would have liked to stay longer at the doctor's and chat away the evening with Mrs. Hedrick and Connie and the doctor as he had often used to do. But a married man didn't leave his wife sitting alone at home, and Alma would rarely come with him, no matter how much he begged.

"Your folks are all so stuck up," Alma said. "They think they're better than I am."

"That's not so, Sweetheart. They're tryin' to be nice to you."

"Well—trying!" said Alma. "I don't like people to have to *try* so hard."

The wind whipped his trousers about his legs and lifted his coat tails. A shower of leaves flew by him, hurrying as if upon important business.

Head down, he nearly collided with another person going in the opposite direction. It was the Catholic priest.

"Oh! McBain! When are you going to come around again for a little chess with me?"

"Och!" said Willie, laughing. "I'm a married mon now. That's like to make me a stranger amongst my old friends, I fear."

"Women! Women!" said the priest in mock despair. "More's the pity! Well, I haven't congratulated you. I hope you'll be happy, my son."

"Oh, I am," said Willie. "You must come and see us, Father." But he said it casually and did not press the invitation. Just in time he remembered that Alma disliked Catholics as well as dogs. "Toe-kissers," she called them. She called the Presbyterians "Blue-noses," but for Willie's sake she sometimes went to church and sat in a back pew with her own nose in the air. She wasn't going to give any of his pious friends the opportunity to snub her. She always had a better feeling if she could do the snubbing herself, before other people got around to it.

As he came near his own house the rain began to fall. Willie lifted his face to it with pleasure. It smelled of wet leaves and dust, but it felt soft and cool like the rain he had known in Caithness. He puckered his lips and began to whistle again:

> "Oh, ye'll tak' the high road,
> An' I'll tak' the low road,
> An' I'll be in Scotland afore ye.
> But me an' my true love—"

He took off his hat and let the rain and wind play with his hair.

Alma's a good lassie, he thought, and I love her more than ever I'd a-suspected I was goin' to. He looked in the window and gave a bobolink whistle to see her head jerk up and her eyes come around to the dark panes. She looked almost frightened, a poor starved girl who trusted no one.

98

"Alma, honey, I hope ye werena lonely. Willie's here now," he said, his arms around her.

20

"Whatever do you do here, Abbie, to keep from drying up and blowing away?" asked Mamie. She was lying on her back on the bearskin rug by the stove in the new parlor, one knee crossed over the other and her shapely legs rather prominently displayed amidst a fluff of petticoats. Abbie was running up curtains on the sewing machine.

"Just what you see," said Abbie. "We go to church and we go to the Ladies' Aid, and sometimes somebody gives a party, and then we go to church again."

"Oh, Lord! does that go on forever?"

"Practically."

They looked at each other with commiserating eyes and burst out laughing. Mamie sat up and began to arrange her hair.

"That social the other night—of all the dreary affairs! I never thought for a moment they wouldn't dance. Doug never told me. After we'd been sitting on those hard pews for hours, listening to old such-and-such and you-know-who make speeches, I said to Doug, 'Listen, dear, when does the dancing start?' 'Dancing?' he said, 'What made you think they'd dance? They don't.' Well, you could have laid me under the violets!"

"I know," said Abbie, "there's no proper society here. It's scandalous!"

"You mean it's sanctimonious! Something scandalous would be quite a treat." They laughed over this for several moments. They were very easily amused.

"Oh, you were funny in prayer meeting the other night!" said Abbie.

"Well, I was bored to tears. I'd have been asleep in another minute if I hadn't done something."

"But what a thing to do. You crazy!"

"It wasn't anything. There was Doug sitting at the other end of the pew looking as solemn as the preacher, and I wanted to put my head on his shoulder. I stood it as long as I could, and then I just gave myself a long slide down the pew and landed in his lap. I didn't think anyone would notice."

"The old ladies are still talking."

"Cluck—cluck—cluck!"

"That's what I say, but, honestly, it doesn't pay to get them down on you in this town."

"I suppose not—nor in any town. I know that pretty well! They've yapped at my heels all my life. But I don't care, really."

"Smoke follows the pretty girl," said Abbie.

"Was Angus shocked, too?"

"Not exactly. I'm always thinking that Angus is going to be shocked at things, and then he isn't. He's a sort of saint himself, but he seems to understand if other people aren't—only he's awfully strong on being reverent in church."

"I know," said Mamie. "He takes God seriously, doesn't he?"

"You know," said Abbie, with a sudden rush of confidence, "the only person I'm ever jealous of is God." A sweep of color went across her cheek, and suddenly she wished she hadn't said that, but the truth would out.

"That's funny, isn't it?" said Mamie. She got up and shook out her skirts. "Don't sew on that any more. You've been a peach. I can finish them after supper. What are you having for supper?"

"Beef stew and vegetables. It's on the back of the stove at home now. If it hasn't burned on the bottom, it'll be all ready to serve up when Angus comes in, and I've got tapioca custard cooling on the back porch."

"Abbie, you're smart! I haven't done a thing, but Doug will bring home some steak. I guess I'll fry some potatoes and open a can of corn."

"I've got enough pudding for you and Doug, too."

"Oh, have you? You're a darling. I'll make gingerbread to-morrow and bring you over some. Connie gave me your mother's receipt. I'm bursting my seams to be domestic these days. Listen, Abbie, if you've got supper all ready, you don't have to go yet. Play something on the piano while I peel potatoes."

Abbie opened the piano and twirled the stool.

"What do you want?"

"Something lively."

"Looks like this piano hasn't been opened since the last time I played it."

"That's right. I'm a ninny on the piano. I didn't need one at all, but I think Doug wants me to have everything you've got." She thought: And a little bit more, but she didn't say that.

"Silly boy," said Abbie. But she was no longer thinking of Douglas or Mamie—only the piano and the feel of the keys under her fingers as she ran her hands experimentally up and down in a series of chords. She began to play "The Kiss Waltz," and, floating on the waltz rhythm, she drifted into "Loin du Bal" and from there to "The Beautiful Blue Danube." There was something about the gay, recurring beat of waltz time that always made her want to weep. It was full of sadness, just beyond the gaiety, something ironic and inescapable. Twilight fell on the parlor, on the sewing machine and the unfinished curtains, on the patent rocker, the bearskin rug, and the ugly stove. The stained glass in the round window lost its color, and the big square pane in the center was filled with the mysterious blue of early darkness. Now Abbie was playing the "Valse Triste," and there were pain and sorrow in it, and the crying of souls lost in uncertainty.

"Goodness!" said Mamie, coming to the door with a potato in her hand, "I thought you were going to play something lively. Here, I'll light the lamp for you, and then do the 'Blue Danube' over again."

Presently there was a noise of feet and voices at the front door.

"I can always locate my wife by the music," said Angus, coming to spread his hands to the fire. He felt the chill of winter before anyone else did.

"Say, Abbie, don't stop! Let's have that again," cried Douglas. "Mamie and I haven't danced in a coon's age!" She went on playing, gaily now, while Douglas swung Mamie into action. Angus laughed and pulled a few chairs out of their way, then stood with his hands behind him and his back to the fire, dividing his attention between their flying feet and Abigail's flying hands.

At last Abbie brought the dance to an end with a resounding chord. There was a smell of burning potatoes from the kitchen, and Mamie flew to the rescue.

"You children are demoralizing me!" said Abbie, shaking her

101

finger at Doug. "I haven't even set the table. Come over and I'll give you your dessert while Mamie puts your steak on to fry."

21

That autumn Douglas had Mamie's picture taken to send to the folks in Scotland. She wore her best dress and took some trouble with her hair, and even the ineptness of a small-town western photographer of the 1890's could not entirely obliterate her sparkle. It shone out bravely from the small oval on the thick white card. There was the well-shaped mouth just beginning to smile, and the brilliant eyes just beginning to crinkle into mischief. One did not stop to analyze the nose, the forehead, the throat, the hair; one saw only that she was lovely and that even in a mediocre photograph she exerted a spell.

The old folks in Scotland were pleased. The mother did not often write letters, but she wrote one now in the clear, cramped handwriting which seemed so foreign to America. Angus and Douglas had both been taught a similarly small, neat hand, but it had already begun to flow more freely with the haste of American expediency:

> "My dear daughter, I hope that this finds you in good health as it leaves us. God has been kind to my three sons to give them good wives in the new country. You are very bonnie. I pray that your heart may be as bonnie as your face—"

Mamie wept a little over the letter, and showed it to Abigail.

"She wrote me something like that, too," said Abbie. "I think she must be kindhearted."

"It's hard for me to imagine Doug's folks," said Mamie. "He's told me about the little stone house with the thatched roof and the midnight sun, but that's like you read about in books. It doesn't seem real—and Lord! what I've had has been real all right."

"They're simple folks, but I think they must be good. Angus and I are going back to visit them someday."

102

"'I pray that your heart may be as bonnie as your face.' It makes me want to cry, Abbie. I don't think my heart is very bonnie, really. But I do want it to be. I'm trying hard."

"Of course you are," said Abbie. "Aren't we all?"

In spite of Mamie's gloomy feelings about Opportunity society and a general lack of dancing, it was a gay winter. There were oyster suppers and sleighing parties and evenings of music and charades. Mamie developed a talent for amateur theatricals; and from playing the lead in a charade on *She Stoops to Conquer* she progressed to playing Portia in the casket scene from *The Merchant of Venice* at an Evening with Shakespeare.

"Heavens!" cried Mamie, sparkling with laughter, "why couldn't Shakespeare say it in plain English instead of going to all this trouble to make things hard to understand?" Still, she learned the lines with patience, and when she didn't understand them she ran across the yard to get Angus to explain them to her. The committee had asked Douglas to play Bassanio, thinking no doubt that even such a restrained love scene as this one was more prudently played by husband and wife. At the same time Mamie and Douglas made such a handsome couple that prudence could also be charming. But Douglas was more intent upon building his business and paying his mounting debts than on playing the lover in doublet and purple tights. His head was full of interest rates and percentages and how he could acquire more good farmland at the least expense and sell it again at a top figure. His days were full, and sometimes he took his problems to bed with him. It worried him a little that he had not yet begun to put anything by for that glowing future. Old A was tucking away a good deal. But Douglas wanted to spend as well as save.

It took time and thought. Play-acting was a folly that he need not indulge in, he decided, for what was to be gained by learning a lot of complicated speeches and making a public spectacle of himself, when he had already opened the leaden casket and won the beautiful woman?

Mamie pouted over his decision, but she was not annoyed for long. They easily persuaded Harry Shepherd, the druggist, to take the part. He was not as good-looking as Doug and he was a deacon of the church, both of which facts seemed to make the affair respectable. Mamie accepted him goodnaturedly and was delighted to find that she could make him miss a cue by giving

103

him a languishing look. It gave her a mischievous pleasure to exercise her natural talents, and the consequences of her brief flirtations were not important to her. The general admiration was what mattered to her, and she was getting more and more of it as time went on. Her Portia charmed almost everyone. It is true that there were differing opinions, and some of the more unpleasant gossips of town claimed that Mr. Shepherd's prescriptions were not to be relied upon during the weeks just before and after the performance. They went so far as to say that his wife was thinking of going home to her mother if he didn't stop saying "Mamie" in his sleep. But, of course, this was a gross exaggeration, and Mamie's friends denied it hotly. Mamie only laughed. She found any kind of spotlight entertaining.

Douglas watched her in the crimson velvet robes, which Abbie had helped her make out of some old portieres, and his heart swelled. The beauty, the sparkle were always there; but to these she had added unexpected dignity and a firm warm rendering of fine sonorous lines.

Douglas watched her walking so graciously across the improvised stage and he was filled with pride and happiness. He had just finished up a particularly good business deal that day, and the satisfaction of that was still warm at the back of his mind as he gave himself over to the delight of watching Mamie. Mamie had not had time to make bread yesterday and had forgotten to tell him to get meat, so they had dined very meagerly before the play. But he no longer felt hungry, only proud, and full of an almost overpowering love.

After the performance Mrs. Hedrick had asked the three McBain boys and their wives and Johnny Buxton in to supper. The Sunday-school room where the entertainment had been given was near the Hedricks', and Douglas had only time to squeeze Mamie's arm and say "Beautiful! Beautiful!"

"That fool Shepherd really kissed me," whispered Mamie, stifling a giggle.

"Did you like it?"

"No. He doesn't know how."

"Do I?"

"You're fishing."

"Well, reward me."

"On the way home. Be good now."

104

Mamie still wore her cap of imitation pearls and her flowing robes of crimson velvet, and she had rouged her cheeks, to the horror of the minister's wife who had been in charge of scenery and costumes.

"I love rouge," said Mamie to Abbie as they took off their wraps.

"You don't need it," said Abbie. "I'm the one who does, with my pale cheeks and black eyes, but Angus would have a fit if he ever saw me putting any on."

"Do you always think about Angus before you do anything?" laughed Mamie.

"I s'pose I do. Tiresome, isn't it?" They were still laughing when they went into the dining room.

Dr. Hedrick insisted upon having Mamie on his right hand and Abbie on his left. Somehow Douglas found himself between Alma and Connie at the other end of the table. Connie was busy telling Angus about her violin lessons.

"I'll never be very good at it, but I want to learn enough so I can teach. I think a girl ought to be able to do something for herself, don't you? Do you think it's unladylike to do something besides housekeeping?"

"No, I do not," said Angus. "If her soul's right, I think a lassie should do whatever she wishes with her hands."

"I wanted to nurse—" said Connie wistfully.

Douglas applied himself to the oyster stew. He was hungry after all, almost ravenous. On the other side of Alma, Johnny Buxton and Mrs. Hedrick were discussing the best way of encouraging her hens to lay more eggs. He felt Alma's narrow eyes upon him.

"That tastes mighty good to you, don't it? I expect Mamie's been too busy to do much cooking this week."

He put his spoon in his dish and reduced his tempo.

"Well, how's my little sister?" he enquired jovially. "Still looking on the dark side?"

"Your wife's quite an actress. She done the family mighty proud tonight, it looks like."

"That's what I thought."

"Actresses are mighty cute, but I thank the Lord He didn't make me one."

"I see you're a pious girl," said Douglas, allowing himself

105

another oyster. "It's better to be thankful for what He didn't give you than wishful for something He might be reluctant to bestow."

"I don't know how you mean that," said Alma suspiciously. "If you mean to hand me an insult—"

"I'm handing you a bouquet, Sister," said Douglas. "Is there any reason why you do not think you should be called a pious girl?"

"Of course not!"

"Then accept the compliment with my best wishes. It's yours for nothing."

"You're a rare one," said Alma. "I'm glad they didn't all grow up like *you* in the McBain family."

"Three handsome boys," said Douglas, "but one was rotten at the core. Yes, I will, Mrs. Hedrick. That's the best oyster stew I ever ate."

"It makes him hungry to see me act," said Mamie. They looked at each other across the table. Her eyes were sparkling with something especial for him, something deeper and sweeter than her laughter. Oh, Mamie! lovely! lovely! None of the irritations and disappointments of the world can matter, while there is a Mamie in it to send a secret message with her eyes!

When they were ready to go home Willie and Connie were suddenly discovered to be missing. They had gone to the wood-shed to look at the dogs. Alma stood in the center of the parlor with her wraps on and a look of resignation on her face.

"It *would* be me who has to wait," she said.

"Never mind, Alma," laughed Abigail. "Angus was late for his wedding, and if he's reading a book, dinner can get cold before he'll stir out of his chair."

But Alma did not laugh.

"I'll see he don't do this again," she said.

When they went out of doors snow had begun to fall. It had blotted out the ugly tin and shingle roofs, covering them with white beauty. The boards of the sidewalks were puffed with it and the cracks were black lines between. Stars of it caught in Mamie's dark hair and clung like real jewels among the artificial pearls.

Douglas put his arm about her and they walked close together, not hurrying because of the snow.

"Do you love me, Mamie?"

106

"What do you think, my silly darling boy?"

It must have occurred to Connie sometimes that, in spite of her hopes, all she had gotten out of the McBain boys was a pair of hound dogs that another woman would not tolerate. But, if it did, she never gave any sign of it. She called regularly on the two wives and helped them to do up dishes after family suppers and took suggestions from them about clothes and showed them how to make cakes.

The doctor liked dogs if they were not underfoot, and Connie devised means of keeping them out of his way and yet giving them the best of everything. Animals always loved and trusted Connie, and after a month or so Willie's dogs no longer yearned for masculine society nor lifted an ear at the sound of a gun.

But Connie liked to have Willie come and look at them.

"They're getting fat, aren't they?"

"Ye're spoilin' them. They're as soft as rotten herring."

"I'll have to take them walking more."

"Maybe I can get off some Saturday to give them a hunt."

"They'd like that, but I'm not sure that I would. They're just beginning to feel at home here. If you take them hunting, they'll be yours again."

But Willie rarely took them hunting, and he came to see them less and less often. Willie was just as jolly as he had ever been, but he did not get around among his friends as often as he had done earlier.

The loafers still hung around his harness shop to bask in his geniality, usually clearing out, however, when they saw Alma coming. She did not like Willie to be too friendly with other people. Whatever Alma did not understand or share became an object of suspicion and exasperation to her. She had no human ties outside of Willie, and she resented his having any.

Winter slipped into spring. Again the streams rushed and sang, and the fields were yellow with buttercups and then with dandelions. Douglas began taking Mamie with him on his drives through the country. Things were booming now and land was moving rapidly. The Territory was on the verge of becoming a state, and people were talking of incorporating Opportunity into a town. It had got along thus far with a marshal to preserve order, backed by a group of citizens who settled things among themselves as best they could. Now they were beginning to want

107

a mayor and council and everything regular. New people were flowing in, and every day saw changes and improvements.

Doc Hedrick was beginning to suggest Angus for the first mayor. "He's young, he's smart, and the Lord knows, he's honest. The devil himself would trust him with the keys to hell."

Angus was not fully aware of this intention of the doctor's, but other matters made him busier than he had ever been and he was glad to turn over all the outside business to Douglas. Douglas enjoyed it and was doing unusually well. Besides the business of the firm, he had his own numerous private enterprises, and sometimes he took a flyer with Johnny Buxton on something a little out of Angus' line.

Mamie loved to be going somewhere. She would fling her clothes into a bag on a moment's notice and begin to sparkle with delight.

"Abbie," she would call across the back yard, "there's a pitcher of cream in the cool box and a half a dozen eggs. Use them up before they spoil. Doug and I are off to Pine Ridge, and then we'll go on to Carfax and spend the night in the hotel."

Then Douglas would be at the door with a livery rig and a couple of horses prancing to be off. She did not mind the heat and the dust and the long rows of rail fences. It was enough to be moving, to be going somewhere, to spend a night in a hotel. What if the pork was underdone and the coffee terrible? She had not had to cook it herself, and praise the Lord for that! They laughed and joked as they rode along, or, if she was sleepy she put her head on Doug's shoulder and slept while he drove. Sometimes they took their lunch with them and lay under the trees in some woodsy place when they had eaten it, looking at the sky and holding hands like the Babes in the Woods. Sometimes, when there was a full moon, they drove by night, stopping occasionally to let the horses crop grass by the roadside while they made love.

Douglas felt more alive then he had ever felt before, and yet he was so deeply preoccupied with Mamie and the sharp joy of making money that the rest of the world went by almost unheeded. It was not often that he remembered Willie and his problems. However, although he was not very knowing in such matters, it did occur to him that Willie had been married now for more than nine months with no increase in his family.

108

"What happened to your bairn, Willie?" he asked one day when they were alone.

"Och!" said Willie, blushing a little bit, "the poor lass hadna even lost her maidenhead. If there's any bairn, 'twill be my own, thank God."

Douglas went away with mixed feelings. There was something comic about it, and yet he was sorry for Willie, too. He would have wrung a girl's neck if she had tricked him into marriage with such a lie.

Something else which had stirred vaguely in his consciousness came momentarily to the surface with Willie's confession. He had had Mamie more easily and happily than a man should expect to have a young girl with no previous experience. A sudden fleeting picture crossed his mind. He saw again Buck Clayborne's possessive hand on Mamie's wrist, and the look of humility upon that face which so often sparkled and was proud. But resolutely he closed his mind against these things.

Mamie loved him and she was all that he desired in the world. He could not imperil the tremendous beauty of their being together by any thoughts like these.

22

Angus had been working all that winter and spring for a new church building. The old one was completely outgrown, and it only wanted someone with resolution to put a shoulder to the wheel and insist upon a new one. The Reverend Mr. Horner did a great deal of talking and fluttering about; but it was Angus who had tramped through the snow and persuaded people to sign their names to papers promising gifts of money. Now that the hot weather had come, he continued to see people and to ask for gifts. The thing must be done right or not at all. He hated to ask people for money, but when it was a question of advancing the kingdom of God, he saw no choice. When he came home at night he often looked worn and tired.

He started making church calendars during that period, also. At first they were only small sheets, written in his delicate, clear handwriting and hectographed, giving the church events of the week and the order of service or the text. But as the idea of the new church grew in him he began to want other people to see it as he saw it. One Sunday the calendar became a folder and on the front was a very creditable sketch of the old church. The following Sunday there was a sketch of the church as the architect would have it look when it was enlarged and remodeled. From that time onward the calendar was usually embellished with some sort of freehand sketch, a bough of apple blossoms, an old man and a little child walking together, a dove of peace, an open Bible with a candle beside it.

Angus had an entirely untutored facility in drawing. The work was often crude and mistaken and then again it was beautiful and suggestive. It gave him a pleasure, which he himself scarcely understood, to design the church calendars; and the congregation was not without appreciation. Many years later attics and old trunks of keepsakes yielded complete files of Angus' homemade church calendars.

Abbie helped him with the hectographing, but she refused to solicit contributions for the new church.

"It's bad enough to have to go to church at all," she said, "with all the old women looking at me and saying: 'Well, she's certainly beginning to show her condition. I wonder how far along she is?' "

"Abbie," he said gravely, taking her hand, "we don't go to church for the old women. We go to worship God. He should be nearer to us now than He has ever been before."

"I know, Angus. But I do wish I didn't look so bad. I guess it's because I'm so thin that it shows up. Wouldn't God understand if I stayed at home?"

"You've never looked more beautiful to me, Abbie," he said, "and I think that you look beautiful to God, too. Forget the old women."

Abbie sighed. She did hate going around and being stared at, but she was happy, too. What fun to make the long, tucked dresses and the pinked flannel bands, to lay the little shirts and petticoats between sheets of tissue paper in the lowest bureau drawer—the baby's drawer! There had been only two of them for so long—and now there would be three. It did seem odd, and very sweet and exciting, too.

110

She took Mamie into her confidence, but Mamie was not excited.

"Any fool can make a baby," Mamie said, "and I do think Angus is mean to make you go to church."

23

Douglas and Mamie had been married about a year when he found the letter from her mother. She was over at Abbie's helping quilt a little comforter when he came home from the office, looking for some clean collars and handkerchiefs. He was going for an overnight trip by himself this time, and he thought he would not bother Mamie to pack for him. But, as sometimes happened, there were no clean handkerchiefs in his drawer. He was a little annoyed and began pulling out drawers and rummaging through them. He opened Mamie's drawer and turned the scented, lacy contents over with a rude hand. It was not orderly anyway and he thought that she might have mixed his handkerchiefs in with her own.

Under everything he saw a letter from her mother. It had no envelope and he wondered why she had saved it. Mamie rarely saved anything except scraps of lace and ribbons and bits of feathers or artificial flowers which might be useful in retrimming a hat. He took the piece of paper up curiously, not meaning to read it, and he saw that it was dated the sixth of last October. A name halfway down the page arrested his attention:

> "Yes, Buck Clayborne came all right, and of course he hotfooted it right out here. I was mighty glad to tell him you were married. He stood and looked at me as if he thought sure I was lying to him, and he looked as sick as a poisoned pup. Well, he had it coming to him, and now you've got you a good man, I hope you put Buck Clayborne out of your mind."

Douglas stood quietly for a moment with the letter in his hand, trying to understand the full importance of it. Then he put it back where he had found it and folded Mamie's ruffles tidily over it.

"Damn Buck Clayborne!" he said between his teeth. "Damn Buck Clayborne!" He did not care now whether he had clean handkerchiefs or not. He could buy something in the next town rather than go dirty. He flung a nightshirt and some toilet articles into a bag and went for his train without kissing Mamie goodbye.

As he rode along his mind grew calmer. There was nothing significant in the letter. A jilted suitor had come back to see his girl and found her married to a luckier man. The only significant thing, perhaps, was that Mamie had kept the letter. Why had she done that? Was it only the vanity that burned so hotly in her, or was it some sentimental impulse to cling to the old love? And she must have asked about Buck first. *Yes,* her mother had said, in evident answer to a question. *He had it coming to him. I hope you put Buck Clayborne out of your mind.* The words repeated themselves with the rhythm of the train wheels, and Douglas thought, "Did Mamie ever really love me?"

He drove a hard bargain in Mountain Center the next day.

"That McBain is as sharp as an old hand at this land game," said the Mountain Center dealer to his partner. "It don't pay to think you can slip anything over on him because he's young."

"Them Scotchmen are all alike. Hard as nails, but they're honest. You've got to say that for them."

"Oh—honest. But they'll take the skin off the pennies for you."

It was a miserable trip. Over and over Douglas went through imaginary conversations with Mamie.

"Just what does Buck Clayborne mean to you? How much do you still care for him? I found a letter—why did you save it?"

But he had rational moments, too. He suspected that to possess Mamie was nine points of the law in more ways than one. Mamie lived in the present. She was neither introspective nor imaginative. The man who held her in his arms was the man to whom she would give her heart, provided he did not force her to be dull. Douglas faced this honestly, for he loved her enough to see her as she was and still want her unchanged.

He was still undecided whether to question Mamie or not, when the train came into Opportunity. He felt tired and disillusioned and he was looking around for the hack when Mamie flung herself into his arms. He couldn't have imagined that she would meet the train.

"Honey! You went away without kissing me! You didn't even say goodbye. Was that nice? I hardly even slept a wink! And you didn't find the clean clothes I left on the ironing board in the kitchen. Oh, I've been desolate!"

"Mamie! Mamie!" He held her hungrily in his arms, closer, closer. There was nothing in heaven or earth but this—to kiss her hair, her eyes, her lips, to feel that she was his again with nothing shadowy and cold to come between!

"Mamie, *darling!*"

The station agent winked at the brakeman, and the brakeman winked back at the station agent.

"Love's young dream," said one of the loafers, and spat a long stream of tobacco juice at the railroad track.

24

It was late December, and a blizzard was blowing around the two pink cottages, when Angus came pounding on Douglas' door in the middle of the night.

"Abbie's taken sick, Douglas. Can you go for her father? I don't like to leave her alone."

"Right away!" said Douglas. "As soon as I can get into my clothes." He went back into the bedroom and woke Mamie.

"Abbie's sick. I guess it'll be the babe."

"It's about time," said Mamie. "It was due before Christmas." She slipped out of bed and began to dress. When they were ready, he carried her across the yard, for the snow had already drifted deep, and set her down on Angus' porch.

Angus opened the door. His voice was as calm and quiet as usual but he was ghastly pale, and his hand shook on the lamp he held. They could hear Abigail crying and moaning in an inner room.

"I'm glad you came, Mamie," said Angus. "Maybe you'll know what to do for her."

"Yes, I know," said Mamie grimly. "I saw my mother through it five times. I know everything there is to know about it."

113

Douglas turned and headed into the storm. He took long, swinging strides, the lantern he had brought from the kitchen bobbing beside him, his head held low against the stinging snow. He felt excited and glad to be doing something to help a new life into the world. In Caithness a man's success in life was measured in sons. Money and land were hard come by and ephemeral; but stalwart and honest sons were a man's assurance of success, of continuity, and of immortality. Douglas laughed aloud. Think of old Angus beating him to it with a son! "Well," he said to himself aloud in the storm, "if it's a lassie, there'll still be a chance for Mamie and me!" He thought of Mamie with tenderness, and he saw for the first time clearly the kind of son they might have—dashing, handsome, with all of Mamie's beauty and sparkle, and stalwart and strong as himself with healthy red blood running hotly in his veins. He laughed again happily, and he was warm in the bitter winter night.

At Hedricks' he banged a tattoo on the door with his snow-caked mittens. Then he remembered that Connie was sick, and was sorry that he had been so boisterous. He was always remembering too late about Connie. She had had pneumonia and was only just pulling through.

Doc Hedrick came to the door in his nightshirt, grotesque in the lantern light with his hairy legs and bristling mutton chops. He was scowling and his eyes were as fierce as a Turk's.

"Abigail?" he said.

"Yes, the baby's on the way. Angus wants you as quick as you can come."

"Here," said Doc, "you hitch the bay to the cutter. Susan and I will be ready as soon as you are."

Douglas plowed through the snow to the barn. There was a warm smell of hay and horses and the soft sound of large animals breathing. The horses snorted and blew at the draft of cold air and the sudden lantern light. He led the bay mare out of her box stall, took off her blanket and backed her between the cutter shafts. She seemed to sense Douglas' excitement and danced and tossed her head, her breath coming out in a thin blue cloud. When she had the harness on her back, she stamped and shook the bells so that they gave off peal after peal of wintry chimes. Douglas folded her blanket under the seat of the cutter, for he suspected that she might have a long stand in the

114

cold at Angus' house. The doctor and his wife were ready when Douglas reached the house. Mrs. Hedrick, wrapped in furs with the doctor's bag and a bundle of her own in her arms, seemed entirely calm, but Doc was as nervous as a cat. He fumbled the reins and dropped the whip in the snow.

"By Godfrey! By Godfrey!" he muttered.

"A body would think it was your first delivery," said Mrs. Hedrick.

"It's the first time I ever delivered my own daughter," said the doctor, slapping the reins across the mare's back. "It'll be my grandchild." There was only room for two in the cutter, but Doug stood on a runner and clung to the side next to Mrs. Hedrick. He could see her breast rising and falling under the furs, but she maintained her air of calm detachment.

"My land, Doctor," she said, "it was you who brought *her* into the world."

"Maybe," said Doc, "but this is altogether different. Altogether different, by Gad!"

When they reached the little house the doctor and his wife took charge, but Mamie had already set things in order. She had fires in all the stoves and a couple of kettles boiling. She had a basin and soap and towels for Doctor's hands and she had clean torn sheets and old cloths.

Douglas felt pleased with Mamie when she made herself useful in the family. He loved her because she was gay and beautiful, and he didn't care too much that his socks were undarned and his meals unpredictable. But, at the same time, he knew that the women of the family and the town thought her a poor house-keeper. All of the women whom he had known in childhood had been useful women, and, while he did not desire that sort of wife for himself, still he was proud of Mamie when she added usefulness to beauty.

"Sweetheart, you're a brave lassie," he said softly, slipping his arm around her. She did not shake him off as she sometimes did when she was preoccupied; but there was a little hard, firm line about her mouth, and her eyes did not sparkle.

"I'm tired," she said.

"Go home now and get your rest, Mamie," said Mrs. Hedrick. "You've done everything you could, dear, and it may be a long time yet. The first one's always the hardest."

115

Mamie got her shawl and pulled on her overshoes.

"All right," she said.

"See that she gets in safely, Doug," said Mrs. Hedrick. Douglas picked her up and carried her across the drifts to the next house. He set her down gently and unlocked the door for her, but deep inside he felt a stab of disappointment. He had not thought that she would go so easily. When he had seen her safe indoors, he went back to sit with Angus.

It seemed a long night with the crying wind outside, and inside Abigail wailing and sobbing like a wounded animal. The doctor and his wife moved to and fro in the bedroom, their faces drawn and watchful, and Angus paced the little dining room from which the bedroom opened. Douglas had never seen Angus so shaken. He put his hand on Angus' arm. " 'Twill be all right, A," he said. "I'm sure of it." He was not sure at all, but he felt that A must have comfort.

"If I could help her!" Angus said in a low voice, full of anguish. "I canna even pray, Doug. I canna even pray."

"Never mind that, A," Douglas said. "She's doing her best." He felt his own nerves shaken by the ordeal Abigail was undergoing. They kept up the fires, and the clock ticked, and every hour the giddy little cuckoo popped open his doors and uttered his shrill report.

Soon after two, Doctor Hedrick stuck his head out of the bedroom door and bellowed: "Bring in another lamp!" The perspiration was running down his face and his great dark eyes were blazing. Angus tried to take the lamp but his hand shook, and it was Doug who took it and held it for the doctor, while Angus sank down on a chair by the head of the bed, gazing at Abigail's ravaged face. She was much quieter now, like something exhausted by a long race. Her moans were gentle, and her head turned hopelessly from side to side upon the pillow.

"Oh, God, dear God," said Angus softly, the tears running down his cheeks.

And then at last the baby was there, a little silent thing that did not cry.

"Stillborn!" said Mrs. Hedrick in a shocked whisper.

"Not yet, by Godfrey!" cried the doctor. He put his rough bearded mouth to the infant's lips and filled its lungs with his

116

breath, working the tiny arms upward and back as he did so. For a few seconds there was only the sound of the doctor's breathing in the room, and then a thin wail rose uncertainly on the air, and a new life was begun. Doc cut and tied the cord and his deep voice boomed in the silence.

"Saved her!" he said. "Yes, sir, my first grandchild. Well, here she is, Grandma. I turn her over to you."

Mrs. Hedrick took the baby in a blanket and carried her into the living room. Douglas followed, helping with the water and the towels. Angus was still kneeling by Abigail's bed, holding her hand, and too thankful that she would live to think about the baby. But the baby was an all-absorbing curiosity to Douglas, and he could not think of going home until he had seen the doctor's wife wash and dress her.

"Och! the mother in Scotland would be proud if she knew," he said. "It's the first grandchild there, too. Angus got ahead of us all, the sly fellow."

"You feel as if it were your own, don't you now?" asked Mrs. Hedrick, smiling. They were both flooded with relief, now that Abigail's ordeal was over.

"I do indeed!" cried Douglas, laughing out with pure pleasure. Shyly he touched the tiny crumpled hand, so perfect in every way, with minute nails and individual whorls on the fingertips. Then his face clouded. "Do they always have such a hard time as that?" he asked.

"No, don't you think it," said Mrs. Hedrick. "Abigail's bones are so small. She's just like Doctor's folks, all nerves and notions, bless her! Connie's built different. She won't have any trouble when her time comes, and I hope she has a lot of them. Mamie, too," she added. "She'll be all right. She has wide hips and a strong back. Some women are built for babies and some—well, some have them anyway."

It had stopped snowing when Douglas finally went home. The stars glittered overhead and the deep snow lay white below. He went in softly and took off his shoes by the living-room stove. Still holding them in his hand, he tiptoed into the bedroom and stood looking down on Mamie. She had left the lamp turned low for him, and he could see her now, curled like a kitten with her hand under her cheek. He felt an infinite tenderness for her to-

117

night, something deep and adult and enduring. He spoke her name softly, and she awoke like a kitten, uncurling swiftly and stretching, staring at him with wide eyes.

"Well, is it over?" she said.

"Yes, they've a nice lassie." He sat on the edge of the bed and took her hands. He was smiling a little to himself. "We've still a chance to beat them to it with a boy."

She drew her hands away and her body was tense.

"You'd like to see me howling and crying like that?" she cried. "You'd like to see me looking like a bag pudding? Oh, no, you won't! Not ever! I won't be tied down like that. I want to see life!"

"But that's life, Mamie," said Douglas, puzzled.

"It's not what I mean by life. It's being a slave, it's being an animal—it's being—it's being a damn fool!" she cried passionately.

"But, Mamie, I thought—"

"Oh, I saw enough of that when I was a girl," she interrupted fiercely. "I married to get away from all that—oh, love,—yes. But first of all I want life, the way I plan it."

Douglas lay beside her thoughtfully. In a few moments she was asleep again, but he could not sleep for a long time. What did she mean by life, if this was not part of it? he thought angrily. She wanted only cakes and ale, not mutton and crowdy.

When the cold light of a snowy morning came in the window he woke again and quietly dressed. Mamie was still sleeping, curled again in the childish attitude. But her face looked pale and the lids that veiled those luminous bright eyes were faintly blue. He looked at her as he had looked a few hours before, and he was tender with her again. He remembered her mother and the horde of ill-clad children. He, too, wanted life that sparkled and was gay, not the life he had known as a child. Could he blame her? He wondered, too, if any man could be brute enough to force childbearing on a woman he loved, if he knew it was against her will?

He started the fire, and through the frosty window he saw that smoke was curling from Angus' chimney and that Mrs. Hedrick was moving about in the kitchen. He knew that she would give him breakfast if he went over.

They were happy there that morning. Angus looked years younger than he had the night before, and, while bacon was

118

sizzling and coffee bubbling, he led Douglas in to see the mother and baby.

Abigail was pale and thin, but her big eyes were shining triumphantly.

"Oh, Doug," she said, "I'm afraid I made an awful fuss last night. They tell me you were here."

"But look what you did for the house of McBain, Abbie," said Douglas.

"That *is* something, isn't it?" she said with her tired smile. "You know we were counting on a boy, but we wouldn't change her for the world now, would we, Angus? We'd much rather have a girl."

"That's so," said Angus. "Look, Doug, she's to be just like Abbie." He lifted the corner of the blanket and disclosed the small wrinkled face of the sleeping infant.

"No, just like Angus, Doug," said Abbie.

"Stop quarreling now, and let my poor girl sleep," said Mrs. Hedrick fondly from the doorway. "Your bacon's burning to a crisp."

"What will you call her?" Douglas asked.

"Christine," said Abbie. "I wanted her for Christmas, but if she's a bit late, the name is just as good."

Douglas looked at A, wondering if he had not wanted to call the baby Jean after the mother in Scotland; but Angus was smiling, and Douglas surmised that, after the events of the previous night, he would have let Abbie name the baby Jezebel without a murmur of dissent.

So the first McBain grandchild was a girl, and, as a matter of fact, it was Willie who gave the family its first boy. But it was several months later before Willie's boy was born. He was a fat, healthy boy with a wide, crying mouth and Alma's high-cheekbones and sly eyes. Angus' little girl was small and pale with blue Scotch eyes, and hair so light that she looked almost bald.

When I remember that I was that little girl I am sometimes surprised. The story of my birth, and how my grandfather Hedrick blew the breath of life into me, was so often told to me when I was young that it became a legend, the history of a stranger with whom I was not acquainted. I seem to have been a spectator rather than the central figure in the scene that I have just set down.

119

25

That winter Mamie had the best clothes Doug's money could buy. She kept herself busy and contented for weeks with mutton-leg sleeves and boning for collars, with *soutache* braid and military buttons, red wings for her hat, and fur for her dolman. It was not a happy period in the cycle of women's fashions, but Mamie liked whatever was new, and whatever she wore looked dashing on her.

Douglas thought that she was prettier in the simple dresses she wore in the mornings, although he knew that it was a man's failing not to appreciate style, and he tried to remedy this as much as he could. When she was dressed to go out, she looked like a fine lady, and that was worth paying for. He bought her a bottle of the most expensive perfume, so that she might give off a genteel aroma of violets as she passed through a room, and, when she walked, she made a little rustling froufrou of taffeta petticoats.

Doc Hedrick, who admired Mamie hugely, said he understood that the Presbyterian services were practically disrupted when Mamie attended church, because the women were so anxious to get a glimpse of her hats and the men of her ankles.

"What do *you* know about it, Doctor? You never go to church," reproached Mrs. Hedrick. But the doctor insisted on repeating his little joke all over town, and Mamie, when she heard of it, was as amused as anyone.

But being the most stylish young married woman in town also entailed many frustrations. Before marriage a girl still had the stimulus of attracting the male with her finery, but after marriage Opportunity society no longer allowed her this satisfaction. Where could one go in a small western town to display pretty clothes? The members of the missionary society and the Ladies' Aid looked as if they had been in mothballs for years, and too fine a display of fashion was likely to turn them sour. Not that Mamie minded how sour they were, but it spoiled the game when there was no competition. One could walk down the street in a purple watered silk with a bustle and be conscious that the men in the poolhall and the drugstore and the barbershop had all admired it; but, after trailing it in the sawdust of the butcher-shop, there was nothing to do but go home again with a terribly let-down feeling.

"Doug, I wish we could live in Manitou City. There's something going on there." But Douglas was firm on this point.

"No, Mamie, not yet. In a couple of years maybe. Right now we're getting along just fine in Opportunity. Here is where the money is, until we've got enough capital to branch out on a larger scale."

Mamie sighed. She did try to be reasonable and see things Doug's way.

"Then let's have dinner at the hotel."

"All right. Come by the office for me at five-thirty."

Mamie spent most of the afternoon in pressing things and dressing, and she put a little rouge on her cheeks for fun. When she was all dressed, she had half an hour to spare and she ran across the yard to let Abbie see how she looked.

The baby was having an attack of colic, and Abbie was carrying her around while she tried to get supper. Abbie looked pale and tired and a little cross.

"The only trouble with the baby is," she said, trying to be facetious, "that she cries flat. She doesn't have true pitch."

"Put her up on your shoulder and pat her on the back," advised Mamie. "She's got gas on her stomach. Look, like this. I'd take her myself, only I'm afraid she'd puke on my dress."

Abbie lifted the baby against her shoulder and patted her back as Mamie directed. The baby gulped a couple of times and stopped crying.

"My goodness!" Abbie said. "You do know about babies! Do you want a job as nursemaid?"

"Not on your tintype! I know when I'm well off!"

"Oh, Mamie, you look wonderful! Where are you going?"

"We're just having dinner at the hotel. There'll be nobody there but a few drummers, I suppose, but I thought I'd have you look me over and see if I'd lost any pins or got my bustle on crooked."

"You're a dream. Everything's perfect."

"Honestly?"

"Honestly. Umm! You smell good, too. How did you fix your hair?"

121

"I put the front part up on kid curlers. I did it all since noon. I guess it will pass."

"It certainly will. The drummers will go over like tenpins."

"Don't be silly. Well, I've got to run. Doug will be waiting for me."

After Mamie was gone, Abigail laid the baby in her cradle and rocked it back and forth a little until the infant was asleep. Abbie did not know why she was such a fool as to cry, but the tears ran down her cheeks.

Connie had been very ill that winter. She looked pale and anemic in the fall, and then before Christmas she had taken pneumonia and Doctor had had his hands full to pull her out of it. Even her wagging tongue had been silenced, and she had lain quietly day after day watching the daylight creep across the wall.

"Gad! What a peaceful house!" Doctor said, but Mrs. Hedrick reproached him.

"Shame on you, Doctor. You know you'll be as glad as anyone to hear her chattering again."

Only one thing seemed to bother her, even when she was the sickest.

"Mama, is someone feeding the dogs?"

"Of course, dear. They're getting everything they're used to."

"I wouldn't want them to go hungry or cold or anything. I know they'll miss me."

"I'm sure they miss you, Constance. But they're having good care. They'll be glad when you're up again."

But, after the baby came, Connie's horizon widened. There was something besides the dogs to get up for now. She must get well enough to go and see the baby.

She began to ask all sorts of questions about Christine, and when she was allowed to sit up in a chair, she began to crochet a baby cap in blue and white wools. Gradually color came into her lips and cheeks as she chattered about the baby.

"Fancy being an aunt! Isn't that funny? And I can't wait to see Abbie being a *mother!* And, Mama, how does it feel to be a grandma? Do you think they will call her Christine? It seems such a long, forbidding name for a baby. I think Crissie would be nice. It's shorter and more like a baby, somehow. Or how

122

about Kit? Don't you like Kit for a nickname, Mama? I think I'll call her Kit."

The baby was almost six weeks old before Dr. Hedrick would give Connie permission to go to see her. Then one February day Mrs. Hedrick wrapped Connie in blankets and the buffalo robe with a hot brick at her feet, and drove her over to Abbie's in the cutter.

The snow still lay deep and white, but the air had softened and the sky was blue. Connie's feet tingled as she walked up the path from the gate to the door of the pink house. How odd it was to be walking outdoors again! She felt as if she were still in a kind of dream. And there was Abbie at the door to greet her, and Mamie standing just behind her.

"Oh, Connie, aren't you the brave one! How wonderful to have you out again!"

"Oh, it's good! It's good!" said Connie, embracing both of them. "And where's the baby? Where's little Kit?"

Coming home early from the office, Douglas saw the mare tied to the hitching block before Angus' door, and knew, without bothering to go home, that Mamie would be there, too. He went in the front door without knocking and found Connie sitting in the parlor holding the baby. A pleasing aroma of coffee floated from the kitchen where the chatter of voices indicated the presence of the other women.

Connie looked up at him and smiled and held up a warning finger. He closed the door very softly. He was shocked to see how thin and pale Connie was after her illness, but she looked happy. She beckoned with the finger which had warned, and laid back a corner of the blanket to disclose the tiny, sleeping face. Douglas came close and looked. The baby's miniature hands and plain, infant face never ceased to fascinate him. She was the first baby he had known with any intimacy since he had stood beside the hearth as a child to watch his sister Jeanie, with her small pink feet extended toward the glowing peat, while his mother held her on her lap and bathed her. The cottage had always been overrun with children, but he could still hear his mother's voice saying, "Look now! What a clever babe it is!" and feel his own pride and satisfaction in the little sister.

He put out his finger now and touched the palm of the little

123

hand that lay outside the coverlet. Involuntarily the small, crumpled fingers closed around his large one.

Douglas looked at Connie, and they smiled knowingly at one another.

"She's got you now," said Connie. "Isn't she cute?"

"She has old A's cleft chin. Did you notice?"

"Yes, and his blue eyes."

"Did she ever take hold of your finger like that, Connie?"

"Not yet," said Connie. "You've all had the fun of her for six weeks. This is the first time I've even seen her."

"Well, I dare say this is the first time she's ever clutched a body's finger. I'll ask Abbie when she comes in."

"Wouldn't your mother in Scotland be pleased if she could see her?"

"Och! she'd be fair daft."

Gently he disengaged his finger.

"Do you want me to put her in her cradle for you? Aren't you getting tired?"

"Maybe I should be, but I'm not," said Connie happily.

"Well! well!" said Mamie from the doorway. "Look at the domestic scene, Abbie. Quick, before it's spoiled."

Over a tray of coffee cups, Mamie's eyes danced and her lively face dimpled into mischief. Abigail, with a plate of tea cakes, looked over Mamie's shoulder, and Mrs. Hedrick came behind them.

"Oh, it's perfect!" said Abbie. "How about making a Roger's group of it, and calling it 'Baby's First Smile,' or 'Mr. and Mrs. Newlywed and Their First-born'?"

Douglas laughed and put his hand on Connie's shoulder after the manner of family photographs.

"Now cross one leg over the other, Doug, and hold your neck stiff, as if you had it in a vise," directed Mamie, setting down the coffee tray to have a hand in arranging the picture.

"But he really needs muttonchop whiskers, doesn't he, Mama?" laughed Abigail. "You remember the tintype you and Papa had taken with me when I was a baby?"

Connie continued to look down at the baby, but a slow flush mounted painfully under her pale skin.

"I think he'd make a lovely papa!" mocked Mamie. "And wouldn't Connie make a lovely mama?"

124

"Hush, now," said Mrs. Hedrick, "you'll be sure to waken the baby, and I don't want Connie to hold her too long, she's still that weak."

"Of course!" said Abbie, taking the baby out of Connie's arms. "No one shall ever have her but her ownest, ownest mother. She's not very pretty but her ownest mother loves her," and she carried the baby away to the bedroom, crooning softly over her as she went.

Douglas began to hand around the coffee cups.

"I see you didn't forget to put my name in the pot."

"We thought either you or Angus would be dropping in," said Mamie. "Where there's food, you know—a man can always smell it a mile off."

"Here's Angus now!" cried Mrs. Hedrick. "I'll make another pot of coffee. This is Connie's coming-out party, isn't it, my dear?"

"Oh, yes, Mama," Connie said. "I'm so glad to be here again." But, in spite of her brave assertions, she was unusually quiet. The merriment of the others flowed around and over her, leaving her silent.

Only Angus noticed how still she sat with her full plate untouched in her lap. The transient color had drained away from her cheeks, leaving them almost transparent in their pallor. She rested her head against the back of the chair, as if her first visit out since her illness had been almost too much for her.

"You're weary, lassie," Angus said, taking her hand and smiling at her. "I know weariness when I see it, for I'm often plagued with it myself."

"Oh, it's not only the body, Angus," she said looking at him with tears in her eyes. "It seems like no one needs me."

He knew what she meant, and he was too honest to dupe her with hearty assurances that the party was in her honor.

"You're young yet, dear," he said. "There's something for everyone, and you'll find your work and your place in time. I'm certain of that."

26

The next summer Opportunity was incorporated as a town in the new state which had been forged out of the Territory. Partly through Doc Hedrick's efforts and partly because of the general esteem in which he was held by the townspeople, Angus became the first mayor. It was not a post invested with great dignity. Abigail and Mamie kept asking him when there would be balls and receptions, with bunting-draped stands for the speakers, at which they could wear their best gowns and stand in line shaking hands; but Angus only smiled and shook his head. He had enough to do, trying to lay out some workable sort of civic machinery, without worrying about balls and receptions.

The new Presbyterian church, with its greatly enlarged floor space, its spire and new hall, and its Sunday-school room with furnace in the basement, was completed. Angus continued making his church calendars and took a modest pride in the new building which he had worked to achieve. But he did not look back in vainglory or regret, and now he went steadily forward in the business of setting the town in order, as he had gone forward in the business of the church.

Among other things he saw that the outlying streets needed to be properly surveyed, laid out, and named. Except for a few central streets, the town had grown up any which way, with "Swede town" to the south and "Dago town" to the west by the tracks, and wavering cart tracks going here and there wherever anyone set up a front door or a picket fence.

Angus got young men to help him and he himself rode with them on horseback all around the town, surveying and straightening or widening or cutting through new streets. When they had plainly established the right of way, they set up wooden posts at the corners indicating the names of the streets. The streets running north and south were named after the presidents of the United States, and those running east and west were named after the trees which had never ceased to be a wonder to the lad from Caithness. Oak, pine, mountain ash, tamarack, cherry, sycamore, walnut, willow: the names were beautiful to him not only for the sound but for the connotation. They brought to his

126

mind's eye forests and vast expanses of fronded tops, or perhaps a single perfect silhouette against the sky.

Once he had written a poem about the American trees, but it was not very good, and anyway, when they were first married, he and Abbie had sat in front of the parlor stove one day and read each other all their school poems; then they had burned them one by one, as a sort of sentimental gesture to close the past and clear the way for their future together.

The plotting and laying out of the town went on all the next winter when Angus could spare the time for it from other matters, and when the weather permitted.

"Angus, you look dead tired," Abigail said one evening, the following March, when he came in from extra hours in the saddle. "Your feet are wet, too, and your clothes are splashed."

"I'll soon dry off," said Angus. "You've a nice warm fire here."

"They ought to pay you for doing all this extra work," said Abbie, running for his slippers. "I don't see that you've got much glory out of this mayor job—just hard work."

"Glory?" asked Angus, a mild note of surprise in his voice. "You never thought I took it for glory, did you, Abbie?"

He sat beside the stove and began to pull off his boots. The baby was toddling by this time, and she came now in her nightgown and stood beside him, holding onto his knees and looking up into his face.

"Good even to you, young lassie," he said. He rarely bounced or tossed her or laughed or kissed, but the baby trusted him. She continued to look at him with wide eyes and a mouth spread in a smile which displayed some newly acquired teeth.

"I think that Douglas is a lot smarter than you are," said Abbie, returning with his slippers. "He's not giving his time and energy away to every Tom, Dick, and Harry in town. He's working for himself."

"I know," said Angus, drawing on his slippers and taking the baby on his knee. "It may be he's right, too. When a man has a wife, he's not quite free to do his own way any more."

"You mean you like working for other people without being paid for it, don't you?" asked Abbie incredulously.

"I never put it just that way," said Angus smiling at her. "I don't know if ye'd understand, Abbie, but years ago I wanted to be a missionary, and, when I gave that up, I promised myself I'd

127

give my services in other ways. Well, I've not done so mighty well with that, I suspect, an' I don't know as you'd call it advancing the Kingdom of God to lay out streets. But the town needs it and can't afford to pay much for it, an' just now I'm trying to serve the town."

"I know," said Abbie, "only it doesn't seem fair for so much of it to fall on you."

"Maybe it's not fair to *you*, Abbie. It's all right with me. But that's what I meant about a man not being free if he has a wife. You've always been behind me, Abbie, but Mamie's not the kind of woman to inspire anything in Doug except making money."

It was the first time Angus had ever said anything against Mamie, and Abigail looked at him in surprise. But the implied compliment to herself softened her dislike of hearing Mamie criticized.

"Doug wouldn't go in for good works anyway," she said. "He's looking out for himself, and I think maybe that's the best thing to do in this world."

"Maybe it is," said Angus. "It's hard sometimes for a man to know."

He laid the baby's head against his shoulder and began to rock gently back and forth:

> " 'Oh, ye'll tak' the high road
> An' I'll tak' the low road,
> An' I'll be in Scotland afore ye.
> But me an' my true love will never meet again
> By the bonnie, bonnie banks o' Loch Lomond.' "

By the time supper was on the table, the baby was asleep, and, when she came to take her, Abbie stooped and kissed the top of Angus' head.

"I like you just the way you are," she said.

27

Douglas and Mamie spent a week in Manitou City that spring.

"A whole week, Abbie! Think of it!" Mamie said as she packed. "Conrad Lauenstein, the big lumberman from the East will be in town and everybody's going to try and sell him timberland. I hate business, but there will be scads of parties. 'Take your best clothes,' Doug says, 'we want to make a good impression.' And I'm the girl who can do it." Mamie laughed with pleasure.

"Well, have fun," Abbie said. "You've got nothing to tie you down, and you look like a princess. I hope you know how lucky you are."

Douglas' anticipation was as keen as Mamie's, but the parties would be the dullest part of it for him. For some time he had been quietly buying up pieces of timberland with just this opportunity in mind. If he could sell them at a handsome profit, and perhaps get a contract to supply more land to an important corporation, he would be well on his way toward the success he craved.

But he knew that he would have keen competition from more experienced city agents. It was going to be a challenge to his ingenuity, and altogether a delicate piece of business, in which he must keep the right balance between eagerness and reluctance. He must appear naïve and friendly and at the same time be ready to match ruthlessness with ruthlessness. It was the kind of operation he most enjoyed.

Other eager young men with land to sell had come up to Manitou City, too, and under the gaiety there was also tension. Liquor flowed freely in the hotel bars, but Douglas took none of it. He was not deterred by his Scotch Presbyterian upbringing so much as by his distrust of anything that robbed him of a clear head. The business in hand sufficiently stimulated him, and he could not risk a moment's carelessness.

Lauenstein was gracious to everybody, with a kind of old-world courtliness that masked his real intentions. He was an old man but extremely vigorous, with the air of a *bon vivant*, and he fell in gracefully with the dinners and parties and drinking bouts afterward in hotel rooms. Yet Douglas noticed that Lauenstein, too, kept a clear head through it all. He was willing to take what was offered and make his own bargains.

Sometimes across a roomful of slightly fuddled people their eyes met and engaged each other in a gaze of level speculation. Doug saw that Lauenstein was cold but terribly aware.

"This is a businessman," Doug said to himself with admiration.

The parties were like manna from heaven to Mamie. Now at

129

last she had some real use for the dresses that usually hung limp and idle in her closet. She laughed and sparkled; she postured and danced. And there were always men to admire her.

"Oh, men!" she said, "the silly creatures!" Mentally she strung them on her string like beads, and it was fun to be a little scornful of them while they danced attendance. Yet she really loved all of them. If they were a little difficult, so much the better. So she set herself out especially to capture the lumber baron from the East. That would be a feather in her cap and Doug's!

That he was old and ugly and married didn't bother her at all. He was important and that was what mattered in Manitou City this week. She got her fun where she could. Fortunately, she was seated next to him at the first dinner party they attended.

Douglas was too busy during the day to bother with her. He saw that she was having a good time and he was pleased, for he knew how often she was bored in Opportunity.

Johnny Buxton was in the city, too, but he had no gift for the social life and he did not appear at the dinner parties or balls. Yet it was Johnny who put Douglas onto the last-minute purchase of the Pine River holdings. Pooling their resources, they were able to present a larger block of good timberland than any of the other young hopefuls.

"You make the best arrangements wi' the old man that you can, Doug. You've got the inside track wi' him, an' I'll be content wi' whatever you can swing for us," Johnny said.

So it was Douglas who finally did the business, and matched his wits with the old lumberman's to get the best profits he could on the lands he had to sell. It was the sort of tightrope walking he most enjoyed. He could see that Lauenstein enjoyed it too, old hand that he was at the game.

On the evening of Lauenstein's last day in Manitou City there was to be a farewell party for him at the Elks' Club. At the end of the business conference which the two men held in the morning, Lauenstein said to Douglas: "Mr. McBain, I should be pleased if you and your charming young wife would dine with me this evening before the party. Just the three of us in my hotel suite. There's a little more business I'd like to go into with you, if you don't mind."

The contract! Douglas thought, but he kept his voice calm.

130

"Why, thank you, sir. I'm sure we shall be able to accept with pleasure."

Mamie was sparkling with beauty and animation. She did not need the rouge she had put on. Her shoulders were bare and roundly white. Her tongue ran loose and wild, and if she did not always speak the language of an eastern lady, the sound was sheer music.

Douglas let her run on. Nothing mattered now with the contract almost in his pocket. He took the first drink he had had in all this week of flowing bowls. It ran sweetly through his veins as Mamie's voice ran through the air, like music. He felt relaxed and content.

"I think you have a great future out here, McBain," he heard Lauenstein saying. "A new country needs smart young men—not gamblers but solid young men who know what they're doing. I think you're one of them. I'd like to put you under contract to buy land for us regularly. We can try it for a year to see if it works."

"That would please me very much, sir," Douglas said.

Mamie leaned forward and put her hand on Mr. Lauenstein's. "You are very good to us," she said. "Do you think we'll be rich someday?"

He took the hand and raised it to his lips. "I don't see why not," he said, "although it seems to me that a man with such a beautiful wife is already richer than most of the other men I know."

After dinner they went on to the farewell party. People were still on their toes, not knowing where the contract would go nor when it would be settled.

It pleased Douglas to know that he had the advantage of them in more ways than one. He felt elated but also tired. There was only one thing he wanted now: to be at home in Opportunity in old clothes and slippers, with bed impending.

He had no real appetite for dancing, and he knew that Mamie would never lack partners. Out-of-town men did not often bring their wives as he did, and Manitou City was still the new West, where men predominated. Yet, even if the men had been scarcer, Mamie would always have had her dancing partners.

Douglas watched the dancing for a while. His head was still full of quarter-sections and percentages. He saw with amusement that Lauenstein relished the dancing as much as the business. He danced with old-fashioned spring and bounce and much courtly bowing from the waist to the ladies. Douglas watched him swing Mamie onto the dance floor, the gray head bent to the graceful dark one, her full skirts flowing about the old man's legs. And this is the mighty lumber baron from the East that we were all afraid of, Douglas thought. Presently he gravitated to the big leather chairs in the lobby below the ballroom. Here the more serious-minded were still talking business among the brass spittoons.

It was after two o'clock when he finally located Mamie. The tired-looking musicians were snapping their fiddles into cases. People were struggling for their wraps in the cloakroom. It was not until he heard Mamie's laugh on the balcony that he knew where to find her. He opened the door and went out, and old Lauenstein was kissing her good night.

Instinctively Doug's fist shot out, hot and hard, but Mamie sprang between them and took the force of it on her uplifted arm. Her laughter never skipped a beat.

"Come now," she said. "I dared Mr. Lauenstein to kiss me, Doug. He said he hadn't kissed a girl in twenty years. Are you going to wait another twenty years, Mr. Lauenstein?"

The older man laughed uneasily.

"Not if I can help it," he said as gallantly as he could.

"Didn't you bring my coat, Doug? I'm freezing, and tired to death. What an evening! And you never once danced with me, Doug! There's a husband for you!"

They were both sullenly silent in the cab which took them back to their hotel. When they were alone in their room, Douglas burst out angrily: "You were a brave sight, my lass, letting that old fool kiss you, and then you lied for him, too, didn't you?"

"If I did, it was to save your contract. What if you'd struck him? That would have been a pretty scandal."

"The scandal was yourself—kissing on a balcony at two of the morn!"

"Would you have me do it in the lobby?"

"And has this gone on all week, and have I been the blind, deluded husband?"

"Of course not, you idiot. He never kissed me before, and I hope he never will again. He's in his second childhood. Ugh!"

132

"But any man will do, eh? Just so 'tis not your husband."

"That's a nice word, isn't it? It seems to me that you were glad to dance with me once, before you became a *husband*. But now you go and sit among the spittoons, and never ask me for a single dance. You're worse than the old men, honest to God!"

"I thought you wanted it that way," he said. "I thought you were having the time of your life."

"Well, I was," she said, "until you spoiled it."

"Listen, lassie—" he caught her roughly by the arm.

"Don't!" she cried. "That's the arm you hit. There's no use being cruel to me."

"Oh, Lord!" he said, flinging her arm away. He stood looking at her, a procession of angry thoughts moving behind his eyes.

Humming one of the dance tunes, Mamie began to undress.

"Men are all alike," she said, "a lot of stupid brutes. What is a girl to do?"

She folded her dress carefully on the back of a chair, and let a couple of petticoats fall about her feet.

"Come and unlace me, Doug," she said.

"Unlace yourself," he said.

She shrugged her smooth, bare shoulders, and got herself out of her fashionable stays. The corset cover, the linen shift, the long white stockings, were discarded in a careless pile. She flung a pink and blue flowered kimono lightly across her shoulders.

"What's a kiss anyway?" she said. "You've got all the rest of me."

She came and stood penitently beside him.

"Oh, Douglas."

He looked down at the flower-clad shoulders, the bare, pink-tipped breasts, the small feet naked on the red hotel carpet.

He could forgive her anything.

28

When they returned from Manitou City, Mamie brought Abigail a red watered-silk waist. It cost her a pang not to keep it for herself, but Mamie saw the fitness of things and she knew at once that this was made for Abbie's dark eyes. She might have got a pink or a yellow one for herself, but Mamie had her moments of generosity. She liked to see Abbie's eyes grow larger and hear her excited cry of rapture at an extravagant gift.

"Just don't let the baby drool on it, and you'll look like a million dollars, Abbie," she said, laughing and showing her lovely teeth.

"Did you have fun?" Abbie asked wistfully.

"Oh, yes," Mamie said. "It was exciting."

It was understood in the family that Douglas had made another good land deal in Manitou City, and that things were more than ever on the upgrade for him; but he did not talk about it as he might have done a year or two earlier. He was growing more and more still-mouthed and quiet-eyed. You didn't know what he was thinking unless he wanted you to know.

Abbie wore her red watered-silk waist to the Ladies' Aid, and some of the women looked at her with eyes that held a dark reserve of censure.

"Abbie McBain is so nice, it's too bad to see her aping her sister-in-law—the fast one."

That winter the three brothers grew further apart than they had ever been before. Alma was having another baby and would not be seen at the family parties, nor allow Willie to go without her.

Angus and Abbie had a little Swedish hired girl that winter, and they might have gone out and had a good time once more, as Abbie said, but there was always city or church business to occupy Angus in the evenings. And then there were the insurance books! They irritated Abbie most of all.

One of the men in a branch office down in Oregon had died of consumption, leaving his books in great confusion. The company had sent the bulky ledgers, together with a mass of ill-assorted papers and account sheets, to Angus to be untangled. Angus spent his evenings for weeks on this business. He would come home wet and tired, and after supper he would sit down by the lamp and spend the evening copying out figures and adding up columns in red and black ink.

"He's always got his nose in those books!" Abbie said. She appreciated the fact that people trusted and relied on Angus. But what about his wife? Was she to be an old woman before she was thirty? Sometimes her patience wore thin.

134

One evening she came in from Mamie's house with a dish of cold roast meat in one hand and a Boston fern in the other.

"Well, they're off again," she said to Angus, who was working over his books. "At least I get their scraps for watering their fern. They do have the best times! I wish that we could go somewhere sometimes."

Angus looked up at her and smiled. Surprisingly he pushed back the ledgers and the red and black ink.

"I've been thinking," he said, his pale blue eyes suddenly alight, "about a long trip, something that would make Mamie's and Douglas' little comings and goings seem like Sabbath-school picnics. Across the sea, it is. Would you like that, Abbie?"

"Angus! You mean—?"

"Aye, Scotland, lassie. To let the granny and grandfather see our little Christine—and *you*, Abbie, my darling. All the way to Caithness—"

"*When*, Angus?"

"Next year we could go."

"You'd really do it? *Really?*"

"Aye. I'll begin to plan my work ahead now, so that we can have a long holiday. 'Twill be good for both of us, Abbie."

"Oh, it would be lovely!" Abbie cried. "Think of seeing Scotland—and the whole world, all of it, waiting for us!"

So they made their plans, and letters of anticipation flew backward and forward between Caithness and Opportunity.

Connie heard of their plans with interest and a little envy. The winter had seemed very long to Connie. This year she had her health back, and she could take part in the social activities that engaged the young people of the town. But she was not the youngest of them any more, and she felt a little out of place. The girls of her age group were already married, and the few bachelors who were left did not please her at all. She had a lot to say about their faults, in public as well as in private, and her tongue, which had never lacked fluency, now began to acquire sharpness. It was not that she had anything to say, but the sound of her own voice gave her a feeling that she was somebody to be reckoned with. She wanted desperately to do something worthwhile for herself. The doctor had sent Abbie away to a finishing school, and, as he often remarked: "She learned to play the piano and then she got married. What was the good of the piano?

I want my girls to get married, and all the training they need for that they can get in their mother's kitchen."

So Connie was never sent away to boarding school. She struggled along with her violin lessons; and when the teacher, who had wandered into town for a short time, went on farther west, Connie took over some of his less experienced pupils. Dr. Hedrick was away from home most of the day, and it was then that Connie received her pupils in the front parlor. The lessons that she gave were very poor indeed, but the children liked her, and it brought in a little money of her own.

When Doctor was at home, Connie took the dogs and went out for a walk. The dogs needed the exercise, and her father's pointed remarks about old maids had begun to poison her leisure hours.

"If she wouldn't talk so much and be so damned critical, she might have got herself a man by now. But look at her! Sawing away on that damned fiddle! What kind of life is that for a woman?"

"She wanted to be a nurse, Doctor," Mrs. Hedrick reminded him.

"You know what I think of *that*," he said. "She isn't reasonable."

Connie went to bed early in the long winter evenings, and read Dickens and Bulwer-Lytton by the light of a kerosene lamp. Her shades were drawn, and nobody, except her mother, who sometimes saw the crack of light under her door, knew how late she read.

"How in tunket have we used so much kerosene this month, Susan?" Doctor Hedrick thundered.

"Well, Doctor, I dare say we've been careless with lamps, and the girl uses it to start the fire. It goes very fast in the winter-time."

After her father was gone Connie said, "Mama, I'll pay for the extra kerosene out of my lesson money."

"No, no, dear," Mrs. Hedrick said. "Your father can afford you a little extra light at night, and you'll need your lesson money for odds and ends. It's only right you should have pretty things like Abigail and Mamie."

"Thank you, Mama."

So her pillow was often wet with tears for Little Nell, for Dora, the child wife, and for the sad old woman in her bridal finery

136

sitting beside the cobweb-festooned banquet table. Life was not at all the bed of roses that Connie had thought it when she was fifteen.

She was learning to suppress her feelings. Yet the more she hid her real thoughts, the more garrulously she chattered about nothing.

29

It must have been that spring that consciousness, or perhaps I should say memory, first dawned in me. I had begun to run everywhere on legs that sometimes betrayed me like a drunken sailor's. Angus had to build a picket fence around the yard to keep me within bounds. It is so long ago and far away, yet I remember how the grass grew in prickly green ridges between the red bricks of the front walk, and how it felt to slide down the sloping cellar doors at the back of the house. I remember squatting in the fence corner to watch the ants working about the little sandy holes they had built in the grass, and how they sometimes crawled up my legs and sent me scurrying for help.

I remember the sound of the piano through the open window while I was out of doors on my own errands; and how I used to watch for my Uncle Douglas and my father to come home in the late afternoon. My father was always grave and kindly with me; but my Uncle Douglas tossed me up and laughed and had little treats hidden for me in his pockets. He never produced them ostentatiously, but gave me a hint and let me forage, so that I knew the inside of his pockets almost as well as he did; or at least so I thought.

Having no other children to play with, I invented one of my own. Her name was Did, and if anyone blamed me for a misdeed I could always say, "Not me. Did did it." How I learned this trick so young, I do not know, except that to avoid responsibility for error is probably one of the first human instincts.

I saw my pretty mother and my even prettier aunt being gay and happy together over clattering teacups in a region beyond my own, while I sat with Did and my dolls on the white bearskin rug beside the stove.

137

Except for the wonderful visits to Grandmother Hedrick's and my Aunt Connie's, the pink house was my world. As long as I live and keep my senses it will exist, the sweet, safe world of the pink house with the yellow climbing rosebush by the door, and the wide domain of grassy bricks and cellar doors and busy ants that was encompassed by the picket fence.

And over the fence someone is smiling at me.

"Hi there, young lassie."

"Uncle Doug!"

30

One day Douglas came into the office where Angus was bending over his desk writing. Angus wrote a beautiful small hand, regular and clear, even when he was racked by the cough that had continued after a bronchial cold. Douglas hung up his hat and shifted his feet uneasily. He had something to tell A, and it was as difficult to put into words as his decision to leave Caithness had been.

Presently Angus looked up and smiled at him.

"You've something to tell me, Doug," he said. "Something's bothering you, lad?"

"Well, Angus, it's true. It's a thing I hate to say. But I've had a good offer from the Westways Land and Mortgage outfit in Manitou City. They've made it very advantageous to me. I can hardly turn it down. Yet you're so pushed here, I can hardly go off and leave you, either. I wouldn't mention it at all were it not for Mamie—"

"Aye, of course," Angus said quietly. "Mamie would like the life in Manitou City better than this, I'm sure. Yes, it will be a fine thing for you, Douglas."

"You won't mind then, A? You won't feel I'm letting you down?"

"Och, *mind*?" A said. "I'll mind very cruelly, Doug. But this is a thing I've seen coming. You're a good businessman, lad, and you need wider horizons. I'll not be the one to hold you back. Just be sure, though, that it's a wise step you're making."

"Does anyone ever know that?" Douglas asked.

"None of us," A said quietly. "But there's One that does, Douglas. I've never urged it on you. But there is a wonderful peace in prayer. Trust the Great Power, whatever it is, that is out beyond us. Ask, in humility, and the answers will come clear to you."

But there was no other power to Douglas but the strong, up-surging power that he felt in himself; and it was not his way to ask anything in humility. He respected A's God but he had no gods of his own. To get through life as best he could under his own steam, that was all Doug asked. And to do a good job of it, in his own way, seemed a much finer thing than to be carried along on the shirttails of an unseen Power.

Yet he did have his doubts about the wisdom of this move. It was only Mamie's joy in the change that swept them both along.

Willie, too, was restless with life in Opportunity. As far as he was concerned, the town had not lived up to its name. As the town grew and separated itself from the country, there seemed to be less demand for the skills of a harness and saddlemaker. It was queer how bicycles were becoming more than a passing craze and how improved railway service was eliminating the long cross-country drives that people used to take.

When it became clear that Doug was going to Manitou City, Angus called Willie into his office one day and proposed that Willie give up the harness business and come into the office with him.

"Och!" cried Willie in consternation. "You don't mean writing mortgages and life insurance and all that business, do you, A? An' rotting off my tailbone on a swivel chair? No, lad, much as I love ye, 'tis not the life for me. I'd ruin your business for ye in a bare six months. I'd help ye out if I could, A, but leather-workin' is what I know and what I'm handiest at. Still, I doot I'd be better off upcountry a bit where the farmers need my services more than they're needed in Opportunity."

Willie prayed over his future as little as Douglas did. His good-natured optimism performed for him the same service as Douglas' sense of power. Neither of them felt the need of Angus' Unseen Presence.

Little as she professed to like Opportunity, still Alma was the one who was reluctant to make a move into the unknown.

"How do you know what it'll be like out to Carfax?" she asked. "How do you know it's going to be better?"

"Why, Alma, lass, it's bound to be better. It's right in the wheat fields, and a fine healthy spot to bring up the bairns. The men I've met there are princes and gentlemen."

"Princes and gentlemen," scoffed Alma. "And who are you, pray, Napoleon Boneypart?"

"Aye," laughed Willie, "that's me, old Boneypart himself, sweetheart."

Aside from his usual roseate view of the future, there were more complicated feelings which urged Willie to move. He did not bring these complications to the surface and call them by name, but, since his marriage, life in Opportunity had somehow lost its flavor for him. Marriage, in a way he could not quite understand, had gradually cut him off from the family and friends he loved. Douglas and Angus had been going up in the world, and, while he would not admit that he had lost ground, at best he seemed to be standing still. Standing still, cut off from the careless sociability that he loved, he was beginning to feel uneasy, like a bird in a small cage. It was only occasionally, when he went to see his dogs and listened to Connie's garrulous tongue wagging on about inconsequential things, that he sometimes recaptured for a moment the fine flavor of happiness that he had known in his bachelor days. When he was laughing with Connie over nothing, the town of Opportunity seemed to be a fine place, and the spot where they stood the exact center of the universe.

Just before their second baby arrived, Willie and Alma moved to Carfax. The young wheat was springing green on the undulating fields. This country was not so flat as Caithness, but there were no mountains here, only acres and acres of rolling black volcanic-ash soil. If Douglas had come to Carfax, he would have begun buying up cheap land with an eye to the future, for a foresighted man could see potential wealth in this black loam. But Willie was satisfied to find more harness work to do, and to have a larger yard for the little boy to play in than he had found in Opportunity. He never asked for much. If the sun shone and people were kind, Willie was happy.

So the good days in Opportunity drew to a close, and the three brothers went their separate ways. Abbie and Angus continued to live in the pink cottage. The second cottage stood empty for a long time after Douglas and Mamie moved away. Abbie used to look at its blank windows and sigh for her dear friend; and for a long time I watched for my Uncle Douglas, not quite understanding why he no longer came to lift me up and let me explore his pockets.

But they wrote glowing letters of their exciting life in Manitou City, where fortune was filling their laps with favors.

The departure of Willie and Alma made less stir in the community. But my father went to see them after they were settled, and reported that Willie was finding a reasonable amount of harness work, and that they had a vegetable garden and a few chickens and another baby boy.

Manitou City

1

BETWEEN THE BRIGHT LIGHTS of city streets, right through the middle of the town, ran a fine western river with waterfalls and bridges and power plants along its banks. Douglas liked that. He liked the movement and the sparkle and the power of turning wheels. Running water pleased him even better than mountains and trees. Mamie liked the river too. Their hotel window overlooked it. After dining in the restaurant at night, they used to walk along the riverbank, or pause on the bridge to look down at the moving water.

"It's going somewhere," Mamie said. "It's on its way to the sea. We're going somewhere, too, aren't we, Doug?"

"Aye, we're on our way, sweetheart."

He felt it strongly now, that they were on their way to a splendid future, and nothing could stop them, nothing could turn them aside.

He was not altogether pleased with the Westways Land and Mortgage Company, where he was working at present, but he felt that this was only a step forward and that he could go up from there as soon as something better offered.

With scarcely a regret, they had disposed of the carefully selected furnishings of the pink cottage. My Grandmother Hedrick purchased the set of Haviland china with the delicate design of lavender sweet peas, and many pieces of it have come down to me from her. Of the poppies and wheat design, which belonged

143

to Abbie and Angus, I have only a teapot without a lid. Still, china, fragile as it is, endures beyond flesh and blood.

2

In Opportunity one day, Dr. Hedrick laid his stethoscope on the desk at his elbow and looked hard at Angus with his angry black eyes.

"You can't go to Scotland, man," he said. "You've got to go somewhere south and try to get over this cough."

"But I've given Abbie my promise," Angus said, "and we've already postponed the trip twice because of business." He paused to draw a difficult breath. "They've built a high chair for Kit."

It was not really what he had meant to say. He knew himself that he was sparring for time, trying to fend off a little longer the devastating knowledge. The pain that he had suffered in his chest, the continued cough, the uncomfortable dry heat that rose in him every afternoon—he had endured these patiently. But now Abbie's father was trying to give some terrible meaning to his troublesome symptoms.

Angus passed his hand across his mouth, still shaken by the memory of the bloodstain on his handkerchief that had sent him to Dr. Hedrick's office.

"Damn the high chair," Dr. Hedrick cried. "Scotland's a cold, damp place. The only cure I know for what you've got is southern sun and not to work so hard. I can give you port wine and extract of beef and pulverized charcoal, but none of it's any good. You and Abbie have to get away. Abbie will understand. Susan and I can keep Christine for you while you're gone. It may be all you need—a rest and a change of air."

"Abbie will be disappointed. I don't like that."

"She'd feel worse if you died," said the doctor brutally. "I'll tell her how it is."

"No," Angus said quietly. "I'll tell her myself, Doctor. Thank you, thank you."

"Why do you thank me?" Doctor cried. That his son-in-law was sick of a disease likely to kill him made Dr. Hedrick bitterly,

144

helplessly angry. He did not want to be thanked for giving such information.

"Why," Angus said mildly, "I thank you for being frank with me, Doctor. There are a great many things that I shall have to see to before we leave."

"Well, Angus," Doctor said, "if we knew more, it might help us to control this thing. But how does a doctor get time to explore the unknown when he's so busy delivering babies and putting on splints and giving out calomel and paregoric?"

"You know much more than I do," Angus said. "I'll try to do as you direct." He put on his vest and coat, knotted the muffler around his throat, and reached for his hat. "Thank you, Doctor," he said again, his mind too busy with other matters to notice that he had repeated himself.

But the anger had gone out of Dr. Hedrick. "Don't be downhearted, Angus," he said. "We'll pull you through this nicely. Just a little southern sun, a change of scene."

"Yes, yes, of course," said Angus gently.

They shook hands, and Dr. Hedrick went to the office window and watched Angus walking down the street, steadily, quietly, as he had seen him pass along so many times before.

Angus was thinking of the many preparations he must make, but among the practical details there were mingled the words he knew so well: "Our Father who art in Heaven . . . Thy will be done . . . Thy Kingdom come . . ."

3

I was just past four years of age at this time, and I loved my Grandmother Hedrick almost as much as I loved my Uncle Douglas. To fill the empty place in my heart when he was gone from the pink house next door, I used to run away to my grandmother's house.

My mother was often busy with housework, or else she sat at the piano making beautiful sounds which did not move me at all. All through my early childhood went the sound of a piano; yet I have never been able to learn to play or even to read music. In other respects I have been a normally intelligent person.

145

To keep me from running away to the Hedricks' they used to tie a rope around the gate in the picket fence. I have often been told about the day when I arrived at my grandmother's house, carrying a croquet ball in my arms, as she said, with my sparse blond hair making my head look as bald in the sunshine as the croquet ball.

"But, Kit," Grandma cried. "How did you get out? The gate was tied."

"I tied it untied," I replied. The saying became a classic in the family.

So it was not difficult to transplant me to the Hedricks' when my parents went south for my father's health. I remember neither happiness nor unhappiness while they were gone. Everything went well. Aunt Connie fussed over me as she did over Uncle Willie's dogs. She kissed me and coddled me and tucked me in at night with appropriate bedtime stories, and got me up in the morning with jolly cries of "Up, up, Mary, and see the sun rise!"

She worried because I did not like to drink milk, and she said it was a shame that my father had taught me to eat only the yolk of the egg and not the white.

One of her favorite anecdotes, even when she was an old woman, was the account of how she and my mother and I were in a store one day. The clerk said to Connie, "Madam, how much your little girl looks like you!" All her life Connie had treasured this little triumph over Abbie and her child.

I could have drowned in Aunt Connie's ministrations had it not been for the life raft of Grandma Hedrick's impersonal good sense. My Grandfather Hedrick was to me only a pair of terrible black eyes and muttonchop whiskers, who cried in a great voice: "Well, child, what are you staring at?" The ladies shielded me from him as best they could. Still, about this time, he gave me a very pretty blue silk dress in which they had me photographed, for the pleasure of my parents. I still remember the dress; in fact, most of my recollections from this period of my life seem to be material ones. So much of what happened while my parents were gone is completely lost to me, yet I remember that they brought me a sailor-boy doll when they returned. I had never had a boy doll before, and I can still see in detail his little white suit trimmed in blue braid, and his cunning blue cap. I remember

146

this so plainly, yet I have forgotten my father's face except as I have seen it since in old photographs.

Everyone was very cheerful when my parents returned, and it was believed that my father was cured of his illness. The piano sounded again, gaily or passionately, in the parlor of the pink house. I sat on the white bearskin rug before the stove playing with my sailor boy. My father came and went again, but more slowly and quietly than before. He had always been quiet, but now there was some deeper stillness in him that none of us really apprehended.

My mother ran about laughing and asking company in, desperately pursuing a solitary gaiety that would shut out other specters. Sometimes she must have longed for Mamie, who would have been gay with her.

And then in a few months winter came again, and it was decided that my father would have to go south once more. I do not know if anyone, even Dr. Hedrick, knew how sick he was. I am sure my mother did not, for this time she decided not to go with him. What decided her I do not know. Perhaps it was because of me, perhaps it was because there was nothing she could do, and the sight of illness must have become painful to her. Perhaps my father asked her to let him go alone.

He got as far as San Francisco on his way to Arizona, and died alone in the room of a hotel.

4

The news of A's death came to Douglas as a shattering blow in the midst of the lighthearted existence he and Mamie had been living in Manitou City. It was the first bereavement he had suffered, the first setback he had encountered in a career which had moved forward almost too smoothly and successfully. Money was flowing in, and his social life was stimulating and exciting. Now he paused as if an unseen hand had dealt him a heavy blow.

Mamie was in bed with the grippe when the telegram came. She sat up on the side of the bed and thrust her feet into her slippers. The tears ran down her cheeks. "Oh, something's awfully wrong with this world that people can't enjoy themselves,"

147

she cried. "Angus was so much better than the rest of us, and now he's gone and I don't like to think there's sickness and death in this world. It's cruel and horrible. I'll never forget my father, how he looked after he was dead. He wasn't my daddy any more. He was someone else, someone I didn't know." She cried in earnest now, sitting on the bedside with her dark hair disordered and her lovely shoulders bent in grief.

Douglas put her gently back against the pillow. "You stay here, dear," he said. "It can't do any good for you to go to the funeral. Stay here and get well." She gave a long sigh.

"Tell Abbie I love her," she said. "Tell her to try and get a little fun out of life now, if she can."

Douglas met the train from San Francisco that carried Angus' coffin, and went on with it to Opportunity. Willie and Dr. Hedrick met them at the railroad station in Opportunity. Abbie was in bed, prostrated by grief, and the little lassie was with Mrs. Hedrick. Alma had not been able to come to the funeral either.

"We've another wean," Willie explained apologetically.

"A girl this time?" asked Douglas.

"No, another boy, fat an' fair," said Willie.

The funeral was held the next day in the Presbyterian church which Angus had done so much to help build. The building was crowded with men and women from all denominations and walks of life, for A had been well beloved.

Douglas remembered that he had sometimes been annoyed with Angus for his deep preoccupation with God. But now, looking at Angus' still white face, he felt ashamed and deeply sad. The face was not much changed since he had seen it last, and it occurred to Douglas that death had been sitting there for a long time, unnoticed by the rest of them. Angus had not had such need of wife and child, of money or power, as he had had of God.

Willie, standing by Douglas' side, sobbed openly, wiping the back of his hand across his eyes, and Douglas envied him his easy tears. Something stable and unchanging seemed to have gone out of the world, something more quiet and honest and upright than most men know on this troubled earth was lost forever. Douglas wanted to weep for it too, but he could not find tears.

After the funeral, Douglas and Willie took dinner together at the hotel. Willie's old black suit was worn and green and thread-

148

bare, but his face scarcely looked older than it had when he left Scotland. He was still a brave young lad but in a suit which had already given him too many years of service.

Douglas was jolted by the sight of him into the realization that people who formerly rode on horses were using bicycles and trolley cars now, and the more advanced ones were talking about horseless carriages and "aerioplanes." It was a dull season for the saddlemakers.

"Why don't you get into some other kind of business, Willie?" asked Doug.

"What would that be?" countered Willie. "I know the harness business up and down, but I dinna ken beans from barley aboot any other."

"Well, you're not too old to learn," said Douglas. "There are plenty of openings for a smart lad like yourself."

Willie shook his head. "A said something of that ilk to me, Doug. But it's no good. The harness business will pick up again soon. You can't tell me horses are done for. We've depended on horses ever since Pharaoh's day!"

Douglas shook his head also. It was like Willie, he thought irritably, to have been apprenticed to a saddlemaker and to keep on being a saddlemaker in a machine age until the last horse had perished. But one could not be angry with Willie long; his smile was too disarming. He was taking a train at seven o'clock, and, when they rose to go, Doug put his hand in his pocket and drew out two gold pieces, a twenty and a ten. He slipped them into Willie's hand.

"Treat yourself to a new suit," he said. Willie opened his hand and looked at the gold pieces with an embarrassed smile. Then he held them out again to Douglas.

"Ye'll no be offended if I dinna accept them, will ye, Doug?" he said. "I've still got the wolf on the run an' enough wool between my back an' the devil to last another year."

Douglas put his money back in his pocket. There was nothing anyone could do about Willie.

Before he left Opportunity, Douglas stopped to see Mrs. Mc-Allister. He had a strong affection for her that went beyond the sentimental gratitude he felt because she had launched him into a successful business career.

Angus' death had been a severe blow to her, too.

149

"He's the first of my boys to go," she said. "So young, so good! 'Twould have been more fit if the Lord had taken an old woman like myself instead of Angus." Her mouth trembled as she spoke and her eyes, which used to be merry, looked tired.

She *is* an old woman, Douglas thought in surprise. But he only repeated a platitude, "We're none of us as young as we once were, Mrs. McAllister."

She put her hands on Douglas' shoulders. "Take care of yourself, lad," she said. "You're like a son to me, and I think ye've a great future. Never stray too far from Angus' goodness, lad. He winna have lived in vain if the rest of us try to carry on for him."

"I've thought of that," Douglas said. "It's the least we can do to try to live up to him."

"Douglas," she said, "I've made up my mind this will be my last year keeping a boardinghouse."

"Boardinghouse?" Doug said. "It's a wee bit of Scotland that you have here, Mrs. McAllister. Boardinghouse is a poor name to call a thing that's meant so much to so many homesick lads. You'll never give over, will you?"

"Aye," she said. "I've prayed an' I've greeted in the dark of the night, but this is the decision I've come to. I'm too weary to go on, and I've money enough to be comfortable in my old age, if I'm canny about it."

"You'll be canny," Douglas said.

"Aye," she said, "but I'll need your help, Doug. When I sell the big house and settle myself in a wee one, there'll be money left over. I want you to invest it for me so I'll be sure of an income for food and taxes and a Sabbath dress when the need arises."

Douglas took her hands from his shoulders and held them in his own. They were knotted with rheumatism and roughened by heavy work. He fell into the old dialect with her as he said diffidently, "Happen ye'll find a cleverer chiel to handle things for ye than I am, Mrs. McAllister."

"No, lad," she said. "You are the one I trust."

Abbie, too, put herself in his hands as far as financial matters were concerned.

"I don't understand a thing about it, Douglas," she said, "but it seems that Angus provided handsomely for Kit and me. I used to be so irked by his economies and the life insurance he was laying up and all the prudent investments, and to think he was only planning ahead for us and making sure we'd be taken care of if anything happened to him."

She wiped away her tears now with a handkerchief which was heavily bordered in black. She was too pale and thin at the moment, yet the high-necked black dress with the tiny white hemstitched turnover collar looked well on her. Douglas had a fleeting thought that she would make a very handsome young widow. The fact that she was well provided for would not make her any less desirable to some men.

"Abbie," he said, "don't rush into anything from loneliness or boredom, my dear. Don't marry too soon, will you?"

Her great dark eyes blazed at him and, as soon as his words were out, he was sorry he had spoken.

"How can you, Douglas?" she cried. "And you Angus' brother! You know he was my life. You know he was everything I had. I would kill myself now and let them put me in the same grave with him, were it not for our child. Oh, Douglas you are very bad to talk like that to me."

"Forgive me, Abbie," he said. "I only had the thought that you are still young and prettier than when A married you. I didn't mean to hurt you. Please forgive me."

"I'll try," Abbie said tearfully, "but you are not very understanding, Douglas. Except for Kit, my life is ended."

He kissed her gently then, and went away to the train with a heavy heart.

5

Douglas had stayed longer in Opportunity than he had expected to and he felt anxious about Mamie. There had been no letters from her, and he was afraid that she had been cruelly lonely, sick in bed in a hotel suite. Still, the maids were devoted to her, and there wasn't anything the manager or the bellboys wouldn't do to please her.

But he had not counted on Mamie's recuperative powers or her delight in meeting trains. She was on the station platform in

151

her modish suit with a fur neckpiece and a small fur hat setting off the rosy beauty of her face. Her eyes were like stars. After the sad and dreary week he had spent in Opportunity, the sight of Mamie's lifted face scanning the car windows for him brought life and hope and gaiety crowding back to him. With Mamie, absence always made the heart grow fonder. When they were together every day there were many little irritations arising from their different aims and characters; but absence erased these and sent them rushing into each other's arms.

In the cab Mamie was full of cheerful news, and he listened with pleasure, glad that she did not ask for detailed accounts of the funeral or the sadness he had left behind him.

"You know the new Hotel Majestic they're building on Water Street? The dining room is to be something beyond anything Manitou City has ever seen. They're importing French chefs and there's a goldfish pond and fountain. Mr. Glover from our hotel took me over to have a look before the doors opened, and it's simply marvelous. They're installing gasoline lamps—yes, really, that's what they told me. They'll give a really brilliant light, far and away better than the silly old gas lights we've been used to. It's going to be splendid, and there's to be a dinner and ball on opening night, and of course we'll go, won't we, Doug?"

"Oh, I dare say," Douglas said. He looked fondly at her glowing face, and a thought crossed his mind: Is it only the opening of a new hotel that can make her so happy? Is there something else too?

She chattered on for some time, and then she said with a little laugh, "You know, the funniest thing happened while you were gone. Guess who I saw on the street one day?"

"I don't know. Who?"

"A voice from the past really. Go on, guess."

"How far back? You might as well tell me. I'm not a good guesser."

"No, you aren't, are you? Well, I'll tell you. This was a fellow I used to know a long time ago. But you ought to remember him. Buck Clayborne. Remember?"

"Yes," he said coldly. "I remember Buck Clayborne. But he doesn't have a thing to do with us now. I don't care if I never see Clayborne again. I didn't like him."

Mamie laughed delightedly. "That's just what he said about

152

you," she cried. "But that's the silliest thing. I'm an old married woman now, and perfectly safe. I'd like for you two to be friends."

"I don't see any reason," Doug said stubbornly. "As far as I'm concerned he might as well get lost in the jungle. Why should you want to see him?"

"W-ell," Mamie said, still laughing a little, "I was a mess when he knew me. I'd like him to see that I've got good clothes now and can afford to have my hands manicured and my hair washed by a professional. When I knew Buck Clayborne, the only thing I owned was that old yellow dress."

"You never looked lovelier, Mamie, than you looked in that yellow dress," Douglas said. "Where is it? What's become of it?"

"I sent it back to my mother," she said, "and she probably made diapers out of it. Lord knows they never had enough diapers in that household."

"Well, as far as Clayborne's concerned, let's forget all about him."

"We can't, Doug," Mamie said. "I've asked him to have dinner with us."

"Oh, Lord!" Doug said. "How long is he going to be in town?"

"Only a couple of weeks. The least we can do is be polite to him. He'd think it very funny if we weren't. He'd think you were jealous or didn't trust me or something. It's just for old times' sake after all."

"All right," Doug said. It seemed to him that he really did not care very much one way or the other. Only, the joy had gone out of his homecoming and the sadness that he had left on the train was catching up with him again.

He left Mamie at the hotel and went on to the office. His desk was piled high with business which had accumulated in his week's absence. He went to work to clear up as much of it as he could before it was time to go to dinner with Buck Clayborne.

If Buck Clayborne had any qualms about dining with the McBains, he did not show them. He was all suave good nature and confidence, and Mamie bubbled with charm. For the most part Doug sat glum and silent. This was a worldly situation that he might have taken in stride, had he not come so recently from the bleak sadness of his brother's funeral. He could have been happy alone with Mamie tonight, but the presence of an old rival set his teeth on edge.

153

When they were alone together at last Mamie said: "Well, you *were* a dolt tonight. And I wanted Buck to see how well I had married. I must say you didn't help me to show off."

"As far as I can see you needed no help from anyone," said Douglas bitterly.

"That's a nice thing to say!" Mamie cried. "I had to be civil for two of us instead of one. You didn't help me a bit."

"But why should I help you to fascinate Buck Clayborne? Do you think I'm daft?"

"I feel very sorry for him."

"Sorry? In God's name, why? He looked to me like a fellow who could take care of himself."

"He's had a very tragic life."

"Indeed? You mean he has a wife and would rather have someone else's?" asked Doug angrily. "That's hard luck, that is!"

"Well, you may be nasty about it if you like, but his wife's been in a mental institution for years. He's got no kind of normal life for a man."

"He'll take care of himself," Doug repeated irritably.

"You've been as cross as two sticks ever since you came home from Opportunity. You purposely misunderstand everything. I know you've had a dreary time down there, but it isn't fair of you to bring it back with you."

"I can't help myself, Mamie," he said contritely. "There are times when the heart can't be light, no matter what. I didn't mean to bring my troubles back with me."

"Well," she said, "I'm sorry, Doug. I shouldn't have asked company the first night. But, if you give in to grieving, it just comes up like a wave and washes you away. I won't be sad! I won't be dreary! Maybe it's all the religion I've got, but my religion is to be gay, and as far as I'm concerned it's the devil himself who goes around in sackcloth and ashes."

"I was brought up on a different philosophy," Doug said. "In Scotland they told the bairns that the devil was gay and the good man cloaked himself in sorrow and repentance."

"But you never believed that, did you?" Mamie asked incredulously.

"No, I don't think I did," Douglas said slowly. "No, I wanted gaiety too and to have the best of everything. I used to say, ' 'Tis my ain life and I'll make the most of it!' "

154

"And it's slipping by so fast," Mamie said, her face suddenly somber. "All of our lives, they're slipping by so fast. Listen, Doug. Call the bellboy and ask him to bring up a bottle of beer. I can't go to sleep feeling like this."

6

Mamie had a new dress for the opening of the Hotel Majestic. She chose a yellow to please Douglas and to remind Buck Clayborne of old times. For Buck was leaving the day after the hotel opening and she might never see him again at all.

He had dined with them several times and Douglas had been civil to him, as became a man of the world. Mamie had driven with Buck twice into the country when Douglas was busy at the office. Those rides beside Buck had given her a strange feeling, the feeling she had had as a girl that his will was her will. Douglas had always left her free and that was how she wanted to be. Yet there was a powerful urgency connected with the surrender of will that she felt when she was near Buck Clayborne.

For the most part they had ridden silently, shoulder to shoulder, in the hired buggy. But once Buck had turned to her and taken her hand.

"Mamie, you still love me," he had said.

"No!" she said, pulling her hand away. "No! Don't spoil a nice ride, Buck. No, you know that's all over."

He laughed then and slapped the reins over the horse's back and they jogged along back to town.

It was Buck who had arranged the party at the new Majestic Hotel.

"I've engaged a table for the three of us right in the center of the dining room near the fountain. They say this is going to be the best-lit dining room west of Chicago. And they've got a string quartet to play during the dinner. We'll have oysters and champagne and whatever you want. We'll have a big time tonight because I'm leaving in the morning. It'll be a real celebration to repay you folks for some of your wonderful hospitality. After dinner, we'll go to the ball and dance. Mamie will like the dancing, won't you, Mamie?"

155

"Yes, I will," Mamie said. "Doug and I have got very stuffy about dancing. After dinner, we're usually off to bed."

"Well," Buck said, "there's something to say for that too."

Douglas had not given much thought to the opening of the new hotel. Mamie attended to having his evening clothes pressed and his good shoes shined and at her request he got his hair cut. But he had other things on his mind. When he had joined the Westways Land and Mortgage Company in Manitou City it had seemed a fine step forward from Angus' small office in Opportunity. But he had soon recognized that the larger office was riddled with carelessness and inefficiency. Golden opportunities for turning land into money were all around them in a booming western city; but there were too many men in the Manitou City firm working for personal interests and not pulling together. Douglas saw that they lacked a strong guiding hand, and he would not have been averse to supplying that hand himself. He was the youngest man in the firm, but he had been replacing some of the confused bookkeeping and waste motion with the sound and cautious business practices he had learned in Angus' office, and he felt that he was making headway. Still he had moments of regret for having involved himself with a group of men for whom he had no great esteem.

And then the week after his return from Angus' funeral, a man from the East had come into the office to see him. Earl Bannerman was a friend of old Lauenstein, the lumberman, and he had capital behind him. He wanted to start a new land-dealing firm in Manitou City, and Lauenstein had suggested Douglas as a good man to consider for one of the partners. The whole thing had been very tentative, and since Mamie was rarely interested in the details of his business, Doug had barely mentioned it to her. He could explain it all later, if the offer became a fact. But the idea of change had occupied his own mind almost exclusively in the last few days. Whether to cling to security in a firm he did not respect with the hope of bettering it, or to take a long chance on a new business in which he might have a free hand? The sporting chance of making a big thing of a new venture appealed to him very strongly. Bannerman had returned east with a promise of telegraphing him a firm offer within a few days.

Belatedly, Douglas decided to lay out the facts before Mamie as they dressed for the hotel dinner. It occurred to him that she

156

must be prepared to help him make the decision, since her future was concerned. He had an uneasy feeling that the telegram might come for him at any time, and that he had not sufficiently prepared her.

However, he realized with irritation that he could hardly expect Mamie to be attentive to matters of business when she was dressing for a ball.

"Well, will it get us more money, Doug?" she called from the bathroom where she was enveloped in a cloud of scented steam. "If there's more money in it, I'm all for it. You ought to know that without asking."

"I'm sure there's more money in it eventually," he said. "But probably not at first. We may have to draw in our horns for a little while. I don't know."

"Oh, draw in our horns!" Mamie cried. "My horns have never got out far enough to bother me, and I certainly don't want to draw them in. What have you done with my comb, Douglas?"

"I haven't touched your comb," Douglas replied irritably. "Why would I use your comb?"

"Well, why shouldn't you? You comb your hair, don't you?"

"Not with your comb." It was really ridiculous. He took himself in hand. "I just wanted to know how you felt," he said. "The telegram might come tonight, and I'd have to decide."

"Well, you might have asked me about it sooner," shouted Mamie through her cloud of scented steam. "How can I decide your problems for you now, dear, when we're busy getting ready? Oh, Glory! Here it is!"

"What?"

"The comb, of course."

But when she came out of the bathroom, radiant as Aphrodite rising from the foam, she said quite positively:

"Yes, I think you'd better gamble on it. I'm sure Buck Clayborne's making more money now than you are. You shouldn't let him get ahead of you."

"Buck Clayborne!" Doug said bitterly. "That second-rate traveling drummer!"

"He's making a whole lot of money. He's not second-rate. You show yourself up as a jealous booby when you talk like that," cried Mamie angrily.

"Praise the Lord, he'll be out of town tomorrow," Douglas said.

157

They had cooled off considerably by the time they went down-stairs. Mamie was happy in the positive assurance her mirror had given her that she had never looked lovelier. Douglas had begun to think again of the things he would do in business with a free hand and some eastern capital to back him. He left a note with the desk clerk as to where he could be found in case the telegram came.

The Majestic dining room was decorated with potted palms and there were cut flowers on every table. A little fountain played in an ivy-wreathed pool. The white tables gleamed almost too blazingly bright under the new gasoline lamps that were suspended from the high ceiling. The novelty of the gasoline lamps provided the first topic of conversation for the guests.

"Did you ever see anything so bright?"

"Beats the old gas chandeliers, doesn't it?"

"Why, they're better than daylight. Wonderful!"

"They're noisy, though. They make a distinct hiss."

"Well, wait. The musicians are tuning up. You won't hear the lamps when they start 'The Blue Danube.'"

"I don't know if I like so much light. It shows up all the wrinkles."

But Mamie loved the light. Her fine complexion had nothing to fear from it. The light, the music, the sound of conversation, laughter, clinking glassware, and splashing fountain—these all added up to the kind of background that Mamie needed to ap-pear at her best. She saw the looks of admiration from other tables, and the appreciation in Clayborne's eyes. That Doug was silent and preoccupied again tonight did not bother her.

Well, let him sulk, she said to herself. Other people appreciate me if he doesn't.

Buck was opening an oyster for her. She leaned toward him to watch, her curly dark hair touching his cheek.

"Is there a pearl in it?" she asked laughing.

"There should be," he said. "We'll keep ordering them until we get a pearl. A pearl for Mamie."

"Do you really mean it?" she asked. "Would you keep on ordering oysters for me until we found a pearl?"

"Sure I would," he said. "I'd go through all the oyster shells in Manitou City to find a pearl for you."

158

"But would I have to eat the oysters?" Mamie asked. "Ugh! No, I hate the slippery things."

"I'd eat the oysters for you," Buck said lightly. "Waiter, here. Bring us more oysters. Bring us a lot of oysters with pearls in them."

"Oh, don't be ridiculous," Mamie cried. "I'd rather have more champagne than more oysters. Pearls are for tears, anyway, they say. Did you ever hear that? Let's skip the pearls."

"Whatever you say," Buck said. "Tonight you give the orders. Isn't that so, McBain?"

"I think likely it is," Douglas said.

"Poor Douglas," Mamie said. "He's very dull tonight. He gets all wound up tight with business and he won't unbend and enjoy himself. Have more champagne, Doug. It will loosen you up."

"I don't want loosening. Thanks."

"He's got some great big business deal cooking tonight," Mamie said. "He thinks the telephone may go ting-a-ling at any moment."

"Something hot, eh?" Clayborne asked.

"It's a private matter," Doug said stiffly.

"You see what I have to put up with." Mamie laughed. "My big dour Scot."

"You and I are Irish, Mamie," Buck said. "We *are* Irish, aren't we?"

"Of course we are. The lucky Irish."

Doug saw them both laughing at him, merry, carefree, and a little malicious. He pushed back his chair and laid his napkin on the table. Anger pounded into his temples. As he rose, with no clear notion of what he was going to do, he heard his name being called. A bellboy in the smart red uniform of the new hotel was going from table to table. "Mr. Douglas McBain? Mr. Douglas McBain."

"Excuse me," Douglas said. "I will be back."

He went quickly out of the dining room, trying to choke down his anger and square his mind around to business. He went to the hotel desk.

"I am McBain," he said.

"There's someone on the line to speak to you."

"Thank you. Where do I take the call?"

159

"There's a private booth just beside the elevator."

The voice of the desk clerk at the other hotel came through to him. "Your telegram has arrived, Mr. McBain. I thought you would want to know right away. If it is urgent I'll send a bellboy over to the Majestic with it."

"Send it over," Douglas said. "I'll wait in the lobby here until the boy comes."

He was standing in the lobby looking at a newspaper, when he heard the first blast of the explosion in the dining room. The whole hotel seemed to rock as if it were being shaken by an earthquake. Then the voices of the diners rose in cries of terror. People in evening dress began streaming out of the dining room, and behind them through the doorway there was a cloud of smoke. The clear white light of the new lamps had disappeared in a blackness lit by sudden spurts and flashes of flame.

In an instant the lobby was full of confusion and terror. Douglas ran toward the dining-room door, thinking only of Mamie in her yellow dress, laughing and chattering beside the flower-decked table under the new lamp. People kept pouring out of the room, some with clothing on fire, crying for help.

Douglas heard himself calling her name, "Mamie! Mamie!" But she did not come. He pushed through the terrified diners, forcing his way into the burning room.

"Mamie!" he called. "Mamie!"

Stumbling over chairs and against tables, he worked his way toward the table where he had left her. There was an instant when he heard the sound of the fountain still bubbling in the midst of the burning cloth and wood, the falling crockery. He found the table where they had been, but Mamie and Buck were gone. He kept shouting her name and trying to fight his way back through the smoke and fire to the door. Then the second explosion shook the floor under him. The walls seemed to tremble and bend inward. He kept stumbling and falling and creeping forward as best he could, feeling the sharp pain of the flame against his skin. He kept calling, "Mamie!"

7

When he awoke he was in pain and he could not see. I am trapped in the fire, he thought. I am blind. This is what came to Angus. This is death.

But a voice said to him: "It's all right, Mr. McBain. You're going to be all right. Don't move, please. You'll be better off if you don't move. We'll give you something to make you sleep again. It's going to be all right."

Beside the pain there was something terribly troubling on his mind. He could not remember at first what it was. Then he said, his lips feeling painfully thick and strange, "My wife. I was trying to find my wife."

"She's safe," the voice said after a moment's hesitation. "She got out through the kitchen. You mustn't worry about anything now but getting better. Doctor will give you something to relieve the pain."

He formed more words, painfully and slowly. "Is she here?"

"No. No, not now. I expect she will be soon. You must lie very quiet now. It's the best thing."

They were speaking to him as to a child. He tried to remember what had happened, but it was very hazy to him. His arms and head seemed to be swathed in bandages. He thought that he must be lying in a hospital from the odor of carbolic acid and the hush of voices. Gradually the pain receded and he drifted to sleep again.

8

Willie put on his old black suit again and took the train up to Manitou City. Was this to be another funeral? Another brother lost to him? He blew his nose and cleared his throat, but he did not shed any tears. In spite of his comfortable optimism, there were moments when he saw clearly that the world was a grim place. There was no use greeting over it. Tears made matters no better. Only he was too distracted to push back the unruly lock of blond hair that kept falling over his forehead, no matter how he tried to discipline it.

He did not like cities, but he had discovered that they were inhabited by kindly individuals who would go out of the way to direct him when he was lost. So, smiling his gratitude, he eventually found himself on the right corridor of the right hospital and crossing the threshold of a small clean room.

Before he went in the nurse said to him in a low voice. "He'll ask you about his wife. But she hasn't been here, you know. We tell him she inquires after him because we don't want him upset."

"But where is she?"

"Nobody seems to know. She got out of the fire without a scratch, they say. But she's checked out of their hotel."

"I see," Willie said.

"Just be careful what you say to him."

"Aye. I'll take care."

So he stood by Douglas' bed and spoke to him.

"What's all this, lad?" he said in a cheerful voice. "They've got ye done up like an Egyptian mummy. You're a bonnie sight, to be sure."

"Och, Willie," said Douglas. "I'm glad you've come. Yes, I'm trussed up for fair. They've even got my eyes bandaged. Am I going to be blind, Willie? No one tells me the truth here, but you will, lad. You will, wi' ye no?"

"Aye, I'll tell ye true, Doug, as far as I'm able."

"Then answer me that first. Am I to be without sight?"

"Lad, I'm no doctor. But they tell me they think you'll see right enough when the bandages are off. They'd no lie to me, I'm sure. In fact, you're a great deal better than I thought ye'd be after the telegram they sent me."

Douglas lay silent for a moment.

"I'd not like to be blind," he said.

"No," Willie said. "God willing, you won't be."

There was another pause and then Doug said, "How's Alma and the bairns?"

"Fine, fine. Alma sent you her best. The wean's growin' like a weed. Did I tell you we'd named him for Angus?"

"You did well," Douglas said. "If I had a son—" he broke off. "Listen, Willie," he went on in a different voice, "there's a thing

162

that worries me greatly. You know I was not in the dining room when this thing happened. But I went back for Mamie. They tell me she's safe, Willie, but I've never yet heard her speak. Why not, Willie? Did she perish in the fire before I found her? Tell me it straight, Willie. I've got to know. I've got to know if she's lying in a hospital somewhere like me, or if she's—dead."

"Douglas, I've only just come into town. I know no more than what I'm told. But they say she got away without a scratch."

"Then why doesn't she come here?"

"They tell me she asks after you all the time, Doug. You've been a very sick man. Happen they won't let her in to see you."

"Then why do they let you come?"

"Doug, you must give me a wee bit of time. But I'll find out for ye. It's the whole truth you want, and I think you had best have it."

Willie could ill afford the time away from his work, but he stayed on in the city for a week. It was not entirely that his work was demanding, but that even the cheapest rooming house he could find in Manitou City was more than he could afford. He was glad to find that Douglas had plenty of money to take care of the medical and hospital bills that were mounting up.

He looked with wonder, untouched by envy, at the fine suite of rooms Douglas occupied in a fancy hotel.

The mither in Scotland would be proud, he thought. The lad's done well in a financial way.

But how his brother had done in other phases of his life it was now his business to find out. Mamie was not in the fine hotel suite. Her dressing table was swept bare. A few dresses hung in the closet to show that she had been there, but that was all. There was not even a note of explanation.

"Mrs. McBain has gone," the desk clerk said. "She didn't leave an address. That's all I can tell you. Right after the fire, that same night, she came in and packed in a hurry. A gentleman that they'd been seeing quite a lot of came in with her, and helped her with her suitcases. We didn't hear until later that Mr. McBain had been taken to the hospital. When I heard it, I thought that she was probably moving to a room nearby so she could be right with him. Her trunk's still in the storeroom. But then the hospital kept calling, and it seems she didn't go there. She was such a beautiful and kindhearted lady. The two of them were so gay and successful, I can't think anything is wrong. Maybe she went to her mother's while he's in the hospital. But she didn't tell us a thing."

Willie talked to the bellboys and the chambermaids. Mrs. McBain's friend had carried down the bags, and the boy had not been asked to handle them. The doorman said they went away in a cab, but he didn't know where. One of the maids said she had found the rooms in disorder in the morning after the fire, as if Mrs. McBain had dressed and packed in a hurry. Mrs. McBain had left a generous tip for her on the dressing table but no word of any kind. "And we was good friends, too," the maid said.

Willie went to the livery stable and found the cab driver who said he had taken a lady and gentleman to the station from the hotel on the night of the fire. At the depot the station agent said that he had sold them tickets on the sleeper to Chicago. The station agent remembered them particularly because the man had exchanged a ticket he had for the next day, and had purchased an additional ticket for the night train.

Willie went to the doctor then.

"I think I'd best tell him, Doctor," he said. " 'Tis harder to be worried than certain."

"None of it's good," the doctor said. "But you have my permission to tell him. Maybe he'll rest easier if he has it straight."

Willie pushed back his lock of hair and sighed. He thought that this was more difficult than anything he had done before. He stepped into the hospital elevator and saw the door slide shut behind him. The four small walls closed him in and the mechanism began to carry him upward. It seemed to Willie that the city was full of these devilish little cages carrying one up and down, up and down, and no escape to the freedom of open horizons.

"Douglas," he said standing by the bedside, "it's Willie again, lad."

"Good," Douglas said. "But you didn't have to tell me you were here. I heard your solid country tread coming up the hall, lad. But I'll see you with my eyes as well as my ears tomorrow. They're taking off the bandages in the morning."

"That's fine news," Willie said, "fine news."

"So what have you found out, Willie? Have you seen Mamie?"

"No, I've not seen her at all, lad. But I've learned a few things. She's away out of town for the present—safe as can be, I've no doubt. She left town on the night of the fire. Happen she didna even ken ye were hurt, Doug."

Douglas was silent for a moment. Then he said in a strained voice, "Where did she go?"

"To Chicago."

"How do you know? Did she leave word?"

"No, she left no word. I've been through your mail. There's nothing from her. But 'twas to Chicago that they bought their tickets."

"*They?*" Douglas said.

"Oh, aye, Doug. I canna hide it from ye. She's away with some man. You know him, I dare say, for the hotel clerk tells me you've both seen a lot of him lately, though the clerk didna ken his name. Happen he's her brother or a family friend and all is well. I dinna ken."

"He's not a brother nor yet a family friend," Douglas said heavily. "What else did you find out?"

"Not much," Willie said. "She's taken most of her things, but not the trunk. Some of her gowns are still in the closet. 'Twas in a hurry she left—on an impulse maybe."

"Aye, it would be in a hurry. When she left it would be on an impulse. That's how she would do things. And she wouldn't want —she wouldn't want a blind husband, someone she'd have to look after."

"Happen she didna ken, Doug."

"She could have remained a few days to find out," Douglas said quietly.

"Oh, the little slut!" Willie said. In spite of all his resolution to keep an even temper and a calm tongue, the angry tears had begun to run down his cheeks. "The dirty little slut!"

Douglas did not speak. He turned his face toward the wall. This was a thing he had foreseen for a long time and now that it had come it was only like the smart of another burn. He thought that he was the biggest fool that God had ever created because, in spite of everything, he wanted for her only that she should be happy.

165

After a time he turned back to Willie and said, "Wasn't there a telegram from a man named Bannerman in my mail?"

"Aye," Willie said. "I'll fetch it."

9

I remember the scars on the backs of my Uncle Douglas' hands and on his temples. Aunt Connie said that the burns had altered the shape of his nose, too, but if that was the case the change was not in any way disfiguring. He was as handsome as ever, and more romantic in the eyes of the women, for they all knew his story. He never mentioned Mamie to anyone, and people did not speak of her to him; but behind his back women shook their heads and said: "Imagine! He went back into the fire to save her, and all the time she was safe and had run away with another man!"

I was a small child but I was feminine enough to love him better than ever because he had been duped and betrayed by one of my own sex.

My mother was the only one who had a good word for Mamie. She had loved her dearly, and she said now: "I don't care. Mamie must have had her reasons. She liked to be happy. What's wrong with that? Don't all of us want to be happy?"

"But not at great expense to others," my grandmother said. "Mamie had duties which she did not fulfill."

"Oh, *duties!*" cried my mother impatiently. "I'm sick and tired of hearing about duties."

That winter my mother took Connie and me to California on some of the insurance money. No one thought it was an extravagance because I had always been a delicate child and there was fear that I had been unduly exposed to my father's fatal disease. It was only right that the young widow should try to save her child. But, although I was the ostensible reason for this journey, more than anyone else perhaps I sensed how glad my mother and Connie were to get away from Opportunity.

My mother was fleeing from memories and from sympathetically watchful eyes; Aunt Connie was fleeing from monotony and her father's complaint that he had an old maid on his hands.

166

I could feel the buoyancy of their spirits as the miles widened between us and Opportunity.

We took a small apartment in San Francisco and began going to concerts and theaters and eating out in restaurants. My memories of that time consist of a few jewel-bright scenes which were almost entirely related to my own childish interests.

I remember that we were in a restaurant with a very high ceiling, and that I had a red balloon of the lovely gas-filled variety which tugged and fretted to be free. While we dined it was tied to the back of my chair, but somehow it came loose and went up, up until it bumped against the ceiling. I remember my despair, and probably I shed tears, although I was in general a very stoic child. And then I remember a kind-faced waiter who took a hooked window pole and somehow snared my balloon for me and brought it safely down and put the string in my hands.

Later I remember being sick and very feverish and uncomfortable, but, worse still, the arms of my doll had come off and that was the final calamity that brought the whole of my troubles into focus. If my mother or Aunt Connie tried to comfort me they left no lasting impression on my mind. But a strange doctor came and made me stick out my tongue. I showed him my doll, and he must have seen that this was my greatest hurt, for he told me that he had a hospital for dolls, as well as for people, and that if I would let him take the doll for a few days he would see that she was made well. I gave him the doll and her arms, and in a few days he brought her back cured and whole. This is a vignette that still brings tears of happiness to my eyes in the recalling. I must have been missing my father very acutely, although I had put him away from me so resolutely that I could not recall the appearance of his face. I missed my Uncle Douglas and my grandmother also. I was not so happy as Connie and my mother were, I think.

It must have been about this time that Uncle Jack began to call on Aunt Connie and Mama. He brought chocolates to Aunt Connie and disregarded me entirely, but he looked very warmly at my beautiful mother in her artfully modified widow's weeds. Perhaps I was jealous that he did not make me the center of his attention, but he never appeared to me in the heroic light of the waiter or the doctor. In fact, I remember him with a distaste which increased rather than diminished with time.

167

But my mother and Connie were greatly taken with him. At first I went out with them a little, but I fell asleep at the theater and had to be prodded awake or carried back to the apartment, big awkward girl that I was. After that the lady in the next apartment was paid to sit with me. But when they returned one night and found me by myself, that arrangement also came to an end. So presently my Aunt Connie stayed with me, and my mother and Uncle Jack went out alone.

One night I was awake when my mother came in. Aunt Connie was awake too, and waiting up for her. Perhaps I had heard the outer door open, but something woke me and I got up to find myself a drink of water. This is another of the jewel-clear memories of that time. I see the broad band of light through the half-open door and my mother and Aunt Connie standing in it in the room beyond. Usually they were at one in their sisterly good nature, but now something seemed to vibrate between them.

"It's you who have the money," Aunt Connie was saying. "It's easy to see that that's what he's after."

"It isn't that at all, Connie," my mother cried. "He's lonely, just as I am. He needs my help and sympathy."

"Well, I'd have given it to him, too!" cried Connie. "I as good as told him so. I'm not dull company. I've really tried—"

"Connie, people have preferences," my mother said. "You can lead a horse to water but you can't make him drink."

Drink, I thought, I wanted a drink. But why were they talking nonsense about horses? I was sorry to see them looking angrily at each other—they seemed to be all I had left in the world. I did not want them to quarrel.

That spring my Grandfather Hedrick died very suddenly of a heart attack. He had not been provident in looking to the future as my father had been. His life insurance had lapsed, and he had rarely bothered to collect his bad debts. My Grandmother Hedrick was left with a big house and almost no income. The doctor had always lived in the moment and expected the moments to go on forever.

When we heard the news we closed the apartment in San Francisco and purchased tickets for Opportunity. I saw my mother and Aunt Connie weeping, and I knew that there was much trouble in the world. It was not an easy place in which to

168

live, but I was here and I felt that I would have to make the best of it.

Uncle Jack and his sister came to the train to see us off. Before the train left he kissed my mother there in public, in broad daylight, on the station platform, while Aunt Connie and I stood stiffly by. His sister had brought us a parting gift.

"Handle it carefully," she said. "I made it myself. It's a specialty of mine."

When we were in the train my mother opened the big, flat parcel, and it turned out to be a lemon meringue pie.

"A lemon pie!" cried Aunt Connie hysterically. "Oh, my Lord! A lemon pie on a Pullman sleeper on the way to a funeral! I never saw anything so crude and inappropriate in all my life. Oh, heavenly days!"

"I don't think you need to be critical, Connie," my mother said coldly. "She meant well. It's the intention that counts."

"Oh, Lord!" Aunt Connie repeated, laughing hysterically. "What, oh, what are we going to do with a lemon pie on a sleeper?"

"I'll give it to the porter," my mother said. "But you needn't be so superior. It's a beautiful pie, and I think she was very sweet to give us something she had made. Be still now, Connie. Everyone's looking at you."

10

In midsummer of that year Douglas had a letter from Connie Hedrick: She wrote:

"MY DEAR DOUGLAS, Abbie is thinking of doing something very foolish. I wish you would come down and try to persuade her that she shouldn't. We met this man in San Francisco last winter, and I think he's really an adventurer and after her money. None of us want her to marry him, but she absolutely won't listen to anyone here. I think she might listen to you, Douglas. Mother thinks so, too. Can you come soon, please? He's here now, and it's really sickening. I could ask Willie, he's Angus' brother too, but she wouldn't listen to Willie either, I know. But you're handling her money and she trusts your judgment. Please come, Douglas. We need you. Yours truly, CONSTANCE"

Douglas turned the letter over and laid it face downward on his desk. Behind the words on the written page, he could hear Connie's voice running on and on like Tennyson's brook. He had not gone to Opportunity for Dr. Hedrick's funeral, although his conscience had said, "Go." Willie, of course, had gone and had been one of the pallbearers in company with the well-dressed and successful men of the town.

But Opportunity meant Mamie to Douglas, and he did not wish to be reminded of her. He had never tried to get in touch with her or find out what had become of her. She had chosen her way and he had written her out of his life as he wrote out a bad debt in his ledgers. The clothes she had left in the closet he gave to the chambermaid. He relinquished the luxurious suite they had occupied and got himself a good single room at another hotel. When he was lonely for a woman's society, he found that there were plenty of women eager to give him their hearts. He was fastidious about women and enjoyed having a selection. He saw that there were other women with equally good bodies and sounder virtues than Mamie's, but he had no intention of becoming deeply involved with any of them at this point in his life. He intended now to devote himself to a career of moneymaking and success. He could take risks by himself that the responsibilities of a family would make unwise if not impossible.

Bannerman's offer of a partnership, with the backing of eastern capital, was still open to him when he came out of the hospital. But now that he was alone in his personal life, he had an urge to go it alone in his business—not to be tied to someone else's capital, even if he started in a very small way. He was not averse to partners, but he did not want to be financed by eastern money. He had driven all through the back country in hired rigs long enough to know that there were wonderful buys in farm land and timberland, and even in potential mining land, readily available to a man who knew where to look. He could think of only one other man who had this on-the-spot knowledge of local conditions, together with a vision of the future and the courage to gamble on it. Angus had not always trusted Johnny Buxton, but then Angus had distrusted all gamblers. Angus had done well in a business way, but he would never have become a rich man because he was unwilling to take risks. Douglas understood that big fortunes were not built with caution; they were built with intuition and the daring but well-considered gamble.

When Johnny Buxton came up from Opportunity to see Douglas in his last days at the hospital, Douglas was ready to broach the subject of a joint business venture to him. Johnny thought well of it. They were both canny Scotsmen. They walked around each other gingerly, viewing the possibilities from all sides, but knowing at heart that their aims and methods would be the same.

While Douglas was winding up his affairs with the Westways Land Company and tactfully disentangling himself from Bannerman without incurring his hostility, Johnny busied himself with renting modest quarters in a good location in Manitou City and having a painter make them a sign; MCBAIN AND BUXTON, LAND SPECIALISTS.

Until Douglas was thoroughly strong again, Johnny had done the legwork and the country driving while Douglas set the office in order. Now they were both out of the office much of the time, while the routine work was turned over to a young man named Plimpton whom Douglas had rescued from a backwater in the Westways Company. He had recognized in Plimpton his own impatience and frustration with the older firm, and had suspected that Plimpton had the initiative and daring to match their own, with perhaps a better knowledge of urban real estate in Manitou City.

Plimpton was a bachelor as Johnny still was. Among the three of them there were no unwieldy family obligations or loyalties to embarrass them in taking chances, and Plimpton brought with him to the office another great asset. Douglas never asked just what relationship existed between Sam Plimpton and Molly Casey outside office hours, but she was a crackerjack secretary and office manager and worth her weight in gold to all of them.

So the new business was getting a good start, and Douglas found his days so filled that he went to bed tired and ready for sound sleep at night. He could conveniently push the image of

171

Mamie out of sight in the back of his mind, and tell himself that he had forgotten her.

To go back to Opportunity now, if only for a few days, would open old wounds. He drummed his fingers absently on the back of Connie's letter while he looked out of the window at the hacks and trolleys rattling along the street, and at the heads of passing pedestrians. He felt annoyed with Abbie for getting herself involved with another man so soon after Angus' death. At the same time a stab of understanding of her loneliness went through him.

"But I'm not lonely," he said to himself. "I've got my business." But what did Abbie have? She had her child, of course. The child? Kit? He hesitated, then turned Connie's letter over and read it again. Connie was apt to make snap judgments or become hysterical, but if it were true that this man was after Abbie's money—the money that Angus had so carefully provided to safeguard the future of Abbie and the child—then he would have to go to Opportunity. Abbie was a woman and must follow her own course, but at least he must do all he could to see that Kit's future was secured as Angus had intended it to be. He sighed heavily and reached for a timetable.

"Molly," he called into the next room, "can you come in and take a letter?"

"Yes, Mr. McBain."

Molly came to the door with a pad and pencil in hand. She was tall and redheaded, made up a little too artfully. Douglas suspected that she was older than Plimpton and did not wish to appear so. Anyway, she was an excellent secretary.

"Molly, I'll give you a letter to Miss Constance Hedrick, 420 Willow Street, Opportunity, Idaho. And then I want you to get me a seat on the Opportunity train for tomorrow afternoon, and a reservation at the Pioneer Hotel in Opportunity for tomorrow night. I'll have to be out of town for a few days."

"Yes, Mr. McBain." She sat down and wrote the name and address he had given her very rapidly on her pad. Then she looked up expectantly, and he began to dictate:

"Dear Connie—In reply to your letter of yesterday, I shall be glad to come down and see what I can do. My influence, I fear, is small, but, in any case, it is time that I saw all of you again, and I shall be glad of this chance to do so.

172

"With best regards to your mother and yourself, I remain, yours truly, DOUGLAS MCBAIN."

"It's a nuisance," he said to Molly Casey, "but you'll have to cancel my engagements for the next few days, unless you can palm them off on Johnny or Sam."

"I'll see what I can do," Molly said.

11

Douglas found Abbie tight-lipped and pale. He did not meet Jack Yancy, because Jack had gone back to San Francisco to settle his affairs before the marriage. Abbie had sold the pink house where she and Angus had lived and was moving her things into a small rented house nearer the center of town.

"Abbie," he said, "is this wise? Are you sure this man is the right one for you?"

"Yes, I am sure," Abbie said. "Even if I were not sure, I should be driven into this by all the petty opposition that has been put in my way. I am sick and tired of meddling people who try to run my life for me. Sick and tired!" Her great dark eyes blazed. She was very handsome when she was angry, and Douglas saw that she was no longer the simple, pliant girl whom Angus had married. She was a woman in her prime, full of whims and passionate desires.

"*Everyone* is against me in this, and now you, too, Douglas! Honestly, I thought better of you. But I suppose that they have written you and asked you to come here to reason with me."

"It's simply that we don't want you to rush into a second marriage that might do you harm, Abbie. Only a few months ago you told me that no one could ever take Angus' place in your life. You said your life was ended."

"So I did," Abbie said. "So it was. That life *is* ended. But I'm young, Doug. I can't go on subsisting on memories. Is it wrong to want to build a new life out of the terrible loneliness?"

"No, Abbie, it isn't."

"Then why do people hound me? What's wrong with trying to be happy?"

173

"Nothing," Douglas said. "But are you snatching at happiness too soon? Is he the right man for you?"

"I see they have been at you," Abbie said. "They say he drinks; they say he hasn't any solid job. They say all sorts of half-true things. But, *yes*, he *is* the right man for me. I don't want another Angus. Forgive me, Doug. This time I want a man with his feet solidly on the earth instead of on the way to heaven. Jack belongs to this earth. He knows how to live on it and enjoy himself."

"I am sorry I can't meet him," Douglas said. "I'd like to form my own opinion."

"But why should your opinion have anything to do with me? I am the one who is marrying him. That's what drives me wild—the consummate nerve of all you people trying to live my life for me."

"We don't want you to be hurt."

"Oh, hurt!" she cried. "And how about you? Haven't you been hurt? Doesn't life hurt and batter us from all sides? But I couldn't expect you to understand. I used to think you were gayer and livelier than Angus—you and Mamie. I thought your life was so wonderful. But it must have been as dull as mine, or why would Mamie have gone and left you? Mamie knew something that none of the rest of us knew. She knew that life was short and going by every day with every tick of the clock, and she wanted to be happy. I'm just beginning to learn a few of the things that Mamie always knew."

Douglas stood silent, looking at the floor.

"I canna argue wi' you, Abbie," he said at last. He had fallen into the old Scotch brogue for very absence of mind.

Abbie was remorseful now, yet she was not prepared to give an inch.

"I'm sorry, Douglas, if I have offended you," she said. "Maybe I'm shouting out of a guilty conscience. But this is something I have to do. There's one thing, though—I'm glad you came for one reason. I'm helping to set Jack up in business here—he'll soon be doing well on his own, just as you and Angus did. But he'll need help at the start, and we want to build a nice house, a really nice one. I'm going to need quite a lot of the money you've been investing for us. It's my money, it's my affair—at least a part of it is my money. What I want you to do for me, Douglas, is to divide what Angus left us, and put aside some for Kit, in a separate

174

fund, for her education and expenses. Then if anything should happen to Jack and me—I want it arranged so that we cannot touch Kit's part. You understand, don't you, Douglas?"

"Yes, Abbie," Douglas said. "I understand."

And he thought that he not only understood Abbie's good intentions but also her secret doubts. This, after all, was what he had come to do, to see that Kit did not lose her financial security. He had not really expected to accomplish anything else. So they met several times in amity to arrange the details of the settlement. At the last of their meetings, Abbie said: "You've been very good to me, Douglas, and I appreciate it. And now I'm going to ask one more thing of you."

"Yes?"

"I want you to tell Kit that I'm marrying again."

"You've not told her?" he said incredulously.

"Douglas, she doesn't like Jack. It's jealousy, I suppose. He's been very nice to her. She knows we're moving to the new house, and she's unhappy about that. It's so odd. Children are so conservative. You'd think they'd be more open to change than older people. But Kit clings to the old pink house as if her life depended on it. I tried to tell her, but she looked at me so strangely, I couldn't make her understand. But she loves you, Doug. Make her see that she'll be getting a new father, someone she can love as she did Angus."

12

All through my life, I think, I have known things before people told me. I have seen the happy things coming and have been quiet and watchful, fearing to frighten them away. The bad things I have turned my back on and refused to anticipate, even though I knew they were coming—until I was told that they could no longer be avoided.

So I continued to live in the pink house, holding onto it fiercely and possessively, until all of the furniture was gone and there was no longer any possibility that I could stay. The pink house is still in my mind, sunny and serene, with the light coming warmly through the bits of stained glass about the round front window.

175

In memory I still sit on the white bearskin rug before the warm stove while the bright snow falls outside; or in fair weather I slide down the slanted cellar doors, or creep along the red-brick walk looking for ants among the spears of green grass that push up between the bricks.

One of the few memories of my father, that I did not sedulously purge, was of a happy time when I met him outside the picket fence as he came home from work. I had a piece of rope and I had been playing that the gatepost was my horse. But now I put the rope around his waist, and he galloped and pranced for me and allowed me to drive him up the brick walk to the front door.

The rented house near town, with my bed in a dark alcove, always remained dark for me. Even the fine big house that my mother later built, in which I had a pretty room of my own, remained for me a temporary abode rather than the sunny home that the pink house had been.

When Uncle Douglas told me that I was to have a new father, I was not surprised. But the telling made a fact of it and allowed me to communicate the fears that I had hidden.

"I don't want him," I said. "I hate him."

"It won't be long until you like him better than you like me," Uncle Douglas said. "Then I'll be jealous, but it will be best that way."

"No! No!" I cried. I flung myself into his arms and buried my face against his middle to hide my tears. The good clean odor of masculinity, of bay rum and woolen tweed and of my Uncle Douglas enveloped me in temporary security and reassurance. He patted my back and stroked my hair.

"All right, honey," he said. "It will be all right."

"No," I sobbed. "No. No."

"Yes," he said. "You are the one who can make it right. You will have to try, Kit. You will have to try. Meanwhile, you want Mama to be happy, don't you?"

I continued to hold him tightly about the waist, but my sobbing gradually ceased.

"Good Kit," he said, stroking my hair. "You are a good little girl, and Uncle Doug loves you." After a time he said, "Let's walk downtown together and get an ice-cream soda."

Soon I was skipping along beside him on the way to the ice-cream parlor. But just beyond my present happiness was a cloud that waited to bring darkness around me again when he had gone away.

It must be difficult for a man to love a former husband's child, especially if that child is silent and resentful.

My "Uncle Jack" and I never liked or trusted each other; and more and more, after the wedding, I walked up the hill to Grandma's house and let Aunt Connie solace me. I loved and respected my grandmother as much as ever, but she would not pity me.

"What's done is done," she said. "Now you must learn to get along with him."

But Aunt Connie hated Uncle Jack as much as I did, and she gave me all her support and sympathy. Although her sympathy was biased and perhaps unjust, I can never regret this, for I needed love and support so desperately at this time in my life that I am grateful for what she gave me. Possibly I could not have survived without her help, for I fell a prey to every stray germ in those days, and was always being pulled through chickenpox or scarlet fever or some other childhood malady. Often when I awoke in the night with an aching ear or a hoarse cough, it was Aunt Connie who was there to smooth the pillow and envelop me in a flood of friendly words while I gagged down the bitter medicine from the tilted spoon. I was glad when she was there.

13

Douglas' life settled into a new pattern of activity and accomplishment which shut out loneliness and regret. He particularly enjoyed the country driving, his eyes busy with the promising contours of the land, his mind concerned with making money from it. He looked at the wooded country with the eyes of a lumberman, and he felt no sentiment against felling the trees. If he remembered the old tales about the vanished forests of Caithness, they did not deter him in his eagerness to turn timber into money.

He bought up old mines that seemed to be exhausted and sent

in young men with modern equipment to see what could be done with them. Some of the old mines cost him money and brought no return, but the Four Leaf Clover Copper Mine came back handsomely and more than made up for all the other losses.

He liked to envision money in any kind of land. He looked at the arid stretches of sagebrush country in central Washington, and thought that if water could be brought to them they would become a garden.

"Lord, man," Johnny Buxton said, "with all the bonnie acres lying idle in good country, why concern yourself wi' sagebrush and sand? Have a little reason, for God's sake."

"But this comes cheap now, Johnny, and the river is not many miles away. Someday they'll get a dam on it, and ditches will bring down water to all these dismal acres. There's power and health in good water—and wealth, too."

So he began to buy seemingly worthless land. He invested some of the money that Angus had left for me in a wheat farm that lay at the edge of the dry belt. The land had no buildings on it, and it was leased for a percentage of the crop to a farmer who owned adjacent land. Because of the dryness, the land lay in summer fallow one year and was cropped the next. This brought in a modest but secure income. With the other money that had been settled in my name, he bought and sold more freely, building a fund for my future security.

It was about this time that he granted Mamie her divorce. A divorce was simple to obtain. Mamie's lawyer wrote from Chicago asking for it, and Douglas granted it. But one thing bothered him.

"Willie," he said to his brother, "never mention the divorce to the folks in Scotland, will you?"

"Rest easy, lad," Willie said. "Do ye think I'd want to break the mither's heart?" Douglas wrote so seldom to Scotland that it was easy to maintain the fiction. A word or two at the end of the letter, "Mamie is well and sends her greeting," was all that was necessary.

One day when Douglas and Johnny were driving across a barren stretch of country, a blowing tumbleweed hurtled into the path of the horses and frightened them. They had been jogging on serenely and Douglas' hand had been slack on the reins. Now the horses suddenly bolted and the buggy careered along behind them and overturned in a dry ditch. Both men were flung out of the rig and Douglas found himself sitting at the side of the road with a sharp pain in his ankle. Johnny was unhurt, and he set out along the road to recover the horses or get help. He was gone a long time, and Douglas lay for a while by the roadside looking up at the vast blue sky. Presently he sat up again and began to work with his ankle. It was painful and beginning to swell, and he could feel with his fingers where one of the bones was broken. He took a firm grip with his fingers and pushed the broken bone back into place. He tore his shirt into strips and bound the ankle firmly. After he had sat a while longer and come to terms with the pain, he cut himself a stick and began to hobble along the road. Johnny met him on his return from the next farm and helped him into the wagon he had borrowed.

Later, when the small-town doctor looked at his ankle, he assured Douglas that he could not have set the bone better himself. But the ankle was always troublesome to Douglas, and he favored it very slightly in his walking.

I remember that in wet weather his limp was more pronounced and that sometimes, with a perverse kind of humor, he used to move his ankle so that we could hear a little grinding sound of misplaced bones moving against each other. This used to send Aunt Connie and me into fits of shuddering reproach that made him laugh at our discomfiture.

He was filling out now into a powerfully built man, and the interesting scars, incurred in trying to save an unfaithful wife, and the slight Byronic limp, added romantic interest to his handsome appearance. Women turned in the street to look after him. This must have been fuel to his growing sense of power.

14

Uncle Willie sometimes came to see us at this time. I still have a little coin purse of saddle leather with my initials tooled on it which he made for me. It was through him that I got my saddle pony. He knew of a small, gentle horse for sale, and although he could not afford to buy it for me he knew that my mother could.

"What in the world will she do with a horse, Willie?" my mother asked.

"She'll ride it, of course," said Uncle Willie. "The lassie needs to be out in the sunshine. She needs to have something of her own to love and tend. Let her have it, Abbie."

So, at an early age, I learned the joy the centaurs must have felt, to have a human mind and hands and four fleet hooves for galloping. As I grew older I sometimes spent whole days on horseback in the hills, and no one ever bothered me or worried if I did not return at a certain hour. Those were the happiest times of my childhood. Beauty, my little horse, was the dearest possession I ever had.

Later Uncle Willie brought me a puppy, which I named Beady because of his bright black eyes. Willie's own two hunting dogs had died of age and soft living. Aunt Connie had nursed them through their final hours, and mourned them when the ordeal was over. Now she and I devoted ourselves to the new puppy.

Uncle Jack would not have a dog in the house, and I was obliged to keep Willie's gift at my grandmother's. As far as Uncle Jack was concerned, a horse in the stable was one thing, but a dog on the neatly tiled hearth in the fine new living room was another.

I do not remember that Uncle Jack was a particularly neat man about his own person, but he keenly disapproved of untidiness in a dog or a child. One day, when I had spread my dolls and their clothes and furniture all around the living room in the new house, Uncle Jack entered in a rage and threw all my gear into the fireplace where the flames consumed it. One of the victims of this holocaust was a rag doll who had been my bedfellow since the days of the pink house. I was silent but I never forgot. On this occasion it was my mother who shed the tears, but it was she who soon forgot.

When Uncle Willie came into town, Grandma and Aunt Connie gave him dinner, and there was much laughing and talking. Connie's tongue ran twice as fast as ever, in a confused jumble of merriment and extravagance, and Willie told droll stories, usually at the expense of Scotsmen, and kept us all jolly.

"Do ye ken why Scotsmen winna smoke tobacco?"

180

"No, Willie. Why?"

"Because to buy it is expensive, an', if 'tis given them, they must pack their pipes so full, the pipes winna draw."

"Oh, Willie!" Connie would cry, "you're so funny! Tell us another."

"Weel, there was this Edinburgh woman who lay dying in Glasgow, an' she said to her husband, 'Jock, lad, I'll no rest easy if ye bury me in Glasgow. Promise me ye'll take my body to Edinburgh for burial.'

" ' 'Twill be expensive, lassie.'

" 'I ken, but promise me all the same.'

" 'Aye, lass, ye've been a gude wife to me,' said Jock. 'I promise I'll take ye to Edinburgh if ye canna rest in Glasgow. But I'll try ye in Glasgow first.' "

"Poor Willie," my mother used to say after he was gone, "he gets seedier and seedier. I don't know what he and Alma live on, with three growing boys and the harness business almost a thing of the past. He never was smart like Douglas and—Angus."

Now, when she spoke of Angus, I noticed a new tone in her voice. It was different from the tone she had used in her first bereavement; different from the tone she had used in the first days of her marriage to Uncle Jack. I felt the difference without understanding it.

"Well, Willie is a good man," Grandma said. "Smart or not, he's a good man. I always like to see him coming."

Douglas had offered Willie help on several occasions, but Willie would never accept it. "Out-at-elbow pride," Douglas called it, and let the matter rest. Now Douglas was putting everything he could get his hands on back into the business, and when at last Willie appealed to him for help he found himself embarrassed to give it.

In fact, the whole affair was embarrassing and unfortunate. The office had just been renovated and redecorated under Molly Casey's expert eye and at considerable expense. They were getting a better clientele and trying hard to encourage it. Douglas was very busy in his inner office, feeling, in spite of his pre-occupation with business affairs, the comfort of a fine new carpet under his feet. Molly had put a vase of flowers on his desk and it was reflected in the well-waxed surface of the wood.

Molly was becoming a dragon of propriety and watchfulness

in the office. She not only took excellent shorthand notes and did beautiful typing but also guarded her employers' time and interests with fierce possessiveness. She seemed to have enlarged her original devotion to Plimpton to include all three of them. She called them all by their first names and had a breezy self-importance that was sometimes trying. Douglas often thought that she assumed too much responsibility and familiarity, and yet it was all working out so smoothly that he had never tried to discourage her.

On this particular morning Johnny was out of the office on an inspection trip and Plimpton was at home with a chest cold. Douglas' desk was full of papers to be gone through, work he detested, and he had asked Molly to screen his visitors as well as she could.

In spite of this she came in at midmorning with a half-smile giving her mouth a sardonic twist.

"I've done my best, Douglas," she said, "but there's a very seedy clown out here who claims he knew you in Scotland. I can't get rid of him."

"I can't be bothered today, Molly," Douglas said. "Put him off, will you? Did he give his name?"

"No, sir, he said you'd be pleased to be surprised, but I must say I doubt it. His dusty boots are all over the new carpet."

"Put him off," Douglas said.

But presently Molly came back looking puzzled and a little chagrined.

"He says he's your brother, Douglas," she said, "and I'm not sure if he's a practical joker or not. You do have a brother, don't you?"

"Yes," said Douglas shortly. "Yes, I have. You'd better show him in." He was annoyed with both of them.

"Well, Willie," he said by way of greeting, "why couldn't you have given your name at once? Can't you grow up?"

The glad look on Willie's face faded. He was cleanly shaved but badly in need of a haircut. His jacket sleeves were frayed and he wore a blue shirt open at the throat. His boots were as dusty as Molly had described them. In a livery stable he would have looked a fine, carefree fellow, but on the new carpet under Douglas' and Molly's eyes, he was uncouth.

Molly went out, closing the door very softly.

182

"I'm sorry, Doug," said Willie humbly. "I was only tryin' to have a bit of fun. It's no so easy to come by a wee bit of fun these days. But happen I worked too hard at it."

Douglas pushed aside the deeds and mortgages in their blue paper covers, and rose. He went around the desk and held out his hand.

"Well, it's nice to see you, Willie," he said rather formally. "What brings you to Manitou City?"

Willie avoided the direct question. He looked about the office, still trying to shield himself in drollery, the only armor which seemed to him to be invulnerable.

"Ye've a verra tacky wee dump here, Douglas," he said. "My! My! I'm fair ashamed o' ye."

Douglas' day, which had been laid out to the minute, pressed upon him and destroyed the keen pleasure he used to feel at the sight of Willie's twinkling eye. He felt the urgency of coming appointments and Willie's backhanded compliment did not amuse him.

"We're satisfied with it," he said shortly. "Is there something I can do for you, Willie? You've caught me on a busy day. Tonight I'll be freer to talk old times. Where are you staying?"

"The fact is I'm not staying over the night," Willie said. "I'm takin' the afternoon train back. I'm tryin' to do all of my business in the one day. 'Sufficient unto the day is the evil thereof,' as they used to say in the Bible. But maybe you dinna read the Good Book these days any more than I do myself?"

"I'm not a great reader," Douglas said. "I never seem to find the time."

"Weel, I've the time, but I've pawned my Bible," said Willie with a last attempt at humor.

"Come to the point, Willie," Douglas said. "What do you want?"

"Och, man," Willie said, the twinkle gone from his eyes, "I need a wee loan to tide me over a rough time, lad. We've a new bairn and Alma's been ailing. There's been doctor's bills an' a hired girl in for the time Alma couldna do for us, and the shop in Carfax hasna brought in enough to keep us in groceries for the past month. I came up here with the thought to find some opening for a leather worker. 'Tis a grand enough place here, but I've been up and down the street, all the addresses I had in

183

hand, and there's no a job to be had. It troubles me to ask for help. But 'tis only to tide me over, for a wee, small time, laddie."

"How much do you need, Willie?"

"That's no for me to say, Doug. It's what ye can spare, man."

"Well," Douglas said impatiently, "do you want a hundred dollars? two hundred? What do you need?"

Relief flooded Willie's face.

"Two hundred would tide us over," he said. "Och, yes. It canna be this bad much longer."

"I'd make it more but I'm pressed myself now," Douglas said. "Why don't you sell the place in Carfax, Willie? I'll give you a big piece of land out in the sagebrush country. I'll give it to you for nothing. I got it for a song myself. It's pretty dreary, but if ever they get water on it, it will be bonnie country. The place I have in mind has a well on it, so you and your animals won't perish of thirst, and there's feed enough on the land itself for some sheep. You could buy the sheep with what you got out of the Carfax place. With four boys coming along you'll have plenty of manpower in a few years. Or is the newest one a lassie?"

"Na," said Willie, beginning to twinkle again. "Alma and me, we havena learnt the trick o' makin' lassies."

Douglas sent Molly out to the bank to get the two hundred dollars in cash for Willie. He did not urge more money on Willie, although, if he had probed his conscience he might have known that more would have been welcome.

When Willie had gone he found it hard to settle down to work again. To make matters worse, Molly came in then and stood beside his desk as if she wanted to say something to him. He did not feel like facing her just now, but she began to speak in a penitent tone.

"Oh, Douglas, I'm sorry—being so flip about him and all. I didn't know, truly I didn't know, and he never told me he was your brother."

"That was his fault, of course," Douglas said. "You did the best you could."

"But I called him a clown, a seedy clown. I'm so sorry." She had lost her Irish humor in self-abasement.

"For heaven's sake," Douglas said, "don't be ridiculous, Molly. The fault was completely his."

184

"Then you don't blame me? You can forgive me, Douglas?"

Molly had recently begun to wear glasses at her work. Usually she removed them with a casual smile when in conversation, but now she had forgotten to remove them and they greatly exaggerated the size of her eyes, the tears which swam in them, and the ugly smear of greasy eye shadow which trembled on her lashes. The look in her eyes suddenly made him think of Connie Hedrick. He was always bored and annoyed by the adoration of plain women. It had never occurred to him that Molly's hardheaded usefulness in the office could be impaired by extraneous sentiment.

He got up and patted her awkwardly on the shoulder.

"Think no more of it, Molly," he said as kindly as he could. "There was never anything to forgive. Now, you know how much we've got to do today. Let's get at it, shall we, Molly?"

"Yes, Douglas," she said in a subdued voice, "and thank you, oh, thank you!"

15

Jack Yancy was a joiner: the Elks, the Woodmen of the World, the Gay Blades Dinner Club—everything in town but the Presbyterian church. Yet Opportunity did not warm to him. It was a small, conservative community, and it remembered Angus better than his widow seemed to.

One day when I went along Main Street after school, an elderly man whose name I did not know came to the door of his office and said, "You're Angus McBain's little girl, aren't you?"

"Yes," I said.

"Here," he said, "I thought you might like these for school." He gave me a pile of blotters with his firm's name printed on them.

"Thank you," I said.

"And there's another thing," he said. "I just wanted to tell you that I used to know your father. Maybe other people have told you this, but I wanted to say it to you myself—that your father was the best man who ever lived in Opportunity; the best man."

I did not know what to say, and I walked on in silence, holding the blotters out in front of me. Yet I have never forgotten this.

My mother set Jack up in a well-appointed office to take over in business where my father had left off. She was naïve in her belief that this could be done. Even if he had possessed the ability and the will for hard work, I am sure that Jack Yancy would have found the going difficult in Opportunity. Most of his business was done with lumber companies outside the town, and much of the profit was consumed by trips to Manitou City or the entertainment of business associates from out of town. He and my mother gave gay parties for these out-of-town visitors and for the faster crowd in Opportunity. The conservative people were either not invited or, more likely, would not come. Connie and Grandma were not often included in these entertainments, and I would be sent to stay with them, so that the ladies could leave their wraps on my bed and so that my sleep would not be disturbed. When I returned in the morning the glamour of the evening before had vanished. My mother was washing glasses and cleaning up stains from the carpet, while Uncle Jack, unshaven and puffed about the eyes, made profane and angry comments on any subject that was introduced. Sometimes he did not go to work on the day following the party but stayed in bed with what my mother charitably called a cold.

About that time Uncle Jack's sister came to visit us. She brought no lemon pies, but she had a very large collection of luggage for a woman on a short visit. Mama gave her my room and put me in the little room which had been intended for a maid. They had never become successful enough to afford the maid, and so the little room was unoccupied. I do not remember that I was offended by this transfer, although it soon seemed likely that it was to become permanent. From the little room I could look across the roofs to Grandma's house, which seemed much nearer than it had from the larger room. "Aunt Chadwick," I was instructed to call Jack's sister. I grew used to the sound of her nasal voice telling us what Jack enjoyed eating and how it was best cooked. Gradually she took things over in the kitchen, and my mother went back to her piano.

In the morning she played bright scales and intricate finger exercises. In the afternoon there were polonaises and boleros and Hungarian rhapsodies that filled the house and the yard with

186

wild, gay music. In the evening when Uncle Jack was at home there was no music. But when he was out, as he more and more often was, there was music again. I heard it in my small room at the back of the upper floor when I was supposed to be asleep. And now in the evening it was "Valse Triste," or Chopin's "Funeral March," or something reeking with fate and sadness. A piano, played at night at a little distance, always fills me with sorrow. My reaction goes back, I am sure, to this period in my life when I knew instinctively that my mother was unhappy, and when I was not very happy myself.

I did not know exactly what was wrong. Sometimes I caught Aunt Connie and Grandma talking together about my mother and Uncle Jack, but they always began to speak brightly of the weather or the canary or the dog when they realized that I was there. Once I heard Grandma say, "Well, sometimes I think it's six of one and half a dozen of the other." I knew what the saying meant and I knew they were talking of Mama and Uncle Jack.

"No, it's not!" Aunt Connie cried. "It's all on his side, all of it!" Then they saw me and spoke quickly of something else. This puzzled me very much, and often it still does, for my grandmother was a very fair woman. She liked to speak in maxims and clichés, and, as she would have said, she prided herself "on giving the devil his due." So I have thought that my mother must have been at fault too, although it seemed to me, as it did to Connie, that all the provocation was on Jack Yancy's side.

I remember one day coming in from play with a bunch of pansies for my mother. The piano was silent and she was not in the kitchen or the living room. I ran upstairs and opened the door to her bedroom. She was lying on her bed sobbing and shaking all over as if she were terribly cold. Aunt Chadwick leaned over her, pulling a quilt up around her shoulders. My mother did not look up when I came in, but Aunt Chadwick said sharply: "Go away, now. Can't you see your mother is ill? Run along now, like a good child."

On another occasion I heard my mother and Uncle Jack quarreling at night. Experience had taught me that his loud, unsteady voice, full of ugly profanity, meant that he had been drinking too much. I heard him go stumbling down the stairs and out the front door, banging it loudly behind him. There was the sound of Aunt Chadwick's nasal voice, as if she were sympa-

187

thizing or trying to smooth things over. Then I heard her go back into my old bedroom and shut the door.

I must have dozed off to sleep then, for the next thing I knew my mother was shaking me and telling me to wake up and to be very quiet. She was breathing heavily and she was in some kind of desperate hurry. She did not stop to put on my shoes and stockings, but wrapped me in a blanket and took me up in her arms to carry me. She was not a large woman and I was large for my age. I remember still how insecure I felt in her arms and that I did not want to be carried. But it was early spring, the night was cold and dark and my feet were bare. She carried me down the stairs and out into the night.

"Where are we going, Mama?" I asked. My teeth were chattering and I was cold and surprised.

"We're going to Grandma's," she said. Halfway up the hill she had to stop and sit on the steps at someone's gateway to catch her breath. I could hear how she was panting and sobbing in a very painful way.

"I can walk, Mama," I said.

"No, no," she said. "Your feet are bare. You will catch cold."

"Why must we go?" I asked.

"I'm afraid," she said.

Her fear went through me, too, like a cold wind. I remember the blackness of the night, the haste and the terror. I no longer have any recollection of what happened after we were safe at Grandma's, but I shall never forget the moments when we sat on a strange doorstep in the darkness and were afraid.

But the next day she went home again, and things seemed to be as they had been before. Summer came and vacation from school. I rode my horse and played in the back yard.

On one of these days when I was playing in the back yard I had made dolls out of hollyhocks turned upside down; and I was making houses for them by digging caves in a clay bank at the back of the lot. Uncle Jack had been away for several days and the house was quiet. I did not hear the piano or Mama and Aunt Chadwick talking in the kitchen. I was happy in the sunshine and absorbed in my play, when I heard a sound from the house that was like a muffled cry. There was the banging of an upstairs door, and then someone was grinding the crank on the side of the telephone and I heard Aunt Chadwick's voice calling for the doctor.

I got up slowly, dropping the red and pink hollyhock ladies one by one as I began to walk toward the house. Aunt Chadwick met me at the back door. Her face was white with mottled splotches of grayish purple on her cheeks. Her lips were quite pale and her eyes looked very strange.

"Run for your grandma, Kit," she said. "Run as fast as you can. Your mama's taken too much of the wrong kind of medicine. She's very sick. Go quick, Kit."

None of the small-town methods of that day could save my mother, and yet it took her two days to die. Uncle Jack did not come back and Aunt Chadwick began at once to pack. Connie came upon her in the kitchen packing a silver teapot into her handbag even before my mother had breathed her last.

"That's not yours," Connie cried.

"It was a wedding present," Jack's sister said defensively.

"I think we've paid for that wedding and everything connected with it," Connie said. "We've paid many times. Leave the teapot on the shelf."

On the nightstand beside my mother's bed there was an empty medicine bottle and a hastily scrawled note on a scrap of paper. The note did not tell us why she had done what she had done. It did not speak to those of us who were left with love or concern for our future. All it said was, "Carve Abbie McBain on my headstone."

So the Yancys went out of our lives, and it soon became apparent that there was nothing left of my father's small fortune but the house and its furnishings and the money Douglas had invested for me.

16

My mother's last days and the time before the funeral were very strange. People were too busy to pay much attention to me, and since I really did not want their attention anyway, I kept as much as possible out of the way and to myself. I went on digging my caves, but I did not pick any more hollyhocks. The hollyhocks were so beautiful when they were freshly picked, like rumpled red and pink silk, but then they began to wilt and lose color and die. I did not want to cause the death of a flower.

When they began to notice me again, the relatives and friends were dismayed. A cold and quiet little girl was going on with her play as if nothing had happened. They could not understand it. There, dry eyed and grim, I moved among the weeping relatives, knowing that they were watching me and clicking their tongues. It was only in this way that I was able to pull what shreds of resolution I had left about my naked wretchedness.

When Uncle Douglas came he brought me a small black and white plaster sow with three tiny pigs. I do not think it was a toy, but some sort of agricultural model, carefully made to scale, a Poland China family to the life. Later, when one of the sow's legs broke, I found that the plaster had been formed around pliant wires. The four small pigs had nothing to do with my catastrophe. I was glad to have them. I felt more love than ever for my Uncle Douglas.

Aunt Connie lifted up her red and swollen face to him, and her eyes adored him, too. He was grave and kind, and the grownups took him into the parlor to tell him all the things they thought I did not know. They need not have closed the door, because I did not want to hear. I took my pigs into the back yard and made them a little pen under the cherry tree. Later, when I came in, the grownups were still talking. I stood outside the door and I knew that they were speaking of me.

"If she would only cry!" Aunt Connie said. "It's like she was made of stone."

I went away again.

I had wanted to see my mother for the last time, but they decided against it. I think it was Aunt Connie who decided, but she left it to Uncle Doug to tell me.

I used to like to sit out on the cement mounting block by the hitching post in front of my grandmother's gate. On the day before the funeral, I was sitting there at sunset time watching the red clouds when Uncle Doug came up beside me and told me.

"Remember her as she was when she was living," he said. "That will be better."

190

"All right," I said tonelessly. But I was angry that they were making all these decisions for me.

"Kit," Uncle Doug said, "this is all very hard for you. If there is anything I can do—"

"No one can do anything," I said angrily. "And they want me to cry. That is what they want. I can't cry. I don't want to cry."

"You don't have to cry," Uncle Doug said. "Believe me, Kit, you don't have to cry."

He put his hand on my shoulder and I did not twist away. We were together there watching the sunset. The great lump of trouble that lay so heavily in my narrow chest grew easier.

17

While Uncle Douglas was in Opportunity it was arranged that we should go to Manitou City to live with him.

"I'm tired of hotel living," he said to Grandma. "I'll get a nice house and pay the rent on it. You and Connie and Kit can move your things in and keep the house and cook my meals for me. It will be a wonderful thing for me to have a family. This eating around in all kinds of restaurants has given me dyspepsia. I need you more than you need me."

I am sure that this was never true, but we all fostered the pleasant fiction. Out of our loneliness and despair, there bloomed a lovely hope. Aunt Connie, in particular, rose from the depths of bitter grieving to a lighthearted buoyancy of preparation. Grandma had seen too many reversals in her life to allow herself the luxury of exaggerated anticipation; and, even at the age of eight years, I was beginning to share her caution. Yet, when it became plain that Uncle Douglas was going to have my horse, Beauty, and my dog, Beady, sent with us to Manitou City I began to skip again and laugh in the sunshine.

I had my troubles that fall and winter in adjusting to a new school in a large city. Everything was strange and frightening to me in the big red-brick building with its swarms of unknown children. Yet I think now, it was a wonder that I adjusted as well as I did, and that the blows I had received left no greater scars.

191

At first I had a recurring dream that I had been obliged to stay after school, and when I tried to leave the building, I found that everyone else had gone and that the great building was locked and I was imprisoned for the night inside it. I never told my dream to anyone, but in my waking hours I planned how, if such a thing ever happened, I would manage to endure the night. I had seen a cot in the basement where the janitor sometimes slept near the great, terrifying furnace. But the furnace would be warm. I would lie there on the cot and I would not allow myself to become panicky. In the lockers I might find an apple or a discarded sandwich and these would keep me from starvation. I could survive alone. Lonely survival—in a sense that is what my life had become for me.

Yet, aside from the gradually diminishing terrors of school, my life now began to change in a surprising way. It began to contain happinesses which I had never known before.

18

Connie did not bring her violin to Manitou City. Her pupils had never been many or gifted, and her own performance on the instrument was lamentable. It had been a weak and futile attempt at flying in the face of her father and at having a respectable career of her own. Now that her poor papa was gone, she still found herself bound by his strong convictions. She was free to go into nursing, but her father had spoiled it for her. Besides, she felt that she must look after Kit now and take care of Mama in her declining years. Talking had taken the place of doing with Connie—it had become a habit to exhaust her unsatisfied energies in vigorous conversation.

But she was a good housekeeper and an excellent cook. She had learned her skills from her mother, and the two of them worked well and happily together in the kitchen and around the house. They had not gone out a great deal in Opportunity, so they did not mind being transplanted into a new environment where the social advantages were few.

Douglas had a social world of his own in Manitou City to which he never introduced them. They seemed not to resent this.

192

For them the great happiness of life in Manitou City was that a man came home every day, praising their meals, telling them what went on at the office, keeping them in touch with the world.

They had not had a man in the house since Dr. Hedrick's death, and often he had been difficult to get along with—particularly for Connie. Now Douglas came in laughing and making jokes. He brought home presents; he praised their roasts and pies. Sometimes he took us all driving on Sunday, if he was not otherwise engaged. Sometimes he took us to see a play at the Stock Company Theater.

It was a wonderful arrangement for everybody. Douglas was happy because he had missed a home for a long time, and because the family did not curtail his freedom by making demands on him. If he found himself a trifle less free than he had been in a hotel, the advantages more than compensated.

As I look back now I realize more than I ever did at the time how much this whole arrangement was planned about me. There were many complicated strands involved, but central to everything must have been the desire to give a lone child a normal and secure illusion of home, with women in the kitchen and a man coming home at evening. Perhaps the test of how well they managed it was that I never thought of it as being contrived. I felt more comfortable, beloved, and secure than I had felt since my father had become ill in the pink house in Opportunity. This was our home and I was a cherished part of it.

I do not remember that I was ill at all in Manitou City. I ate well and played heartily and gradually made friends of my own age. Connie sang as she worked and Grandma whistled.

The house that my Uncle Douglas rented for us was roomy and pleasantly situated in a good residential district. At the back of the lot was a stable for Beauty. They did not let me ride or drive far alone in the city, as I had done in the small town when my mother was in charge. But Aunt Connie or Uncle Doug often went with me for long drives, and I did not miss the extensive liberty I had had, a liberty which may indeed have been too much and too lonely for a little girl. The cart we had for Beauty was small and only one person ever rode with me. In fact, it was one of our amusements to see Uncle Doug telescope his large frame into the small rig behind the little horse.

"Some day," he used to say, "I'll get between the shafts and let Beauty ride." This always made me laugh, no matter how many times he said it. Whatever he said was amusing and precious to me. In the morning at breakfast, if there was a jar of honey on the table, he used to look at me very gravely and say, "Pass the honey, honey." This used to seem so amusing to me that I would burst out laughing. It has come through life with me as a very great joke. I used to repeat it to my own children until their blank looks informed me that it had no real intrinsic humor. But Uncle Douglas had made it up for me, and I remember it.

Uncle Douglas was proud of my appearance, and he did not entirely trust Connie in the selection of my clothing. All of Connie's life as a dependent had trained her in economy, and when Douglas wished her to be extravagant in the matter of my dresses, she inclined toward ruffles and bows and garish colors. I remember that once when I was dressed too fussily for him, instead of complaining to Connie or Grandma, he said to me, "Next time we'll tone you down a little, honey. I'm going to buy you some dresses myself." So then he brought home, in the gaily flowered boxes of expensive shops, the artfully simple frocks of wealthy children. I am not sure that Connie ever saw the difference or understood why Douglas took over the purchasing of my clothing.

"He's simply crazy about our little Kit," she said, "even to buying her dresses. It's dear of him, but so odd."

One gift that he brought me troubled me a little, but it filled Connie with joy, and without ever saying as much in words, I relinquished it to her. This gift was Dickie, the canary bird. Uncle Doug came home carrying the cage proudly and set it on the table, calling "Kit! Kit! Look what I've got for you."

I was devoted to dogs and horses and, probably because of my lonely condition, I felt a strong bond between myself and animals. I loved birds in trees and chipmunks on fences.

I cried out in delight, when I saw Dickie in his cage, and I gave Uncle Doug the usual hugs and kisses of happy acceptance. But the more I saw of Dickie, the less I cared for him. He fluttered about the cage and screamed in distress when I came near him. When no one was close to him, he sang stridently and ambitiously like a prima donna in a music hall. He had to be fed and cleaned and given water everyday. I saw that he belonged

194

in the trees and not in this dreadfully exposed and tiny prison. And he was alone here, like a child without brothers or sisters. I began to feel so guilty about him that I could scarcely bring myself to feed and tend him. He became a blind spot for me, like the dreadful blind spot I had for the piano, a thing that had to be practiced upon but could never, never be enjoyed. The piano continued to torture me, but now Connie took over the canary bird and loved and tended him and whistled and chirped to him. Finally he would allow her to come near him without having a crisis of nerves. She did not seem to mind that he was caged; in fact, I sometimes thought that his terrible plight endeared him to her.

But, although the gifts that Uncle Douglas gave me were many and delightful, I was not a completely mercenary child. I loved him best for the times he took me on his lap in the big Morris chair, and told me about Scotland or sang or recited verses to me.

Some of the nursery rhymes that Connie had taught me became more delightful to me when recited in a Scotch brogue.

"'Wee Willie Winkie rins through the toon,
Oopstairs an' doonstairs in his nicht goon,
Tirlin' at the window, cryin' at the lock,
Are the weans in their beds, for noo 'tis ten o'clock?'"

Not very different, but wonderful in Uncle Doug's voice that rumbled in his deep chest beneath my listening ear. So I lay back, drowsy and happy against his breast, and heard him sing,

"'Oh, ye'll tak' the high road
An' I'll tak' the low road.
An' I'll be in Scotland afore ye,'"

even as my father had used to sing it.

19

Aunt Connie's hopes must have been very great when she came to Manitou City. A man in the house is worth two in the bush, and marriage must have seemed only a step away. She sang and laughed around the house. When she remembered, she even tried to bridle her tongue, but she did not often remember.

Soon after we were settled Uncle Douglas began bringing Johnny Buxton around to the house. Johnny greatly relished the home-cooked meals, but Connie saw to it that he got the smallest pieces of pie and the less succulent portions of meat. She was hardly civil to him.

"Connie," Douglas said, "you ought to be nicer to Johnny. He's looking for a wife now, and he's going to be a very rich man one of these days."

"I don't care," Connie said, tossing her head. "He has disgusting table manners. All he talks is business. He makes horrible noises with his soup. Besides, I simply don't like him."

"Did you ever hear about the man who went into the woods looking for a straight stick?" asked Grandma. "He went all through the woods looking, and he picked up a crooked stick at last."

"Yes, I've heard," cried Connie. "I've heard that story many times and if I never hear it again I'll be just as glad. And I'd rather come out of the woods with no stick at all than Johnny Buxton."

Douglas sat back laughing at her. "Well, don't say I haven't done my best for you," he said.

"Oh, you're impossible!" Connie cried, but her eyes were soft as she said it.

A few months later Johnny married a small, plump woman, somewhat older than he was. But they had both come from Glasgow and she made excellent scones. Through all the vicissitudes of Johnny's later business life, it was a permanent and happy marriage.

Occasionally Douglas brought Sam Plimpton home with him to dinner also. Plimpton was developing into a very eligible young bachelor, good-looking and talkative. He seemed mildly interested in Connie at first, but unfortunately they both talked at the same time. It became a kind of unacknowledged contest to see who could talk the other down. When Connie had talked him into silence for the third time, Plimpton ceased to come to the house even for a good dinner.

The loyalties at the office had shifted very greatly since the partnership had first been formed. Plimpton and Molly were now

196

on a very formal basis. She took dictation from him in a dignified dudgeon, and made more embarrassing mistakes in the transcription of his letters than in the others. He treated her with offhand kindness and avoided being alone with her. If he realized that she had been very good for him at one time, he now saw that she was too old and too lacking in social position to do him any good as a wife.

He was receiving invitations to all of the debutante and charity balls now, and he realized that the city was full of charming young girls with wealthy fathers who could be very useful to him in a business way. He had outgrown the help of plain and unimportant women like Molly, and Connie Hedrick.

Douglas felt sorry for Molly. That was the chink in his armor, feeling sorry for people. But it was only a chink, and he did not let it get him into serious trouble.

He found Molly weeping over her typewriter one day when she thought herself alone in the office. Instead of walking by as if he did not see her, he went up and put a friendly hand on her shoulder.

"Come on, old girl," he said. "What's the trouble anyway? Get it off your chest, Molly. I'm a good father confessor."

"Oh, Douglas," she sobbed, "I haven't gone to confession for years. Maybe that's what's the trouble. But there's too much to tell and it's all working out the wrong way."

"Sam's disappointed you, hasn't he, Molly? You thought you had him, and he's given you the slip."

"Yes, it's true, but I've seen it coming a long time. I've known it all along really, and I guess it's my pride more than my affections that hurts now."

"You did a lot for him, I know," Douglas said. "But it doesn't look as if you ever had any real strings on him, Molly. You should have pinned him down when he first fell for you. Married him when he was in the mood."

"That's easy to say, Doug. But neither of us had any money then and we thought we'd go up together. Only, you know, a man can go faster than a woman. Still, I'm glad we aren't tied up now. We've both changed our minds, I guess. But it's hard to see him dancing around with rich young girls and me still clicking the keys of a typewriter. I guess that's what makes me mad."

197

"He's looking for someone higher up the social ladder, Molly," Douglas said.

"I know," she said, "but it didn't have to be that way. Out here in the West people don't go asking into every woman's background. My sister Sheila has done all right for herself. Of course, she's younger and prettier than I am, but she's always played it smarter than I have. Her boss was an old rich fellow instead of a young one. She married him after his wife died. She even had a son for him, and now she's a rich widow and still pretty enough to attract a man her own age. Nobody asked about *her* social background. Some women have the luck."

"You'll have it, too, some day," Douglas said kindly, patting her shoulder. He doubted if she would, but he could not help feeling sorry for her. And now he wanted to terminate the scene and get on to his work. But Molly embarrassed him by catching his hand and pressing it to her cheek.

"Oh, Douglas! Douglas!" she said. The tears streaked unattractively down her cheeks. "You are very good to me."

"Forget it now, Molly," he said. "You've got a lot of letters on your desk. Better get at them."

20

Christmas that year was one I shall always remember. The smell of the balsam tree filled the house, and Connie and I made strings of popcorn and cranberries for it. Uncle Doug saw to the placing of the candles, for he had a fear of fire, and although he liked to take chances, he surrounded his chances with a sensible precaution. When he came home in the evening on the days preceding Christmas, he was loaded with mysterious packages which he hustled in to his bedroom closet. On his closet door appeared a notice which said:

> *Miss Christine McBain, keep out.*
> *Bogles at work.*

"What are bogles, Uncle Doug?" I cried in delighted expectation.

198

"Bogles?" he repeated. "Do ye no ken bogles, lassie? I thocht ye was a Scottish bairn."

"Oh, I am, Uncle Doug, but I dinna ken bogles. What are bogles, Uncle Doug?"

"Spirits, lassie, and not the kind that come out of a bottle, neither. But ask me no more aboot bogles, Kit. They dinna like to be mentioned. If there's too much talk about bogles they're like to take offense and turn haggis an' crowdy into stanes an' peat ash. Let's hae nae mair haverin' an' claverin' aboot bogles."

"Oh, be careful then. Be careful," I cried. "You said it again, Uncle Doug."

"Whisht!" he said, laying his finger on his lips.

But he took me into his confidence about the beautiful Edison phonograph with the blue morning-glory shaped horn. This was for Grandma and Connie, and he would not have been able to smuggle it into the house without my delighted complicity.

Every month from my own money, Douglas made me a small allowance so that I should feel independent and learn the value of money. I saved it for October, November, and December that year, and bought a muffler for Uncle Doug, a lace-trimmed handkerchief for Connie and a pair of bed socks for Grandma. At the last moment, I realized that I had purchased nothing for Beady and Beauty, and my money was nearly all used up.

So on Christmas Eve Uncle Douglas took me out to the shops, and we purchased a half-pound of cube sugar for Beauty, and for five cents the butcher gave us a very large soup bone for Beady. At the same time we picked up the handsome big turkey Uncle Doug had ordered. Grandma had already prepared the stuffing, and the week before had made her annual plum pudding. Connie was in charge of vegetables and relishes and pumpkin pies.

Now, besides the scent of balsam, there was the tantalizing odor of Christmas cookery.

Before bedtime I put the presents I had purchased under the magic tree. Then I wrapped Beady's bone and hung it on one of the branches. Beady sniffed the air with great interest. Grandma, who was celebrated in the family as a trainer of dogs and horses, had taught Beady to watch but not to touch until he was given permission to do so.

"Watch, Beady!" I said, holding up an admonishing finger.

199

Like the knight before the altar in the old tale, poor Beady spent the dark hours in solitary vigil beside the Christmas tree. When I came down in the morning he was still sitting there, hopefully savoring the increasing ripeness of the butcher's bone. I was merciful enough to take it off the tree and let him have it in the back yard before plunging into the splendors of my own Christmas.

This was *the* Christmas of my childhood. Other Christmases have faded from my memory or they are colored with loneliness or sadness; but this one remains with me, complete and joyful. There were games and books, which I loved, and a wonderful box of water colors, and there were dolls. I was a big girl but I still enjoyed dolls. The dolls, like Beady and Beauty, gave me an illusion of family. They were creatures which belonged to me.

Grandma and Aunt Connie gave me a baby doll for which Aunt Connie had made a complete layette even to the small crocheted booties. Uncle Douglas gave me a boy doll in a plaid kilt and velvet bonnet, a bonnie Scotsman.

The candles shone and sparkled on the tree, more lovely than any electric lights I have seen since. This, I suppose, was because they were ephemeral and dangerous. The Edison phonograph played "Liebestraum" and "Uncle Josh at the County Fair," and the "Sextet" from *Lucia*.

While I was setting the table for dinner and Connie and Grandma were bustling about the kitchen, Uncle Doug put on the record of "The Beautiful Blue Danube," and tried to get Connie to dance with him. They took three laughing turns around the kitchen and then Connie cried, "The gravy's burning!" and ran away from him. So then he took me around the waist and we whirled dizzily about the dining table for a few moments, until his ankle gave out, and he sat down laughing in the big chair by the fireplace.

Then the doorbell rang and Molly Casey came in carrying a fruitcake she had made. It was all wrapped up with a sprig of holly tied with red ribbon on top of the package.

I think it was Grandma who had suggested that we ask Molly to dinner, because she must be lonely. I had seen her sometimes at the office when I had gone there with Uncle Douglas, and I had never thought much about her in her plain office clothes. But today she had got herself up like a fashion plate, in an

200

expensive green suit with a red hat and red shoes and a bobbet of artificial cherries on her lapel. Even I thought that the red hat did nothing for her bright auburn hair, which was frizzled and curled in a fine confusion of ringlets.

"My God, Molly, what have you done to yourself?" Uncle Douglas cried. But she looked so piteous at that, that he added hastily, "Why, you're a Christmas dream, Molly. You're as bonnie as Erin go bragh."

Connie came from the kitchen in a gingham apron with perspiration on her upper lip and her hair straggling down at the back from the whirl to the music of "The Blue Danube." She and Molly looked at one another for the first time as Douglas made an awkward introduction.

"Connie, this is Molly Casey, the best secretary a man ever had. And Molly, this is Connie Hedrick, the world's best cook. Shake hands. You're going to be friends."

They had heard a great deal about each other, and they were already disposed toward suspicion and dislike. Now, with Doug's words echoing in her ears, Connie saw a woman in an expensive suit and hat which she knew she could have chosen with better taste, had she been able to afford them—a woman who spent every day in the same office with Douglas, doing everything for him with a secretary's skill and care.

In her turn, Molly looked at Connie and saw a woman younger and better-looking than herself, without make-up, one securely intrenched in Douglas' kitchen, almost as intimately a part of his life as a wife would be. They took an instant dislike to one another, and a fraction of the innocent pleasure vanished from the day for all of us.

Still it was an excellent dinner. Douglas joked and teased and praised and cajoled, while Grandma radiated an aura of substantial good sense, and all of us overate.

When the meal was over Molly rose and said, "Well, I know it's not nice to eat and run, but I've got to go along to another engagement."

"For goodness sake!" Connie cried. "I thought you were going to stay the afternoon and listen to all the Edison records. What's your great hurry?"

"Well, I'd like to stay and help you with the dishes," Molly said. "But my sister Sheila is coming in town tonight with her

201

boy, and I'm going to meet them at the station and take them to the hotel. She's engaged the best suite in the hotel, my sister has. My sister's a really wealthy widow—her husband left her very well fixed, if you know what I mean, and the best is none too good for her. Some time I'll have you over to meet her, if she's not too busy."

"I have nothing in common with rich people," Connie said. "I find that the simple pleasures of life suit me far the best. And, as for the dishes, I wouldn't think of letting you touch them, anyway, in all your fine clothes. It might spoil your hands for the typewriter."

Douglas looked from one to the other in puzzled surprise.

"You girls are going to be the greatest friends," he repeated. "You must get together oftener." But somehow the ring of confidence had gone out of his voice.

"It's been a lovely party," Molly said. "I thank you all so much."

"We've enjoyed having you," Connie said, "and thank you for the fruitcake. We'll put it away and let it age. That's the best thing to do with a fruitcake, as you know. It's so nice you can cook as well as type, isn't it?"

"I think so, too," Molly said. "But how did you know, since you do not type?"

I could see a tart reply rising to Connie's lips, but Grandma stepped between them and took Molly's hand.

"It's been real nice to have you," she said. "Come again soon, my dear."

Douglas saw Molly to the door; when he came back Connie was in the midst of a tirade. "Her rich sister, the best suite in the hotel! And that suit and hat she wore, they must have cost all her month's wages! You'd think she'd have got something suitable, something that went better with her hair—or maybe she should have colored her hair a little less blatantly. She looks like a fast woman."

"Constance!" Grandma warned.

"Your tongue's off the rail again, Connie," Douglas said shortly. "She's a real good woman and I couldn't get along without her. You've no call to be hard on her."

"And *you* expect *us* to be friends!" said Connie haughtily.

"Well, you've a lot in common," Douglas said.

202

"Too much," said Connie cryptically. She tossed her head and went into the kitchen to do up the dishes. I followed her out and dried them for her. At first she would not talk but kept humming "Jesus, Lover of My Soul" off key, while the phonograph in the next room played "Auld Lang Syne." But after a while her good humor came back and she began to talk about Beady and the dolls and to tell me the story of The Princess and the Pea. This was a story she seemed to like, although I could not understand why a pea should be felt through so many mattresses or why it made any difference to anybody. I thought the princess was a snob.

But the good humor of the lovely day was restored. In the evening we lighted the stubby candles again and had cold turkey sandwiches, and I carried my baby doll and my Scotch doll up to bed with me, and all of my dreams were sweet.

21

Uncle Douglas liked to take me with him when he went out to places that were suitable for a child—even to some that were perhaps not so suitable. At night when he went out, I was snugly in bed; but I remember the matinees, the drives, the daytime visits to friends when I was dressed in my best and went proudly beside him.

"Get her some pretty clothes, Connie," he said. "Don't spare the expense, but get them in good taste. I want her to look nice."

He took me with him to the photographer, and I still have the picture of myself, rather pale and blond, dressed in a pretty plaid dress, leaning back against his shoulder. He looks so sturdy and prosperous and proud in the photograph, exactly as I remember him best.

At the time it all seemed natural and right to me. I never questioned how it was that I had found the father I had longed for. It did not seem odd to me that Connie and Grandma stayed at home when Uncle Doug and I went out. Only now does the oddness strike me. But I think he was afraid of Connie. One of Grandma's maxims was, "If you give her an inch, she'll take an ell," and this I am sure was one of Connie's faults. A kind word

203

set off a chain reaction of anticipation and hope and effusive response in Connie that knew no proper bounds. By the uninhibited flow of her compulsive talking she dominated any group she was in; she brought the conversation down to her level and resolutely kept it there.

If Douglas had taken Connie with him into his social world, she would have ensnared him beyond escape, and he was not ready for that. He liked Connie, but her very eagerness drove him in the opposite direction.

Yet he was a very lonely man, as I was a lonely little girl. Suddenly we meant a great deal to each other. We were proud of each other and happy in each other's company. He could use me as a shield against matchmaking ladies or their daughters, yet I rarely took part in the adult conversations, nor did I hold him back when he wished to be alone with other people.

Connie brushed my curls until they shone and dressed me prettily in clean dresses and little fur-trimmed coats. "Be a good girl, Kit. Mind what Uncle Doug tells you." She kissed me lovingly and sent me off as Cinderella sent off the stepsisters to the ball. If she envied me, she did not let me feel it. For all her surface faults Connie was the soul of goodness. Yet she must have wrung her hands and wept in secret, watching her life go by so emptily from day to day.

When the horse-racing season started Uncle Doug and I went every Saturday afternoon to the races. We both loved horses; and to see them fidgeting and fretting at the line-up and then dashing away in the splendid competition of the race filled me with excitement and delight. We knew most of the horses by name and what were their gaits and how they had clocked.

We usually shared a box with some of Uncle Doug's friends. Uncle Doug presented me to them formally, as if I were an adult. "Mr. and Mrs. Beach, my niece Christine McBain. Kit, Mr. and Mrs. Beach raise horses on their ranch. 'Lightning' out of 'White Star' is their filly."

"How do you do?" I said politely, holding out my hand. They shook it gravely, smiling over my head at Uncle Douglas.

"Such a nice little girl, Douglas!"

They gave me the front seat in the box where I could see everything, and Uncle Douglas furnished me with a bag of peanuts or a paper of caramels. Soon I was lost to their adult world in my own delighted observation of the horses, of the jockeys in their brilliant satin costumes, of people with hopeful or troubled faces milling up and down beside the track, of all the excitement of Saturday afternoon at the races.

I knew that Uncle Douglas placed bets on the horses and that he sometimes won and sometimes lost. When he won we had an ice-cream soda on the way home. When he lost he said we must do penance by getting along without. I accepted this philosophically, as I had come to accept the many ups and downs of life as I had experienced it. Connie, and sometimes even Grandma, used to quiz me about Uncle Doug's losses, but I could not have given them exact figures if I had wished to.

Once, however, I remember asking him: "Aren't you afraid to gamble, Uncle Doug? Connie and Grandma say it's not like a Scotsman to risk his money on horses."

"Ah," said Uncle Doug, laughing, "but I don't often lose, do I now, Kit? How many ice-cream sodas have you done without?"

"Not very many," I said.

"No, you see, I'm a very lucky fellow, Kit—at least where money is concerned. *You* must never gamble because it's wrong and not thrifty business for a lassie. But *I* have the devil's luck, and 'twould be sinful not to make the most of it."

I had not had any such result in mind when I spoke to him, but after that I never missed my ice-cream soda on the way home.

Sometimes in the box with us at the races there was a Mrs. Rossiter for whom I did not particularly care. She rarely spoke to me or I to her. She had a full but graceful figure and auburn hair brushed up from a high, pale brow. She wore black, with sparkling rings on her fingers, and she did not put any color on her cheeks, but her lips were very red. The gentlemen in the box with us seemed to be quite entranced with her, although to my mind some of the other ladies were far prettier. I was glad to see that Uncle Douglas did not pay a lot of attention to her, as the other men did. He sat by me, pointing out the good qualities of the horses, and when she spoke particularly to him, he turned his handsome profile toward her and answered her casually over his shoulder. Yet she called him "Douglas" instead of "Mr. McBain," and he called her "Sheila." This made me a little uneasy, although I could not have said why.

205

22

The next autumn, for very desperation I suppose, Connie began to branch out a little by herself. We had never led an active church life in Manitou City. All of my memories of Sunday school and church are connected with Opportunity. In Manitou City, Grandma and Uncle Douglas seemed to have abandoned church-going altogether, whether from disaffection or strangeness or apathy, I do not know. Careful as they were of me in most ways, they seem to have let my religious life lapse at this point. But now suddenly Connie began to go to church, especially to the evening services, and often elderly gentlemen, widowers or silent bachelors, saw her home.

We would hear them coming up the front walk after service, Connie talking a blue streak in her carrying voice and laughing a great deal between bursts of words. There would be an occasional rumble of masculine acquiescence, but no lingering on the porch. Either the gentleman came in for cocoa and a slice of Connie's excellent cake, or he said a brief farewell and left her at the door.

Gradually Mr. Cushing came more often, and he always stopped for cocoa and cake. Grandma, who had studied a book on phrenology and had opinions about people's bumps, inspected Mr. Cushing and said that he had a good character. He was a bookkeeper in a grocery firm, and he had no observable bad habits. It is true that he was much older than Connie, but he was certainly an eligible bachelor.

He was a tall, thin man, making Connie, who was falling a victim of her own good cooking, look like a small round ball bouncing along beside him. He had shy, dark eyes under beetling brows and a tremendous, black handlebar moustache spread, like a *Danger* sign on fragile ice, across his vulnerable face.

"He's absolutely grotesque," Connie babbled to Grandma, "but possibly he could be induced to shave off the moustache if I got to know him better. He seems quite nice in every other way. Actually, his eyes are very kind, and a little Sen-Sen would take care of his breath."

Mr. Cushing was kind to me and I remember that he brought

me a box of candy, but it had been on the grocery shelf too long and one of the candies had a worm in it. I never mentioned this to anyone, but it may have colored my opinion of him, for Uncle Doug had been spoiling me and I was snobbish about the gifts bestowed upon me.

I am sure that it weighed strongly with Connie that Mr. Cushing was polite to me. Although I was not her own child she loved to play that I was. This put her in the disadvantageous position of the unmarried woman with a child, but without the usual preliminary satisfactions of the flesh which would have preceded the child. Poor Connie was hedged about by emotional difficulties which grew more complicated instead of less so.

Douglas was usually out on a Sunday evening and he had never happened to encounter Mr. Cushing. But finally Mr. Cushing broke all precedent and invited Connie to attend the theater with him on a Wednesday evening. Connie was in a flutter of anxiety and suspense. She was delighted to be invited to the theater by no matter whom, and she was glad that Douglas would be at home and would see her go out in the company of another man. Yet she was frightened, too, because Mr. Cushing was really not a very good catch and Douglas was critical. She did her hair very carefully and pressed three dresses, not knowing which she would finally decide to wear, and she made a very delicious apple pie for Douglas' dessert.

Grandma and I had promised to wash up the dishes, and Connie appeared at dinner in all the glory of the pale-green dress with the black braid trim, and with her hair piled high like a woman of the world.

Douglas looked at her in surprise.

"Connie, you look real nice," he said. "What's the occasion? Are you off to a Sunday-school picnic?"

"I'm going to the theater," Connie said, and she could not help adding, "with a man," although she knew at once that her hasty tongue had betrayed her.

"With a *man?*" laughed Douglas, "and what's become of all the lassies? A man! Take care of yourself, Connie. These men are not to be trusted, as you certainly must have been told."

"Oh, shut up!" Connie said. "If I'd had a brother, he couldn't have been a meaner tease than you are. It's not very fair of you."

"Well, if I approve of him, Connie, I'll put in a good word

for you. I'll tell him you're a peerless cook, and that you'll take a lot of teasing before you get throwing mad."

Connie lifted a plate with a menacing gesture. "Look out!" she said. "I'm pretty near throwing mad now."

The doorbell rang and Connie ushered Mr. Cushing into the living room. He was wearing a long black overcoat and had a black derby hat in one hand and a black umbrella in the other. His moustache seemed even more imposing than we had remembered it. When Connie introduced him to Douglas, he handed Connie the umbrella so that he could shake hands.

"We aren't going to need it, are we?" asked Connie dubiously.

"It's in the paper," Mr. Cushing said. "Rain is predicted, and it's a good bit to the streetcar. I like to be prepared."

"That's right," said Douglas heartily. "There's nothing like being prepared."

"If it rained, we could call a cab, I suppose," said Connie, with bravado.

"Cabs are a little out of my class, I guess," said Mr. Cushing mildly. "The streetcars can always be depended upon, fair weather or foul."

"Exactly my opinion," said Douglas, who never rode a streetcar if he could avoid doing so.

"I'll get my coat and hat," said Connie.

After they had gone, Douglas' mood changed. He said irritably to Grandma, "Connie isn't serious about this fellow, is she?"

"I don't know," Grandma said, "but I think it might be a very fortunate thing for her if she were."

At that they let the matter drop.

Connie and I shared the same room and I was so accustomed to having her in the next bed that I slept badly when she was out. On that particular night I awoke when I heard the front door close and I got up and went to sit on the top step of the staircase to greet Connie when she came up. There was a light downstairs, and I heard Connie say in surprise, "Why, Doug! You're still up?"

"I was waiting for you to come in," he said.

"Oh, that was kind of you, I'm sure," said Connie in a mocking voice. "I see that you don't trust men either."

"This one looked harmless enough."

"He's very nice," Connie said. "He doesn't plague the life out of me like some people I know."

"Look here, Connie," Uncle Doug said, "you aren't going to accept attentions from that shoddy old fossil with the handlebars, are you?"

There was a silence. Then Connie cried out in a tortured voice, "My Lord! Can I help it if men like that fall in love with me, and the men I love don't? I've got to have something. *I've got to have something!* What business is it of yours?"

"I suppose it isn't," said Douglas stiffly. "But I have your welfare at heart. I—"

"Yes, you do, don't you?" Connie cried. "Yes, I suppose you do." Suddenly she began to laugh very hard. "But it's so funny! Really, so very funny!"

I had heard Connie laugh like that before, and I was not surprised when the laughing turned into sobbing. "Oh, dear," she sobbed. "I'm all tired out. I must get to bed."

I got up from the step where I was sitting because now I did not want Connie to find me sitting there. I had not intended to eavesdrop on a private conversation, and I sensed that to find me listening would have made her humiliation complete. Yet I could not quite tear myself away. I heard Uncle Doug's voice now, lower and nearer to Connie. I visualized him putting his hands on her shoulders. He said, "I didn't mean to make you cry, Connie. If you want this fellow with the handlebars—"

"Oh, no, Doug," she said. "You don't understand. I don't want him at all, but, of course, I'll keep him around in case of emergency. Only I'll see that he doesn't come when you're here."

"Don't be ridiculous!" he said.

"It's too late, Doug," she said. "I've been ridiculous too long. I'll go on being ridiculous the rest of my life, I suppose."

I heard her coming toward the stairs, and I ran and crept into bed and pretended to be asleep. She came in very quietly, except for an occasional sobbing breath, but Uncle Douglas slammed his bedroom door. I already understood that he did not like women who cried and were humble. He preferred them vain and contemptuous and even cruel, rather than silly.

The old weight of trouble came back to lie on my chest. I loved both of these people so much, yet I saw that they were as they were and that nothing was likely to change them.

209

23

The next year in Manitou City was a very good one, but it had lost the magic quality of the first year. Again I had a happy Christmas with candles on the tree and turkey and pudding. When I came down to breakfast there were many presents under the tree, particularly books, for I was becoming a serious child. Aunt Connie had dressed a small doll for me in the costume of a fairy, complete with sparkling crown and star-tipped wand. It was very pretty.

When we sat down to breakfast Uncle Doug said: "Kit, why don't you run upstairs for your old Scotch laddie doll. He'd like to meet the new fairy doll, I'm sure."

I ran upstairs, and when I returned with my Laddie, someone seemed to be sitting in my chair. I ran around and looked and there was the largest doll I had ever seen. She was almost as large as a small child, and she had curly brown hair and very large brown eyes that opened and closed. This was the last doll that was ever given to me, I think, and although I was delighted at the time, I kept her sitting in my bedroom and did not really play with her. Because of her big brown eyes I named her Abigail. Perhaps that also made her strange to me.

Now that I had begun to read so many books I played with my dolls in a new kind of way. They became characters in plays which sometimes continued for weeks, carrying the same set of characters through different adventures and vicissitudes. Some of the plays were simple ones about princes and princesses and wicked enchanters. But, if the grownups had known, I think they would have been surprised and possibly worried to discover how sophisticated and true to life some of my plays were.

In the spring, when the weather grew fine, Uncle Douglas sent me to the barn one day on some kind of errand for Beauty. I came out of the sunlight into the mote-filled dusk of the barn, and there I saw, leaning up against Beauty's stall, a wonderful blue bicycle, the most beautiful bicycle that any child had ever owned. I had a friend who owned a red bicycle, smaller and not so fine as mine. Now my friend and I rode up and down the neighborhood sidewalk, splashing through puddles and calling

210

out to one another as we raced. She called her bicycle "Red Racer" and I called mine "Blue Streak."

So I was happy and did not really notice that I was dressed and brushed less often to go out with Uncle Douglas.

There was one Saturday in the spring, however, when he hitched Beauty to her cart and said that we would go driving into the country.

"How am I to dress her?" Connie asked. "Is it to be a picnic or a party? Do you want a picnic lunch?"

"No picnic lunch," he said. "We're to have lunch at the Beaches' country place—where they raise the race horses."

"Oh, good!" I cried. "We'll see the horses."

"As to what she shall wear," he said, "it must be nice but not fussy. The kind of thing a country gentleman's little girl would wear in the country, if you know what I mean."

"How should I?" Connie said. "I've never been to a country gentleman's place where they raise horses. I'll have her clean, if that's what you want, and her curls nicely brushed, but don't ask me for any miracles." Connie's tongue was getting sharper than it had been. She had always had a retort, but now the retort was sometimes tinged with bitterness. She had given up church at this time and we never saw Mr. Cushing any more.

I shall always remember that day as a day of running water. It seemed to me that every lush and greening hillside gurgled with tumbling brooklets, running downward and away with hasty and heedless joy.

We saw the stables and the wonderful frolicking colts in the pasture lots. Some of the guests went riding, but since the time he had hurt his ankle Uncle Douglas did not care for horseback riding. He and I walked away from the paddock and sat in the deep grass on a hillside with water running in ditches above us and at our feet. The sun was warm and glorious and the air was almost steamy with moisture. It was a lovely day.

Uncle Douglas always respected my intelligence, and now he explained to me about irrigation, and how this lovely running water that pulsed around us was pumped up from the river and guided into these tiny rushing streams to make the hills green and the pasture secure for the horses. He went on and told me the vision he had for the desert country in the drier regions of the state.

211

He said that someday there should be a great dam built, in those places, which would keep the river water from running away and being lost in the spring floods. Someday, he said, irrigation ditches would carry this stored water from the dam all over the desert and make crops flourish where now there was only sagebrush and sand and a little feed for sheep.

"Even your Uncle Willie will be rich when that happens," he said. "He's making a fair living with sheep, now that the harness trade is gone. But some nice ditches like these on his place would put him on easy street. He could raise wheat or corn or any kind of garden stuff."

"We haven't seen Uncle Willie for a long time," I said wistfully.

"No," he said, "he doesn't often get to town. But I do what I can for him. I send him money two or three times a year. I want you to know that, Kit. I do what I can for him." He seemed to want very much that I should understand this.

"I know you do, Uncle Doug," I reassured him.

The green, lush hillside, the far blue hills across the distant river, the happiness and peace of that moment come very strongly back to me. I hear the rush and gurgle of the sweet, life-giving water that seemed to be almost a part of the moist bright air. I am sure that Uncle Douglas was happy too. Running water had played a greater part in his life than I knew at that time. Now there was a footfall behind us, and Mrs. Rossiter had come to join us. She wore a black riding habit and her auburn hair was massed up neatly under a severe small hat.

I was angry with her for intruding on my perfect happiness and I turned sullen and had only monosyllables to give her in reply to her bright words of greeting.

"Kit," Uncle Doug said sternly, "where are your manners?"

I tried to do better then, and if not behave like my usual self, at least to behave like the little girl of a country gentleman. But what I did or said mattered not at all after that, for Mrs. Rossiter scarcely gave me another glance, and all of her pretty looks were for Uncle Douglas.

24

I was the only child at the luncheon, but Mrs. Beach had arranged for me very charmingly—almost too charmingly perhaps. When the grownups had liquor to drink before luncheon, I was given a glass of lemonade which was colored a charming pink; and at my place at the table there was a little red ball and a very large glass of milk, a beverage that I detested and rarely drank at home. Under Uncle Doug's eye, I gulped this one down and put the ball in my pocket.

After luncheon, which seemed to me to last a long time and to be full of the meaningless laughter of grownups, I found a charming corner arranged for me with a jigsaw puzzle on a small table, and two picture books of a kind I had long outgrown. This was to keep me amused while the ladies and gentlemen played cards. The afternoon was longer than the luncheon, but I was the only one who did not seem to enjoy it.

All the other guests had come in the fashionable new motorcars. When Beauty and her childish cart were brought around for Uncle Doug and me, Uncle Doug was the butt of a great deal of good-humored ribbing. He took it all in the greatest good spirits, and threw out his usual promise to get between the shafts some day and let Beauty ride. But perhaps because I did not enjoy it myself, I felt that he was not as amused underneath as he appeared to be on the surface.

He was quiet most of the way home, but at last he said, "Well, we'll have to get one of those monstrosities ourselves, won't we, Kit?" I knew, of course, that he meant the motorcars.

"I like Beauty best," I said staunchly.

"Yes, so do I," he said, "but I also notice that you like your bicycle. A motorcar would be even more modern and stylish than a bicycle, Kit."

"Uncle Doug," I said, "I don't think I'll go to any more luncheon parties with your friends."

"Eh?" he said. "Why not?"

"I don't know exactly. I liked the horses and the streams very much. But I'm either too little or too big for luncheon parties. I don't know which."

213

"I guess you are right, Kit," he said. "I guess you are right. But we've had a lot of good times, haven't we?"

"Oh, Uncle Doug!" I cried, rubbing my cheek against his rough sleeve. "Yes, we have!"

25

One day Connie came in from a Ladies' Aid Tea or some sort of women's party, and Grandma and I could see at once that she was upset.

"Kit," she said to me, "do you know a Mrs. Rossiter?"

"Yes," I said. "I know her."

"Then why didn't you tell me?" she cried.

"I don't know why," I said. "I see a lot of people when I go out with Uncle Doug. I didn't think you wanted to know."

"What does she look like?" Connie asked.

"Well, she's sort of tall and her hair is reddish. All the men seem to like her."

"Ah!" cried Connie triumphantly. "So you noticed that too, Kit? Oh, Mama, the shame and degradation of it!"

"What is the matter, Constance?" Grandma asked.

"The whole town is talking," Connie said. "The whole town!"

"Talking of what? Be reasonable, Connie."

"Oh, it was humiliating," Connie said. "These women were talking about Douglas and this Mrs. Rossiter. They didn't even know I knew Douglas—that's how thoroughly he has kept us out of his private life, although we wash his clothes and cook his meals as if we were his servants. And for once I kept my mouth shut. I really did. I stood there listening and they went on talking. It seems she's a very notorious character—*all* the men know her, and now she's going everywhere with Douglas. 'Such a handsome man,' they said, 'and the scars on his hands and temples, you know how he got those?' And they said he's on his way up to be very rich, and now he's fallen head over heels in love with this notorious woman."

"Come, come, Connie," Grandma said. "They were gossiping and you are exaggerating. Do you know who she is?"

"Yes, I am going to tell you, and that is the most disgusting

214

part. She's a younger sister of that redheaded Irish secretary of Doug's, the one with the green suit and the red hat and shoes. Only this one married a rich old man and inherited all his money. She's got a son, but she keeps him away at school so that she can carry on her own affairs, blatantly, in front of the town."

"Poor Molly," Grandma said.

"I don't know why you say that," Connie cried. "It's the very thing she's been scheming for, I expect. This is the woman who was going to have the best suite at the hotel, if you remember. But think of him letting Kit meet her! Our innocent little Kit. He owes us all more than that. Oh, I shall have it out with him when he comes home tonight!"

"You'll do no such thing, Constance!" Grandma said in the voice that she seldom used but which we always heeded when she did. "And he owes us nothing. You know that very well, Constance. He's given us more than we can ever repay, as it is. And he never made any promises that he hasn't kept. It was all on a temporary basis, as you well know."

"Then I won't come down to dinner," Connie said. "I can't sit at the table with him, in all his terrible duplicity, and not speak my mind."

"I'll tell him you have a headache," Grandma said.

Connie stormed upstairs and we could hear her slamming doors and running water very noisily into the bathtub.

"Kit," Grandma said, "you know Aunt Connie is very excitable. You must try to forget about all these things she has said."

"Yes, Grandma," I said.

But when Uncle Douglas failed to come to dinner, I sat at the table alone with Grandma and there was a very cold and heavy stone at the pit of my stomach.

"Eat your dinner, Kit," Grandma said gently. "No trouble should be great enough to keep a person from eating." So I choked down the food on my plate and it joined the cold stone in my stomach.

While Grandma and I were doing up the dishes, I heard the front door open. I dropped my dish towel and ran to meet Uncle Douglas. I threw my arms around him and crept under his coat to press my face against the tweed and the hard buttons of his vest, as I used to do when I was a very little girl.

"Honey! Honey! You're crying," he said.

215

"No, I'm not," I said fiercely, hiding the tears against his vest. When Grandma came to the kitchen door, he said, "I'm sorry I didn't call you. I usually do, don't I? But something came up unexpectedly. I'm really sorry."

"Have you eaten? I can heat up a plate for you in a minute."

"No, no," he said. "I've already eaten, and I have to go out again soon. I just came back to change clothes. What's wrong with my little Kit?"

"I think she was worried when you didn't come or call."

"Hey, Kit," he said, trying to turn my face up so he could look at me. "You never need to worry about me. You know that, don't you? I have the devil's luck, Kit, in everything I do. In everything," he repeated positively. "You know that, honey."

He sat down in the big Morris chair that he liked when he was at home and he took me on his lap as he used to do when I was smaller. He pulled my head back against his shoulder and stroked my hair, and began to go through the old routine:

> " 'Wee Willie Winkie rins through the toon,
> Oopstairs an' doonstairs in his nicht goon—' "

He had taken off his coat, and where his shirt sleeve was pushed up, I could see a part of the tattooed anchor on his arm. I touched it gently with the tip of my finger. An anchor for adventure on the high seas; an anchor for security at home. I loved the anchor.

Then he began to sing, and soon my voice joined his:

> " 'Oh, ye'll tak' the high road
> An' I'll tak' the low road,
> An' I'll be in Scotland afore ye;
> But me an' my true love will never meet again,
> On the bonnie, bonnie banks o' Loch Lomond.' "

The time went by and I was lost in happiness. But after a little Grandma said, "Kit, Uncle Doug has to go out again. He came to change his clothes. We mustn't keep him."

"Thank you, Mother Hedrick," he said, smiling at her. "I might have forgotten, if you hadn't reminded me."

He went into his room, and in a short time he came out again, freshly shaven and resplendent in evening clothes.

216

"Pop my hat, Kit," he said. He had a wonderful collapsible opera hat which it was my duty and pleasure to open for him. When he came in late, he would leave the hat on the hall table for me to pop shut the next morning.

I opened it now and set it jauntily on his head. He had called a cab, and it was waiting for him at the door. He kissed both Grandma and me before he went out, and we both said, "Have a good time!"

The house was very still after he had gone.

"You'd better go up to bed now, Kit," Grandma said, "and be as quiet as you can, because I expect that Connie is asleep. Don't forget to say your prayers."

So I went quietly up the dark stairs alone.

26

Uncle Douglas bought a motorcar soon after that. He took us all riding with him on the day he brought it home. We tied our hats on with scarves and held fast to the sides of the seats and felt the quiet air rush by as if it were a high wind. Uncle Doug looked flushed and excited.

"How do you like it?" he kept asking us, over the noise of the motor. "What do you think of it? Did you ever go this fast with Beauty, eh?"

Connie and I were in ecstasies, uttering cries of terror and delight, and assuring him over and over that we liked it very much. Grandma held her hat with one hand and the seat arm with the other, and she looked a little pale and tired.

"Speed isn't everything," she said. "People are better off if they don't try to go too fast."

"Oh, Mama!" Connie said, "you're very old-fashioned. This is simply heavenly."

It was a hot summer and sometimes in the early evening just after supper and before the sun went down, Uncle Doug took us riding in the motorcar to cool off after the sultry day. But he always brought us back by dark.

"It's Kit's bedtime," he would say. "Wee Willie Winkie's abroad." Then we three womenfolks got out of the car at our

217

front door and I kissed him good night, and he would drive off with a gay wave of the hand.

From the exultation of the drive, Connie's spirits would now sink very low.

"He'll be in at three in the morning," she said one time, bitterly, "when that woman is through with him. I suppose she sleeps all day, but he's got to go to work as usual. How is he going to stand it?"

Often he was gone for the whole weekend, after he bought the motorcar.

"It's a house party at the Beaches' place out at Lake Vivienne," he said, once.

"I thought they ran a horse ranch," said Connie, trying to catch him in a lie.

"This is their summer place," he said. "They have everything."

After he had gone, Connie would say ominously, "He's with that woman."

I had heard Mrs. Rossiter spoken of so often as "that woman" that I began to think of her as a kind of monster.

One Sunday in early fall soon after school had started, Uncle Douglas said to Connie: "I'd like to take Kit calling with me this afternoon, Connie. See that she's dressed nicely. I want her to make a good impression."

I stood by listening, but I did not say anything. I had not gone alone with Uncle Doug for a long time.

"Where are you taking her?" Connie asked. "She's my child, too, you know."

"I'm not going to contaminate her, if that's what you mean," Uncle Douglas said. "I love her, too, remember. Just have her ready, please."

"I don't think I'll let her go this time," Connie said.

"Kit, you'd like to come with me, wouldn't you?" Uncle Doug asked.

I felt trouble in the air, but I said, "Yes, I'd like to come."

"All right. You always win," said Connie bitterly.

Connie pressed my best dress and brushed my coat and polished my shoes.

"Wash yourself well, Kit," she said, "really well, behind the ears and back of the neck. And clean your fingernails. I'll do your curls on my fingers the last thing. It seems you have to uphold

218

the honor of the family and make a good impression." I scrubbed myself well, at the same time filled with chilly apprehension. I had had a date with the owner of Red Racer to ride Blue Streak to the park. That would have been simpler and gayer than this unknown mission; but Uncle Douglas wanted me, and nothing in the world would make me disappoint him.

In the car on the way Uncle Douglas said to me, "Kit, I am taking you to see a very fascinating lady. I think you have met her before, but probably you don't remember her."

"Mrs. Rossiter?" I said.

"How did you know?" he said, looking at me in surprise.

"I remember pretty well," I said.

"I want you two to love each other," he said. "It's very important, Kit."

I have sometimes thought since then that the course of my life may have hinged on that afternoon call. But, if it were a crossroads of decision, I was happily unaware of it at the time.

Mrs. Rossiter lived on the second floor of an impressive new apartment house. There was an elevator to save us climbing stairs, and she had a doorbell on her door as if this were a house.

It seemed dark inside the apartment after the crisp, fall sunshine out of doors. I had never seen a place like it. The walls were a dark, deep red, and the furniture was black and some of it was carved into the shapes of dragons and flowers. On the floor there was a very deep red carpet and the windows were hung with some kind of dark hangings, so that most of the light came from lamps with heavy silk shades and fringes. In one corner of the room there was an Oriental god sitting among ferns and artfully lighted so that his half-closed eyes looked wise and mysterious. There was a smell of cut roses and of incense or perfume of some kind.

I stood in the middle of the strange room with all of my senses alerted, like an alarmed turtle ready to draw in its head.

"So here we are!" Mrs. Rossiter said. "How charming she looks, Douglas. Such a nice little girl, and you dress her so tastefully. And how do you like it, dear? My pretty room?"

I turned my eyes to Mrs. Rossiter, and I saw that she was wearing something loose and black and very glossy that seemed to flow about her rounded figure and set off her pale face and high forehead and very red lips. Suddenly her eyes reminded me of the eyes of the Oriental god. I had not noticed this on the other occasions when I had met her. But then I had not seen the god, either. In this light her auburn hair appeared to be made of burnished bronze or antique gold. I looked at her for a moment before I could bring myself to speak, then I said in a voice that was strange to my own ears, "It is very nice."

"I'm glad you like it," Mrs. Rossiter said. "Your uncle likes it, and I know he'll be pleased that you do, too."

"Sit down, Kit," Uncle Doug said, "and tell Mrs. Rossiter about your school."

"Yes, do," Mrs. Rossiter said. "Sit here, dear, and tell me."

I sat on the edge of a hard black chair that was a little too high for me. To speak of school in an atmosphere like this seemed fantastic even to me. "Well," I faltered. "I go to school. I'm in the fifth grade."

"She has the best report cards," Uncle Doug said. "I never have to take her behind the woodshed and use the birch cane, do I, Kit?"

"Hardly ever," I said with a faint smile at his humorous sally.

"She paints, too, with water colors and makes up poems, don't you, Kit?" Uncle Douglas said proudly. I had never heard him boast of me before. I was inexplicably filled with shame for my accomplishments, and hung my head.

"And of course she plays the piano, I expect," said Mrs. Rossiter brightly. "Won't you play some little piece for us, darling?"

I saw then to my consternation that there was a grand piano in a dark part of the room. The piano was my shame and degradation—I could not learn to play it. Everyone said to me, "But your Mother was such a beautiful musician, Kit. Surely you can learn to play." I had dutifully taken lessons once a week since I was small, yet only the faultiest and most elementary trickles of sound came from the ends of my fingers. When I sat at the piano my head was filled with cotton wool, my hands were made of lead, my heart was a stone.

Usually Uncle Douglas was on my side in the controversy as to whether the piano lessons should be continued. "Let her stop it, if she wants to," he said to Connie. But Connie always answered, "Abbie would have wanted her to play."

But now I looked in vain at Uncle Doug for help. This after-

220

noon he wished me to please and impress, and he said, kindly, "Go ahead and try, Kit. You do the 'Pixie's Waltz' quite well."

I sat more firmly on the hard black chair. "I would rather not play," I said, "if you don't mind." I was familiar with the sad tale of Elsie Dinsmore, whose papa had made her sit on the piano stool until she fell off in a faint because she refused to perform on the Sabbath day. I did not intend that such a thing should happen to me.

"Oh, do play, dear," said Mrs. Rossiter brightly. "I should love to hear the 'Pixie's Waltz.'"

"I can't," I said in desperation. "I'm very sorry, but I can't."

"Another time, Sheila," Uncle Douglas said. "There are going to be lots of other times, I hope. She's shy, and the place is strange."

"Of course," Mrs. Rossiter said. "Now I'll get you a cookie and a glass of milk, Christine, and then I'll tell you about my own little boy while we have our party."

The "cookie" was a very fantastic French pastry which I enjoyed, but the glass of milk was real and had to be downed before their eyes. They drank small glasses of a deep red liquor which seemed to me to match the room.

Mrs. Rossiter brought me a picture of a fox-eyed boy with freckles, and said: "This is my Richard. He's away at school. He's only a year older than you, dear. When he's at home next summer the two of you might be the best of friends. This summer he was at a camp at the lake where he learned to be an excellent swimmer. Do you swim, dear?"

"No, I don't," I said.

"If we got the lake place," Uncle Doug said, "we'd all do lots of swimming."

"Are we going to have a place at a lake?" I asked, surprised. I had never heard him speak of this before. He exchanged glances with Mrs. Rossiter, and they smiled.

"It's an idea," he said.

"My poor little boy lost his father a long time ago," Mrs. Rossiter said. "He likes your Uncle Douglas very much. Do you know what he called him one day last summer? He didn't think what he was saying and he called your uncle, 'Daddy.' Wasn't that a funny thing?"

221

"You know this boy?" I said to Uncle Douglas.

"Yes," he replied. "Richard was here between his camp and his school. I'm sure you will like him, Kit."

"Perhaps," I said.

Except for the large pastry this was not a successful visit. Possibly I have recorded it unfairly, but I can rely here only on a transcription colored by my feelings.

Mrs. Rossiter soon tired of wooing me, and I could see that Uncle Douglas was annoyed with me. I sat stiffly and silently on the edge of the hard black chair, while they chatted together, and until Uncle Douglas felt that we should leave.

At parting Mrs. Rossiter presented me with a beautiful little silk-covered box.

"Here is something pretty for a pretty little girl," she said coaxingly. She was trying harder than I was to please my uncle; but then she was more experienced than I and she realized more clearly what was at stake.

I opened the box and saw that it was empty. "What did it have in it?" I asked. "It must have had something in it."

"It had a bottle of rare perfume," she said. "But you are too little for that. Little girls like you don't wear expensive perfumes."

"I'm really not so little," I said. "I'm almost eleven."

"I call that little," Mrs. Rossiter said icily, and then she added, "I thought you would like the pretty box, but, of course, if you don't—"

"What do you say, Kit?" prompted Uncle Douglas ominously.

"Thank you very much, Mrs. Rossiter," I said with stiff politeness. "I can use it for a trunk in my dollhouse. It will be very elegant." The word "elegant," I thought, was enough to placate both of them.

On the way home Uncle Doug and I rode in silence. Even the fresh air and the cheerful noise of the car failed to animate me.

Finally he asked (but as if he already knew the answer), "Well, Kit, what do you think of her?"

I continued silent, twisting my feet under the car seat, then I said formally, "She is a handsome woman."

His eyes blazed at me. It was the only time I had ever seen him angry.

222

"They've been poisoning your mind against her," he cried.

"Why do you say that, Uncle Doug?" I asked coldly. "All I said was she was a handsome woman."

Again we rode in silence, and, also for the first time, there was a wall of reserve between us. It is true that I had uttered nothing but praise, but I had taken my first step toward adulthood, by aligning myself with the smug and virtuous women against the charming and unvirtuous.

When I reached home I ran indoors and threw my arms around Connie.

"Did you have a good time?" she asked anxiously.

"Oh, yes," I lied, and that was another step out of my childhood.

27

A few weeks later Douglas told us that he was going to be married. We were at supper, I remember, and he was nervous and ill at ease as he told us, but none of us cried out or seemed surprised. Grandma said very cordially, "My dear, dear boy, I hope that you will be very happy. You deserve it if anyone does."

Connie said, "Oh, Douglas, did you have to *marry* her? Couldn't you have had her without that?"

"Constance!" Grandma cried, sincerely shocked.

Uncle Doug was very pale, but he said quietly, "Connie, I want to marry her very much."

"Well, that's all I want to know," Connie said, pale too, and without tears. "God knows, I want you to be happy, Douglas."

"And Kit shall come to visit us often," Uncle Doug said, looking at me gently and propitiatingly. "Sheila loves Kit almost as much as I do. When she knows her better she'll love her just as much."

Grandma said, "You will want this house, Douglas."

"Oh, no," he said. "Sheila has all kinds of plans for a larger apartment where we can do a lot of entertaining. We're going to have a place at the lake for the summer as well. You can stay on here, of course, as long as—"

"Thank you, Douglas," Grandma said, "but we'll move soon now. We won't stay on beyond the month that's paid for. It was only while you needed us."

"But where shall we go?" burst out Connie. "Where in the world shall we go?"

"Why, back to Opportunity, of course," said Grandma quietly.

"But so much has happened there! How can we ever go back? It won't be fair to us—to Kit."

"Kit is a sensible child," Grandma said. "She knows that grown-ups must live their lives the same as children must. Isn't that so, Kit?"

"Yes, Grandma."

I sat quite still and heard their voices going on about me.

Uncle Douglas was at home less and less frequently during our days of packing and preparing to leave. When he came he brought presents and was gentle and kind, and Connie held her tongue and behaved like a sister-in-law. But there were moments alone with Grandma and me, when she could not contain her wounded feelings. Usually I ran out of doors when one of her tirades started. Yet some of her complaints still linger in my ears.

"She's a rich widow," was one of her favorite accusations, "a rich widow. It's easy to see why Douglas is going to marry her. He's crazy for money. He'd do anything to get a little richer."

"Be sensible, Connie," Grandma said. "We both know Doug better than that. Money comes easy and goes easy with him, but that's his own affair. He wouldn't marry for it."

"Then why?" asked Connie miserably. "Why?"

"Douglas has been a long time without a woman," Grandma said. "I think she fascinates him."

"But he could have had women," Connie said. "You know he could."

"Yes, Connie," said Grandma dryly. "I know that he could."

"He made one horrible mistake in his first marriage," cried Connie. "Now to see him make another!"

"A man's entitled to his own mistakes," Grandma said.

We never questioned Grandma's wisdom and strength. She took this blow as she had taken all the others. We brought her our heartaches and rebellions, and leaned against her sturdy virtue. If it was hard for her, she did not let us know.

28

I do not remember if we were invited to the wedding. In any case I am sure that Aunt Connie would have refused to attend. All I remember is that we finished packing our belongings before the wedding, and took the train for Opportunity.

We shipped Beauty and the blue bicycle. The dolls and the pretty dresses that Uncle Doug had bought for me were packed with the household goods. We planned to carry the canary and cage in hand, and at the last moment Aunt Connie became emotionally stubborn about the old dog, Beady. She said he would die of fright if he were left alone in the baggage car, and she did not care what the railroad regulations were, she was going to take him into the coach with us.

The idea frightened me, but I loved Beady dearly, and I thought that Aunt Connie was good and heroic to care so much for his welfare.

"But you can't take him with you in the cars, Connie," Grandma said. "They simply won't let you get onto a train with a dog." Her voice was tired. She was the conscience and the common sense of all of us, and we did not notice how sad she was, how tired, how reluctant to return to the big empty house in the small town where life had dealt her so many blows.

"I will smuggle him in," said Connie. "I can do it perfectly well. I won't have an animal suffer because of human vagaries. *He* doesn't understand why we must take this train journey. *He* doesn't know that our lives are all broken and disrupted again. It isn't his fault. Poor Beady!" Her voice rose almost hysterically. "*People* have to suffer, but it isn't fair for us to make innocent animals suffer too. I won't—I won't be unkind to an innocent animal, no matter how unkind—"

"Hush, Connie," Grandma said. "Do anything you like with Beady."

So we took Beady into the car with us, and I do not remember at all how it was done, although I do remember with the most detailed clarity the ensuing events of the journey.

We smuggled Beady under the seat by the window, and Aunt

Connie sat next to him, holding his leash and spreading her ample skirts over him. He was a good old dog and he lay still as he was told to do.

Any triumph, however small, was sweet to Connie at that moment, and she said to Grandma, "You see. It was perfectly simple. There was no trick to it at all."

"We're not there yet," Grandma said wearily.

I sat next to Connie holding the bird cage. Dickie fluttered and cheeped under his muslin cover. I could hear him cracking seeds and swinging on his swing in mindless unconcern. Yet we were going back to Opportunity. Never again at breakfast and dinner would we see Uncle Douglas. *Pass the honey, honey. Do ye no ken bogles, lassie? Did you ever go so fast with Beauty, eh? Wee Willie Winkie rins through the toon—Oh, ye'll tak' th' high road an' I'll tak' th' low road, but me an' my true love will never meet again—*

Grandma sat opposite us, surrounded by last-minute parcels. She was riding with her back to the engine, which made both Connie and me carsick, but Grandma always said that she did not mind riding backward. She leaned her head against the cushion now, and closed her eyes. Her face was sallow and wrinkled against the dusty red plush.

Soon after it leaves Manitou City the train begins to climb toward the Idaho mountains. The change of altitude is scarcely noticeable from the train window. The wheat fields roll away on either side, but each roll of horizon is a little higher. Pine trees line the more distant ridges; finally one sees the far blue mountains.

Presently Grandma rose unsteadily and went to the ladies' room. She was gone a long time. The moments passed and passed.

"Why doesn't Grandma come back?" I asked.

"I don't know," Connie said.

Finally Aunt Connie gave me Beady's leash and asked me to move over and spread my skirts. "Don't let anyone see him," she said, "whatever happens." She went down the aisle after Grandma. I put down my hand and Beady licked it, but I was filled with a deep foreboding. My foreboding was correct.

Grandma had had a heart attack and fallen against the door of the ladies' room so that they had great difficulty in getting her

226

out. I heard Aunt Connie's cries and the commotion going up and down the aisles. I saw them removing the hinges of the toilet door and bringing Grandma out. They asked for a doctor, but there was not one on the train. They wired ahead for a doctor to be at the next stop. Curious people pushed past me in the aisle, talking and wondering. They put Grandma across the seats in the first compartment after the ladies' room. From somewhere came a bottle of brandy.

Idaho was a prohibition state then, one of the first in the nation, and it was illegal to be found in possession of liquor once the state border had been crossed. This was an hour of illegal transactions. Stiff with fear and anguish I sat mute in my seat, trying to conceal the fact that we were illegally sheltering a dog who belonged in the baggage car. To hide Beady was all that I could do for Aunt Connie and Grandma at this moment. I sat tight-lipped and terrified. For an eleven-year-old child, I knew bereavement intimately. I knew that quite possibly Grandma, who was all-wise and my only sure protector, would die as my father and my mother and my grandfather had died, and Aunt Connie and I in our helplessness would be left to face the world alone. Not even Uncle Douglas—

Beady was panting, his tongue lolling. A little drop of his saliva trickled down my leg. The canary chirped and cracked seed, and swung upon his swing.

The brandy at last brought Grandma around. When the excitement was over, the conductor went through the train trying to return the brandy bottle to its owner, but no one would claim it. The train was in Idaho now. At the first stop a doctor boarded the train, but Grandma by this time had begun to gather her many strengths together. There was little he could do except warn her against future activity and anxiety. Shrunken and pale, she was half carried from the train in Opportunity. Attention was focused on her alone, and somehow I was able to remove the dog and the bird cage from the train without anyone knowing that a dog had been there.

I cannot even imagine what Aunt Connie felt that day, for whenever I return in my mind to that journey, I am immersed in the complicated anxieties and griefs of an eleven-year-old child, and my imagination refuses to go further.

227

Lake Vivienne

1

THERE WAS SOMETHING about the desert country of central Washington that reminded Willie of Caithness. The sagebrush gave the air a spicier tang, but the long reaches of barren land had the same wide sky and unobstructed view. A man could almost imagine the sea in the distant blue haze that made a kind of mirage on the horizon. Birds sounded high and far, and the hoot of a train could be heard for miles on a clear day. But there was no midnight sun here in the summer, only a nearly intolerable heat and a glare of white light on pale, tawny soil that made the sheep huddle in the shade of the few scraggly cottonwood trees in the dry stream bed.

If the summers were hotter, the winters were colder here than in Caithness. Snow often fell and again the sheep huddled close under the cottonwoods or around the barn to share a common misery. In the spring the soil produced a brief crop of grass and wild flowers, and the streams rushed and roared and tore out bridges and cut away eroded pasture land. Then the water was gone as precipitately as it had come, and only the deep wells with their creaking windmills kept the small farms in operation the year around.

But Willie felt at ease here doing the best he could to accommodate himself to whimsical nature. Everything was within his grasp in a place like this. There were no complications of the imagination to disturb him. When he thought of Douglas in his

229

city office, surrounded by secretaries and partners, his desk cluttered with deeds and mortgages to other peoples' land; with other peoples' money put out here and there to make more money, and with drink before meat and a shave and change of clothing before going out for an evening of complicated social encounters, he did not envy Douglas at all.

Hoeing a garden patch or standing among his sheep, Willie sniffed the clear, sage-scented air with pleasure, and sang or whistled as he worked. The two older boys rode a pony the mile and a half to school now. When they were not in school, they helped him hoe or they wrestled or played nearby or went hunting for rabbits in the sagebrush or rattlesnakes in the rocks above the dry gulch. The two youngest were still about Alma's skirts in the large kitchen where they all ate their meals.

Alma was full of daily complaints for the life they led.

"This is a fine place you've brought me to," she said. "I sure got myself taken in by the wrong McBain boy, the one that couldn't never make ends meet. I'd have had a better chance to wear silk with either one of the other two."

"Weel, lass," said Willie with a good-natured laugh, "one was already married, when you came on the scene, and t'other one had his eye elsewhere. You'd no one to pick but me, poor lass."

"*I* pick *you?*" said Alma haughtily. "And you was chasing after me as if I was the only thing in a petticoat you'd ever seen in your life. *You* picked *me* and don't you never forget that."

"Ah, weel," said Willie, still in a pleasant humor, "my grandmither used to say, there's as mony versions of a tale as there be people to relate it."

"I don't know what you mean by that," Alma said, "but if it's something nasty—" But Willie was off to the barn with one of the weans on his shoulder and his mouth puckered into a whistle.

He was obliged to have a sheep dog here as part of his farm equipment, and he and the dog were on the most excellent terms of friendship. They worked together with the sheep and lay down together in the shade of the barn on hot days, or struggled through the blizzard together in winter.

Once Willie lost his way in a blinding storm and might have perished if he had been alone; but the dog, with a keener homing instinct than his own, guided him safely back to the farmhouse.

"My lord!" Alma said when they came in, plastered with wet snow, "I just got through wiping up the floor after the kids, and now you and that dirty dog! You stayed away so long, we et supper without you. But I'll warm you up something. I'm not mean."

Willie had no retort that time. He unwound his snow-encrusted muffler with stiff fingers, and sat in a chair by the kitchen stove to pull off his boots. The dog came up beside him and licked his hand, and Willie patted the dog on the head.

The little boys came too and stood around them.

"Where was you, Pa?"

"Is the snow deep?"

"I was out dancin' the Highland Fling on th' shed roof, my bairns," said Willie. He was improvising in good humor rather than in bitterness, and the children laughed delightedly.

"*You!*" said Alma scathingly. But she brought him a plate of *good* hot stew to eat by the fireside.

They heard of Douglas' marriage with characteristic reactions.

"Some highfalutin' lady, I suppose," said Alma. "He couldn't never be satisfied with a good, sweet, simple girl. He'll pick one with her nose in the air to lord it over all his relatives."

"Well, I'm glad," Willie said. "He got a bad deal the other time, although she was so bonnie to look on. I dinna ken whatever went ill with them. If they'd had a bairn all might have been well, perhaps. But this time I hope 'twill work out for the best."

Willie thought about Douglas and his intended bride a good deal.

"I'd like to give them a wedding present, Alma," he said.

"What have *you* got that either of *them* would want?" asked Alma.

"But that's no the point," Willie said. "It's the thought o' giving that counts. Doug's done so much for us."

"Much!" Alma said. "If you call this God-forsaken desert *much*."

"We've had a good potato crop this year," Willie said.

"Yes, an' we can use it, *all*," said Alma.

"We'll take a bushel of the best ones, Alma, washed and packed like something choice, and ship it up to them. Every man eats potatoes, be he ever so fortunate. Doug will understand, and 'twill carry our kind wishes."

231

Willie sorted over the potatoes with care, washed them and packed them nicely in a new bushel basket. He tied a clean burlap sack over the top of the basket, prepaid delivery charges, and saw it into the baggage car of the train himself. How it was received would depend on the understanding of Doug's new wife. But Willie always hoped for the best.

2

The bushel of potatoes was delivered at an awkward time to the new apartment. The wedding had been solemnized in the mayor's office at the city hall. Both Sheila and Douglas had long discarded their Catholic and Presbyterian backgrounds, and the mayor was a friend of Doug's. Only the Beaches had stood up with them, but all their friends, and Molly, of course, were invited to the apartment for champagne and lobster salad afterward.

Sheila wore a champagne-colored silk suit and a little toque of the same material, and Douglas had procured with considerable difficulty and expense a sheaf of tawny-golden orchids to cascade down her shoulder. Her wedding ring was set with small diamonds and a large diamond blazed in her engagement ring.

Sheila had relegated the rings Mr. Rossiter had given her to her red velvet jewel case, but Douglas was nervously aware that his diamonds hardly came up to those in Mr. Rossiter's rings. He had tried everywhere to procure a stone as fine as the one in Sheila's first engagement ring. But Sheila laughed and said, "Darling, the diamond may be smaller than his, but you're bigger than Rossiter was. You're handsomer, you're younger. I never really loved him very much, but you—well, *you* know how you can flip me over, don't you?"

"Yes!" he said, "*I* know. That's one of the best things about the marriage. We know all about each other, don't we?"

"Oh, well," she said, "yes. But all the same I may be able to surprise you."

He laughed and kissed her. Part of the pleasure and satisfaction of this marriage lay in the anticipation that she would.

232

Later, Mr. Rossiter's rings came out of the jewel case again to sparkle beside Douglas' rings on her white, white fingers. Sheila liked the effect of a simple, dark, expensive dress together with a blaze of jewels.

On the day of the wedding they returned from the mayor's office to find the apartment crowded with the people they knew best—people with motorcars who liked horse racing and dancing. The men amused themselves with sports and good eating and drinking, but their religion was making money. The women amused themselves in spending the money, and their religion was keeping the men, and keeping themselves young. They laughed a great deal and talked rather loudly—at least so it seemed in an apartment, even a large apartment.

Sheila had abandoned the heavy red velvet and carved teakwood of her former apartment. She was thrifty, and she meant to use some of these things at the lake house. The Buddha would sit in the garden there, and she had plans for the red draperies. But the new apartment was all light and champagne color and Louis XVI furniture and little carved cupids and garlands of roses. It had cost a good deal of both her money and Douglas', and she was nervous about liquor rings on the tables and spots on the delicate carpets. But, after all, these people were celebrating in her honor, and they had given a lot of cut glass and sterling silver bowls, cold-meat forks and Battenburg lace. There was nothing she could do but smile her reserved smile.

"Mona Lisa," Harry Beach sometimes called her, and the others had changed it to "Mona Sheila," a nickname she liked. The only other she had had was "Reddy," the nickname she had been called by as a young secretary in John Rossiter's office. But she had hated that, and now she never thought of those days at all if she could help it.

Molly was the only relic of that past at the wedding party today, but there was no way around good old Molly. However, Sheila had bought her a plain, expensive dress of soft woodbrown, forestalling any red and green fantasies that Molly might have devised for herself. Molly did not look as out of place as she felt. She saw many of these men in the office at work, and she knew how to meet them in a hardheaded, fast-quipping, business way. But here, with champagne glasses in hand and pretty women eyeing them, they became unpredictable strangers. The women she partly envied, partly scorned. They were like the mistletoe that sucked the sap out of the oaks.

All her feelings were harrowed and mixed up today anyway. She was constantly on the verge of tears, thinking that since some other woman besides herself was to have Douglas, it was, at least, her little Sheila.

She had helped Sheila along all her life as best she could, and if it seemed at times that her sister had got all the breaks that she herself had longed for and never had, still, Molly wanted Sheila to be happy.

"She was always smarter than I was," she said to herself with a sniff and a tear, "but there's no use blaming her for that."

It did Molly's feelings no good that day to see Sam Plimpton there with his young wife. She had read all about her in the newspapers; "charming debutante, Vassar graduate, daughter of R. C. Hollander of the Hollander Lumber Company."

And now Plimpton accidentally bumped against her in the crowd, and, "Well, well, Molly!" he said. "You're looking fine—just fine. Molly, I want you to meet my wife."

Molly saw that she was prettier than the newspaper pictures had indicated.

"What was the name?" the girl asked, holding out her hand to Molly.

"Miss Casey," Sam said hastily. "She's Sheila's sister, you know. She works in our office, too, dear."

"Oh, yes," Mrs. Plimpton said. "How happy you must be today, Miss Casey. I'm very glad to have met you."

They did not stay long. Molly suspected that Mrs. Plimpton thought Sheila's crowd a little old and fast and vulgar, but she was doing her social best by Sam's business associates. Anger and hurt and Irish sentiment harrowed Molly, but the champagne was free and plentiful. "That's something," Molly said to herself, as she took another glass.

The door of the apartment was left open for comers and goers, and in the midst of the celebration a delivery man from the railway express came and stood in the doorway with a burlap-covered bushel basket in his arms.

"Mrs. Douglas McBain?" he said.

"Sheila!" someone cried. "Do you recognize yourself? You're

234

Mrs. McBain now." They pushed her forward and everyone stood around laughing and expectant.

"Doug," Sheila said, "it's another wedding present. But what in the world?"

Douglas took the bushel basket while Sheila signed for it. He carried it in beside the long table loaded with silver and cut glass and costly linens. The cramped, careful handwriting of a Scottish schoolboy on the label made his heart sink unreasonably.

"We'll open it later," he said. But they were all very gay now and determined to see what the basket contained.

Molly, walking a little unsteadily, brought scissors from a kitchen drawer and cut the heavy twine that tied the gunny sack on top of the basket.

"Potatoes!" everybody whooped, and Molly cried, "Irish pataties, be gorrah!"

"It's somebody's idea of a joke," said Sheila coldly.

"No, no," said Douglas going red to the ears, "it's nobody's joke. They came from my brother Willie down in the country."

"Oh," said Molly slowly, "the little one in the blue shirt who said he knew you in Scotland."

"Take them into the kitchen," said Sheila. But then she remembered the caterers. "No, out on the back landing."

"You can give them to me," said Molly. "I'll use them, if you don't want them."

"I don't want them," Sheila said. Then she looked around and smiled her reserved smile, and slipped her arm very snugly through Doug's. "Somebody get me some lobster salad," she said. "I've had nothing but champagne, and I know I shouldn't be hungry on this day of days, but I am."

People came and went, but Molly kept staying on and drinking the little shallow, open-mouthed glasses full of champagne. She had spilled some on the front of the brown dress, and she was beginning to feel very much at home and to talk.

"Sheila was always the lucky one—yes, she was. But I promised Mama I'd look out for her and by the Holy Mother, I have. He came into the office and he said, 'Tell him it's a man he knew in Scotland,' and I never tumbled—all the time it was brother Willie."

"She's had too much, Doug. Get her a cab," Sheila said.

"I'm just beginning to have a good time, Shee. Let me alone, do."

"Go quietly now, old girl," Sheila said. "You'll be sorry tomorrow if you don't."

"Come along, Molly, be a good lass," Douglas said, putting his arm around her and propelling her toward the door.

Molly turned her face to his shoulder and began to sob.

"Oh, Douglas!" she said. "Douglas."

Douglas put her into a cab.

"Send the potatoes with her," Sheila called.

A couple of hilarious guests carried the basket of potatoes out and put them in the cab at Molly's feet. The cab drove away, and one of the laughing guests threw a handful of rice after it.

Douglas stood on the curb and in spite of the exhilarations and anticipations of the day, he felt momentarily depressed.

Why are we here? What is the use of it? What is to become of us? he thought. But then Sheila came and put her arm through his and drew him indoors.

"Let's forget it," she said. "*Darling*, the party's almost over, and there'll be just the two of us alone in a few minutes."

So he pressed her hand and remembered that he was a bridegroom.

3

Lake Vivienne in the early 1900's suddenly became accessible and a social asset to Manitou City. For years it had been wild, remote and beautiful, known principally to lumberjacks and hunters. Now an electric railway to the mill town of Lakeside made weekend commuting from Manitou City possible; and the roads were being improved to such an extent that the more adventurous motorists sometimes drove their own automobiles from the city to the lake.

The dark northern waters began to blossom with sailboats and small launches, and expensive cottages began to be built among the pines. Because of the difficulty and expense of transportation, life at the lake became a symbol of luxury and privilege which was hard for ambitious people to resist.

The Beaches had a charming houseboat on Lake Vivienne. It was moored near some property which they owned on the wooded shores of the lake, and they reached it by motor launch from Lakeside. They called it *The Ark*, and all around the inside of the large main saloon there was painted a frieze of animals going two by two. Every weekend during the summer season the Beaches entertained at charming small houseboat parties. Sometimes the women remained to sun themselves and gossip and swim during the week, while the men returned to their offices in Manitou City.

It was on a weekend in *The Ark* that Douglas and Sheila had come to the conclusion that they would be conventional and marry and live the good life. The lake had a special significance for them, romantically and ambitiously.

So, although Sheila seemed to be a city dweller to the core, she reached for the prestige of a place at the lake. Douglas had the same desire for the symbols of social affluence. But even more than for Sheila, the lake in itself fulfilled for him the deprivations of his childhood. Here were mountains and trees and water. He could drown his memories of the dwindling rain-water barrels of Caithness in this prodigal abundance of water. He could forget Willie sweating in the desert places of the state, in the sound of waterfalls gurgling and foaming into the dark mysterious lake. At night he heard the water lapping on the shore. He bathed in the lake on hot weekends when he had left the city behind him; and after they acquired a motorboat he heard the waves beating against its sides and foaming out behind in a white plume of energy across the dark mirror of the lake. The *Imp* was the fastest motorboat on Lake Vivienne. There was no other that could touch her for speed, and Douglas liked that. They had considered a houseboat like the Beaches', but that would have been an imitation, and they wanted something less casual and more substantial. So the "cottage" went up somewhat away from the shore among the pines. It had a large fireplace and screened porches and plenty of room for weekend visitors. There was a combined bathhouse and boathouse on the lake with docks and a diving raft. Graveled paths led upward in devious ways among the trees to the low brown shingled house.

Sheila had a flair for architectural planning and a high hand with workmen. Douglas left much of the supervision of the building to her. She liked to do it, she was willing to stay in Lakeside all the week to see that the work was done, and she was furnishing an equal part of the cost. They had agreed before the wedding that she should keep Mr. Rossiter's money in a separate fund in her own name, because of Richard, and Douglas never interfered with that even to advise her on investments. She had learned a good deal about investments in her days with Mr. Rossiter. She did very well for herself with no help from anyone, and she liked to keep it that way. She was so yielding and passionate on the personal side, so unyielding and cool on the business side! The contrast amused Douglas greatly, and constituted much of her allure. But, when she wanted something, she could be generous, and she wanted the summer place to be finer than either of them could afford alone. So they managed the planning and the financing of it jointly, in a medley of encounters, both passionately sensual and coolly calculating. Douglas laughed when he thought of those days of planning the summer place. Sheila was always presenting new and surprising facets. He felt well-satisfied and conscious that they were both headed in the same direction.

Sheila had strong ideas on the interior decoration of the cottage. She wanted it smart and daring and sophisticated. Actually, her daring was stronger than her sophistication, and her taste was still rooted in her childish impulses.

For a long time she had been in revolt against the church in which she had been reared and in which she felt that her instincts had been stifled. The Buddha in her first apartment was not a decorative accident—it was a part of the revolt, a kind of artistic thumbing of the nose at her past. If she had been reared a Buddhist, she might have hung a colored picture of Jesus and the Sacred Heart in her living room to tell the world that she was a nonconformist.

At the summer place she decided to relegate Buddha to the garden and to decorate the house with red lamps and little grinning imps and devils. Douglas was somewhat puzzled, but he believed that interior decoration was a woman's province. His idea of a summer cottage was something rustic and clean and uncluttered, with a breeze sweeping through it from the lake.

"Can't you be wicked without advertising it, darling?" he asked lightly. "After all, you aren't running a bawdy house."

238

"*That's* not amusing," she said. "But the house *will* be, if you let me handle it. It will be as amusing as the Beaches' *Ark* and animals, and more unconventional. I'll pay for it all myself if you're going to be stuffy about my ideas."

"Have it your own way," he said. "If *you* are in the house, I won't look at the imps. You're the one to be pleased."

She pulled his head down and kissed him. "You'll like it," she said.

When it was done, he decided that he did like it. They had left the rafters bare and stained the wooden walls dark. It was cool and dim inside the cottage among the trees. The red curtains and big red divans and the imps perched on mantel and shelf and over doorways, the red glow from the lamps at night, all made a striking effect.

Their friends were delighted. People stopped exclaiming about the Beaches' animals and said, "But have you *seen* the McBain's demons?"

Douglas remembered Tam O'Shanter, and it began to please him to have his own collection of devils dancing and fiddling on the rooftops. So they called their place Brimstone Manor and christened the motorboat the *Imp*.

It was only very rarely, when he came home tired and exasperated from a hot week in town and saw Sheila sitting so cool and sardonic among her demons that he was annoyed. But a swim in the lake usually put him in a good mood again. If that failed, she had whiskey and ice waiting for him on the porch before dinner.

In the summer when Richard came home from school there was a slight embarrassment in their way of living, but they adjusted that by letting him invite his school friends to the lake and by making a continual party of it. Sometimes Douglas had an uneasy feeling that they were making a guest of Richard, and he tried heartily to be a father to him. He had always wanted a son of his own, and now he had one. But he and Richard had missed all the tender encounters of childhood, and, beyond the hearty conviviality of their surface relationship, they sometimes looked at one another with the appraising eyes of strangers. Having reached the secretive years of adolescence without any close parental relationship, Richard had no intention of surrendering his privacy to the man with whom his mother was currently in love. He was not bitter, only realistic, and the cottage and speedboat on Lake

239

Vivienne represented a great improvement over a commercial camp. He was perfectly willing to play along with them.

4

It was not until the second summer that they invited me to come to visit them. I was not quite sure that I wanted to go. I was nearly thirteen and desperately shy and self-conscious. The vicissitudes of my life had not given me confidence. Because of Grandma's heart condition, because of all the memories the town held, because we had no man coming and going at regular hours, we led a very secluded life in Opportunity. But I had friends of my own age, I did well in school, and all summer long I rode Beauty over the beautiful country roads and hills in perfect contentment. The thought of leaving this contentment behind, even for ten days, frightened me.

But Uncle Douglas had sent money for my train ticket and for a new dress. On a Friday afternoon I was to go to Manitou City where he would meet me and take me to Lake Vivienne. He would have to go back to the city on Monday morning, but he would be with me again on the next weekend at the lake, and then I should return with him to Manitou City and he would put me on the train for Opportunity. His letter sounded pleased and excited, and the joyous prospect of seeing him again was greater than my apprehension of the unknown.

"Will you go?" asked Connie in excitement.

"Yes, I will go," I said.

We went to town and Connie bought yards of material at the dry-goods store. She sewed me a red plaid dress for traveling and a white lawn dress for a possible party. She bought a pattern and made me a bathing costume of blue twill with long bloomers and a sailor collar trimmed in white braid. The bathing costume turned out to be large, and the red plaid dress, which had been made from an old pattern, was a trifle small. Connie faced the hem of the dress so that it was the right length, but it was skimpy across the chest where I was beginning to have small, rounding breasts. I was terribly conscious of these and the dress embarrassed me, but I could not bring myself to point out the difficulty to Connie, who was trying so hard to make me presentable. I wore it as it was, and as often as I could remember I kept my arms folded across my chest. I wore a large straw hat with a turned-up brim and an elastic band under my chin.

Connie wept when I left.

"Don't forget us, darling. And do be so *very* careful of that treacherous lake. I'll never have a moment's peace until you are back. Write us, darling, do."

Connie had told me many times about her terrible experience in trying to learn to swim in the Natatorium at the Golden Gate Park in San Francisco. They had been on a trip when she was young and her father had said that every young female should learn to swim in case she ever needed to save her life in water. And she had gone down the chute with every confidence that swimming would be easy, but her head had gone right under and she had nearly drowned.

"I could *never* learn to swim," she said, "*never!* I tried and tried. It was impossible."

I have had only two unreasonable fears in my life, the fear of water and the fear of snakes. Both of these were fixed fears of Connie's which she implanted in me early, along with the many good enthusiasms with which she also endowed me. I have had a hard time getting over these two phobias.

5

I saw Uncle Douglas through the train window before he saw me. My heart began to pound with happiness. He stood on the platform at ease, looking prosperous and self-assured. He wore a light summer suit and a panama hat, in the best fashion. Yet there was something strange about him, too. Perhaps it was only that I had not seen him for two years; but he seemed heavier to me and somehow puffy about the eyes.

He was looking eagerly along the car windows, but he did not see me until I was coming down the car steps. Then for an instant it was as if he did not recognize me. Whether it was the plaid dress and the turned-up hat or the fact that I had grown four inches, I don't know. I realize now that he had last seen me as a

241

pretty little girl with blond curls and that now I was a hobble-
dehoy, awkwardly between pretty childhood and confident adolescence.

Yet he only hesitated an instant. Then he held out his arms.
"Kit!"

I ran to him eagerly.

"Oh, Uncle Doug, I'm so glad to see you!"

"Kit! Kit! My little honey!"

I bobbed along beside him joyously while he carried my suitcase.

"First we'll go to the office for a minute. Then we'll have lunch.
You can order anything you want—anything."

"Anything?" I cried blissfully.

"Caviar and champagne if you like," he said. "Neither your
Aunt Connie nor your Aunt Sheila is here to stop us."

"Then I'll have a hot tamale and a French pastry," I said.

"Good!" he said. "Good! That sounds unusual enough to come
from the heart."

They had enlarged the office a great deal since I had seen it
last. Two pretty secretaries had new desks in the office, but Molly
still sat behind her typewriter, pegging away.

"Here she is!" Uncle Doug cried proudly to Molly. "Isn't she a
fine big girl?"

"I should say so," said Molly. "Otterson called while you were
out, Doug, and he won't talk to anyone but you."

"He can wait," Uncle Doug said. He began to go through the
drawers of his desk for things that would please me, a new pencil,
a bunch of varicolored rubber bands, a blotter with a picture of a
steamship on it. It was an old routine which he had always gone
through on my visits to the office.

I opened my suitcase and brought out a pen wiper which I had
made for him and a small clay tray for paper clips. It had occurred to me that we always accepted gifts from him but never
thought that there was anything we could give him in return. I
was pleased to see how delighted he was.

Presently he dictated a letter and made a few telephone calls
while I sat in the best client's chair looking about the office.
There were large charts on the walls showing new land develop-
ments divided off into many small lots—Sunnyvale Addition,
Buena Vista Homes, Castle Manor Park. With the telephone re-

242

ceiver still at his ear, he pointed out another chart which I had not quite understood.

"It's a preliminary drawing of the dam," he said, "the one that's going to turn the desert into good farm land. Remember? I told you once."

"Yes, I remember," I said, hearing again in my mind the rushing of many little streams among lush grass.

"We'll call it the Garden of Eden Dam. Eden Water! How about that? Oh, yes, yes, this is McBain. When did you want to see me? No, I can't. Not until Monday morning. Nine o'clock then? Fine. I'll see you."

He hung up the receiver and turned to Molly.

"We're going to lunch now, and then we'll take the trolley to the lake. Won't you come with us, Molly?"

Molly looked up from her typing.

"What *is* this? Poor-relations week?" she asked casually. I do not think that she meant to be unkind; she was used to depreciating herself and she thought of me as a child. But I was of an age to understand as much as an adult, and I was unduly sensitive. Still, I kept a blank face, and I thought proudly: I'm not really a poor relation. My father provided for me.

Uncle Doug said hastily, "No, this is not poor-relations week, Molly. It's a very special week that I've been looking forward to for a long time. It's Kit and Douglas week. But you'd better join us anyway."

"Thank you," Molly said, "but I've got an appointment to have my hair dyed. All your plush clients would leave you if they saw me sitting here as the good Lord intended."

On the electric trolley the conductor came up to us and shook hands with Uncle Doug and patted me on the head.

"This is my niece, Christine McBain, Jim," Uncle Douglas said. "And this is Jim Broderick, Kit. Jim is the smartest conductor on the line, and a real good friend of mine."

"I'm pleased to meet you," I said. I was impressed by the uniform and flattered that the conductor of a train should take any notice of me.

"You've got a mighty fine Uncle, little girl," Jim Broderick said. "I'd trust him with my bottom dollar. We've been riding together several years now, and I'm proud when he calls me friend."

All three of us were happy. Uncle Doug had the gift of making

243

unimportant people feel appreciated. At the same time, he was not immune to a feeling of pleasure when they appreciated him.

When we left the electric train at Lakeside, three large, gangling boys suddenly sprang up around us and grabbed our luggage.

"This is Kit," Uncle Douglas said to them, and to me, "This is Richard, and his friends Bill and Charles."

The boys looked at me with curiosity and then with disdain. They had expected something a little more mature and worldly-wise. I had twittered like a canary all the way out in the train, but now I lost my voice completely.

At the dock the *Imp* was rocking gently on dark waters. Uncle Doug helped me to step down into her from the solid planks of the dock.

"She's the fastest boat on the lake," he said proudly. I had enjoyed the train ride, but I had never been on water before and everything seemed very strange to me. Richard started the motor and one of the other boys cast off. There was a great sound of motor and rushing water and a froth of spray. I clung wildly to my hat as the dark waters rushed away behind us.

Uncle Doug leaned forward and shouted above the noise of the motor, "Take it off."

At first I could not think what he meant, but he shouted it again, and I took off the hat and let the wind blow my hair.

It was even stranger to find myself stepping out onto a narrow dock that also seemed to me to be rocking in the midst of swirling water. We went up a path among trees and Aunt Sheila sat on the wide, screened porch, sipping something out of a tall glass. She pulled Uncle Doug's head down to her without bothering to rise and gave him a long kiss.

"Here's Kit," he said to her.

"How are you, Christine?" she said, holding out her soft white hand with the jewels.

"I'm fine," I said.

"You've grown," she said. "You were quite a little thing when I saw you last."

"Yes," I said, folding my arms across my chest.

"I thought your Uncle sent you money for a new dress," she said.

"This is new," I said. "Aunt Connie made it."

"Oh, I see," she said. "Well, dear, have a good time. Mary will show you where you are to sleep."

Mary was a large black woman, the first Negro I had ever been near enough to speak to. She wore a pale-green uniform and a white cap and apron. She led me back through the house to a small bright bedroom with red curtains at the windows. A little red imp sat grinning on a shelf beside the bed.

"You-all better get into your bathing dress now, Miss," she said. "Everybody go in the lake before dinner."

In silent apprehension I took off my clothes and got into the heavy blue twill bathing costume which Connie's loving hands had made for me. I knew with a sinking heart that it would be as wrong for me as the red plaid dress. And then there was the horror of the dark cold lake.

They were all as much at home in the water as fish, or so it seemed to me. Uncle Doug tried at first to teach me to swim, and the boys made a few playful lunges at me which filled me with panic. I remembered Connie's dreadful experience at the Natatorium, and I was stiff with terror. Presently Uncle Doug and the boys began a wild game of waterball, while I sat shivering on the dock, hating myself and not knowing what to do. Aunt Sheila did not come down to bathe now. It seemed that she preferred to swim in the morning.

While we were in the water a motor launch full of people arrived. They seemed to be old friends, and some of them trooped to the house with laughter and conversation, while two young women in bathing suits joined us on the dock. Their bathing suits seemed to me very brash and daring, and I wondered what Connie would have thought of them. They were soon in the water playing waterball with the boys. Uncle Doug came and sat beside me on the dock, breathing hard from the exercise, the water streaming from his hair.

"Ah," he said, "that's good after a week in the office! If I did this every day I'd keep my sylphlike figure."

In my discomfort I could not think of anything to say.

"You're shivering, Kit," he said. "Better go in now and give yourself a good rub. We'll try again tomorrow. You'll soon learn."

But I was a complete dolt. This week stands out as one of the most unhappy of my life. I had weathered far more dreadful things, but I had always before been in proud possession of

245

myself. Now I felt abased and inadequate and homesick, and after Uncle Doug went back to the city no one lifted a hand to help me. The only thing that saved a shred of my self-respect, was that they paid little attention to me. Company came and went, the boys shouted in the lake or took the *Imp* on long excursions. Aunt Sheila said to me in the morning, "Have a good time, dear," and washed her hands of me for the day.

There was one time when they noticed me for a moment. Because I could not or would not swim I sometimes sat timorously on an air mattress that floated on the water. But one day I suddenly realized in panic that it had drifted out from shore and that I was beyond my depth. I swallowed my terrible pride and called for help, and, laughing, they towed me back to shore.

At home, whenever I felt unhappy I was accustomed to solace myself with reading. So now, having plenty of time on my hands, I began to look for books. There were some current magazines, but nowhere any books. I was surprised, because Grandma's house in Opportunity had many shelves of books, books which had belonged to my grandfather and my father, and other books which, for all our frugality of living, we had purchased for ourselves. I had never thought of a house without books. The idea seemed fantastic. I asked Mary if there were any stored away.

"Books?" she said, surprised. "What you-all want of books?"

"To read," I said, feeling ashamed again that I should be different from everybody else.

After a while she came back with a book in her hand.

"Here one," she said.

It was a copy of *The Houseboat on the Styx* by John Kendrick Bangs, which, I suppose, had been given to the house by some jocose guest who admired the small red devils sitting in their niches. So all that homesick week I read *The Houseboat on the Styx*, glad to find Shakespeare and Milton and other old friends there, although I expect that most of the satire and fantasy was lost upon me. I have never seen a copy of that book since, but it will be with me as long as I remember anything.

246

6

The long, long week that seemed as if it would never pass, passed. I went with the boys in the *Imp* to meet Uncle Douglas on Friday afternoon, and I made a brave show of doing what other people were doing and of having a good time. I hoped that Uncle Doug was deceived.

I counted the meals, the hours, the minutes until we could leave on Monday morning, and Monday morning finally came. Aunt Sheila turned a cool, pale cheek for me to kiss. "Have a good time, dear," she said. It seemed to me that she had said no other thing to me since she had condemned my dress. On the train coming out to the lake I had chattered happily, secure in the belief that I had found my Uncle Doug again. On the way back I was silent and shy, convinced that I had lost him. I am not sure that Uncle Douglas noticed any difference.

When we came into the office, Molly said: "There's a stack of mail on your desk, Doug."

"I'll see to it," he said. "And, Molly, Kit's train leaves at eleven-thirty. There won't be time for a hot tamale and a French pastry." He winked at me conspiratorily. "But I want you to order her a nice box lunch, sandwiches, and grapes and cake—something good. And don't make any appointments for me after ten o'clock. Kit and I are going shopping and then I'll see her to her train."

He went into his inner office and closed the door, and Molly said, "Cheese, beef, or ham?"

"Ham, please," I said.

She called a number and ordered a box lunch to be delivered as soon as possible. Then she turned to me and looked me over.

"What kind of a time did you have out there?" she inquired curiously.

"Fine," I said.

"Well, that's better than I do," she said. "When I go out there, all the little devils begin crossing themselves, and that's embarrassing for everybody. Now, I'm busy. You'll find some magazines on the table in the corner." Over a magazine I stole occasional glances at Molly, typing away in all the glory of her newly dyed hair, and I found that I liked her better than I should ever have thought I could.

247

A few minutes after ten Uncle Doug came out of his office, looking as pleased as a boy playing hookey from school.

"Tell anyone who inquires that I'm out of the office on very important business," he said to Molly, winking at me again and making me smile and feel excited too.

We walked down the street to a jewelry store. It was a large store, with gleaming plate-glass windows. The windows displayed a great deal of black velvet and a few very exquisite jewels sparkling against it. I had never before been in such a store. Even in summer daylight it was lit up by many lights in crystal chandeliers, and the cases on either side of the aisles sparkled with many jewels against velvet. Along the walls there were glass cupboards full of silver dishes, and all sorts of handsome clocks were hung above them. Some of the clocks were chiming the quarter-hour as we entered. The whole place seemed to twinkle and glitter with wealth and opulence.

A bald man, who seemed to me also to glitter, from his shiny forehead to his gold teeth and polished nails, came forward and greeted us very warmly.

"But I'm terribly sorry," he said, "Mrs. McBain's brooch hasn't come in yet. There was a little delay in finding the right stone for the central petal."

"Never mind," Uncle Douglas said. "It wasn't about the brooch that I came in this morning. I'm looking for something pretty for this young lady. This is my niece, Christine McBain, Mr. Cully. Kit, this is Mr. Cully, who has one of the handsomest stores in Manitou City, don't you think so?"

"Oh, yes," I said breathlessly.

"Thank you very much, Mr. McBain," said Mr. Cully, "coming from you, such a compliment really touches me, because I have no customer with better taste than your own. Had you something special in mind, sir?"

"A watch, I think. What do you say to that, Kit? Would you like a watch?"

"Oh, yes," I said, "but it would cost too much, wouldn't it?"

"She's a Scotch lassie, you see," said Uncle Doug, laughing. "Yes, it must be a watch. Let's see what you have, Mr. Cully."

From a dazzling array of watches we chose a small gold one with a pin shaped like a fleur-de-lis. Uncle Douglas pinned it awkwardly to my dress.

248

"How's that, eh?"

"Oh, it's beautiful! Oh, thank you, Uncle Doug. Thank you!" I felt the terrible inadequacy of any words I could say, but he seemed very happy.

He gave Mr. Cully a large bill, and while we waited for the change he looked about the shop with frank pleasure.

"A bonnie shop!" His gaze came around to me and he said apologetically, with a smile almost as shy as my own, "I've always been fond of glitter. It's a strange fancy in a man from Thurso."

We went along to the train and I was plagued again with the new shyness that tied my tongue.

"You've got your lunch box all right?" he said.

"Oh, yes. I ordered a ham sandwich."

"Ham is always tasty."

"I like it."

"Mind you don't get carsick. Connie will meet you, I suppose?"

"Yes. If she doesn't, I know my way."

"Give them my kind regards."

"I will."

He settled me in a seat and kissed me. Then he stood outside the train, waiting for its departure. We could not hear each other through the window glass, but he winked again and smiled and gave me a comical imitation of the porter who had just gone by trundling a trunk. The train began to move and he waved both hands at me and threw me a kiss. I pressed my face against the glass, so that I could see him as long as possible. I saw him going away, limping a little—with the limp one forgot when he was approaching because then one only saw his eyes and his smile. At the barrier he turned and waved once more and then he was gone.

I sank back in the seat, sick with misery because I had been too shy to tell him how much I loved him.

7

My watch caused a sensation among my friends, and Connie was enchanted by it. Grandma admired it, too, but she said, "Poor Douglas! He gives out of arrogance and pride, because he was once so poor."

249

"That's not fair, Mama," Connie said.

"Maybe not," Grandma said.

"And anyway, you shouldn't say it before Kit. You'll spoil all her pleasure in this exquisite gift."

"Kit is a sensible girl," Grandma said. Sometimes Grandma's confidence in my good sense was a severe trial to me. Yet perhaps it was this confidence which gave me the ability to differ with her. I thought now that, even if my uncle did give out of arrogance and pride, there was a wonderful sweetness in the giving.

Early the next summer I received another invitation to spend ten days at Lake Vivienne.

"Of course you will go," said Connie. "We'll make a new traveling dress, but I think the bathing costume will be good again. It was a little large last year."

I had never told Connie and Grandma anything but that I had had a fine time at the lake. There was no use worrying them, and I felt that most of my trouble had been due to my own inadequacy.

"No," I said, "I don't think I'll go again."

Connie was very much surprised.

"But he's sent you the money and everything."

"I'll send it back," I said, "and I'll write him a real nice letter so he won't feel badly. I don't think any of them will mind."

"Well!" Connie said. "You're a funny child, Kit."

"I'm not a child," I said resentfully. "I'm nearly fourteen."

I am sure that they did not mind. They were already planning a trip to Europe for that summer.

They went on the *Mauretania*, the fastest boat on the high seas—on the maiden voyage of the fastest boat. One could scarcely do better than that.

Uncle Douglas rarely wrote letters unless they pertained to business, and then he dictated them to Molly and signed them with his beautiful clear, flowing hand. But I had many picture postcards from him that summer. I treasured all of them. There was the *Mauretania*, of course. On the card he had written: "the *fastest* steamship on the ocean." There was the Tower of London, and an Irish jaunting cart, and Edinburgh Castle, and the Eiffel Tower. There was one from the battlefield of Waterloo in Belgium, and that puzzled me a little because I did not know much about Waterloo nor why anyone should visit it. Aunt Connie was fond of saying that someone had "met his Waterloo," and I knew that it meant some sort of humiliating defeat. She used it chiefly of cocky young men who got shrewish wives.

But I was a methodical girl, and before the summer was over I had read Victor Hugo's description of the Battle of Waterloo, and I went on and read about Napoleon and all the things that happened to him. I thought somehow that it was a natural thing for Uncle Douglas to be interested in the fate of a man like Napoleon. They had both started so humbly and gone ahead so rapidly.

There was a picture postcard of the Casino at Monte Carlo, and I read that from there men often went out and shot themselves because they had lost their fortunes at the gaming tables. I followed Uncle Doug to Rome, too, and lying in the hammock under the crab apple trees on hot summer afternoons, I read about Caesar and all the glories and splendors that had fallen into ruin.

Perhaps, I thought, I am learning more from his travels than he is. But that was my own personal brand of arrogance and pride.

8

At Southampton, Douglas and Sheila stepped from the first-class splendor of the *Mauretania* into the boat train, and went up to London. After a week of sight-seeing and good living, they crossed to Dublin, and there, with very little discussion, they decided to part for a few days while each one visited his ancestral home.

Sheila had not been born in Ireland but she still had aunts and uncles and cousins living in a small village in County Mayo. She wanted to see whence she had come, but she could not quite risk having Douglas see it with her. There might be pigpens and filth and poverty and coarseness that would color his image of her.

Douglas, in his turn, was just as concerned that Sheila should not see the half-empty rain-water barrel, the peat fire, the oat-

251

straw mattresses, and the outhouse in the corner of the stable that he remembered in Caithness. They went their separate ways, relieved, and did not stop to examine the failings of a marriage built on pretense.

Douglas had sometimes sent money home to Scotland, but he had written very little. Because of his mother he had never told them about his divorce from Mamie, and now that his mother was dead, it seemed useless to speak of a thing that had happened so long ago.

Jeanie had replaced the mother as letter writer for the scattered family. The letters she wrote were very simple:

> "DEAR BROTHER, The gift you sent was needed and has been well spent. God bless you. This leaves us well and hope it finds you and Mamie the same. We would love to see you. Never forget us, though the great Pond divide us. We pray for your good health and happiness. Your sister,
> JEAN"

Douglas was still in his secure world of ease and accomplishment when he reached Inverness. But there he had to spend the night before he could get the slow train that would crawl northward across the flat, bleak land, stopping at every little station along the way. Inverness was still in the Highlands, a bonnie town with trees and hills, but, walking down the street at ten o'clock of the night, he could read his newspaper in the bright, clear twilight of the summer evening. There was something in the sky, the crisp air, the smell from the gutters and the little tobacconist shops that stirred a kind of homesick foreboding in him. He asked himself: Should I have stayed in London? How far away is Manitou City? Am I indeed the man I thought I was?

The feeling increased almost to panic, as he crawled northward the next day. A man should never try to go backward, even condescendingly, as a tourist. There are forces we do not understand, old corpuscles still moving in the blood from other men's genes. He had tried so hard to get away from this place, and now, voluntarily, he was coming back. But only for three days, he told himself. To feel like this is absurd.

When at last he got down from the train at Mid Kirk, he felt stiff and tired, and his lame ankle pained him; but his head was clear again and the depression of the journey had left him.

252

The wind swept across the long stretches of flat land, bending the oats in pale green ripples, smelling of the sea. His brother Davie, who had been a small boy when he left, came to fetch him in a high, two-wheeled cart. Davie was a man now, fair-haired and lean, the most like Angus in appearance of any of the brothers. He ran the home croft with the help of the old father. His wife and two small sons and sister Jeanie all lived with them in the old home. Charley, the other younger brother, rented a farm nearby. Geordie, the next brother after Willie, was a watch and clock repair man in Glasgow.

At the farm they had a high tea ready for Douglas with hot scones and pancakes, jam and crowdy, and strong hot tea. The kitchen seemed crowded with honest, smiling faces; his father, Jeanie, Charley with a wife and two lassies, and Davie's wife and two small sons.

He found that he was not lost among them, as he had feared he might be. His passionate desire to be somebody had borne fruit. They looked at him with admiration and respect; he had become a great man who deserved their pride.

"Ye've done weel, Douglas," his father said. "There was a time when I thought ye would stand firm at nothing, but your mither was right. She said, ' 'Tis Douglas will go beyond any of them,' she said. My poor, lost lass, she was right in that as in so mony ways."

At first they were shy and diffident, but soon they began to ask him questions and put out sly sallies of humor. He could laugh at the wit, but the questions were difficult to parry. He found himself describing Mamie's latest costume to the women-folk and expatiating on the details of the indisposition which had prevented her from leaving London.

"It'll no be a bairn, will it? after a' these years?" asked the father.

"It's no a bairn," said Douglas heavily.

He was on safer ground when it came to talking about Willie and Kit. He spoke of them in detail. That he had not seen either for over a year amazed the home folks greatly.

"You've no idea of the distances in America," he explained. "We live apart and all of us are busy."

One of Charley's little flaxen-haired girls came up beside him and gazed at him shyly.

253

"Do ye see redskins?" she asked.

He took her on his knee, trying to remember when he had last seen an Indian.

"Once," he said, "when Kit and I were driving Beauty out from Manitou City into the country, we came to a spring near the highway, and there were redskins camping." He saw by her wide eyes that she imagined painted warriors on horseback. Actually, it had been a very bedraggled, small encampment but he remembered that Kit had been impressed.

"Beauty would not go near them," he said. "She kept whirling around in her tracks, until we had to let her make her way back as she had come. Why she should behave so I dinna ken. Some odor of wildness must have struck her nostrils and filled her with fear."

The little girl put her head back against his shoulder. "I would'a been afeared too," she said softly.

"What like is Willie's wife?" asked Jeanie. "Her letters are verra woefu' with troubles an' complaints. Is their croft so poor an' sma'?"

"They have a hundred and sixty acres," Douglas said.

"Ah!" they all said. "A bonnie lot of land—and in America!"

" 'Twill be bonnier, when I've put a dam in there to spread the water over the land."

"You?" they cried in admiration.

"Aye," Douglas said, "myself alone. I've great plans for the future."

"Ah," they said again, lost in admiration.

Douglas slept very well that night, even in the perpetual daylight, even on the oathusk mattress, even with Mamie's photograph upon the mantel shelf. The many little tensions and anxieties that he lived with daily, fell away here. It was a complete holiday. When he got up the next morning the men had already gone to the turnip fields. "Swedes," they called the turnips, he remembered, but he did not remember why. Jeanie had gone with the men, for as an unmarried woman she had to pull her share of the load. Mary, the wife of Davie, had milked the cows and prepared the breakfast, and now she served him shyly.

"We never get porridge like this in the states," Douglas said,

254

smacking his lips over the great steaming bowl of oatmeal that was so familiar.

"Do ye no?" Mary asked, "and why not?"

"They fancy their oats steamed and rolled out flat instead of steel cut," Doug said. "It's not the same thing at all."

"Then I doot it's the one superiority Scotland has over America," Mary said. "We've no verra much to offer in any other way."

He walked out into the cool bright morning with Davie's two little boys running beside him. "Where are they working?" he asked.

"Over yon field," answered the elder boy. "Do ye no see them?"

The smaller one took his hand. "Come," he said, "We'll tak' ye there."

The workers in the field greeted him genially.

"Keeping American hours, eh, lad?"

"You must have been up at dawn," said Douglas.

"Dawn?" they said, laughing.

"Well, all night then with your midnight sun."

"The swedes never stop growing in midsummer, nor the weeds neither. Winter's the season to lie abed."

Douglas tried to take the hoe from Jeanie's hand, but she said, in a low voice, "Take father's. He shouldna be doin' this, but he's a stubborn auld mon for the work."

"Nae, lad, ye'll spoil your city shoes," said his father, but he gave up the hoe nevertheless and Douglas bent his back to the work. It was like old times with the larks singing, and the Johnny-jump-ups blooming in the corners of the slate-slab fences.

At midmorning they returned to the house for a second breakfast. At this season they worked almost the clock around and regaled themselves with five meals during the waking hours.

He remembered it all so well, and the disgust he had felt for the meanness of it. How had he come by that disgust when he had never known a better life? Now that he had experienced the better life, he somehow felt less repugnance for this primitive way.

In fact he was surprised to find how little the lack of modern sanitary convenience disturbed him. He had an unexpected sense of coming home, of belonging in the circle about the peat fire in the kitchen. There was something here which he could not

255

analyze. Was it only acceptance? Lack of ambition? He did not know. Certainly there was no striving or crowding, no rivalry or dissension. They live like animals, he thought contemptuously. Yet in the same instant he knew that there was a calm content among them that was above price.

It was a content which he had missed in the champagne-colored apartment and the summer place with the little devils. It took him back to the pair of pink cottages in Opportunity, yet even there—. Perhaps the secret lay in the fact that all ages accommodated themselves to the same fire, and children stood listening by the knee of age.

Yet in America there had been Kit, and now he had Richard and his friends. The thought of Richard, regarding him with the cool eyes of a stranger, suddenly revolted Douglas. For a moment he was caught off guard, and he thought: He is not *my* son. We are not even friends. But this was an attitude which he had studiously purged from his mind, and he set it aside now. He thought, instead, that he was glad he had not brought Sheila with him. Much as he loved her, had she been with him he knew that he would have missed this sense of homecoming, and that he would have been overwhelmed by the lack of plumbing.

After the noon meal, in Douglas' honor, the others left off working in the fields. The men sat in the front dooryard while the women cleaned up the dishes and tidied the kitchen. The talk was slow and thorough. It ranged from the price of tups and ewes in America (a subject on which Douglas was sadly uninformed) to the world situation in politics and economics.

Charley and other neighbors came and joined them, squatting on boxes and tubs about the doorstep. These men read the newspapers; sometimes they asked Douglas questions he could not answer, and advanced ideas which surprised him. He wondered fleetingly, if, preoccupied as he was with the transactions of McBain, Plimpton and Buxton, and the continued need and desire to make money, he was more insular than they were. He was puzzled and slightly annoyed.

They moved back into the house for tea and other neighbors joined them. The little kitchen and parlor were full of friendly, simple people come to look at the magnificent prodigal who had appeared again in their midst.

One of the chiels who came was obviously a simpleton, a tall gawky fellow with wide blue eyes and a hairless chin. "Welcome, Robbie," they said to him kindly, but they smiled and nodded to Douglas in apology for him. "Pay no heed to him," they seemed to say. "The poor lad's daft, but we canna turn him away."

"Och," said Robbie, "I was fair run down by a cycle on my way here. Bicycles is an invention of the devil, seems. Do ye have bicycles in the States, Douglas?"

"Aye," Douglas said, laughing. "We have bicycles."

"Och, then I winna go there. Why does a mon hae two gude legs, gin he winna walk? E'en a horse is a bonnie thing. But the roads is nae mair safe for simple folk, wi' bicycles wheelin' to an' fro like mad. What is the world comin' to, an' nae but cycles gangin' back an' forth?"

"Why, man," said Davie, "Douglas here has e'en a motorcar to ride in. What do you say to that, Robbie?"

"I say 'tis a sin," said Robbie. "A motorcar is no better than a bicycle. Still Douglas is a famous mon they tell me. Could be I am wrong. What else do ye have, Douglas?"

"Oh," said Douglas, smiling, "I've a house by a loch, and on the loch the fastest boat anyone has there."

"The fastest boat? And do ye row it then?"

"No. It has a motor in it—a kind of engine-like. It goes of itself."

"The devil it does! Ye put something into it."

"Aye, petrol."

"And then it goes of itself. Ach! God!"

"Ye see, Robbie," said Davie, "in America men have a great mony more things than we have here in Caithness."

"Aye, I believe that," Robbie said seriously. "Bicycles an' motorcars an' fast boats. But where are their stout legs?"

"Well," Douglas said, "the distances are very great. I used to go by horseback, but it took a long time. A motorcar gets over the miles and doesna weary."

"Aye, ye've got mony things," Robbie said admiringly. "The only thing a mon in Caithness has is his soul."

Everyone laughed, and one of the men said, "And what is the soul, Robbie?"

"I dinna ken," Robbie said. "That's the great mystery, I believe. Gin I kenned wha' was the soul, I'd be a famous mon, like Douglas here. Why do ye no ask him?"

257

"Douglas," they said to him, laughing, "can ye no explain the soul, mon?"

"I've not thought a great deal about it," Douglas said. "I'm content with my life as it is."

"Oh," they all said, envying him his good life.

"But never say there's no such thing," said Robbie. "Maybe you canna see it. But once in his lifetime every true mon feels it in him, wrigglin' and squirmin' to be free."

"Give the lad a cup of tea," someone said, "an' a scone to keep his soul in his body." They laughed again; and Douglas thought: in America they'd have the good sense to shut this fellow in a madhouse. It's Scotland, for sure, when they smile and tolerate such a one, and let him run loose, prattling of souls and bicycles.

Still, he woke in the night and lay in the half-light of the little parlor, thinking of Robbie and the soul, and the half-forgotten precepts of his childhood. He had never willingly faced up to the nightmare of the Calvinistic concept: the immortal soul, hell and damnation, and the horror of eternity. He enjoyed living from day to day, and sometimes the days slipped by too fast; yet, he thought, when they were over, he would prefer oblivion to some eternal hell or heaven.

Douglas arose very quietly so that he should not awaken the other sleepers in the house. He pulled on his clothes and went out into the quiet yellow light of the first hour of morning.

Suddenly he was a boy again, full of desperate ambition, stealing away to the glories of an unknown future. " 'Tis my ain life, an' myself the only one wha's got to live it." And his mother looking at him so sadly and saying, "Och, Douglas, if I never see ye again, lad!"

He strode out along the country road in the sharp air from the sea, and it seemed better to think of these things while walking than in the restlessness of a bed without sleep.

My ain life. Mysel' the only one wha's got to live it. This was the mystery beyond all mysteries. *Myself*, no one else—and yet each living man a self, a mystery shut into a rind of flesh. Why? For what reason?

But, after he had walked a little, he ceased to think, and only relished the brisk air and the vivid sense of movement. The light

258

from Dunnet Head flashed monotonously in the twilight, warning ships away from the distant rocks. He kept walking until he reached the cliffs above the sea, and there he stood watching the miracle of the returning sun, palely golden as it lifted through shrouds of mist out of the north sea. Its long, pale rays fell slanting across the flat fields. The Orkney Islands caught its rays and loomed suddenly clear and purple in the far blue water. A lark rose singing from a dusky field, and long blue shadows lay behind the slate fence slabs that outlined the narrow, rutted road behind him.

Myself, only myself, alone, he thought, breathing the pure cold air. No other can ever know this moment, breathe this same air. He was filled with joyous terror.

It is this, he thought. If there is a soul, it is this. He could not put it into any clearer words, but he felt a kind of splendid exultation. "Myself," he said aloud, "alone." But that did not entirely satisfy him, and he said, "If there is some God who made me, then he is with me, too."

He turned back, thinking that he was uncomfortable in Caithness but that it was a sweet discomfort. The long flat horizons and the smell of burning peat had brought back his boyhood; the picture of Mamie on the mantel had brought back his early manhood. The three days he was spending here were timeless. He felt suspended in some sort of purgatory, awaiting he knew not what.

"A man needs these times," he said to himself, "to get a new hold and find out where he is." He remembered that Angus had said, "I could think better in Caithness." That was true. The Scotch were a slow race; they were better with a large sky overhead, and time to think. How little thinking he had ever done, really!

Biblical phrases from his childhood came back to him. "For what shall it profit a man, if he shall gain the whole world, and lose his own soul?" The old Calvinistic instincts were hard to root out, and as he walked he kept wondering about the soul. Was it only an invention of the black-frocked ministers? It seemed too subtle an idea to be without foundation. Was it what he had felt just now, a happiness of existing, a throbbing sense of being alive that had nothing to do with externals and seemed

259

capable of going on beyond the limits of the flesh? Could one lose it? Not in another life but in this? It was a secret thing that he desired to keep.

But he was a fool to have any fear. He had certainly not gained the whole world, only a precarious sliver of it that moved like a treadmill under his feet, and what he had wanted most had often turned to ashes.

By the time he reached the farm again, he was limping painfully and he felt very tired. Everyone was in the fields and the house was empty. He went into the parlor and flung himself on the bed to rest. His body lay quiet, but his mind went restlessly on.

Presently someone tapped on his door, and before he could get up to answer it, Jeanie came quickly in and closed the door behind her. She held an unopened letter in her hand, and he saw at once that it was from Sheila. There was always something exotic and passionate about the bold black handwriting on the expensive notepaper that Sheila used. It was unmistakable.

Jeanie sat down beside him on the bed.

"I've a letter for you, Douglas," she said. "I wanted to give it into your own hand, lad."

He turned the letter over and read the address of the sender on the back, *Mrs. Douglas McBain, Imperial Hotel, London.* So Sheila had come back from Ireland already! She could scarcely have spent a night in County Mayo.

"It's no Mamie's hand, Douglas."

"No, 'tis not."

"But you've naught to hide from me, brother," Jeanie said. "I've kenned this long while. I read the change in your letters, in what ye didna say."

"Shall I tell you all about it, Jean?"

"No, Douglas. 'Tis no affair of mine, lad. I just want to be sure if you are happy."

"Aye, Jean," Douglas said. "I'm very happy, But it was hard to explain. I decided it was better to say nothing." He felt himself flushing under her steady eyes. She looked at him so searchingly, trying to read him, and yet she did not want his explanation. At last she smiled and drew his head down until she could kiss him.

260

"Aye, 'tis better so, Doug," she said. "We need say no more."

He found himself alone with the envelope in his hands. When he opened it a faint odor of sandalwood arose from the loosely written sheet.

"Darling! I am dying of boredom. Ireland is all finished. How soon can we go on to Paris?"

Douglas got up and began to pack his things. Suddenly he was in a hurry to be going. He had had as much of Caithness as he could endure.

9

So they went on through Europe, eating and drinking well, seeing the tourist sights, and spending more money than they had intended.

There was only one time when he remembered his curious experience in Caithness. He was alone on the deck one night on the return voyage. He had been thinking of the amount of money they had spent, and wondering if they had in any way got the value of it. "That's a Scotsman's thought," he said to himself bitterly. He often overspent, rather than let anyone say he had a Scotsman's thrift. He did not wish to lay by useless money for the sake of thrift. Money was to spend and to enjoy, and thrift seemed despicable to him. But now Sheila had the idea of building a town house when they returned to Manitou City, and she had ordered furniture and rugs in Paris. The costs had been mounting up. He would have to hustle a lot of new business when he got home to pay for it. His mind was busy with ideas for opening new tracts of land, putting up low-cost housing. If they could get the dam in operation and turn that vast desert region into habitable country—.

He stood by the ship's rail in the darkness and felt the steady wind on his face. Below him the black waves rushed by, laced with white foam that caught light from the portholes until they seemed almost luminous.

He had a sudden sense of the strangeness of this palace of light and luxury floating between the immensity of dark heaven and fathomless sea. Was it not a very fragile thing which the elements tolerated? A bubble of sophistication which might easily be annihilated?

Yet inside the ship Sheila was playing cards with the wealthy New Yorkers whose diamonds matched her own, and there was light and security, and no one gave a thought to the wind and waves that snarled outside in the darkness.

Again Douglas felt very much alone, but not with the deep joy he had experienced in Caithness. He tried now to recapture the sensation of beneficent completeness which he had felt in the early morning by the North Sea. But there was only the dark and the wind and the sound of the waves.

"A Scotsman never gets over his yearning for an immortal soul, poor fool!" he said to himself with a brief laugh. "If he's not counting his ha'pennies, he's trying to talk himself into a meaning for his life. It's time I grew up and became an American."

10

Willie was delighted when Douglas came to visit him one hot weekend in early fall. Alma complained of the extra work and the scant hospitality she had to offer, but she would complain of something else, if it was not that. Willie had learned to turn a deaf ear to her complaints.

Douglas drove down from Manitou City in his motorcar, bumping along the rough country roads in a cloud of dust. What he wanted to do was drive up and down more rough roads, and even into the desert where there were no roads. He wanted to go to the river where it trickled mildly now between eroded banks. He had come down for business rather than for social reasons.

"You'd best leave the motorcar in the dooryard," Willie said, "an' we'll take the horse an' wagon from here. 'Tis a bit slow, but we'll see the country better."

Douglas saw Willie's boys swarming over the red leather seats of his car with some trepidation.

"Don't crank it up or touch the wheel or gears, boys," he

warned. He was surprised at himself for speaking sharply, but the car was new and he wouldn't even let Richard drive it.

"They're good lads," Willie said. "They'll no harm it once their curiosity is satisfied."

"Pa, can we go with you in the wagon?"

"No, you bide at home an' do your chores. Happen your mama may need your help, lads."

Once they were away from the untidy farmyard, the complaining wife and the importunate children, the brothers felt at ease with each other. Douglas could tell all the recent news of Caithness at first hand, and this broke down any barriers between them. Willie felt no resentment at his brother's better fortune. He was grateful for what he had and glad that he was not plagued by the obligation to strive beyond his abilities.

"But what do ye want with this desert land?" he asked. "Ye've a bonnie place at the lake, so I hear, and surely Manitou City ain't spreading its suburbs out this far."

"It's a wonderful opportunity," Douglas said. "I own a lot of land out here, thousands of acres, that I got for almost nothing. Now, you see, if I could put water on the land, I'd really make some money."

"But water, man! You see it. It's bone dry in summer, a desert for fair. How can you water all of this?"

"A dam will do it," Douglas said. "It's the dam I've dreamt of ever since I first laid eyes on this country. It's why I sent you here, Willie. Someday your land will blossom and be worth money."

"Aye, a dam would help," Willie said, "but will it no cost a lot of money to put in the dam?"

"Yes," Douglas said, "a lot of money. It takes money to make money. That's what you have to understand, if you want to be rich."

"Well, I'd be glad to be rich," said Willie, "but I'd be unco' canny aboot the risks involved."

"I know," Douglas said. "It's a risky business, but that's the fascination of it. I enjoy risks. It's like walking along a high ridge in a wind. You have to step carefully, and look sharp, but you feel very good when you've made it safely across."

"And if you don't make it?"

"I have the devil's luck. You know that, Willie."

263

"Aye, you've the devil's luck."

"This summer we went into the Casino at Monte Carlo. We stood watching for a few minutes and there were all these old duffers with their 'systems,' making little marks on charts whether they won or lost. As far as I could see everyone was losing. 'Try a ten-franc note,' Sheila said. 'You're always lucky.' I ran a ten-franc note up to a thousand francs. I never stopped winning for a single play. Sheila wanted me to go on playing. 'Our fortune's made, Angel,' she said. But I wouldn't push it too far. I knew when to stop. It's the canny Scot in me." Douglas laughed. He had enjoyed telling his friends about Monte Carlo ever since his return from Europe.

"Aye, you'll pull it off," said Willie confidently.

"But I can't do it without help," Doug said. "I'm going to survey the land out here and divide it up into small tracts. I'll have to begin selling it on faith for lower prices than I'll get after the dam's in. The first takers will get a bargain, but they'll also help to pay for the dam."

"And what does Johnny Buxton think of all this? He's a canny Scot, too."

"Johnny's a good man," Doug said. "But he lacks vision. This project is my own particular thing. Johnny and Sam both want to be sure. They're both conservative, but they're willing to let me take the risks if I want to, and I've never noticed them balking at a percentage of the profits that I bring into the firm. It's been a solid partnership."

Before Douglas left the next day, Willie brought him two hundred dollars that he had saved up toward the future. It had grown out of a good watermelon crop, and a couple of years' shearing and slaughtering.

"It's no a great bit, Doug," he said, "but invest it in your dam and I know 'twill come back to me with interest some of these days. I put more trust in you than in the country's banks."

Douglas was touched. He gave Willie a promissory note, and tucked the money away. But he was used to the confidence of other people. Without his ever striving for it, little people came to him with their trust. Mrs. McAllister had begun it, and he thought of her with affection. He still handled her affairs and sent her the profits of the small investments he made in her behalf. He was confident that people would buy the desert land

he offered on the strength of his assurances that he would build
a dam.

11

It was nearly noon before Douglas got back to the office on
Monday morning.

"Madame La Grande has been calling you every half-hour,"
said Molly.

"Who?"

"Your wife, my little sister."

"What did she want?"

"How should I know? Remember? I'm only the secretary. Not
the cute little one who takes dictation from the boss's knee. I'm
the old maid who sets everybody's teeth on edge."

"Come off it, Molly," Doug said.

He went into his office and called Sheila at the apartment.

"Darling, how are you? Is anything wrong?"

"It's just that you took a terrible weekend to go away, Doug.
Remember the Endicotts? The nice New York couple we met
on the *Mauretania*? She had the handsome diamonds, you remember?"

"Yes, of course."

"Well, he was in town on business. On business with J. W.
Carnahan, the big mining man."

"I know J. W."

"Yes, you know him, only you've never been to his house,
Doug. But you would have been if you'd stayed in town. I went."

"I thought you were going to the Beaches' this weekend."

"Do you think I'd go to the Beaches' when I could go to the
Carnahans', Doug?"

"When you say it baldly that way, it sounds terrible."

"It's not terrible at all. The Beaches understand. They're old
friends. They've never been at the Carnahans' either."

"Well."

"But it's the house I wanted to tell you about. The Carnahans'
house is wonderful, Doug. I've seen it on the outside many times,
but you can't imagine what it's like inside. It's given me a lot of

265

new ideas for our house. That's why I called this morning. I want to talk things over with the architect before the plans are finished."

"Listen, Sheila, my desk is piled high with business. I just this minute got in. We can talk this out tonight just as well, can't we?"

"All right," she said, "if that's the way you feel about it."

"It's not the way I *feel*, dear. There's work I've go to do or we'd better forget the new house."

"I'm sorry. But come home early if you can. This is really important to *me*, whether you care or not."

He hung up irritably and turned to his letters. But the thought of the new house weighed on his mind. Such a large, pretentious house for two people—and Richard, when he was at home for an occasional weekend!

When Molly came in for dictation, he said impulsively, "Why do two people need a great big house, Molly?"

"So, that's what she was after!" Molly said.

"She's been inside the J. W. Carnahan house," Doug said.

"Och," said Molly. "She's not the girl to let anyone get ahead of her. But, Faith! Why should she? They say Mrs. J. W. Carnahan was taking in washing in the mining camp not more than twenty-five years ago, before J. W. struck the mother lode of silver. There's one thing, though, Mrs. Carnahan's always stuck with her church and she's as respectable as a lace altar cloth."

"Well, *I* haven't struck the mother lode of silver," Douglas said irritably.

"Did ye ever hear the old tale of the fisherman and his wife, Doug? The fisherman caught a big, white talking fish, and when he let the poor creature go, it promised to give him anything he wanted. The man asked only for a better hut with no leaks in the roof, but, when his wife heard, she was fit to be tied. She kept sending him back to the sea to ask for finer and finer houses, 'til finally, when the poor fish had turned himself inside out to give her a palace, and still she wasn't satisfied, the fish put her back in her leaking hovel and there was an end to it."

"How did we get started on this? We have letters to do."

"I was just giving you a word of warning."

"Sometimes I wonder why I don't fire you, Molly," Doug said, grinning at her.

266

"I wonder the same thing," Molly said. "If herself had been running your office, I'd have been fired a long time ago."

"You're bitter about Sheila," he said. "You used to be devoted to her."

"It's no good," Molly said. "She's come the lady of the manor over the poor secretary to me several times too often. I've got my own sort of prickly pride, funny as that may seem."

"I'm sorry she's hurt you, Molly."

"Och, hurt!" said Molly. "I'm not so easy hurt. I've been knocked about quite a bit in this life. But I thought we had letters to get through."

"We do," said Doug. "Take a letter to Larson and Saar, 1721 Tenth Street, Seattle, Washington. Dear Sirs: In reply to your letter of September seventh—"

Molly began to write very quickly and efficiently on her shorthand pad. She was a good secretary. Buxton and Plimpton had taken on the attractive new young secretaries, so that now Molly devoted nearly all her time to Douglas' business. It was the most varied and complicated business of the three, and she watched over it with a jealous eye. She saw, perhaps more clearly than Douglas did, that he was spending too much and taking too many risks, but she had no way of telling him so except by means of fairy tales.

Eden Water

1

MONTHS LATER, when the crash came, Douglas was less prepared
for it than any of the people in the office. He had seen the falling
stock market as an unfortunate phase that could be weathered if
he were given time. He was the only one who knew how deeply
he was involved; but a stubborn optimism and faith in his un-
failing luck kept him hoping for a sudden change that would
sweep him on top of the wave again. The awkward thing was that
people began to ask for the return of their money. It took all of
his persuasive charm to stall them off so that he could get time—
a little more time.

His voice was hearty and confident, his appetite good. He
would not allow himself to imagine defeat. It was only Molly who
began to look worn. She forgot to dye her hair; at the roots near
her scalp, it showed thin and yellowish-gray while the ends were
still a rich auburn.

It was curious that the avalanche should have been precipitated
by one man. A very small stone was dislodged on the mountain-
side, and the whole ephemeral accumulation crashed down with
a sound like thunder. In a few months, if the small stone had
never been dislodged, everything would have melted away harm-
lessly and no one would have suspected the peril.

Jim Broderick, the conductor on the interurban train between
Manitou City and Lakeside, had given Douglas money to invest,
but now he wanted his two thousand five hundred dollars to buy

a small chicken ranch. He was looking forward to retirement, and he was tired of waiting for the large profits he had been promised in connection with the Garden of Eden Dam project.

All he wanted was his money back with the interest that had accumulated. Two thousand five hundred was a drop in the bucket to all the money McBain handled. Broderick thought it should be an easy matter to get it back on short notice. McBain was such a nice, good-hearted fellow.

But, oddly enough, McBain stalled him. "Now, Jim," he said with an arm about his shoulder. "Leave it a little longer. You'll make big profits, if you do. This is a slow time in business for all of us. But I hate to see you withdraw your capital before it has doubled itself."

Broderick went home convinced, but he awoke in the night and thought to himself: No, I'd rather have the chicken ranch now than the big profits later. After that he kept going to the office, but McBain was out and the red-haired secretary appeared to be stupid and not very helpful. He did not get his money, and he was a quick-tempered and impatient man.

He forgot all the times on the train when he had come and sat in the seat with Douglas McBain and been proud to have other passengers see him discussing financial affairs with a big business-man who treated him as an equal. He panicked and began to tell his troubles all over town to anyone who would listen.

"Doug," Molly said, "You've got to find the money for that old so-and-so. There's going to be trouble if you don't."

"Another week," Doug said, "and I'll be out of this jam. Those bonds are due—"

"I wouldn't wait a week. Go to Buxton or Plimp. They'll tide you over."

To go to Johnny Buxton and say, "Look, I'm momentarily strapped. Give me twenty-five hundred to tide me over?" Or even to Plimpton? No. He had been the venturesome and the success-ful one too long. The other two had drawn back from the slim chances he had taken; they had washed their hands of the Garden of Eden Dam. If he had succeeded he could have been genial with them, but in his temporary embarrassment, he would not go to them to beg. He was already overdrawn at the bank, but he did not think that Jim Broderick would plunge into any hasty action.

"Another week," he said to Molly.

"Go to Sheila then," she said, urgently. "Don't wait."

Well, where but to one's wife? Yet he was curiously reluctant to tell Sheila what had happened to him.

"It's only temporary," he said. "Just a loan for a week or two."

"I'm surprised you should come to me now, Doug," Sheila said. "You know how much I've got tied up in the new house. I'm doing more than my share on that, as you very well know."

"We may have to scrap the new house," he said harshly.

"Don't be absurd," she cried. "We've gone too far to pull back now."

"Listen!" he said, "raise me twenty-five hundred dollars tonight. We'll talk about the house later."

Sheila took out her check book. She was pale and her lips were compressed into a thin line. "I never thought you'd be such a fool as to get yourself into a corner," she said.

He took the check and made it over to Broderick.

"Thank you," he said, and tried to kiss her, but she turned her head away.

Broderick was satisfied, but he had spread the word all over town that you couldn't get your money out of McBain these days, and now all sorts of people besieged the office for money. Private individuals and companies began to threaten suit. The engineering firm which had made a preliminary survey for a proposed railway and observations for a dam site suddenly brought suit for $965.30. Then a man named Morgan swore out a complaint that McBain had obtained five hundred dollars from him through fraudulant misrepresentation.

"It's larceny," he said.

The deputy sheriff, an old friend of Doug's, was apologetic when he served the warrant.

"I know you can clear this up, Doug. But we have to do what the law requires."

"Certainly, Tom. I know," Douglas said. But he was sick with chagrin. He saw the headlines in the paper: *Manitou City Businessman Charged with Larceny.* He saw the hail-fellow-well-met friends storming the office with demands and charges and warrants; he saw Johnny and Sam disclaiming any part in his downfall; he saw Sheila's cold white face turned away from him.

He spent a night in jail, and even beyond the chagrin, was the

271

terrible weight of his astonishment. That life, that luck, which had been so very good to him, could suddenly strike him down! It was a thing he could never have imagined until it happened.

In the welter of disillusionments and false friends, Perry Beach came forward with four thousand dollars' bail. For a moment it restored Doug's confidence in the good life. He had one friend who was willing to take a chance on him. Perry did not come in to see him, but put the bail money into the hands of Douglas' lawyer.

2

After his release Douglas went home jubilant. This could all be cleared up in a short time now. It had been terrible; it had taught him a costly lesson, but he had a friend who believed in him and he would weather the storm. Sheila would lend him the money to settle his debts now, and when he was on his feet he would make it up to her a thousand times. They would sell the lake cottage, the boat, the many costly things. They would start over—he felt it in himself that he could start over.

When he unlocked the door, he saw trunks in the hall and everything in disorder.

Sheila came to the door and looked at him. She had on her hat and coat. Her gloves were in her hands.

"So you are back again, I see," she said.

"Where are you going?" he asked.

"I'm going to San Francisco for a little while, until this all blows over."

"Well, I don't blame you," he said. "This hasn't been fair to you. But it's all unnecessary and ridiculous. I'll be on my feet again in a short time. If you'll just stand by me and help me now when I need it."

"I gave you a check last week when you asked me," she said. "But how long do you think that kind of thing can go on? I want to tell you something now. There won't be any more. Do you hear? There won't be any more."

"You mean that you won't help me even temporarily?"

"I mean I can't give you any more money."

"I don't ask for a gift—only a loan."

"Isn't it the same thing? Look what you've done to all these other people."

"Very well," he said angrily. "But you needn't use that tone to me, you know. Have I ever tried to take advantage of you, Sheila?"

He went to her now and put his hand on her arm. The soft wool sleeve of the coat slipped on the soft silk of the dress on the soft smooth arm that he knew so well.

"Sheila!" he said.

"Please don't touch me," she said. "I can't afford to be pulled down by you now. I've got where I am by tooth and nail, and I won't be pulled down now."

"Do you think I want to pull you down?"

"I don't know what you want, but I'm a realist. I've learned to look out for myself. It's the one thing life has taught me."

"Sheila!" he said. "My God! I'm not down permanently. You know me well enough for that. And I've got friends. Perry Beach put up four thousand dollars' bail."

"I know," she said. She had begun to pull on her gloves.

He had a moment of wonder and uncertainty.

"Maybe you gave him the money, Sheila?"

"No," she said, "but I arranged it. Perry would do that much for *me*."

"For *you*?" he said. "I thought he had done it for me."

"You *are* naïve," she said. "If you knew the world a little better, you might not get yourself into a jam like this."

Douglas took her by the shoulders and shook her. "What's the matter with you?" he said.

"I'm only trying to tell you," she said coldly, "that I can't be responsible for any more of your follies. I'm just going to take a little trip, that's all; and when you've got things under control again I'll probably come back—if there hasn't been too much scandal in the meantime." He took his hands off her shoulders.

"That's considerate of you," he said in chilly fury. "I'll have the welcome mat on the doorstep for you and a big candle burning in the window. I'll—"

He pushed her away from him and turned and went out of the apartment, slamming the door behind him.

Sheila stood still for a moment. A kind of uncertainty crumpled

273

her smooth, cold face. Suddenly she ran to the door and down the stairs, calling "Douglas!"

But he was already cranking the car at the curb. She stood in the hallway and watched him, annoyed at herself for running all the way downstairs.

"Let him go," she said to herself.

He got into the car and began to drive. All he could think of was that if he had stayed in the room with her any longer he would have killed her.

"I would have killed her," he kept saying to himself in surprise. "I would have killed her."

He turned the car northward and began to drive toward Lake Vivienne. When he came to a gasoline pump, he had the car filled with fuel. At a grocery in the outskirts of the city, he bought bread and cheese and cold meat as if he were preparing for a summer outing. He could pick up blankets, old clothes, and a gun at the lake cottage. He did not examine his motives, because he did not care.

He had not known that it was in him to run away. But he found that it was.

3

We took the *Manitou City Star* because the Opportunity paper specialized in local news and Grandma liked to be informed on world affairs.

It was a winter afternoon when Aunt Connie brought the newspaper in from the porch where the paper boy had flung it. Grandma was sitting by the stove in the dining room, as she often did now, with nothing to occupy her hands. I sat at the dining table with Caesar's *Commentaries* and a Latin grammar and dictionary spread before me. I did not care for Latin. It seemed to me to be as remote and unnecessary as the piano practice which they had finally allowed me to give up. But I was in high school and I had the firm intention of going to college. I was grimly at work.

Connie had unfolded the paper, and she stood just inside the closed door staring at the headlines. Her face had gone white and strange, and she said in a queer voice, "Mama! Something terrible has happened. I knew it would happen. I knew."

Grandma turned her head slowly.

"What is it, Connie?" she asked.

I felt cold apprehension going through me. How could any headline in The *Manitou City Star* possibly affect us? We led such quiet lives here, so far out of the world. Yet I knew that thunderbolts could strike, even in remote and quiet places.

Connie spread the newspaper on the table beside my Latin books.

"It's incredible," she said softly. "It was bound to happen; and yet, now that it has, it seems as if it can't be so. It's too fantastic."

Grandma rose from her chair, and the headlines leapt to meet her. The three of us read them in silence:

Douglas McBain Arrested
MANITOU CITY BUSINESSMAN CHARGED
WITH LARCENY AND FRAUDULENT MISREPRESENTATION

We looked at each other in silence. We did not know what towers of speculation had fallen about his ears, or where his devil's luck and the stock market had parted company. Perhaps it was only that the people who had been buying desert land on the promise of water had lost patience and begun to press for a return of their money. Did they not know that it took money and time to build a dam? Could they not have waited a little while before crying fraudulent misrepresentation and larceny?

We stood about the table staring down at the newspaper, and we were pale with incredulity and shame. Honesty had always been a fetish with us. "As honest as Angus McBain," people in town said, as they might have said, "Honest Abe." And now Douglas McBain's name was spread across the newspaper in tall letters of disgrace.

With her usual inconsistency, Connie now cried, "I will not believe it! It cannot possibly be so!"

"Poor Douglas!" Grandma said. "Poor dear, good Douglas."

"Well, Mama!" Connie said. "If he has done these things, how can you pity him? Oh, what are we to think? Kit, you had better not read any more, dear."

But I had already read the whole account, and my heart was very sore.

275

It was only later that our own possible involvement began to occur to us.

"Mama, what about Kit's money?" Connie said slowly. "He has all of it. But he never would have taken chances with that! You don't think he would, do you?"

"I don't suppose that he intended to lose anybody's money, Constance," Grandma said. "We can only wait and see."

Suddenly I hated my money. Little as it was, necessary as it was, I hated it. In some inexplicable way it seemed to have come between Uncle Doug and me to cut off our love and friendship.

4

That day Mrs. McAllister came to see us. She lived as secluded a life as we did, and I suppose that she and my grandmother had not seen each other since the time of my mother's funeral.

She came slowly and heavily up our front walk and rang the doorbell.

"I cannot see her," Connie said.

"Of course you can," said Grandma. "Open the door, Kit."

Mrs. McAllister sat down heavily in the chair which was offered her. She looked very much older than she had when we had seen her last.

"Ye've been reading the papers, I dare say?" she said.

"Yes, yes. It's hard to believe."

"I'll not bother you long," she said, "but a thing has been fretting me beside my own troubles. It's about Christine, Angus' lassie." She looked at me with her gentle blue eyes half lost in wrinkled lids. "I know Angus took care of her, and I couldna rest until I knew that her wee bit was safe for her."

"We don't know yet," Grandma said. "We let him invest everything for her."

"Och, indeed. You would, of course," she said with a deep sigh. "Then we must only hope for the best."

"And you, Mrs. McAllister," Grandma said. "Had he money of yours invested?"

"Aye," Mrs. McAllister said. "But I do not blame him. He never once asked me for a penny. It was I, myself, who always forced it

276

on him. I trusted him too much, because he was like the son I never had. There was something about him that was different from a' the rest."

"We loved him, too," Grandma said.

"We *still* love him," I said fiercely.

Suddenly Connie ran upstairs with a stifled sob, and we could hear her fling herself onto the bed and give way to crying.

"Well, I must get on back the way I came," Mrs. McAllister said. "I didna mean to disturb you. I thought happen you might know more than I do."

"I wish that we did," Grandma said.

The two old women shook hands at the door, and we could see Mrs. McAllister going away slowly and painfully down the hill. Neither Grandma nor I spoke, but we could hear Connie sobbing upstairs.

We hated to see the newspaper on the doorstep after that; yet every day the boy delivered it, and almost everyday there was something about the case. The preliminary trial had been set for early February; before that time we read the terrible news that Uncle Douglas had disappeared.

Molly Casey, Douglas McBain's secretary, was quoted as saying that Mr. McBain would be back to stand trial. She was sure of it—sure. She claimed that she had talked to him on the telephone and that he would be back. But she could not or would not tell where the telephone call had come from.

One issue of the paper carried a story which almost stopped our heavily beating hearts:

McBAIN SUICIDE, IS RUMOR

As a possible explanation of the disappearance of Douglas Mc-Bain, accused real-estate promoter, friends have suggested that he might have drowned himself in Lake Vivienne.

In support of this theory his automobile was found one day on a woods road near Lakeside, apparently abandoned.

Connie and I, with still, white faces, looked at Grandma when we read that.

"I do not think so," Grandma said in her steady, sensible voice.

"Oh, Mama," cried Connie. "It might be so, mightn't it?"

"No," Grandma said. "He loves his life too well. Somewhere he will start again, or he will come back."

The warm blood began to return to my heart, but I did not say anything.

At the end of the newspaper story there was a single sentence that read:

Mrs. McBain still has her apartment at the Winchester Arms, but she is visiting in San Francisco and is unavailable for comment.

"Oh, that woman!" Connie said. "Do you think he has gone to her there?"

"It's unlikely," Grandma said. "He will try to keep her skirts clear of this, I should think."

"*She* will keep her skirts clear, you mean," Connie said. "Why is she in San Francisco? Why isn't she in Manitou City standing up for him? She's a selfish woman."

"We know nothing, Connie," Grandma said. "We must not be hasty in condemning anyone, when we don't know."

So the day of the trial came and still Douglas did not appear. His lawyer asked for an extension of time, and it was granted. But now a nationwide hunt for him began. "Like a common criminal," Connie said. They printed a picture of him in the paper. We looked at it sadly trying to see him in it. But it was badly reproduced and it did not even resemble him. He seemed too heavy and his hair had a solid look like a black cap on his head. The mouth that I always remembered smiling was firmly set and there was no twinkle in the eyes. The eyes looked out under level brows like the eyes of a stranger.

This was a man who had squandered other people's money, and who had run away after a friend had put up four thousand dollars' bail for his release from prison.

It was the running away that hurt us most. We knew that he had had an honest vision and a dream of water on dry land which he had tried to realize. We knew that he had gambled, for that was in his character—only this time the devil's luck had deserted him. But we had not known that it was in his character to run away. That was the surprising and the dreadful thing.

The suicide theory was somehow dropped and, so far as I

278

know, the lake was never dragged for his body. Others besides ourselves knew how he loved his life.

Gradually the affair began to be referred to in smaller head-lines, farther back in the newspaper. There were a robbery, a murder, and a railroad strike that pushed the missing business-man into the back pages of the news. But we always opened the paper with trepidation, hoping that they had found him, hoping that they had *not* found him.

Only once did we see Mrs. McBain mentioned again. She had given up her apartment in Manitou City and settled in San Francisco. She was quoted as saying: "We kept our money strictly separated. I have sold our lake house, and his part of the proceeds will go towards settling his debts. My part was mine before I met Mr. McBain, and I am in no way involved in his financial diffi-culties. I have no idea where he is, and I do not wish to know."

"Oh, the slut!" cried Connie angrily. "Now! You see?"

Grandma did not reprove her, nor did she think of an appro-priate aphorism.

5

Uncle Willie read the papers too. He read them with shock and sorrow and a gnawing concern for his two hundred dollars that had been so laboriously put by and so confidingly risked. He must have wanted to keep the news from Alma, since he knew how she would leap on it and tear it apart. But the newspaper was one of her few diversions. At night by lamplight, she first went through the comic strips with a look of grim concentration on her face; from there she turned back to the murders, rapes, and scandals, and these seemed to give her more joy than the Katzenjammer Kids or Andy Gump. Politics she left to those who relished them. In her opinion politicians were all scalawags and up to no good. But larceny interested her as much as murder, and there was no use cutting out an item, because her curiosity would only be the more aroused.

So Willie laid the first account of Douglas' trouble before her in silence and let her do the talking. She had a great deal to say. She recalled all the suspicions she had had of Douglas' integrity;

they were many and went back to the very first time she had seen him in the hotel dining room at Wapago. All of her envy and anger at pretense and high living flowed out now in an excited flood. "They, with their place at the lake and their fastest boat, their diamonds and their motorcars! And look what it's brought them to. Stealing to make ends meet! I'm not surprised. And trips to Europe and a dam for the river. Your brother's overreached himself. I could have told you all along he would."

It had been a winter of heavy snows and dark, forbidding weather. But Willie could not stay indoors and listen to Alma talk. He took the dog and his gun and tramped off across the frozen fields. The river was still rimmed with ice, a small silver thread in a wide, eroded gully; but he knew it would be a roaring torrent when the snow began to go out of the distant hills. The promise of the dam had become a deep hope which he hated to relinquish. He had seen the new people buying up dry land with the expectation of irrigation, and he had dreamed his own dreams of a green farm with good crops and plenty of water. To lose this dream of greenness was worse than to lose the two hundred dollars, worse even than the knowledge that Douglas had played too recklessly with other peoples' money.

When they read that Douglas had disappeared, Willie set the boys to cleaning up the barnyard and doing little chores about the house, so that the place would look as well as possible.

The farm had gone down badly in the last two months. During the late summer and fall they had had an extra hand on the place and things had looked considerably better. The young hand had worked for his board and keep, asking no more than a place to stay and die in. He had come with the harvesters and been too ill to leave, and Willie had befriended him. Alma scolded and complained, but Willie said: "We canna turn him away, girl. He's got the same fever of the lungs that Angus had, poor lad. The tools can go in the barn an' we'll give him a bed in the toolshed." So Gabe Broman stayed and seemed to grow stronger for a while. He was grateful, and he worked hard when he was able.

In the evenings Willie used to enjoy talking to him. They had the doctor out to see him once, but there was little that could be done.

"It's tuberculosis," the doctor said. "I could tell him to go to

Arizony or put him in a sanitarium, but all that takes money, and it probably wouldn't do any good."

"I thought they called it consumption," Alma said, getting as much pleasure as she could out of this morbid break in her domestic routine.

"Well, they used to," said the doctor, "but now it's tuberculosis. It sounds more scientific. Give him milk and eggs, if you can spare them, and as much rest as possible. It's only a matter of time."

If Gabe Broman had kin, he never mentioned them. When, in late November, he suddenly died, Willie had the doctor out again to sign the death papers, and they buried him quietly beyond the east field under some stunted cottonwoods. The little gear he left scarcely paid for the plain pine coffin, but he had kept the place neat and tidy while he lived. He had even talked of painting the house if there had been ready money for paint.

But Willie liked the house as it was, gray-weathered wood inside and out. It was almost the color of the land that stretched away on all sides, gray in winter and early spring, and baked gray again in autumn, after the brief greening and yellowing of late spring and summer.

It was rare for Willie to look at his farm with critical eyes. But the day he heard that Douglas had disappeared, he did look at it so. He saw that Gabe Broman's extra hands were missing, and that in winter this was not a very pretty place. But a little tidying was all that he could do.

Alma came out to him as he worked around the barn. She was carrying the newspaper in her hands, and she said suspiciously, "It looks as if you're getting fixed for company."

"Not at all," said Willie. "I was only thinking we missed the extra pair of hands that poor Gabe lent us."

"Well, you'll never take in another man in trouble, I hope."

"I hope I won't need to," Willie said.

"And as for your brother, Douglas," Alma said. "He had better not show *his* face around here. I never did trust him nohow, and it would be just like him to come here now and expect you to feed and clothe him and hide him. If he does, I'll send him packing in a hurry, you can bet your life on that!"

"What if he *should* come here?" Willie said. "Where else would

a man go but to his brother's? And, should he come, you'll take
him in, and treat him good, and keep your angry mouth quiet.
I mean this, every word."

Willie was easygoing, but when he finally spoke out in earnest,
Alma accepted his decision.

She said now, sullenly: "You're so darn honest, it hurts a normal
human being to live with you, and yet you're ready to take in
your brother who's no better than a thief. I never saw such a
man."

"Don't speak of it before the bairns," he said. "Should he come,
let them think what they will of him."

"You'd let your children be charmed away and turned into jail-
birds, too, wouldn't you?"

"They'll learn no harm from him," Willie said. "Remember now,
Alma, we'll do the best we can and say the least. I mean this."

"And what if the police find him here? You'll be in it, too, right
up to your neck."

"Dinna jump ahead," Willie said. "We'll face each thing as it
comes."

6

Douglas told himself later that he had never consciously
planned to run away. It was an inexplicable wild impulse born of
his need for time and a quiet place to face himself. He had only
meant to go to the lake cottage for a few days to plan how he
could recoup his unexpected losses and mature his many unfinished projects; to look squarely at a future without Sheila or
any other woman.

Perhaps, if he had met anyone he knew in Lakeside, he would
have gone back to Manitou City the next day. But freedom beckoned to him from the lake and the woods. Here was the beginning
of a vast wild country where a resourceful man could lose himself
for a long time without the need for explanations and regrets.

He left his car in deep woods on a dead-end road and made his
way to the cottage. He slept in a bed that night, and before light
the next day he made a pack of what blankets and supplies he
could carry on his back, slung a gun over his arm, and started

282

to walk. The ease of escape made it seem foreordained. "Predestination?" he thought. "My God! I'm still a Presbyterian!"

And the bond? "Beach did it for her," he said. "I was blind even to that." He remembered, too, that he had left the Thurso gardener before the promised year was up, and the sky had not fallen. When you have broken faith, you go on living, and the sky is the same blue, the bruised pine needles underfoot smell as sweet. There is no thunderbolt from overhead. A man has to do what he can, and some get by without dishonor though others do not.

The winter woods were cold, and Douglas was soft from easy living. He found soon enough that he had not made the easiest decision. But, having chosen a way, even though it might prove the wrong one, he stuck to it.

But he was disappointed in his hope that this would clear his thoughts. While he walked he kept going over the many projects and intrigues and intricacies of his business, and asking himself in bewilderment why or how they had gone wrong. And bitterest of all was the thought of Sheila in San Francisco with her jewels and her private bank account. How had he failed so miserably with women? He could not understand that. There had always been women who seemed to love him, and he had been generous to the two he had loved. But somehow they had been like the diamonds and furs and fast boats and motorcars: lovely and expensive and in the end unsatisfying.

So, as he walked, his thoughts went around and around among large and small matters and he saw no clear answers to any of his problems. His mind pained him more than his feet, swollen with chillblains and blisters. When he slept, huddled in his blanket in the shelter of a rock or a fallen log, he dreamed horrors that were worse than the daytime reality. He awoke, sweating, in the freezing cold, and got up and stumbled on to another place which offered him no more comfort.

He met no one at all in the woods, and that finally became the most frightening trouble he had to face. He was miles from anyone, alone.

"Only myself alone—'tis my ain life to do with as I choose." So he had done *this*.

One day he stopped walking and laid his cheek against the rough bark of a pine tree and began to sob.

He had been going north for four silent days, but now taking hold of himself, he turned south again, and began heading, as nearly as he could tell, toward civilization. Still he had no plan, except that he hoped to keep alive and that he wanted to see some human face. For the first time he thought of Willie. He saw the rough shock of blond hair falling over the forehead, the merry blue eyes and easygoing mouth. If anyone forgave him, Willie would. If anyone could help him back into the civilized world of men, it would be Willie.

7

One day as I was coming home from school, I saw a strange woman going up the street ahead of me. Strangers in Opportunity were rare, and this one was noticeable because she was more smartly dressed than most of the women we knew. I was surprised when I saw her turn into our gate. She stopped then and stood looking down at the purple and yellow crocuses that had begun to bloom on either side of the walk. Winter's ice still lay gray and hard under the trees on the shady parts of the lawn and on the north side of the house; but a few days of Chinook winds had brought out the snowdrops and the crocuses.

I entered the gate and came up beside the strange woman.

"Did you want something?" I asked, looking up into her face. Although she had seemed a stranger from behind, there was something vaguely familiar about the face. It resembled some old picture I had seen, or was it, perhaps, that somewhere I had seen the lady's daughter?

"Yes," she said. "Yes. I wanted to see—" She broke off and looked at me very strangely. Her face, which was beautiful in a faded, artificial way, began to pucker and fold into some unexplained emotion.

"Oh, Lord!" she said. "You must be the baby, Christine. You're a big girl. You're nearly grown. Oh, Lord!"

Suddenly she began to cry. It was very embarrassing to see her and I did not know what to do. She began hunting through her handbag, and although it contained many miscellaneous items, she did not seem to find what she wanted.

284

"Shall I call Grandma or Aunt Connie?" I asked in some distress and puzzlement.

"Yes, do," she said. "Please do."

I started to run into the house, but Connie was already at the front door. She came onto the porch and looked down at the visitor. I was used to reading Connie's face, and I saw surprise and anger there at first, and then a sudden softening that turned into tears to match the visitor's. Connie ran down the porch steps to the walk crying, "Where have you been? Oh, Mamie, where, oh, where have you been?"

"Everywhere," Mamie said. "Don't ask me." They clasped each other and mingled their tears. I stood, amazed, watching them hugging each other and crying there on the narrow walk between the tiny green spears and the yellow and purple crocuses.

At last Connie, ever mindful of the town's opinion, said, "Come on in. The neighbors will be watching. There's been enough for them to talk about without this."

"Do you have a handkerchief? I left mine somewhere."

"Yes. Take this."

As I followed them into the house, I heard Mamie ask, "Where is he, Connie? Do you know where he is?"

"No," Connie said. "We don't know. We don't know any more than the police or anyone. We don't know anything."

"Oh, I thought you might," Mamie said. "All the way I kept on hoping."

"Why didn't you write?"

"Oh, Lord! You ought to know I never write—when I can come."

"You've seen all the papers, I suppose?"

"Oh, yes, I think so. I didn't see them at first, and then I ran onto an item one day. I was in Helena, Montana, and I packed up my duds and went to Manitou City, and there I got all the back numbers of the paper and read the whole thing. I went to his office, and they'd taken his name off the sign over the door. Just Buxton and Plimpton now. That Johnny Buxton! I never liked him. I went in to see him and there he was on the other side of a wide polished desk, as cold as yesterday's potatoes. 'My dear Mamie,' he said, 'you're about twelve years too late, aren't you? But you were smarter than the rest of us, my good woman. You saw him for what he was a long time ago.' I picked up an ink pot

285

to throw it at him, but what was the use anyway? He told me to go to a Molly Casey who had been Doug's secretary."

"Molly!" Connie said. "Didn't she know where he was?"

"If so, she wouldn't tell me. She was living in a messy little room, half filled with filing cases and papers of all kinds. She was ruder to me than I was to her. 'I'm busy,' she said. 'I've a job to do, and the ex-wives may form a line to the right of the doorway and sit there all night, but they'll get nothing out of me,' said she. So then I came on here."

Grandma entered the room then. Her face was a study of surprise, and I hoped her heart would stand the strain of this new turn of events. Mamie kissed her and said, "I'm trying to find where Douglas is, Mother Hedrick."

"A lot of people would like to know," Grandma said. "I expect the police have more resources than we have."

"Numbskulls," Mamie said, dismissing the police. "But where is Willie? You can tell me that at any rate, I expect. And Willie'll know."

"Willie is living on some kind of sheep ranch out in the desert —out where the dam was supposed to be. I can give you the address. But wouldn't that be the first place they would look?" said Connie.

"Maybe so," said Mamie, "but I've got to try."

"But, Mamie, *why*?" asked Grandma. "After these years? What can you do for or against him?"

"Oh, not against him!" Mamie said.

"But *why*?" repeated Grandma.

"I don't know," Mamie said. "I've always been a damned fool. You know that as well as I do. So I'm at it again. But you saw the papers. 'Mrs. McBain is in San Francisco,' they said. You saw her own words; 'I am in no way involved. . . . I do not wish to know where he is. . . .' She ought to be with him, helping him. It isn't fair that a man should have two women run out on him when he's in trouble. That's why I've got to find him. It isn't right to let it happen twice."

"She's a no-good, selfish woman," Connie said bitterly, "a regular scarlet woman, but still this is a time when he probably couldn't take her with him if he would. Maybe he's better alone."

"No. I won't believe that. Twice to the same man! It isn't right."

286

"And what about you, Mamie? What have you done all these years?"

"Don't ask me," Mamie said again. "I've had good times and bad times. But it's a funny thing—the only home I ever really had was with Douglas, and I was so damned anxious to run away from it. How crazy can a woman be?"

Mamie stayed for supper with us. I looked with admiration at her brightly colored, pretty clothes, so different from Connie's and Grandma's genteel shabbiness and austerity. Yet she had had to borrow Connie's handkerchief.

The company of older people was familiar to me and I sat quiet, drinking up their stories of the past. I was past fourteen now and I knew, better than many fourteen-year-olds do, how sorrowful and strange life could be. Yet I loved it. I was a quiet spectator, listening and watching, smelling and tasting, storing the troubles and gladnesses of other people away in my mind beside my own. To sit unnoticed at a table where grown people conversed or told old tales had almost never bored me. If it did, I could slip out quietly and find my pony or my dog or my dolls to play with. It was an unnatural childhood, yet I have not regretted it.

This evening I did not slip away, for this was conversation I could not miss. It was about my Uncle Douglas and then here was Mamie, the fabulous Mamie of whom I had heard so much. She had an air about her of places I had never seen, of lavish extravagances that my prudent grandmother had kept hidden from me, of follies and charms and strange emotions. Even the vulgarity I recognized for vulgar; yet I gloried in it.

"Isn't she quiet?" Mamie said, noticing me at last.

"She's my little darling," Connie cooed. "Aunt Connie's lovey-dove."

"How much she looks like Angus," Mamie said. "I remember the night she was born. How it snowed that night. Fourteen years! It's too long. It isn't possible. What's to become of all of us?"

"We learn to make the best of things," Grandma said, "or we don't survive."

Mamie looked at me again, very searchingly, and I turned my eyes aside in embarrassment.

287

"I don't see any of Abbie in her," she said. "Poor Abbie! Dear Abbie! How beautiful she was. What a good time we had in those funny little pink houses!" She wiped her eyes again on the borrowed handkerchief, and gave a long sigh. "But I'll make it right," she said.

She took the midnight train out of Opportunity with Uncle Willie's address in her handbag.

"Do you think she'll find him?" Connie asked Grandma. I was not sure whether Connie hoped that she would or that she would not.

"I don't know," Grandma said. "Maybe she will. She's aged but she hasn't really changed. Most people would have written, but she took the train and came."

"But will he want her now?" Connie asked in a low voice. I think she hoped that he would not.

"I don't know," Grandma said again.

In the following days I thought of Mamie's search with great intensity. To be able to go to him! I would have gone if I could. But I was bound by shackles of youth and inexperience, by fear, and Latin grammar, by lack of money, and the final, terrible thought that, should I find him, I would only be an embarrassment to him. If Mamie thought of that, she did not let it stop her.

Suddenly I saw her as the sort of person I should most have liked to be: a woman who did what she wanted to do when she wanted to do it. Much as I admired this courage and certainty, I could never adopt it. For, between me and my desired goals, there were so many other people who desired things, too, that I lacked the heart to be ruthless. I think that Mamie never saw the other people at all, but went straight for her goal, however whimsical or wrongheaded it might be.

So all my life I have been a prudent Scotswoman, but I have had this vision of recklessness and freedom that I saw one night in Mamie Stephens.

The following days I shall always remember as a time of darkness. The spring rain came down in torrents, but it was so cold it did not melt the hard ice in the fence corners. Instead of soaking into the ground, the water rushed away, carrying broken twigs and debris down the gutters and into the larger streams. The precocious crocuses were bruised and battered down by rain and

288

hail. I went to school in my rubbers and waterproof coat and my heart was heavy.

8

There are many things that I do not understand about the events which followed, and I am reluctant to let my imagination tamper with what I know. We heard several versions of the story, and I have chosen among them and pieced them together as best I could.

Uncle Willie never told us about how Douglas came to the farm, but years later Aunt Alma did.

"He scratched on the window one night," she said, "like a lost dog."

" 'Don't pay no heed,' I said to Willie; but Willie got up out of bed and went to the door and let him in. You never saw a man so worn down as he was. He'd lost all his fine, rich flesh. His shoes were wore clean through and his feet swelled up. He hadn't shaved his face in a long time, and he'd lost that better-than-thou, smart-aleck look I used to hate in him. Oh, he had come down, I tell you. Maybe that's why I let Willie talk me into takin' him in. I'm a charitable woman, an' I see he wasn't goin' to lord it over us again—at least that's what I thought then.

"The police all over the country was lookin' for him an' they'd been out an' talked to Willie a couple times before he came. I don't know how they missed him—except he'd been in the woods and he didn't look like he did when he left town.

"He hadn't eat for a couple days an' my cookin' that he used to turn up his nose at when he was fillin' his belly at the fine hotels sure went down fast.

"We had a hired hand that died of tubercolosis that fall. I was afraid I'd caught the tubercolosis myself, an' I was in no condition to take on a man wanted by the police an' another mouth to feed in my condition of poor health. But Willie says, 'He's my brother, Alma,' and so that was *that,* and nobody asked *me* was I dying or not. But what I started to say about the hired man, very few folks even knew he had died, and Willie put Doug in the tool shed to sleep where the kid had slep', an' we went right along as if Doug was the hired man. Nobody ever asked us questions. So there we had him, an' nobody never asked how *I* felt neither, with another mouth to feed and laying ourselves liable to all kinds of trouble. It's just what comes of marrying a soft fool like Willie."

About this time Molly Casey wrote Grandma a letter, and I still have it somewhere among my things, but I do not need to get it out to remember what it said. Molly wrote:

"DEAR MADAM:

"I thought I ought to tell you how all this trouble of Mr. McBain's leaves the little girl. Well, everything's gone except the wheat farmland he bought for her out in the Eden Dam country. That's in her name and his bankruptcy won't touch it. Because of lack of water it lies fallow every other year, but it may just yield enough to see her through school and up to where she can get a job or marry. He meant her no harm, because I know he loved her dearly.

"I don't know where he is, but I'm working full time every day on his affairs, and, the good God with me, I hope to pay off some of the losses, so it won't go quite so hard with him if they ever find him.

"Respectfully yours,
"MOLLY CASEY,
"Secretary to Douglas McBain"

I had never seen Connie so bitter as she became after that. Two things rankled in her—that he had lost money for me, her darling, and that other women, Mamie and Molly, had the courage to try to help him.

About this time Connie gave me a little book which explained to me the facts of life. It was a book she had seen recommended by *The Ladies' Home Journal* on "how to tell your child," and perhaps she learned as much from it as I did. But, in spite of my embarrassment, she could not give it to me in silence. She felt that she must back it up by warning me against men so that I would be prepared for life.

"Men are cruel and selfish, Kit," she said, "like your mother's husband, Jack Yancy. You can't trust them, and they demand dreadful things of you. Your Uncle Douglas even—"

"My Uncle Douglas is good," I said.

290

"Your Uncle Douglas is a thief," said Connie. "He has stolen other people's money, and run away; and he has always been full of lust for lightheaded women, just like every other man."

"Constance!" Grandma warned.

"She's old enough to know," Connie said. "I wish someone had told *me* about men, when *I* was her age."

Grandma rarely said anything to Connie when Connie was in one of her tirades. We both knew it was better to agree or be silent than invite more trouble by arguing.

But this time when Connie had gone out of the room, leaving me awkwardly holding the book of enlightenment in my hand, Grandma said to me very quietly, "You know the story about the fox and the grapes, Kit. The fox couldn't have the grapes, so he told everybody that they were sour."

"Yes, I remember, Grandma," I said.

"Pity her, Kit," Grandma said, "and make your own decisions."

Mamie had told us herself that she never wrote if she could possibly go, but it seems now that she did write a couple of letters. She went to the town nearest Willie's farm and got herself a room at the hotel. She was there for several days, as the hotel register still testifies. "Mrs. Mamie Stephens," she signed herself. She went out to the drugstore and bought herself a tablet and envelopes and a new pencil which they sharpened for her. Then she must have sat a long time in the bleak little room thinking what to say and how to say it. She wrote two letters and put one in a sealed envelope inside the other.

First she wrote to Willie:

"DEAR WILLIE

"Well, this is a voice from the past I guess (ha ha!). But really I'm serious this time and sorry for the things I did. I really want to help him if I can, if only by standing by him when he's alone. I think you'll know where he is, Willie, and can give him this letter. Please do, because I'm serious this time, and I would like to see him. I can only stay here a few days, so please let me know soon if I can see him somewhere where it's safe. I wouldn't do anything to put him in any danger. God knows I only want to see and help him.

"MAMIE STEPHENS."

291

Alma showed us this letter years later, but what Mamie wrote to Douglas no one knows because the letter was lost in the flood. Whatever it was, it made Douglas want to see her.

Willie wrote to her in reply:

> "Walk out the main road running west from town on Monday afternoon for a half a mile to the crossroad and my hired man will pick you up in the wagon and bring you here."

So it was arranged.

9

A cold wind was blowing over the empty fields when Mamie left the hotel. It had rained all night, but now there were patches of blue among the dark, swiftly moving clouds, and always optimistic, Mamie believed that the storm was over.

She dressed lightly and brushed her hair and made up her face so as to cheat the damage that the years had done. The dim hotel mirror gave back a reflection that satisfied her. She had not thought about the mud that would be in the road after the plank sidewalk ended. But nothing daunted her, and when she found herself slipping in yellow mire, she worked her way along beside the barbed-wire fence at the edge of the road where dead weeds and matted grass made little islands of safety. She had worn her pretty, high-heeled, high-laced shoes with the white kid strips between the patent leather toes and heels, and she saw the mud ooze over them with regret. Doug liked things neat and pretty. He noticed what a woman wore. Most men didn't, and that was one of the things she hadn't realized when she had left him. So many things she had not realized. It had been a kind of madness between her and Buck Clayborne, a thing unfinished from her extreme youth that she had had to finish. She had craved Buck's cruelty and ruthlessness, tempered for her alone by his infatuation, until the infatuation ended; and then she had seen how gross an interlude it had been. Thinking back, she remembered that Douglas had always given and never exacted much, that he had been kind, and not really a fool, only preoccupied with business—and she remembered how badly she had treated him—and herself. Oh, herself! The tears were starting now, as they always did when she thought of herself, but she fought them back, because she wanted to be calm and quiet when she met him, and as neat and pretty as possible. Her heart beat heavily, because she did not know whether or not he would want her. But Willie's note had made her hope.

The road was perfectly deserted and he might have come safely into town for her, she thought, but one never knew who might have recognized him, even in a hick town like this. And she would walk anywhere to meet him now. So she kept going along the roadside, holding her long skirts up as best she could to keep them out of the mire, and away from the burs that waited on the dead weeds to be caught and borne away to other seeding grounds.

As she walked the sky grew darker and the patches of blue disappeared. A thin mist of rain began to fall.

Oh, God, my feather hat! she thought. Why couldn't it have been a sunny day? And she wondered in a kind of desolation if she might not have taken the wrong road? Because it seemed to her that she must have been walking for more than a half-mile and there had not been a crossroad. All of the country was bleak and flat and utterly drab, and perhaps he would not come at all—perhaps it might even be a hired man, only a hired man as the note had said.

When she thought this, the tears began to run. But it made no difference now. The rain was spoiling her makeup anyway.

And then ahead of her she saw the crossroad and a small farm wagon hitched to a single horse waiting where the road turned off. At first she did not see the driver, but as she drew nearer it became apparent that a man was standing in the road beside the horse. He did not call out or come toward her, but stood there waiting for her.

It seemed to her still to be a very long way that she had to walk, and her steps dragged more and more slowly. It was not that she was tired, only at the last moment she was somehow reluctant. And he was not going to help her.

So they came face to face at last, their eyes searching each other for vulnerability and clues.

"Douglas?" she said in a faltering voice.

293

"You came back," he said, as if to himself. "I never thought you would."

"Yes, as you see," she said, trying to laugh. "Yes, I am here. You really are surprised, aren't you?"

"Nothing about you ever should surprise me," he said. "I thought I had seen everything."

"No, no, not quite. I surprise myself sometimes."

"Get in," he said. "It's not a smart rig, but it's all I've got to offer, and it's Willie's, not mine."

"That's all right."

"A little while back I could have offered you a motorcar, the fastest boat—"

"I know. Don't bother now. We've both come down a peg or two."

"Get in," he said again, taking her hand and helping her over the wheel into the wagon seat. "I'm sorry it's raining. Take off your hat. There's some clean gunny sacking in the wagon bed. You can put it around your shoulders, over your head if you like. You still want to go with me? You don't want me to take you back to town?"

"No. I want to go with you."

He took up the reins and spoke to the horse. It began to move forward, straining to pull the wagon through the heavy mire.

"This is a nasty country," he said. "It's all muck now, but for most of the year it's a desert, dry as a bone. I had a crazy dream of a dam, because the soil itself is good. I gave it a crazy name— the Garden of Eden. Now I'm running from the law. You understand that, don't you? I can't give you a thing—unless you want to turn me in for a reward. I hear a reward is offered."

"You ran a risk picking me up this way, didn't you? Maybe I have the police following me."

"I don't think so," he said. "Still I'm not sure. I don't know why you came back now. A year or so ago you might have got something handsome out of me. At that time I was giving away diamond brooches and earbobs and all sorts of things that pretty ladies like. Now I've got a clean gunny sack for you, and it will soon be wet through."

"All right," she said. "That's good enough for now. I just can't promise anything for the future. You've known me long enough to know that, I guess."

294

They drove in silence for a while. The horse moved slowly, making difficult progress in the mud. The wheels of the wagon creaked and the mud splattered against the dashboard in little staccato sounds above the lighter, staccato beating of raindrops. The rain was coming more sharply and persistently now. It shut out the long view of desolate country and enclosed them in a lonely intimacy.

At last Douglas broke the wordless gap between them with an anguished question. "*Why*, Mamie? What have you come back for? Why?"

"Well, why do you think? For you, for you. You won't believe it, maybe, but it's true. It isn't too late now, is it? Is it, Doug?" she cried, searching his face.

"I think so," he said gravely. "If we could have had a regular life, a good home, children perhaps . . . If we had both tried harder . . ."

"I know, Doug. I've thought that lots of times since. But I'm the same as I've always been. I guess I'd have flown off the handle in one direction or another no matter how we tried. But now—*now*, can't we go on from here some way?"

"I don't know," he said. "I don't see how. Could a time for making up be any worse? If we were foolish before, now we would be daft. Surely you see that."

"I see nothing. I just feel, and now I feel this in my heart, Doug. If everything had been going fine with you I wouldn't have come no matter how I felt. You had her, another woman, then. But, God! I couldn't let two women run out on you, without your knowing how bitterly one of them regretted it."

"I see," he said, looking away over the horse's head. "But possibly now, I don't need anyone—or don't want anyone."

"I don't believe that," Mamie said. "Maybe I'm not the one, but you can't go on alone. It takes two, Doug—a man and a woman."

Again they rode in silence.

Yesterday he would have said that he had reached the very dregs of humility, that he had no false pride left. But he saw now that one small pride still bristled in him. It was the pride of going alone, of not succumbing again to the overwhelming feelings for Mamie that had once engulfed him so deeply. He turned his face away from the gray eyes that were still beautiful in spite of the makeup over the little lines. Something in his heart stirred, but he would not let her see it.

10

The flood swept down the gully past Willie's farm in a wall of muddy water. It had been building all winter in the far-off hills. The melting snow and the incessant rain together had built it up, and there had been no dam to hold it back. At first it had been only a rising and quickening of water in the sloughs and washes, and then it came faster and faster, swifter water pouring down upon slower water until it surged forward like a reaper, cutting away banks and willows and pieces of grazing land, sweeping sheep off their feet and swirling them away, eating the underpinnings from sheds and privies so that they toppled and fell and were carried down on the dirty, foaming tide.

Willie and the boys and the dog ran out, when they heard the roar of water, to save the sheep, but there was little they could do. Heavy with unsheared wool, the ewes on the verge of lambing, the sheep scarcely struggled against the flash flood that took them by surprise. Willie's dog ran yelping above the thunder of the water into the torrent, trying to drag back the helpless sheep, one by one. At last he, too, still yelping and trying to swim against the current, was sucked under and whirled away.

It was then that Willie gave up, and, shouting to the boys, ran to get Alma and try to make the higher ground on which the next farm stood. In a few minutes, behind him lay the ruins of all he had built and struggled for during the last few years of his life.

The flood reached the farm first, but it swept on toward the road where Douglas and Mamie were riding. An hour before, Douglas had crossed the wooden bridge over the gully that was dry for nine months of the year, without thinking of the rising waters below. But now, when they came to the bridge, he saw that the water had risen to the level of the planking and was filling the whole gully with foaming, seething water.

The horse stopped on the slippery bank shaking its head and

shuddering so that the rain sprayed out from its rough coat like a fine mist.

Shaken out of their emotional preoccupation, Mamie and Douglas looked at each other.

"I don't know if we can make it across," Douglas said.

"Is this the only way to Willie's farm?"

"Yes."

"Then where else could you go?"

"I could take you back to town."

"No," Mamie said. "Let's try the bridge. It looks sound."

"It looks dangerous."

Mamie's eyes had begun to sparkle, her color to come more warmly into her cheeks.

"I like things dangerous," she said. "You know that, Doug. Let's go on."

"What do we have to lose?" Douglas asked.

He urged the reluctant horse onto the bridge. They could feel the planks quaking under the hoofs of the horse and the ironshod wheels of the wagon. The bridge was shaken also by the fury of the water rushing below. It began to tilt and sway sideways as they saw the greater wall of water bearing down upon them. The wall of water came fast, with the roaring of a flood tide. There was the sound of crashing and splintering wood, the despairing shriek of the horse. And they were struggling in icy water among broken timbers. Douglas heard his own voice crying, "Mamie! Mamie!" The cry seemed to be echoing from some distant corridor of his mind, far, far away. Somewhere he had been hunting for her, and she had not been there.

But now his hand closed on a piece of her dress and he caught her and drew her to him. He began to swim, holding her against him. He was a strong swimmer, but the current was different from anything he had ever experienced. Beams and timbers and drowned sheep rushed down on the turbulent water. He was choked with swirling sand and straw from flooded barnyards. Mamie clung to him, heavy and helpless in her long wet garments. Her clinging arms had a terribly familiar feel. It seemed to him that there had always been a woman, demanding, helplessly clinging, pulling him down in turbulent water.

Yet he could only think now of the necessity of reaching the other side of the gully. He had sought her in vain through the horror of fire, and now in the horror of water he had found her. If he did not reach the other bank it could mean nothing to either of them. So he struggled and fought the water with the best strength he had, and he could feel that he was making headway. The edge of the torrent was just beyond, a strip of wet earth that appeared to be the one solid and silent promise in this heaving turmoil of water. It was the world that he and Mamie had left so long ago as well as the uneasy Eden that might hold some future for them.

But, while he saw the land ahead of him and strained to reach it, a shadow loomed at the edge of his vision. Something large and dark was rushing toward them. A part of a henhouse? A shed torn loose from some meager barnyard? He could not tell what it was, but he felt that it was the thing that could kill them. He made the greatest effort that he had yet made, and, for an instant, he thought that they were free. Then a corner of the rapidly turning building struck them as it roared past. The blow went all through him. Mamie's weight grew heavier but he did not let her go. For now, vaguely at first and then more solidly, he felt shifting ground under his feet.

Relief began to surge up in him as he fought his way out of the water, knee deep in quaking mud. With a hoarse cry of triumph, he struggled onto solid ground and laid Mamie down to ease his aching arms.

Her hair fell all about and across her white face. Her head hung loose as if some stem inside her had been snapped. For an instant she opened the wild gray eyes and looked at him, but then the eyes glazed into unconsciousness.

He did not know how far he carried her, searching for help. But at last he staggered into a farmyard and was able to lay her on a cot in a strange house. He had known for some time that she was dead.

11

Willie's friends and neighbors, poor as they were and despoiled by the flood, rallied around to feed and clothe him and his family and make up a small purse for them. The farm had been so badly washed away that there seemed no chance of trying to reclaim it.

"You had a hired man, didn't you?" they asked.

"Och, God! I did," Willie said. "I think he was lost in the waters. I havena seen him." He sobbed as he spoke, and Alma put a hand on his arm.

"Don't take it so hard, honey," she said. "You done everything you could for him." But still Willie sobbed.

Among the many casualties of the flood, Willie's hired man was listed, as well as an unidentified woman whose body was brought by an unidentified man to a remote farmhouse during the peak of the flood. This was the perfect solution for a man who wished to lose himself to the world. It was the last, supreme temptation.

But two days after the flood Douglas McBain walked into Molly Casey's little office, and stood among the filing cabinets and papers and flotsam and jetsam from the office of better days, looking at Molly with quiet eyes.

"Douglas!" she cried, "Oh, Holy Mother. What has happened to you? You're so thin. You look like a ghost."

"Never mind," he said. "But I'm back, Molly, and I want you to help me."

"It's all I've ever wanted to do, Doug," Molly said.

"Then you're to notify all the proper people," he said. "Tell them I've come back to stand for whatever I'm guilty of. Tell the newspapers, tell the police, tell all the people whose money I've squandered. I'm through with running." He sat down wearily in the old desk chair that Molly had salvaged for him.

"I think it's the best way, Doug," Molly said. "And I can tell you that it isn't all lost. I've been working on the business while you were away. The stock market's come back. Really, it doesn't look so bad. Some things we can settle out of court."

"You're the world's wonder, Molly," he said. "It's myself has been the perfect ass."

"No, no, Douglas. Please."

"And there's another thing," he said. "I've to arrange for my wife's funeral."

"Sheila?" Molly cried, looking at him in astonishment. "But she's getting a divorce, surely she isn't—"

"No. Mamie," he said. "My first wife, the one I loved first."

They were silent for a few moments, and then Molly said:

299

"Where is she, Doug? I'll call and make the arrangements for you."

"Thank you, Molly," he said.

12

There were some people who never got their money back from Uncle Douglas. The big accounts were settled, most of them out of court. It was the smaller accounts, the bits of money from people who loved him that never came into court and were never settled out of it. Thus many people were the poorer for having trusted him. Yet, if the purse was leaner, perhaps the heart was richer—or so I thought, being myself one of those who was never repaid, and being also a sentimentalist. I had still the farm he had bought for me, and the proceeds from it saw me through college and a little way beyond, so that I was more fortunate than many people were.

It would be gratifying if I could say that he devoted the rest of his life to repaying even the last and least of those who had trusted him, but it was not so. Yet he must have suffered his own private torments.

I remember when poor Mrs. McAllister died. It was much later that spring. The rains and floods were forgotten and yellow roses hung in bowers over the wooden gates in Opportunity. The poplar trees rustled and turned their shining leaves in the sunshine.

Connie and I attended the funeral together, for Grandma never went out to anything those days, even to the funeral of an old friend. The cemetery was well out in the country on a hillside where wild flowers were thick in the long, coarse grass. Connie and I rode there in the procession of town hacks, and stood by the graveside while the coffin was lowered.

The Presbyterian minister was slow and long in his committal of the old Scotchwoman's body to the earth. I do not know what made me raise my eyes during the prayer to look across the open grave at the folks who stood beyond. But I did, and there at the crowd's edge I saw a man in a dark suit with his hat in his hands. There were tears on his cheeks, and although he was so

300

much thinner than he had been I knew it was my Uncle Douglas. I had a dreamlike feeling that this could not be, yet I remember that I started violently and would have gone around the grave to him. But Connie's hand closed fiercely on my arm.

"*No!*" she whispered. "No, Kit. Not before everybody."

The prayer went on a long time, and when I looked again he was gone.

Connie and I went home silently and we did not mention the incident to Grandma or to each other.

But Connie kept on her good dress as if she were expecting company. She was nervous and distraught after dinner, and during the evening she paced restlessly up and down.

"What is the matter with you, Constance?" Grandma asked.

"Nothing," said Connie. "The funeral upset me, that's all." But I knew she was thinking that he might come to see us. And I hoped so, too, with all my heart.

After Grandma had gone to bed, Connie still paced and fidgeted. At last she went to the telephone. She turned the crank that rang the bell, and the sound was loud in the room. When the operator answered, Connie asked to be connected with the hotel. I stood by watching her with wide eyes, hoping and wondering.

Her voice sounded angry and defiant as she inquired if Douglas McBain of Manitou City was registered there. I could not hear the answer, but I read it in Connie's face.

"Thank you," she said, putting the receiver back on the hook. "He's not there," she said as if to herself. Then she saw me watching her, and she said violently, "Maybe, if *we* died, he'd come for *us* too. But I won't give him the satisfaction of dying! Thief! Murderer!"

I did not think of anything to say, and after a while we went to bed. The whole incident seemed to me like a dream. In time I might have come to believe that I had imagined seeing Uncle Douglas at the graveside, had it not been for Connie's telephone call—had it not been for the very real ringing of the telephone bell in the silent room.

13

It was a good many years before I saw my Uncle Douglas again, and then it was very briefly.

As I grew older my life was satisfying without him. My college days were not affluent, but in better ways they proved rich and exciting, for they were filled with new friends and small personal triumphs. If I had had a lonely and sometimes unhappy childhood, it proved to be an excellent conditioner for life. I had learned to recognize and seize upon the good and fortunate when it came, and to weather the tiresome and unrewarding without rebellion. So I made a happy marriage and had a son, whom through some excess of sentiment on my part we named Douglas. This use of a name which I had loved was to have been the period that closed a portion of my life and opened up a new future. Our little Douglas was a brave laddie, as the Scotch would have said, and we were happy with him.

Our home was in New England, and the West seemed very far behind me in both time and space. But I wrote regularly to Aunt Connie and Grandma, who still lived quietly in Opportunity. Connie had softened again and mellowed, but her tongue ran on as wildly as ever. Even her letters, written in a spidery, vertical hand, were garrulous and wordy. She never missed a week in writing to me, and I always tried to reply, for even when I was deeply involved in my own affairs I remembered what she had done for me and how few people had ever returned the floods of love that she had offered.

It was from Connie's letters that I learned how things had gone with my uncles. She corresponded with Alma, and in any case she had her ways of finding out what happened to anyone in whom she took an interest.

After the flood Willie had taken his family to Seattle and secured a job as a stevedore on the docks. The older boys were able to work now, too. They bought a little house with a garden plot, and Alma was happier than she had been in years.

When Douglas was at last released from his obligations and involvements, Willie got him a job on the docks, wheeling crates, carrying parcels, loading coal on tramp steamers. So for a few months they worked side by side, Willie laughing and whistling and trading jokes with the other stevies, Douglas silent and withdrawn. And then there was a clerkship vacant in one of the warehouses, and Douglas applied for it.

I do not know by what rapid stages of chance, merit, or luck, my Uncle Douglas climbed the ladder of success for a second time. But when I visited Seattle some ten years after the Eden Valley flood, my Uncle Willie was still a stevedore on the docks, and Uncle Douglas was the chief wharfinger of the port of Seattle, and sat behind a fine desk in a large office overlooking the sound.

That summer my husband was sent on business to the Orient, and my little boy and I went as far as San Francisco with him. While he was abroad, we traveled to Opportunity to visit Connie and Grandma. Then a college friend of mine invited me to visit her in Everett. I thought I would not go, but Connie said: "Yes, you must go. And then you can stop in Seattle and see your uncles."

"I'm not sure that I want to see them now," I said. "All that belongs to my childhood."

"Yes, you must see them," Connie said, "and then you can tell me all about them. They say that Douglas has married again—not Molly Casey, who helped him out of his troubles, nor anyone else he used to know who might have been expected to be close to him. No, Alma says, he married his landlady at a boarding-house where he stayed. Imagine! Well, I must say he has always dignified his lusts with marriage, which is more than some men do. But three marriages—really! So you must go and see, Kit, truly you must."

Whether because Connie's tongue could still hypnotize me into a child's acquiescence or because of some unfinished emotional experience of my own past, I cannot say, but the fact remains that little Douglas and I arrived in Seattle one fine summer morning with a free day ahead of us and nothing to prevent me from calling my uncles.

I called Uncle Willie's house first, and Alma answered.

"Well, Christine!" she said. "We thought you'd forgotten your poor relations since you come up in life and moved back East and all. But Willie won't forgive you (nor me neither) if you don't come out to have a meal with us. It won't be much; we

303

don't go in for all the fancy food I guess you're used to. But we won't starve you. Douglas? You'll find him at the wharf office, no doubt. His wife's out of town now, so he prob'ly won't ask you out. They're way above us now, of course, though I never forget she was only his landlady, and older than he is too. But he goes his way an' we go ours. I've got my pride, too, even if Willie hasn't never been a financial success. At least he's good an' honest an' he's stuck to his one faithful wife."

When I heard my Uncle Douglas' voice on the telephone, many long-forgotten things rose up in me. I felt my child's heart beating in my breast once more.

"Kit?" he said. There was the tiniest pause before he went on, and I knew how all of it must have come back to him, too, the good and the bad. I could even understand that, although it was he who had squandered the money my father had left me, my very innocence and trust might have made it seem to him, sometimes, as if *I* had sinned against *him*.

Then his voice came heartily: "Why, Kit! This is a real surprise. Will you take a cab and come out to my office? I've some free time this morning. I'll have Willie in to see you too."

"I've talked with Aunt Alma," I said. "Willie had already gone to work."

"Yes, he starts work early," he said. He paused again. Then: "Ella, my wife, is out of town just now. I can't very well have you out to stay, and I'm tied up with business at lunch."

"That's all right, Uncle Doug," I said. "I'll keep you for only a few moments this morning. It was just to see you once again, after so long a time."

"Yes, Kit," he said. "Come then as soon as you can."

So little Douglas and I took a taxi to the port.

"Who shall we see now?" asked Dougie, to whom our pilgrimage back into my youth was a checkered affair of sugar cookies and kisses and long, dull conversations.

"He was like my daddy," I said.

"Will there be ice cream?"

"I don't think so."

"Or toys?"

"Probably not. But you must be a good boy. We won't stay long."

I think that Uncle Douglas had never properly assimilated

304

the fact that I was grown and had a child. He looked at us so strangely as we came in the door of the office.

But somehow I felt at home sitting beside his desk with type-writers clicking in the next room. He was leaner than he had been, and his hair was quite gray.

He kept looking at Dougie with admiration and surprise.

"And you named him Douglas, Kit?" he said. "I wonder at that."

"I always liked the name," I said.

"Yes, it's a good name."

It seemed to me that we had nothing to say to each other. My eyes wandered across his desk to a single rose in a vase. It was a perfect hybrid tea, just opening from the bud and of the most delicate flesh pink. It must have been cut that morning in a dewy garden.

"You like the rose?" he asked.

"Yes, it is beautiful."

"I grew it myself," he said. "I've taken a fancy to roses. This one reminds me of a young girl's cheek. You'd such a cheek yourself, Kit, when you were a wee lassie."

"I didn't think you cared for gardening."

"It's an odd thing," he said. "Possibly you never heard it. But I was apprenticed to a gardener once in Scotland. I ran away because I hated it. So now the wheel comes round and I take pride in growing roses that remind me of a young girl's cheeks." His tone was light but he did not smile.

"What do you have in your desk?" little Douglas asked. My uncle's eyes rested on the child again, and now he began to smile. He looked at me with a conspiratorial wink, and as he used to do for me he began to open desk drawers in search of things a child would like. He found a brightly colored steamship folder, some odd-shaped paper clips, and a little bundle of colored rubber bands.

Little Douglas accepted these with pleasure.

Then Uncle Douglas found a new red pencil which he sharpened with a sharpener that stood on his desk. He gave my son the pencil and a little pad of paper.

"Can you draw an elephant?" he asked.

"I can draw a ladder," Dougie said.

"Let's see."

305

They were already good friends. I was in some way the stranger, and our conversation fell into banalities about weather and trains and my husband's business in the Orient.

"I have asked Willie to come in," Uncle Douglas said. "He will want to see you."

"It will be good to see him."

"He hasn't changed."

"I can't imagine that he ever will."

Then he said, irrelevantly it seemed: "You know the government is planning to build a dam in there now. In the Eden Valley, you know."

"Really?" I said.

"Yes, it's true. Do you still have the farm I bought for you in there?"

"No," I said. "We sold it after I married. You see, we had moved so far away, and we needed the money to buy a house."

"Too bad," he said. "It might be worth something if you had waited."

"I think that a dam in the Eden Valley will make you happy, Uncle Douglas."

"Yes and no," he said. "I've always liked to do things myself—my own way. Still, this is a kind of justification. It makes me appear less of a fool or a scoundrel. I don't know which. Possibly both."

Just then the door opened, and Willie came in with arms outstretched for me. His face was beaming with pleasure. His blue shirt was open at the throat and his old corduroy pants sagged and flopped about his legs. His shoes were cracked and broken. I have a notion that he was usually more restrained in the wharfinger's office, if he came there at all, but my presence made him forget for the moment that he was only a dockhand.

"Och! My lassie!" he cried, "what a day this is! And you so finely grown and with a son so brave an' bonnie! If only Angus were here to see you, too, my dearie!"

It was easy to talk to Willie. He had a lot of questions about my life, my home, about Grandma and Connie.

"And how *is* Connie?" he asked, looking, it seemed to me, as if he really wanted to know.

"Why, she's the same," I said; and then I added, laughing, "She's a bit prickly sometimes, of course."

306

Uncle Willie looked at me with an expression at once shy, sad, and somehow ardent. "She liked dogs," he said simply. "When she was young, had not life gone sour for her, she would have been a verra comfortable an' loving lass to live with. Or so I've always thought."

Douglas' telephone was ringing, and he excused himself to answer it. I realized that we had stayed our time for a busy man and that I should not linger over this.

"I must call a cab," I said. "I didn't intend to stay."

"Willie will look after you now," said Uncle Douglas.

"But I can't take you away during work hours, Uncle Willie," I protested.

"Yon Douglas has given me the half day off in your honor, Kit," said Willie gleefully, "an' I'll no quarrel wi' him for that, lassie." He laughed, and nodded his head at me, just as he used to do, and his unruly blond hair fell over his forehead in the same brave disorder. He was getting a little wrinkled about the eyes, but the wrinkles were pleasant ones and age had really touched him scarcely at all.

"Wait but a minute now," he said, "an' I'll bring round my bonnie chariot. If ever ye've ridden in a sonsier combination of rattling parts I'll be much surprised, Kit. And Douglas," he said, "you'll be with us the night for dinner, will ye no? Alma's preparing a banquet, I believe. We'll be expectin' you."

"I'll come if I can manage it, Willie," Douglas said. "But I've a lot of letters to get out and a man from the East coming in about some importations. Two ships are due on the late tide."

"I know," Willie said, "only I thought, this once, possibly—"

When Willie had gone after his car, Uncle Douglas said to me with a touch of embarrassed formality, "I'm sorry Ella was not in town. I'd have liked to have her meet you."

"I'm sorry, too," I said. But the sorrow in our hearts was not for that.

"So we won't see you tonight at Uncle Willie's?" I said.

"No, I'm afraid not," he answered. The telephone on his desk had begun to ring again.

"Then probably never again?"

"Oh, there will be other times and other places, Kit, I hope."

He went with us to the door. "Willie will be here any minute now."

"Uncle Doug—" I said. But I did not know what I wanted to say. I could not go on. He patted Dougie on the head. "Be good," he said. "Take care of your mama. I've been very fond of her."

"I will," Dougie said.

There was a pause, and I heard his telephone still ringing. Then he said to me: "Kit, because you have Scotch blood I'll tell you something I've never said to anyone before. We've a curse of Calvinism in our blood, all us Scots, and whether we believe in a loving and all-powerful God, as your father did, or whether we play at worshiping the devil as Sheila taught me to do, a Scotsman wants to be thrifty with his life. In the end he must have a reckoning and tote up the assets and the debits. The easiest way is to lay the reckoning in the hands of the angels; the hardest way is to have the reckoning with himself. I don't know exactly what I'm saying—except that you will find Willie living very poorly and cheaply; yet I would like you to know that I know that he has made a greater success of his life than I have made of mine."

"No!" I said. "No! To me, Uncle Doug, to me—"

But he turned back then to answer his telephone, and I heard Willie's old car rattling around the corner.

"He was a nice man, Mama," Dougie said. "He gave me all these things. Why are you crying?"

I did not answer at once, because he was too young to understand that I had just said a last farewell to my second father, my innocent first love, my Uncle Douglas.